Just One Damned Thing After Another

THE CHRONICLES OF ST MARY'S
BOOK ONE

JODI TAYLOR

Published by Accent Press Ltd 2015

ISBN 9781910939529

Copyright © **Jodi Taylor** 2015

First edition published 2013

I made all this up. Historians and physicists – please do not spit on me in the street.

Jodi Taylor

'History is just one damned thing after another.'

Arnold Toynbee

Dramatis Thingummy

Dr Edward Bairstow

Director of St Mary's. Tall, authoritative. Early 50s. Holds together a volatile mix of technicians, historians, kitchen staff, security teams and the sometimes explosive Research and Development Section.

Mrs Partridge

PA to Director. Not to be crossed.

Historians

Madeleine Maxwell (Max)

Historian. In her late 20s. Short, red-haired, engaging, impatient, self-deprecating, with a murky past and a precarious future.

Tim Peterson

Historian, late 20s. Tall and shaggy. A good friend.

Kalinda Black

Historian. Blonde and blue-eyed. Looks like a Disney princess. Possibly drinks the blood of recently qualified trainees. Recipient of Mr Dieter's affections.

Sussman

Max's fellow trainees.

Grant

Rutherford

Stevens

Nagley

Jordan

Technical Section

Leon Farrell

Chief Technical Officer. In his mid-30s. Dark hair, blue eyes, competent, calm, quiet.

Mr Dieter

Farrell's number two. Built like a brick shi – a very large young man.

Medical Team

Dr Helen Foster

Early 30s. Medical doctor and with the people skills of Vlad the Impaler. Recipient of Mr Peterson's affections.

Nurse Hunter

Recipient of Markham's dubious affections.

Security Section

Major Ian Guthrie

Head of Security and whose unenviable task it is to keep St Mary's safe, despite all their best efforts. Late 30s.

Mr Markham

Security guard. Small,

	grubby and disaster prone. Reputedly indestructible – which is just as well.
Mr Whissell	Nasty piece of work.
Big Dave	Murdoch Gentle giant.

Research and Development

Professor Rapson	Head of R & D. Age unknown. Lives in his own world. Responsible for the destruction of the Clock Tower and the disastrous Icarus experiment. Apparently unaware of the properties of methane.
Doctor Dowson	Librarian and Archivist. Age unknown. Also not quite up to speed re methane.

IT

Isabella Barclay	Head of IT. Professional bitch. Short, spiteful and redheaded. Gossip says she harbours an unrequited passion for Farrell.
Polly Perkins	Technician

Others

Mrs Mack	Kitchen Supremo. Mid 40s.

Jenny Fields	Kitchen Assistant and dodo advocate.
Mrs De Winter	Retired schoolteacher.
Turk	Officially a horse.

The Villain

| Clive Ronan | Dark, non-descript, impassive and deadly. |

Plus, assorted armies, raptors, stonemasons and hostile contemporaries too numerous to mention.

One

There have been two moments in my life when everything changed. Moments when things could have gone either way. Moments when I had to make a choice.

The first occurred when, after another disruptive day at school, I stood in front of my head teacher, Mrs De Winter. I'd done the sullen silence thing and waited for expulsion, because I was long past three strikes and you're out. It didn't happen.

Instead she said, with a strange urgency, 'Madeleine, you cannot let your home circumstances define your entire life. You are intelligent – you have abilities of which you are not even aware. This is the only chance you will ever have. I can help you. Will you allow me to do so?'

No one had ever offered to help me before. Something flickered inside me, but distrust and suspicion die hard.

She said softly, 'I can help you. Last chance, Madeleine. Yes or no?'

No words came. I was trapped in a prison of my own making.

'Yes or no?'

I took a huge breath and said yes.

She handed me a book, a notepad, and two pens.

'We'll start with Ancient Egypt. Read the first two chapters and Chapter Six. You must learn to assimilate, edit, and present information. I want 1500 words on the precise nature of ma'at. By Friday.'

'Is this a punishment?'

'No, Madeleine. This is an opportunity.'

'But … you know I can't take this home.'

'You can use the school library and leave your stuff there.

Miss Hughes is expecting you.'

That was the first moment.

The second one came ten years later. An email – right out of the blue:

My dear Madeleine,

I am sure you will be surprised to hear from me, but I have to say that, since you left the University of Thirsk, I have followed your career with great interest and some pride. Congratulations on your academic record at Thirsk, Doctor Maxwell. It is always gratifying to see a former pupil do so well, particularly one who laboured under so many difficulties in her early years I am writing now with details of a job opportunity I think you will find extremely interesting.

You will be aware, from your time at Thirsk, of the existence of a sister site – the St Mary's Institute of Historical Research – an organisation I think would appeal to anyone who, like you, prefers a less structured existence. Their work inclines more towards the practical side of historical research. This is all I can say at the moment.

The Institute is located just outside Rushford, where I now reside, and interviews are on the fourth of next month. Do you think you would be interested? I feel it would be just the thing for you, so I do hope you will consider it. Your travels and archaeological experience will stand you in good stead and I really think you are exactly the type of person for whom they are looking.

The pay is terrible and the conditions are worse, but it's a wonderful place to work – they have some talented people there. If you are interested, please click on the link below to set up a possible interview.

Please do not reject this opportunity out of hand. I know you have always preferred to work abroad, but given the possibility that America may close its borders again and the fragmentation within the EU, perhaps now is the time to consider a slightly more settled lifestyle.

With best regards,
Sibyl De Winter

I always said my life began properly the day I walked through the gates of St Mary's. The sign read:

University of Thirsk.
Institute of Historical Research.
St Mary's Priory Campus.
Director: Dr Edward G. Bairstow BA MA PhD FRHS

I rang the buzzer and a voice said, 'Can I help you, miss?'

'Yes, my name's Maxwell. I have an appointment with Doctor Bairstow at 2.00 p.m.'

'Go straight up the drive and through the front door. You can't miss it.'

A bit over-optimistic there, I thought. I once got lost on a staircase.

At the front door, I signed in and was politely wanded by a uniformed guard, which was a little unusual for an educational establishment. I did my best to look harmless and it must have worked because he escorted me through the vestibule into the Hall. Waiting for me stood Mrs De Winter, who looked no different from the last time I saw her, the day she took me off to Thirsk. The day I got away from that invention of the devil – family life.

We smiled and shook hands.

'Would you like a tour before the interview?'

'You work here?'

'I'm loosely attached. I recruit occasionally. This way please.'

The place was huge. The echoing central Hall was part of the original building with medieval narrow windows. At the far end, an ornate oak staircase with ten shallow steps and a broad half landing branched off left and right to a gallery running round all four sides of the hall.

Various rooms opened off this gallery. Through the open doors, I could see an entire suite which seemed to be devoted to costumes and equipment. People trotted busily with armfuls of cloth and mouths full of pins. Garments in varying stages of completion hung from hangers or from tailor's dummies. The rooms were bright, sunny, and full of chatter.

'We do a lot of work for film and television,' explained Mrs Enderby, in charge of Wardrobe. She was small and round, with a sweet smile. 'Sometimes they only want research and we send them details of appropriate costumes and materials, but sometimes we get to make them too. This one, for instance, is for an historical adaptation of the life of Charles II and the Restoration. Lots of bosoms and sex obviously, but I've always thought Charles to be a much underrated monarch. This dress is for Nell Gwynn in her "orange" period and that one for the French strumpet, Louise de Kérouaille.'

'It's lovely,' I said softly, carefully not touching the material. 'The detail is superb. Sadly, it's a bit modern for me.'

'Dr Maxwell is Ancient History,' said Mrs De Winter. Apologetically, I thought.

'Oh dear,' sighed Mrs Enderby. 'Well, it's not all bad news, I suppose. There'll be drapery and togas and tunics, of course, but even so…' She tailed off. I had obviously disappointed her.

From there, we moved next door to Professor Rapson, in charge of Research and Development. He was so typically the eccentric professor that initially I suspected a bit of a wind-up. Super-tall and super-thin, with a shock of Einstein hair, his big beaky nose reminded me of the front end of a destroyer. And he had no eyebrows, which should have been a bit of clue really; but he smiled kindly and invited us in for a closer look at his cluttered kingdom. I caught a tantalising glimpse of a buried desk, books everywhere and, further on, a laboratory-type set

4

up.

'Dr Maxwell hasn't had her interview yet,' said Mrs De Winter in rather a warning tone of voice.

'Oh, oh, right, yes, no, I see,' he said, letting go of my elbow. 'Well, this is what I tend to think of as "practical" history, my dear. The secret of Greek Fire? We're on it. How did a Roman chariot handle? We'll build you one and you can find out for yourself. What range does a trebuchet have? Exactly how far can you fling a dead cow? How long does it take to pull someone's brains out through their nose? Any questions like that then you come to me and we'll find your answers for you! That's what we do!'

One of his expansively waving arms caught a beaker of something murky that could easily have been embalming fluid, the Elixir of Life, or Socrates' hemlock and knocked it off the workbench to shatter on the floor. Everyone stepped back. The liquid bubbled, hissed, and looked as if it was eating through the floor. I could see many other such damp patches.

'Oh, my goodness! Jamie! Jamie! Jamie, my boy, just nip downstairs, will you? My compliments to Dr Dowson and tell him it's coming through his ceiling again!'

A young lad nodded amiably, got up from his workbench, and threaded his way through the tangle of half-completed models, unidentifiable equipment, tottering piles of books, and smudged whiteboards. He grinned at me as he passed. In fact, they all seemed very friendly. The only slightly odd thing was Mrs De Winter preceding every introduction with the warning that I hadn't had the interview yet. People smiled and shook hands but nowhere did I get to venture beyond the doorway.

I met Mrs Mack who presided over the kitchens. Meals, she informed me, were available twenty-four hours a day. I tried to think why an historical establishment would keep such hours but failed. Not that I was complaining. I can eat twenty-four hours a day, no problem.

The bar and lounge next door were nearly the same size as

5

the dining room, showing an interesting grasp of priorities. Everything was shabby from heavy use and lack of money, but the bar was particularly so.

Further down the same corridor, a small shop sold paperbacks, chocolate, toiletries, and other essential items.

I fell in love with the Library, which, together with the Hall, obviously constituted the heart of the building. High ceilings made it feel spacious and a huge fireplace made it cosy. Comfortable chairs were scattered around and tall windows all along one wall let the sunshine flood in. As well as bays of books they had all the latest electronic information retrieval systems, study areas, and data tables and, through an archway, I glimpsed a huge archive.

'You name it, we've got it somewhere,' said Doctor Dowson, the Librarian and Archivist who appeared to be wearing a kind of sou'wester. 'At least until that old fool upstairs blows us all sky high. Do you know we sometimes have to wear hard hats? I keep telling Edward he should house him and his entire team of madmen on the other side of Hawking if we're to have any chance of survival at all!'

'Dr Maxwell hasn't had the interview yet,' interrupted Mrs De Winter and he subsided into vague muttering. In Latin. I stared somewhat anxiously at the ceiling, which did indeed appear to be blotched and stained, but at least nothing seemed to be eating its way through the fabric of this probably listed building.

'Did they tell you?' he demanded. 'Last year his research team attempted to reproduce the Russian guns at the Charge of the Light Brigade, miscalculated the range, and demolished the Clock Tower?'

'No,' I said, answering what I suspected was a rhetorical question. 'I'm sorry I missed that.'

I was moved firmly along.

We stopped at the entrance to a long corridor, which seemed to lead to a separate, more modern part of the campus. 'What's down there?'

'That's the hangar where we store our technical plant and equipment. There's no time to see it at the moment; we should be heading to Dr Bairstow's office.'

I was still thinking about the Crimean War and the disasters of the Battle of Balaclava when I realised someone was speaking to me. He was a man of medium height, with dark hair and an ordinary face made remarkable by brilliant, light blue-grey eyes. He wore an orange jump suit.

'I'm so sorry,' I said. 'I was thinking about the Crimea.'

He smiled. 'You should fit right in here.'

'Chief, this is Dr Maxwell.'

'I haven't had the interview yet,' I said, just to let them know I'd been paying attention.

His mouth twitched at one corner.

'Dr Maxwell, this is our Chief Technical Officer, Leon Farrell.'

I stuck out my hand. 'Pleased to meet you, Mr Farrell.'

'Most people just call me Chief, Doctor.' He reached out slowly and we shook hands. His hand felt warm, dry, and hard with calluses. Working man's hands.

'Welcome to St Mary's.'

Mrs De Winter tapped her watch. 'Dr Bairstow will be waiting.'

So, this was Dr Edward Bairstow. His back was to the window as I entered. I saw a tall, bony man, whose fringe of grey hair around his head rather reminded me of the ring of feathers around a vulture's neck. Away off to the side with a scratchpad in front of her sat a formidable-looking woman in a smartly tailored suit. She looked elegant, dignified, and judgmental. Dr Bairstow leaned heavily on a stick and extended a hand as cold as my own.

'Dr Maxwell, welcome. Thank you for coming.' His quiet, clear voice carried immense authority. Clearly he was not a man

7

who had to raise his voice for attention. His sharp eyes assessed me. He gave no clue as to his conclusions. I'm not usually that good with authority, but this was definitely an occasion on which to tread carefully.

'Thank you for inviting me, Dr Bairstow.'

'This is my PA, Mrs Partridge. Shall we sit down?'

We settled ourselves and it began. For the first hour, we talked about me. I got the impression that having no acknowledged next of kin and a lack of personal ties constituted a point in my favour. He already had details of my qualifications and we talked for a while about the post-grad stuff in archaeology and anthropology and my work experience and travels. He was particularly interested in how I found living in other countries and amongst other cultures. How easy was it for me to pick up languages and make myself understood? Did I ever feel isolated amongst other communities? How did I get around? How long did I take to become assimilated?

'Why did you choose history, Dr Maxwell? With all the exciting developments in the space programme over the last ten years and the Mars Project in its final stages, what made you choose to look backwards instead of forwards?'

Pausing, I arranged and edited my thoughts. I was nine. It had been a bad Christmas. I sat in the bottom of my wardrobe. Something unfamiliar dug into my bottom. I wriggled about and pulled out a small book – *Henry V and the Battle of Agincourt*. I read and re-read it until it nearly fell apart. I never found out where it came from. That little book awoke my love of history. I still had it: the one thing I had saved from my childhood. Studying history opened doors to other worlds and other times and this became my escape and my passion. I don't ever talk about my past so I replied with three short, impersonal sentences.

From there we moved on to St Mary's. Dr Bairstow gave the impression of a large, lively, and unconventional organisation. I found myself becoming more and more interested. There wasn't any particular moment I could identify, but as he talked on, I began to feel I was missing something. This was a big campus. They had a Security Section and twenty-four-hour meals and plant and equipment and a Technical Department. He paused for a moment, shuffled a few papers, and asked me if I had any questions.

'Yes,' I said. 'What's Hawking?'

He didn't answer but pushed himself back slightly from his desk and looked across at Mrs Partridge. She put down her scratchpad and left the room. I watched her go and then looked back at him. The atmosphere had changed.

He said, 'How do you know about Hawking?'

'Well,' I said, slowly. 'It's not common knowledge of course, but …' and let the sentence die away. He stared at me and the silence lengthened. 'It just seems strange that a hangar in an historical research centre is named after the famous physicist.'

Still no response, but now I wasn't going to say anything either. Silence holds no fears for me. I never feel the urge to fill it as so many other people do. We gazed at each other for a while and it could have been interesting, but at this moment, Mrs Partridge re-entered, clutching a file, which she put in front of Dr Bairstow. He opened it and spread the papers across his desk.

'Dr Maxwell, I don't know what you've been told, but perhaps you could tell me what you do know.'

He'd called my bluff.

'Absolutely nothing,' I said. 'I heard the name mentioned and wondered. I'm also curious about the large numbers of staff here. Why do you need security or technicians? And why do people need to know I haven't had "the interview"? What's going on here?'

'I'm quite prepared to tell you everything you want to know, but first I must inform you that unless you sign these papers, I shall be unable to do so. Please be aware these documents are legally binding. The legal jargon may seem obscure, but, make no mistake, if you ever divulge one word of what I am about to tell you now, then you will spend the next fifteen years, at least, in an establishment the existence of which no civil liberties organisation is even aware. Please take a minute to think very carefully before proceeding.'

Thinking carefully is something that happens to other people. 'Do you have a pen?'

The obliging Mrs Partridge produced one and I signed and initialled an enormous number of documents. She took the pen back off me, which just about summed up our relationship.

'And now,' he said, 'we will have some tea.'

By now, afternoon had become early evening. The interview was taking far longer than a simple research job warranted. Clearly it was not a simple research job. I felt a surge of anticipation. Something exciting was about to happen.

He cleared his throat. 'Since you have not had the sense to run for the hills, you will now have the "other" tour.'

'And this is the "other" interview?'

He smiled and stirred his tea.

'Have you ever thought, instead of relying on archaeology, unreliable accounts and, let's face it, guesswork, how much better it would be if we could actually return to any historical event and witness it for ourselves? To be able to say with authority, "Yes, the Princes in the Tower were alive at the end of Richard's reign. I know because I saw them with my own eyes."'

'Yes,' I agreed. 'It would; although I can think of a few examples where such certainty would not be welcomed.'

He looked up sharply.

'Such as?'

'Well, a certain stable in Bethlehem for instance. Imagine if you pitched up with your Polaroid and the innkeeper flung open the door and said, "Come in. You're my only guests and there's plenty of room at the inn!" That would put the cat amongst the

10

pigeons.'

'An understatement. But you have nevertheless grasped the situation very clearly.'

'So,' I said, eyeing him closely, 'maybe it's good there's no such thing as time travel.'

He raised his eyebrows slightly.

'Or to qualify further, no such thing as public-access time travel.'

'Exactly. Although the phrase "time travel" is so sci-fi. We don't do that. Here at St Mary's we *investigate major historical events in contemporary time*.'

Put like that, of course, it all made perfect sense.

'So tell me, Dr Maxwell, if the whole of history lay before you like a shining ribbon, where would you go? What would you like to witness?'

'The Trojan War,' I said, words tumbling over each other. 'Or the Spartans' stand at Thermopylae. Or Henry at Agincourt. Or Stonehenge. Or the pyramids being built. Or see Persepolis before it burned. Or Hannibal getting his elephants over the Alps. Or go to Ur and find Abraham, the father of everything.' I paused for breath. 'I could do you a wish list.'

He smiled thinly. 'Perhaps one day I shall ask you for one.'

He set down his cup. With hindsight, I can see how he was feeling his way through the interview, summing me up, drip-feeding information, watching my reactions. I must have done something right, because he said, 'As a matter of interest, if you were offered the opportunity to visit one of the exciting events listed, would you take it?'

'Yes.'

'Just like that? Some people feel it incumbent to enquire about safe returns. Some people laugh. Some people express disbelief.'

'No,' I said slowly. 'I don't disbelieve. I think it's perfectly possible. I just didn't know it was possible right now.'

He smiled, but said nothing, so I soldiered on. 'What

11

happens if you can't get back?'

He looked at me pityingly. 'Actually, that's the least of the problems.'

'Oh?'

'The technology has been around for some time. The biggest problem now is History itself.'

Yes, that made everything clear. But as Lisa Simpson once said, 'It is better to remain silent and be thought a fool than to open your mouth and remove all doubt.' So I remained silent.

'Think of History as a living organism, with its own defence mechanisms. History will not permit anything to change events that have already taken place. If History thinks, even for one moment, that that is about to occur, then it will, without hesitation, eliminate the threatening virus. Or historian, as we like to call them.

'And it's easy. How difficult is it to cause a ten-ton block of stone to fall on a potentially threatening historian observing the construction of Stonehenge? Another cup?'

'Yes, please,' I said, impressed with his sangfroid and equally determined not to be outdone.

'So,' he said, handing me a cup. 'Let me ask you again. Suppose you were offered the opportunity to visit sixteenth-century London to witness, say, the coronation parade of Elizabeth I –it's not all battlefields and blood – would you still want to go?'

'Yes.'

'You understand very clearly that this would be on an observation and documentation basis only? Interaction of any kind is not only extremely unwise, it is usually strictly forbidden.'

'If I was to be offered any such opportunity, I would understand that very clearly.'

'Please be honest, Dr Maxwell, is this admirable calm because deep down, very deep down, you think I'm clearly insane and this is going to be one to tell in the pub tonight?'

'Actually, Dr Bairstow, deep down, very deep down, I'm having a shit-hot party.'

He laughed.

Waiting in Mrs Partridge's office sat the quiet, dark man with the startling eyes I'd met on the stairs.

'I'll leave you with the Chief,' Dr Bairstow said, gathering up some papers and data cubes. 'You're in for an interesting evening, Dr Maxwell. Enjoy.'

We left the office and headed down the long corridor I'd noticed before. I experienced the oddest sensation of entering into another world. The windows, set at regular intervals along one side, cast pools of sunlight along the floor and we passed from light to dark, from warm to cool, from this world into another. At the end of the corridor was a key-coded door.

We entered a large foyer area with another set of big doors opposite.

'Blast doors,' he said, casually.

Of course, what was I thinking? Every historical research centre needs blast doors. On my right, a flight of stairs led upwards with a large, hospital-sized lift alongside. 'To Sick Bay,' he said. On the left, a corridor with a few unlabelled doors disappeared into the gloom.

'This way,' he said. Did the man never say more than two or three words together?

The big doors opened into a huge, echoing, hangar-style space. I could see two glassed-in areas at the far end.

'Those are offices. One for IT,' he gestured at the left room. 'And one for us technicians.' He gestured right. An overhead gantry ran down one side with three or four blue jump-suited figures leaning on the rail. They appeared to be waiting for something.

'Historians,' he said, following my stare. 'They wear blue. Technicians wear orange, IT is in black, and Security wears green. Number Three is due back soon. This is the welcoming committee.'

'That's … nice,' I said.

He frowned. 'It's a dangerous and difficult job. There's no support structure for what we do. We have to look after each other, hence the welcoming committee; to show support and to talk them down.'

'Down from what?'

'From whatever happened to the crew on this assignment.'

'How do you know something happened?'

He sighed. 'They're historians. Something always happens.'

Ranged down each side of the hangar stood two rows of raised plinths. Huge, thick, black cables snaked around them and coiled off into dim recesses. Some plinths were empty; others had small hut-like structures squatting on them. Each was slightly different in size or shape and each one looked like a small, dingy shack, stone-built, flat-roofed with no windows; the sort of structure that could be at home anywhere from Mesopotamian Ur to a modern urban allotment. Prop a rickety, hand-made ladder against a wall and with a broken wheel by the door and a couple of chickens pecking around, they would be invisible.

'And these are?' I asked, gesturing.

He smiled for the first time. 'These are our base of operations. We call them pods. When on assignment, our historians live and work in these. Numbers One and Two.' He pointed. 'We usually use them as simulators and for training purposes, because they're small and basic. Pod Three is due back anytime now. Pod Five is being prepped to go out. Pod Six is out. Pod Eight is also out.'

'Where are Pods Four and Seven?'

He said quietly, 'Lost.' In the silence, I could almost hear the dust motes dancing in the shafts of sunlight.

'When you say "lost," do you mean you don't know where they are, or they never came back for some reason?'

'Either. Or both. Four went to twelfth-century Jerusalem as

14

part of an assignment to document the Crusades. They never reported back and all subsequent rescue attempts failed. Seven jumped to early Roman Britain, St Albans, and we never found them either.'

'But you looked?'

'Oh yes, for weeks afterwards. We never leave our people behind. But we never found them, or their pods.'

'How many people did you lose?'

'In those two incidents, five historians altogether. Their names are on the Boards in the chapel.' He saw my look of confusion. 'They're our Roll of Honour for those who don't come back, or die, or both. Our attrition rate is high. Did Dr Bairstow not mention this?'

'He …' I was going to ask how high, but a light began flashing over the plinth marked Three. Orange figures appeared from nowhere it seemed, lugging umbilicals, cables, flatbeds and the tools of their trade. And quietly, with no fuss, no fanfare, Pod Three materialised on its plinth.

Nothing happened.

I looked up at the Chief. 'Um …'

'We don't go in. They come out.'

'Why?'

'They need to decontaminate. You know, plague, smallpox, cholera, that sort of thing. We shouldn't go in until they've done that.'

'But what if they're injured?'

At that moment, the door opened and a voice shouted, 'Medic!'

Orange technicians parted like the Red Sea and two medics trotted down the hangar. They disappeared into the pod.

'What's happening? Who's in there? Where have they been?'

'That would be Lower and Baverstock, returning from early 20th-century China, the Boxer Rebellion. It looks as if they require medical attention, but not seriously.'

'How do you know?'

'When you've seen as many returns as we have then you get a feel for it. They'll be fine.'

We both stood in silence watching the door until eventually two people, a man and a woman, dressed in oriental clothing, limped out. One had a dressing over one eye and the other's arm was strapped up. They both looked up at the gantry and waved. The blue people waved and shouted insults. They and the medics headed off. Orange technicians swarmed around the pod.

'Would you like to have a look?'

'Yes, please.'

Close up, the pod looked even more anonymous and unimposing than it had from the other end of the hangar.

'Door,' he said and a battered-looking, wooden-looking door swung soundlessly open. After the enormous hangar, the inside of the pod seemed small and cramped.

'The toilet and shower room are in there,' he said, pointing to a partitioned corner. 'Here we have the controls.' A console with an incomprehensible array of read-outs, flashing lights, dials, and switches sat beneath a large, wall-mounted screen. The external cameras now showed only a view of the hangar. Two scuffed and uncomfortable looking swivel seats were fixed to the floor in front of the controls.

'The computer can be operated manually or voice activated if you want someone to talk to. There are lockers around the walls with all the equipment required for your assignment. Sleeping modules here pull out when needed. This pod can sleep up to three reasonably comfortably, four at a push.'

Bunches of cables ran up the walls to disappear into a tiled ceiling.

In amongst this welter of slightly scruffy but undoubtedly high-tech equipment, I was amazed to see a small kettle and two mugs nestling quietly on a shelf under a rather large first aid locker.

16

'Yes,' he said, resigned. 'Show me a cup of tea and I'll show you at least two historians attached to it.'

The tiny space smelled of stale people, cabbage, chemicals, hot electrics, and damp carpet, with an underlying whiff from the toilet. I would discover all pods smelt the same and that historians joke that techies take the smell then build the pods around it.

'How does it work?'

He just looked at me. OK then, stupid question.

'What now?'

'Is there anything else you would like to see?'

'Yes, everything.'

So I got the 'other' tour. We went to Security where green-clad people were checking weapons and equipment, peering at monitors, drinking tea, running around, and shouting at each other.

'Is there a problem?' I asked.

'No, I'm afraid we're a noisy bunch. I hope you weren't expecting hallowed halls of learning.'

I met Major Guthrie, tall with dark blond hair, busy doing something. He broke off to stare at me.

'Can you shoot? Have you ever fired a weapon? Can you ride? Can you swim? How fit are you?'

'No. No. Yes. Yes. Not at all.'

He paused and looked me up and down. 'Could you kill a man?'

I looked him up and down. 'Eventually.'

He smiled reluctantly and put out his hand. 'Guthrie.'

'Maxwell.'

'Welcome.'

'Thank you.'

'I shall be watching your progress with great interest.'

That didn't sound good.

We finished with a tour of the grounds, which were very

17

pleasant if you discounted the odd scorch mark on the grass and the blue swans. Even as I opened my mouth to ask, there was a small bang from the second floor and the windows rattled.

'Hold on,' said Chief Farrell. 'I'm duty officer this week and I want to see if the fire alarms go off.'

They didn't.

'That's good, isn't it?' I said.

He sighed. 'No, it just means they've taken the batteries out again.'

This really was my sort of place.

Two

They say owners get to look like their dogs but at St Mary's it was a case of the trainees getting to look like their institute. St Mary's was shabby and battered and after a few weeks, so were we.

Only seven of us trainees turned up on Day One. Apparently, there should have been ten. It seemed an average of only 3.5 trainees actually graduated from each course.

'You'll be the point five, then,' said a tall guy to me, presumably alluding to my lack of height. I ignored him. He rammed paperwork into his folder, seemingly not noticing most of it falling out of the bottom as he did so. His nametag said Sussman. He had dark eyes and hair and looked almost Mediterranean – the sort who gets a tan just by looking out of the window.

Next to him stood Grant, a stocky lad with sandy hair and steady blue eyes. He stacked his paperwork neatly with broad, blunt hands and inserted it carefully into his folder, his square, pleasant face thoughtful. He stood next to Nagley and listened as she spoke. She had a clever, intense face and her eyes and hands moved continually. She was as highly strung as he was placid. They made a natural team.

The other girl, Jordan, stood slightly apart, and almost poised for flight, her body language uncertain. I guessed she wasn't sure she wanted to be there. I was right. She remained aloof and left in the first week. I don't know what happened; one day she was there and the next day she was gone. There was no point in asking because they never told you. I can't remember even hearing her voice.

The other two, Rutherford and Stevens, talked together as

19

they sorted their papers. Stevens was a little older than the rest of us, small, chubby, and enthusiastic. He looked excitedly round the room, taking it all in. Rutherford had the big, blunt look of a rugby player.

The first shock was that we lost our academic titles and I became Miss Maxwell again. Only heads of departments had titles. I quite liked that. I could see Miss Maxwell would have far more fun than Dr Maxwell would.

We were shown to rooms in the newly built Staff Block. Mine was small and shabby and I shared a bathroom with the two other girls, Nagley and Jordan. Laid out on my bed were sets of grey jump suits, possibly the most unflattering garments in history. A neat electronic scratchpad fitted snugly inside a knee pocket. Heavy-weather gear, wet-weather gear, grey T-shirts and shorts, socks and boots completed the set. I unpacked my few belongings and changed. Surveying myself in a mirror, I looked like an excited, grey sack with ginger hair.

We met again downstairs and shuffled off for our medicals. I didn't bother trying to hide my dislike of doctors because Dr Foster didn't bother trying to hide her dislike of patients. The white coat and stethoscope looked incongruous on her. Closely fitting black leather and a short hunting crop would have better suited her stern expression.

The medical paperwork seemed endless. My life had been comparatively blameless so far, but despite that, I was vaccinated for and against everything, and I mean everything. We were also encouraged to give blood regularly – as an investment for the future.

After the medicals, we trooped back to the Hall, rubbing the bits that still throbbed, and sat while Dr Bairstow gave his welcome speech.

'Congratulations to those of you here today. You constitute the best of the candidates interviewed, but only the best of you will complete your training. You should be aware that not all of you will make the grade. You have tough times ahead of you. Of course, you may resign whenever you wish. There is no compulsion. If you wish to leave, you should be aware that the confidentiality documents you signed today apply in perpetuity and, again, the consequences of divulging any information of any kind to anybody will be very, very clear to you.'

He paused and eyed us all individually. I made myself stare calmly back.

'We work in conjunction with the University of Thirsk, whence some of you graduated. We enjoy considerable autonomy, but we are answerable to them for our funding. They in turn answer for us to a small and discreet government body who, as far as I can tell, answer to no one below God.

'You, however, answer to me.'

He paused again for this to sink in.

'Our public image is of a charmingly eccentric historical research organisation which is of no harm to anyone but itself. This view is particularly prevalent in the village, especially as the echoes of our latest explosion die away. Strive to maintain this image please, ladies and gentlemen.

'I hope to get to know you all better over the coming months.' His eyes crossed slightly and he said, in the voice of one who has committed something distasteful to memory, 'Please remember my door is always open.' Then he was gone.

After this we grappled with yet more hand-outs, schedules, organisational schematics, and even more forms to complete. The concept of the paperless office never really made much headway at St Mary's. I leafed through the papers in my folder until I found my timetable. The first lecture started at 09.00 the following morning with Chief Farrell, who I remembered, followed by a session with the Head of IT, Miss Barclay, who I didn't.

We assembled, bright-eyed and enthusiastic, the next morning. Chief Farrell, calm and authoritative, was easy listening and pretty easy on the eyes as well. Izzie Barclay was another matter, rendering her subject so completely devoid of interest and relevance that you could practically hear people's eyes glazing over. I listened with only half an ear while watching her pose in the sunshine so everyone could admire the glints in her red hair.

I suppose that because, with the exception of Smartarse Sussman, I'd rather liked everyone I'd met so far, I was lulled into a false security when it came to Barclay. My own fault. I could have kept my mouth shut. I should have kept my mouth shut, but I'm stupid and never learn. Third in command at St Mary's after Dr Bairstow and Chief Farrell, her approach was a contrast to everyone else's easy-going style; she was unpopular, self-important, and lacking the sense of humour gene.

Without warning, she wheeled and pounced. 'You! Stevens! What did I just say?'

If he'd had any idea of what she'd been boring on about, it must have flown straight out of his head with the sharpness of her question. He stared at her; a small furry woodland animal hypnotized by a ginger cobra. The silence lengthened.

I looked up. 'You were describing the position of a point as relative. No point can ever be regarded as solid or fixed but must always be viewed in relation to everything else.'

More silence. 'Is your name Stevens?'

Good God, it was like being back at school.

'No,' I said, helpfully. 'I'm Maxwell.'

'I suppose you think you're clever.'

More silence.

'Answer me.'

'I'm sorry; I didn't hear a question there.'

Mercifully, the clock struck, signifying the end of the lecture and lunchtime. No one moved.

At last, she stepped back. 'Dismissed.'

So that was my card marked; second period on the first day. Way to go, Maxwell.

St Mary's consisted of a warren of dark corridors and small rooms. Only the Staff Block, Hawking Hangar, and the kitchens were less than two hundred years old. The walls showed barely a lick of paint below shoulder height. The lovely old panelling was gouged and scraped and successive generations had carved their names and dates all over it. Such carpet as remained was old and worn. All the furniture sagged. We could see through the curtains they were so thin, and an overall smell of damp stone and whatever we'd had for lunch that day hung in the air.

Regular soft explosions from R & D didn't help with the preservation of the building. One memorable day, early in our training, Professor Rapson put his head round the door and said, mildly, 'If it's not too much bother, may I recommend you evacuate the building right now, please.'

Chief Farrell paused from revealing the secrets of the universe and said, 'Right, everyone out. Immediately. No, not the door, Miss Nagley, use the windows. Move!'

We clambered out of the windows and joined the rest of the unit on the South Lawn. Major Guthrie's team, wearing breathing apparatus, threw open windows around the building. Something greenish wafted out. We all got the afternoon off.

It was exhausting. It was exhilarating. And uncomfortable. I hadn't realised how closely together we would live and work. Historians work in pairs. We weren't assigned a partner because St Mary's believes the best and strongest partnerships are between those who choose each other. Like marriage, I suppose, but with a lower attrition rate. Where possible, the traditional pairing was one man and one woman. Grant and Nagley took to each other straight away and Rutherford and Stevens seemed to hit it off, which just left me and that cocky bastard, Sussman. The circumstances of my life before St Mary's had made me solitary but now wherever I looked he was there. He and I were the only unallocated singles so we seemed to be stuck with each other.

'What's the problem with working with me?' he demanded, after I'd spent an entire day trying to avoid him. 'Have I said something? Do I have bad breath? What is it?'

I tried to marshal some words. 'It's not you ...' I started to say.

'Oh, come on, you're not going to follow that up with, "It's me," are you?'

'Well, yes,' I said, stung. 'But I can lie to you if you prefer,' and went to step past him.

'No, look, I'm sorry. Just wait a minute. Have I done something? Sometimes, you know, I can be a bit ...'

'No, I'm ...' I struggled for words.

He smiled and said, 'You're not a team player. Yet. You don't trust people enough to place your safety in their hands. You don't like relying on other people and you especially don't want to rely on me because you don't know me, you don't like me, and you don't trust me. At this very moment you're wishing I'd drop dead so you can vanish back to your room and enjoy your own solitary self, doing whatever you do in there every night.'

'Well, nearly right. I'm actually trying to vanish to the dining room, but the rest was spot on.'

'Look, we two are on our own here. I've been watching you, Maxwell, and you're as good as I am. And I don't say that often because I've got a big head as well as a big mouth. At the moment, we need each other, and I think together we could be pretty good. You want to be the best and so do I, but we can't do it separately. I'm not asking you to tell me your life secrets or sleep with me; I just want to work with you. What do you say?'

I'd once over-ridden my instincts and confided in Mrs De Winter and that had changed my life. Maybe I could do it again. Looking at his feet, I nodded. He was too clever to push it any further. 'OK, I'll see you tomorrow, at breakfast,' and disappeared.

Once that barrier crumbled, others followed. On the whole, the people at St Mary's were a good crowd. Volatile, noisy, eccentric, argumentative, loyal, dedicated, and impatient as well, of course, but also the best bunch of people you could hope to meet. I began to relax a little. The strange chaos of the first few weeks unravelled into order and routine and we began to get the hang of things.

The mornings were mostly devoted to lectures on temporal dynamics, pod procedures, maths, and the history and structure of St Mary's. We spent our afternoons in the Library, keeping abreast of developments in our specialised areas – Ancient History in my case – the latest thinking in archaeology and anthropology, together with intensive research on the other two specialities in which we were required to be current.

'What did you choose as your other two specialties?' asked Sussman one Friday lunchtime as I staggered to my room, legs wobbling under the weight of books, papers, and boxes of data cubes and sticks. My scratchpad was banging in my knee pocket and I was desperate for tea and a pee and not in that order, either.

'Middle Ages and the Tudors,' I said. 'How about you?'

He opened the door for me. 'Roman Britain and the Age of Enlightenment.'

I was impressed. His main area was Early Byzantine. These were big subjects. He wasn't just a pretty face. I was glad now I'd taken a chance on him. He wasn't everyone's cup of tea, but I liked him better as I got to know him. Except on Fridays.

On Fridays, he was just a pain in the arse.

'It's Friday,' he said, passing me a sheet of paper and we sat down.

'Oh, for God's sake, Davey.'

'Come on, Max, it'll only take a minute.'

'Why don't you revise like the rest of us?'

'That's no fun. This is much more of a challenge.'

'Not as much of a challenge as that blonde admin clerk

25

you've been chasing all week. How's that working out for you?'

'I'm quietly confident,' he said, rolling up his sleeve and picking up a pen.

Every Friday afternoon after lunch, just when normal people were looking forward to the weekend, or feeling sleepy after too many helpings of Mrs Mack's treacle tart (or both), they would shove us into the small training room and hit us with unending questions on all the topics covered that week. Essays, multiple choice, the occasional practical demo – it all came thick and fast. One thing after another. Bang, bang, bang. And we had to pass. Failure was not an option, as the famous saying goes. Fail just one weekly test and you were out. No re-sits, no second chances. You were gone.

Consequently, every Friday lunchtime was devoted to the Sussman Method of Exam Preparation which basically consisted of writing things on his arm. This was irritating enough, without having to watch him achieving higher marks than those of us who'd toiled at the bookface, which was really bloody annoying.

He began to write.

'Come on, Max. Read me that bit about temporal and spatial co-ordinates and I'll buy you a drink.'

He found me one afternoon in the small classroom on the second floor where I was hiding from a cross-country run.

'Have you heard?'

'Obviously not,' I said, marking my place with a finger so he would take the hint and go away. 'Heard what?'

'Rutherford's broken his leg.'

'What? Is he OK?'

'Well, no. He's broken his leg, you daft bat.'

I picked up my McKissack's *The Fourteenth Century* and hefted it in a meaningful manner. 'Is he here in Sick Bay or have they taken him away?'

'Oh, they took him to Rushford. It was nearer. He'll be back soon.'

But he wasn't. We never saw him again. Rumour had it he went off to Thirsk as a post-grad assistant, which left poor Stevens pretty exposed. I really felt for Stevens. He wanted this so badly and he struggled with nearly everything. Academically he was fine, but with everything else he was a complete disaster and worst of all, that bitch Barclay, scenting blood in the water, was making his life a misery. This brought out the side of Sussman I didn't like very much. I asked him to tone things down a bit because he couldn't – or wouldn't – see that his careless brilliance and effortless achievement were a bit insensitive when Stevens was struggling so hard.

'Why should I?' he demanded. 'There's only three, or at the most, four of us going to complete our training. Me, you, Grant, and probably Nagley. What's the point?'

'Are you suggesting we throw Stevens under the bus?'

'What do you care?'

'He's one of us, you insensitive pillock.'

'Well, now who's suddenly a team player?'

'He'd do it for you.'

'He wouldn't have to.'

I said nothing, which was usually the best way with him.

'Oh, all right, then.'

After a morning running simulations, I was sitting at my favourite data table in the Library, trying to work out exactly where I had gone wrong when Sussman came and plonked himself opposite me.

'So, how did your first simulation go?'

'Oh, really well,' I said, inaccurately.

'Where did you end up?'

'Minoan Crete, Bronze Age.'

'Wow,' he said. 'Well done.'

'Yes. Sadly, I was aiming for early fifteenth-century

27

Constantinople.'

'Ah. Oh well, never mind. You'll get it right next time. Did you hear about Stevens?'

'Oh, no. What now?'

'He wanted Tudor England. 1588 to be precise.'

'And?'

'He ended up right in the middle of the Spanish Armada.'

I thought quickly. 'No, that's good. 1588 *is* the Spanish Armada.'

'No, *right in the middle* of the Spanish Armada. About eight miles off the east coast with the San Lorenzo bearing down on him with all guns blazing as he and his pod disappeared beneath the simulated waves. The Chief is still trying to work out how he accidentally managed to override all the safety protocols and Barclay's got a face like a buggered badger. He's a bit depressed, so we're off to ply him with alcohol before he loses the will to live. Coming?'

'Yes,' I said, stuffing my gear into my bag and following him to the bar.

Nagley and I put our heads together and did what we could. We gave Stevens extra sessions, extra revision, and helped him with his notes. Grant and a muttering Sussman tried to make him look good physically, but probably our efforts only served to highlight his deficiencies.

We were finishing one of the sessions with Chief Farrell on closed timelike curves when the door opened and Barclay marched in. I saw Stevens go pale. He'd been expecting this, but now the reality was upon him.

'Mr Stevens, a moment please.'

Whether by accident or design (and you never knew with her), the door didn't close properly behind her and we heard every word.

'Stevens,' she snapped, 'get your gear together, please. I'm sorry to tell you – you're chopped.'

28

It was brutal. The class gasped. We looked at each other. Chief Farrell, his lecture now lost beyond recall, got up and stepped out into the corridor. We could hear voices. Eventually silence fell. Chief Farrell brought Stevens back into the classroom. He dropped blindly onto the nearest chair. The Chief placed a sympathetic hand on his shoulder, said, 'I think we're finished here today,' and went quietly out of the room. I suppose it was too much to hope he was giving her a good kicking in the corridor.

Stevens was devastated. Grant and Sussman rushed him to the bar for emergency treatment. Nagley and I did his packing for him and spent an enjoyable half hour dreaming up a series of elaborate and painful deaths for Bitchface Barclay, as she was everlastingly known.

He cried when he left and, to my amazement, so did I, but we didn't have much time to mourn Stevens. Now we moved into the physical part of our training. Apparently, up until now we'd had it easy.

'Good morning, everyone,' said Major Guthrie, trying not to grin evilly and failing. 'Up to this moment, I'm sure you've all enjoyed the cut and thrust of academic debate, but the time has come to embark on the more "hands-on" part of your training. I see there are just the four of you remaining, which gives my section the opportunity to ensure each of you will receive extensive, thorough, and frequent attention. You will find your new timetables in the folders in front of you. Please study them carefully. The consequences of non-attendance, for whatever reason, will not be pleasant.

'Your primary survival strategy will always be running away, which brings me to the running schedules you will find in Appendix C. Those of you who have hitherto avoided our jolly cross-country sessions,' he smiled unpleasantly, 'will be sorry.'

Oh, bloody hell.

Now I got to know the security section rather well. As well as you usually get to know people who have their hands all over you five times a week. I suspect there are married couples who have less intimate physical contact than we did. I met Big Dave Murdoch, Guthrie's number two, a real gentle giant, calm and polite.

'Good morning, Miss Maxwell. Today, I'm going to rob, rape, and strangle you. Shall we begin?'

I also met Whissell, our other unarmed-combat specialist, small and runty with bad teeth and a habit of standing too close. They said he liked the girls a bit too much, but I suspected he didn't like girls at all. Sessions with Whissell and his hands were always a little too real to be comfortable and one day, enough was enough.

I reached down, grasped, and twisted.

'Aarghh,' he yelled. I saw the blow coming but didn't quite manage to avoid it.

He closed in.

'Very good, Miss Maxwell,' said Murdoch, appearing from nowhere. 'But a more effective response would have been to catch his wrist – like this – and follow through – like this – finishing with the heel of the hand – like this.'

We both regarded the groaning heap of Whissell.

'Most instructive,' I said. 'Thank you, Mr Murdoch.'

'An honour and a privilege, Miss Maxwell. And keep that thumb un-tucked.'

After that, I always tried to make sure I got Murdoch. Weasel, as we called him, was the type to hurt the things he feared. I tried to keep a discreet distance from him and remain politely aloof, but he had sensed my dislike and I suspected that I would pay for it one day.

They kicked up the simulations programmes until we were in Hawking morning, noon, and night. I loved these sims sessions. I loved walking down the hangar, joking with Nagley or Sussman. I loved entering the pod and smelling that special pod smell. I loved checking the lockers and stowing my gear, settling myself in the lumpy chair, beginning the start-up procedures, laying in my pre-calculated co-ordinates under Chief Farrell's watchful eye, taking a deep breath and initiating the jump. I loved dealing with the hair-raising scenarios that followed. The sims were so real to me that I was always surprised to open the door and find myself still in Hawking.

We simulated missions where everything went according to plan, but only a couple of times because that almost never happened.

We simulated missions where we were attacked by hostile contemporaries. That happened a lot.

We simulated missions where we became ill with something unpleasant. That happened a lot too.

We simulated missions where the pod caught fire.

And, everyone's favourite, we simulated missions where we all died. These were usually scheduled for a Friday morning so we finished in time for the afternoon exams. Nothing good ever happened on a Friday morning.

The final exams loomed ever closer. Not long to go now – the culmination of all our hard work. Unless you were Sussman of course, in which case, you'd barely worked at all. They posted the exam schedule. Every single one had a pass mark of 80% and we had to pass every single one.

First, on the Monday, was Weapons Expertise. I laid about me happily, smiting hip and thigh with enthusiasm. I got Big Dave Murdoch and not only could I hold him off, but I managed to land a couple of good blows as well. I felt pretty pleased with myself and he winked at me.

Archery was a doddle, as was target shooting. Guthrie scribbled away and I hoped this was a good sign. They gave me a pile of miscellaneous tat and fifteen minutes to fashion a weapon. In the absence of any fissionable materials, I came up with a pretty good slingshot that David himself would have been proud of and when asked to test fire, I took out the small window in the gents' toilets on the second floor. Much more scribbling happened.

Fire fighting was easy. Electrical, chemical – you name it, I doused it. There was good scribbling for Fire Fighting.

Wednesday was Self Defence. I made no headway at all with Weasel as he none too gently chucked me around all over the place, grinning his stupid head off all the time. I waited until a particularly heavy fall then placed my hand on my lower stomach, curled into a ball and uttered, 'Oh God, the baby!'

Weasel stopped dead, saying, 'What …?' and I hacked his legs out from underneath him, leaped to my feet, ran across his chest, and rang the bell, which was the whole point of the exercise. Weasel shot me a filthy look and, at this point, there was no scribbling at all. Major Guthrie threw down his clipboard and walked off.

'Oh dear,' I said to a watching Murdoch.

'No, you're OK. He's gone round the corner where no one can see him laugh.'

So I felt quite pleased with myself and then, on Thursday, it was time for the Field Medic Test.

We started with theory: plague, cholera, and typhoid symptoms, how to treat simple fractures, shock, resuscitation, no problem at all. In fact, I enjoyed it. Then, in the afternoon, we had to go out and find ourselves a body. A number of volunteers lay scattered around the place and we had to find one. They had a label tied to one arm with a list of symptoms and injuries so we could diagnose and treat. With my usual luck, I fell over Izzie Barclay.

We didn't like each other. I had still not forgiven her for Stevens and she definitely didn't like me. Physically, we looked alike: both of us being short and ginger. Maybe that was it. Maybe because I didn't find her as fascinating as she thought I should. I don't know.

She lay stretched out near the entrance to Hawking, muffled up to the eyebrows against the cold and reading *Computing for*

Geniuses, or some such thing. Her label said she'd been in an explosion. With dear old Mr Swanson from R & D looking on, I questioned her closely and got to work. Severe head trauma, broken limbs, burns; I worked away, bandaging, improvising splints and doing a good job. Mr Swanson scribbled away again. I sat back on my heels, satisfied, and then the sackless bint said, 'Oh, by the way, I'm on fire!'

My heart stopped. I'd failed.

I checked her label.

'No, you're not.'

'Yes, I am.'

'You didn't say.'

'You didn't ask.'

I took a deep breath. She was smirking. Everyone knew this was our examination. Everyone cut us some slack, Murdoch falling over more times than he had to, Guthrie rounding people's scores up instead of down. I bet Professor Rapson held up his broken limbs for bandaging without even being asked. And I'd got Bitchface Barclay and she'd screwed me.

I said, 'Oh dear,' deliberately omitting the 'ma'am' she so coveted. 'This is an emergency. I must deal with it at once.'

I stepped away to the outside tap, filled a bucket with ice-cold water, and emptied it all over her. She screamed and shot to her feet, soaked to the skin. It was bloody excellent. I didn't dare look at Mr Swanson. She had to drip her way past a small crowd of interested techies who had turned up to see who was screaming. Someone sniggered. I swear it wasn't me.

I waited all evening expecting to hear I'd been failed.

'Don't panic,' said Sussman. 'Why would they fail you for something so trivial? They've invested hugely in us. And it's not as if you actually set her on fire, which is what I would have done. You put her out. Don't expect any gratitude from the rest of the human race.'

He was right. I'm sure she filed her own body weight in yellow disciplinary forms, but I never heard a word about it. Of course after that day, she loved me even more!

And so we came to the dreaded Outdoor Survival, appropriately scheduled for Friday and all over the weekend. I'd survived unarmed combat. I'd even survived First Aid and Fire Fighting. So I was feeling pretty pleased with myself until Major Guthrie knocked the smirk off my face. Apparently, we would be driven to places unknown and left for two days to die of starvation and exposure. I hate the cold and wet and when I discovered this would be part of the final examination in November, I started to make plans. Not to cheat exactly, because that would be wrong, wouldn't it? More like dealing with the situation on my own terms.

I had already made some plans. Actually, I'd been making provisions since they first told us. We would be dropped off separately and make our way back somehow, to arrive before Sunday lunchtime. That wasn't going to be a problem because I planned not to leave the building in the first place.

I acquired one of Barclay's black jumpsuits. She was such a Grade-A bitch that I had no qualms at all in stealing from her. People see what they expect to see. Take away the greys and I was no longer a trainee. If I put on a techie-style baseball cap, grabbed a clipboard, slipped my scratchpad in my knee pocket, and looked as if I knew what I was doing, then I might just get away with it.

Next, I needed to avoid getting on the transport. I slunk into admin, brought up the lists, deleted my name, and re-printed. Hopefully, each driver would think I was with one of the others. Whenever anyone asked me which transport I was on, I said vaguely, 'The other one.'

So far, so good. Now I needed somewhere to hide for two and a half days. I planned to use the time studying for my pods exams, which followed immediately afterwards, so it couldn't have worked out better. I started poking round in odd corners.

Obviously, I wanted to avoid the main building, the Staff Block, and the public areas.

I remembered the dark corridor opposite the Sick Bay lift and went for a wander one evening. The best bet was at the end, in the paint store. The badly lit room, cluttered and dusty with disuse, had a large, empty area at the back, cordoned off by yellow and black tape.

A notice on the wall said:

NO STORAGE IN THIS AREA.
L. FARRELL (CTO)

It wasn't visible from the door, which made it ideal.

I started stockpiling. Sleeping bag, water, chocolate, torch, batteries, pods revision notes, and backpack. Food I would get the night before, pack it all away, and hide the backpack in the store. So long as I kept quiet, I should be OK. After all, I would be revising. It was practically my duty to cheat.

The others were strangely evasive about their own plans. I suspected they all had their contingencies stashed away around the countryside. I could only hope they weren't planning something similar. It would be a bit of a bugger if no one at all got on the transports.

I breakfasted ostentatiously in woodland camouflage gear, making sure I packed away enough to keep me going for the day, then slipped quietly away. I never thought I'd say this, but nothing you learn at school is ever wasted! Years of bunking off had finally paid off. In the toilets, I stood on the cistern, bundled my camouflage up into the false ceiling, and pulled out blacks, a cap, and a clipboard.

I wandered slowly down the long corridor, consulting my clipboard, occasionally peering at a fire alarm point, and making a tick on my paperwork. I felt horribly vulnerable, but no one so much as looked at me. No one came racing down the corridor shouting my name, so presumably I'd not been missed at the transports, either.

I strolled into the paint store and closed the door behind me. Retrieving my backpack and stuff from behind the cobwebbed tins of Battleship Grey at the back, I made my way to the empty corner. And a door opened in the middle of nowhere and Chief Farrell stepped out.

It would be hard to say who was the most gobsmacked. I stood rooted to the spot, waiting for him to realise where I should be, compare it to where I actually was, and fire me on the spot.

It didn't happen. Long seconds ticked by with nothing happening and it slowly dawned on me that he looked as guilty as I felt. And where had he come from? He just appeared. There was nothing. Then there was an open door. Then he stepped out. And here he was. In the middle of the room. We stared at each other.

'Miss Maxwell,' he managed, eventually, ignoring the fact I appeared to be disguised as the unit's IT officer.

'Good morning, Chief,' I said politely.

What now? While we were grappling with this social crisis, I heard sudden voices in the corridor outside. Panic gripped me and I stared wildly around for somewhere to hide. He grabbed my arm.

'Come with me. Door!'

Four strides and I was inside a pod. I would have known that even with my eyes shut. The smell was unmistakable. I looked around. This one was small. Maybe a single-seater. The layout was different, with the console on the left-hand wall. The colour was different – a boring beige instead of the standard grim grey. Everything was different, not least the fact it appeared, from the outside, to be invisible.

I couldn't think of anything to say that wouldn't get me into even deeper trouble, so I shut up. I suspect something similar flitted through his mind and he was a man of few words anyway.

Eons passed. My backpack slid off my shoulder and hit the floor with a thump that made us both jump. At last, he said, 'What are you doing here?'

'Looking for somewhere quiet to do my pod revision,' and pulled out a folder, as if that would convince him.

'Shouldn't you be ...?'

I cut him off with a gesture and a complicated, ambiguous noise intended to convey – if you don't ask then I won't have to lie and you won't have to take any action we might both regret, because, let's face it, I'm not the only one up to no good here.

We both paused to contemplate the massive rule-breaking going on here.

'Would you like some tea?'

'Oh. Yes, please.'

There was only one seat so we sat on the floor and sipped.

'You picked the wrong day to ... study ... in the paint store. It's inventory day and people are going to be in and out all day, counting things.'

Bloody typical. It had been such a good plan, too.

He sighed. 'You can stay here.'

I looked around.

'In my pod.'

I looked at him.

'This is my pod. My own pod. I keep it here out of the way.'

I carried on looking at him.

'It's experimental.'

'Ah. That accounts for some of its more unusual features.'

'Yes, I use it as a prototype. If things test OK then I incorporate them into the mainstream pods.'

I nodded.

'Only it's not generally known.'

I nodded again.

He turned and looked at me directly. 'Is this likely to be a problem for you?'

'No.'

37

'Edward mentioned this.'

'Edward?'

'Dr Bairstow. The Boss. He said he found it one of the most unusual things about you. He said the more extraordinary things he told you, the quieter and calmer you became. You're doing it again.'

'I'm sitting here in an invisible room!'

'Only from the outside and invisible is not a good word.'

'Don't tell me we're "cloaked".' I did the hooked fingers thing.

'No, it's camouflage. Simply a combination of high def. cameras and a sophisticated computer putting it all together and projecting the images back again. It works well against simple backgrounds like plain walls, less so against complex subjects – a leafy jungle for example.'

I nodded and looked around. A small telephone-like object resting on a stand caught my eye. 'You have a telephone?'

'Funny you should pick up on that. It's a remote control. Someday you'll be using one yourself.'

I nodded again, having no idea what he was saying.

'I'll leave you then to get on with your ... revision. You'll probably find around six thirty on Sunday morning will be the best time to finish and take a walk in the woods, coming in through the East Gate.'

'OK. Thanks.'

'Leave the place tidy,' he said, paused as if to say something else and then left. I made myself comfortable in his chair and pulled out my pod files.

He was right about the inventory. People wandered in and out all day, including Polly Perkins from IT and a small, dark girl and they had a very interesting conversation. They were counting tins of Sunshine Yellow, which is, apparently, the colour of the cross-hatching outside the hangar, when the Chief stuck his head round the door and without even a glance in my direction, asked them to count Lamp Black as well.

After he'd gone, they put down their paperwork and prepared for a good gossip.

'Is he shagging Barclay?'

I turned up external audio and stared at the screen.

'No, that never really got off the ground, although not for want of trying on her part. She did everything she could and at the last Christmas party, it was just plain embarrassing. But fun to watch.'

'Whatever did he do?'

'Nothing. He was polite but distant. You know how he can be.'

'Yeah, and I know how she can be as well. Don't tell me she's given up.'

'She might as well. The word on the street now is that he's very interested in someone else.'

'Oh? Who's that then?'

'Can't you guess?'

'What? Her? You're having me on!'

Her? Who's her? Why does everyone always know what's going on but me? Come on, ladies! Clarify for the confused eavesdropper.

'Well, she'll lead him a merry dance.'

'Already is by the sound of it.'

Why was I so upset?

'No wonder Barclay's so pissed.'

'Yeah, great isn't it?'

'And they say,' she continued, 'that cocky git Sussman's sniffing around as well.'

What? Who?

'Did you hear she chucked a bucket of cold water over Barclay the other day? Apparently they all nearly wet themselves trying not to laugh and old Swanson doubled her score on the spot.'

Wow! 'She' was me. I never saw that coming. An inner

voice said, 'He's not interested in you. Who would be?' But inside, a little warm glow spread.

I had nearly forty-eight hours solid revision time in this oasis of peace. I un-jangled my nerves, gave my aching body a rest, drank an ocean of tea, made sandwiches, ate chocolate, slept, and revised big time. And spent some time thinking about what I'd overheard. I did try to concentrate on operations, procedures, and protocols but snippets of that conversation kept intruding. Occasionally, I grinned to myself.

I eased myself out of the building at six thirty on Sunday. The Chief was right; it was a good time. Hardly anyone was up and paying attention at that time on a Sunday morning. The night watch, in their last hour of duty would be thinking of breakfast and writing their logs and everyone else was still in bed. I changed back into camouflage gear and strode confidently towards the woods. The rain bucketed down; thus confirming my decision to give the whole exposure and hardship thing a miss. It was three long miles to the East Gate. By the time I'd hacked my way through wet woodland, tripped over roots, fallen into boggy patches, had my face whipped by branches, and been splattered with mud, it looked as if I'd been out there for a fortnight. I was soaked to the skin.

I got lost twice – I'm not good with directions, eventually arriving at the East Gate. They laughed at me but gave me a slurp of hot tea while I signed in. They must have rung ahead because Major Guthrie was waiting for me. I knew he was suspicious, but I looked so authentic: wet, muddy, bleeding, limping, and I'd only gone three miles.

'How did you get back?'

'Found a stream and followed it down.'

'How did you find the stream?'

'Fell in it.'

'How did you get in?'

'East Gate.'

'How did you find the East Gate?'

'I was looking for the South Gate.'

'Where were you dropped?'

'Some God-forsaken, windswept, rain-lashed, barren landscape not previously known to man.'

'I can't seem to find your name on the transport list.'

'Bloody hellfire, sir, does that mean I didn't have to do this?'

Long, long pause. I returned his stare with a look of blinding innocence and batted mud-clogged eyelashes at him. I'd cheated. He knew I'd cheated, but I stood before him, authentically bedraggled and there wasn't a lot he could do.

'Go and get cleaned up and get something to eat.'

'Yes, Major.'

Yay!

Afterwards, I said to Sussman, 'How did you do?'

'I paid a guy to follow the transport at a discreet distance. He picked me up and I spent the weekend clubbing in Rushford.'

'What? Baby seals?'

'Very funny.'

'What about Grant and Nagley?'

'They planned ahead, planted two mobile phones in the transports, used the GPS, rang for a taxi, booked into a small hotel, and shagged themselves senseless for forty-eight hours.'

And I'd spent forty-eight hours living off sandwiches and sleeping on the floor. Alone.

'Does anyone actually take this bloody exam?'

'Not in living memory. That's the whole point. It's an initiative test. They know we all cheat. It's expected. The trick is to look them in the eye and lie right down the line.'

Well, bloody, bollocking hell!

I was still somewhat aggrieved over the Outdoor Survival thing, but the three-day pod exam was a triumph, as were Thursday's simulations. The end was in sight, which was just as well, because I was absolutely knackered. It would be typical if I fell at the last fence. Only the sims weren't the last fence. The last fence was on Tuesday. Tuesday was the real deal.

Three

Tuesday was the day when we finally found out if we had what it took. No more hiding behind the theory or the lectures or the sims. No more hiding from our own fears. This was it at last.

I kicked off the covers and bounded out of bed. Not something that happened too often. After a quick shower I dressed, with luck for the last time in the now-despised greys. Skipping down the corridor, I banged on Sussman's door. 'Come on! Today's the day.'

I heard his door open behind me, but didn't stop. Dancing round the corner, I ran into Chief Farrell. It was like hitting a warm wall. He steadied me and we smiled at each other. I wouldn't have thought my heart could beat any faster without flying out of my chest altogether. 'Sorry, Chief. Did I hurt you?'

He smiled patiently. 'No, Miss Maxwell, I have survived. Your big day, then?'

'You betcha, Chief. Shrewsbury, circa 1400. Can you believe it?'

'I seem to remember you mentioning it almost incessantly this last week. You're in Number Eight, by the way.'

'Great! Eight is my lucky number.' I grinned like an idiot and hopped from foot to foot in my impatience to get going.

'Go, Miss Maxwell, before you break something.'

'Bye, Chief.' And I was gone.

I helped myself to eggs, bacon, hash browns, and grapefruit juice. The others did the same, although Nagley just pushed hers around the plate. I thought she looked a little pale and when I spoke to her she only nodded. Sussman, naturally, was nearly as full of it as me.

As soon as we finished, we set off to Wardrobe. I was issued a thick, coarse, brown woollen dress of ankle length.

'Forget sweeping around with a long dress,' said Mrs Enderby, supervising my transformation. 'This is not the movies. Nothing picks up dust, dirt, wet, excrement, and the occasional dead dog as much as a sweeping hemline. You'll thank us when you're tip-toeing through the delights of a medieval street.' She was kind enough not to mention occasionally having to run for my life as well. The look we were going for was a young, respectable housewife, maybe a journeyman's wife or an upper servant to a prosperous household. A young, unmarried, and seemingly unprotected girl wandering around the streets would be asking for trouble.

Underneath I wore several linen shifts and, underneath them, a sports bra and modern thermal underwear. There was no way I would be wandering around medieval Shrewsbury in early spring with no drawers on. And, as Mrs Enderby so cheerfully said, if things got bad then the wearing of anomalous underwear was going to be the least of my problems.

I also got a linen wimple to show my married status, a pair of stout leather shoes, a dark green cloak, and a basket. We always carry something. It helps us blend in and gives us something to do with our hands.

They showed me the waterproof matches, compass, and water purification tablets all carefully sewn into concealed pockets.

Sussman was off to a Victorian village cricket match, Nagley to Restoration London, and Grant got Roman York. All quiet and unspectacular jumps since we were, for the first and last time, going solo. It only ever happens on the first jump; for all other jumps there are always at least two historians.

Wardrobe checked us over for watches and jewellery and then despatched us to the hangar. Of course, everyone knew where we were going and why. Best wishes and good luck calls followed us down the corridors. I don't know how the others felt, but my insides were somersaulting and I was equally torn between fear and excitement.

We entered the noisy hangar. All the pods were in on that day so there were a lot of people around.

We scattered towards our respective pods. Number Eight was at the end. Chief Farrell was waiting. The computer read the codes and opened the door. I climbed in and looked around. The console sat to the right of the door in this pod and I could see the co-ordinates already laid in.

'All done,' said the Chief. 'It's all on automatic for this jump. There's really nothing for you to do but sit back and enjoy the ride. Let's just rein you in a bit so we can go through the pre-flight checks.' He pulled his scratchpad from his knee pocket and began punching keys while I walked around checking everything. Opening a locker door I was surprised to see it fully stocked with rations; lots of rations.

'What's all this?'

'Oh, I forgot to say. We're turning this one round as soon as you come back, so it's ready loaded for fourteen days.'

'The toilet's working. Try and keep it that way. So is the incinerator. The tanks are full and the cells charged. It's the easiest jump you'll ever have; absolutely nothing for you to do. How long are you going for?'

'Only six hours. I used to know Shrewsbury quite well, so I'm looking forward to having a good wander round. They won't let me stay any longer.'

He smiled. 'Six hours is long enough for your first trip.'

'Am I going in real time?'

'No. Six hours for you and thirty minutes for me. After I've seen you off, I'm going to make myself a cup of coffee and wait over there for you to come back. You'll be back here before I've finished it.'

'If you have a cup of tea ready for me, then I'll tell you all about it.'

He looked at me with his head on one side. 'Yes, all right.'

I was suddenly embarrassed. 'Oh, no, it's OK, Chief. I just thought ... you know ... of course, it's nothing special for you, is it?'

'I shall demand a blow-by-blow account from you in return for a mug of tea. Now, are you all set?'

Putting the basket on the second chair, I settled in the left-hand seat and checked the read-outs. I took a deep breath, turned and grinned at him. 'Yes!'

'Good luck! See you later.'

After he had gone, I said, not without a bit of a wobble, 'Computer, close the door.' The door shut. Well, so far, so good. Across from me, Pod Three disappeared. I said, 'Computer, confirm co-ordinates are laid in.'

'Confirmed.'

Another deep breath. 'Initiate jump.'

'Jump initiated.'

There were no flashing lights, no calendars with the dates peeling away, and no dramatic music. The world went white for a few moments and then cleared. I peered out eagerly at what had to be the most un-Shrewsbury like landscape on the planet.

Green grass flowed as far as the eye could see. On the horizon, huge snow-capped mountains jutted up into a clear blue sky. I didn't know where or when I was, but it sure as hell wasn't Shrewsbury.. It probably wasn't Kansas, either. I'm pretty sure I said, 'Shit!' and switched on the other cameras, in case Shrewsbury was hiding round the corner. But there was no corner. No Shrewsbury. No nothing. Only waving grass.

I sat for a bit and had a think. After a while I said, 'Computer; confirm date and location.'

'Shrewsbury, England. 1408.'

'Computer; confirm time of jump remaining.'

'Five hours, fifty-six minutes.'

Given the socking great Shrewsbury-shaped gap in the landscape and the fact that my plans for the day had been kicked into touch, I really should go home now. On the other hand …

'Door.'

The door opened and cold, fresh air flooded in. I stood up slowly. Standing in the doorway, I put one hand on each side of the door jamb and cautiously peered out.

In front of me, the grass rippled and shimmered in the breeze. The sun beat down from a cloudless blue sky. Apart from the hissing wind, it was utterly silent.

I turned back into the pod, paused, and then looked to the door again, considering my options. I could demand emergency extraction from the computer, which would whirl me back to St Mary's at nose-bleeding speed almost before the words had been uttered. It's quick and definitely not painless. That's why it's for emergencies only. I certainly wasn't where I should be and it would be the cautious, the sensible thing to do. But, for God's sake, I was an historian and cautious and sensible were things that happened to other people. I wasn't in any danger; the worst that could happen would be an afternoon of mild tedium.

People usually only shrieked for emergency extraction when they were actually on fire or bleeding from multiple wounds. What would I say? What emergency could I declare? 'I'm not in Shrewsbury,' hardly seemed to cut it. What was the point of doing this if not to explore a little? And the pod wasn't going anywhere for five hours.

On the other hand, there had obviously been a major malfunction. If I went outside and the stupid thing went off without me then I was in deep shit. Presumably it and everyone else thought I was in fifteenth-century Shrewsbury. Yes, a sensible person would definitely not go outside.

I picked up the basket and wedged it in the doorway. If the door couldn't close then the pod couldn't jump. Theoretically.

Standing in the doorway I took a long step outside. Nothing changed, so I took another. Even not knowing where or when I'd landed could not detract from my excitement. I was in another time! I was an historian! I held out my arms and twirled around and around. I was an historian! The sights I would see. I shouted, 'Yes!' turned a cartwheel, and my coif fell off.

It seemed wise to calm down a little. I didn't want my first jump to be my last. Protocol says the first thing to do is to establish personal safety – often a bit of an optional extra for historians. I scrambled up on to the roof and revolved slowly around 360 degrees. Shading my eyes, I turned around the other way. The computer remained silent. None of the proximity alerts went off. I still had no idea where I was, or when, but this world was empty. Nothing impeded the view from horizon to horizon; nothing in the sky; no smoke; no vapour trails; not even a bird. Only the swaying grass moved in the wind. I was completely alone.

It could have been frightening, but the assignment was only for six hours and after all those years at Uni, more years post-grad work, archaeological work, and then all that training at St Mary's, I found it very pleasant just to stand, eyes closed, with the sun on my face, and listen to the silence.

After a while I decided I could improve on this so I jumped down, made myself a cup of tea, snagged a bar of high-energy chocolate from the rations locker, spread my cloak on the ground, and sat with my back against the sunny side of the pod.

I was happily sunning myself when the computer cleared its throat and announced sixty minutes to the return jump. I'd done it! Assignment completed!

I did a quick tidy round because historians never go back with a messy pod. I picked everything up, did the outside FOD plod (Foreign Object Drop) to check nothing had been left behind and the inside POD plod to make sure I hadn't inadvertently picked something up: very important that, because the pod wouldn't jump if I had. I put the folded cloak inside my basket and placed it on the second chair, incinerated the chocolate wrapper, washed my face and hands, settled myself in the chair, and watched the numbers count down.

At thirty minutes the computer reminded me again. And

again at ten minutes, five minutes, one minute, and finally, at thirty seconds. I'd be back in seconds, shout at the techies for not knowing their Shrewsbury from their elbow, have a brew with the Chief, check in with Sick Bay, sign something official, exchange the despised greys for blues, drop the word 'trainee' from my life, and become a proper, fully-fledged historian. Look out world.

'Ten, nine, eight,' said the computer. 'Five, four, three,' and the voice stopped as the entire console went dark.

The entire bloody console went dark.

This time I did panic. My heart stopped and it wasn't until my chest began to hurt that I remembered to breathe. Gripping the edge of the console, I shouted 'No, no, no, no!' and began to thump the panel. Strangely, this failed to work at all.

I struggled to stay calm. I kept staring at the console, desperately willing it to fire up again. This was unheard of. I'd never seen a dark panel because no pod had ever failed before. This could not be worse. I was stranded at an unknown destination. The pod had malfunctioned and thought it was in Shrewsbury in the 1400s and so any search initiated by St Mary's would go there. If I didn't know where I was then how would they? And it was all my own fault. If I'd gone back immediately when it became apparent the jump had gone wrong, then I wouldn't be here now.

'Computer.'

No response.

'Computer, status report.'

Nothing.

'Computer, open the door.'

The door stayed shut.

I pushed the manual control and the door slid open. So, I still had power and I still had life support. I just didn't have a working pod. For all intents and purposes it was now just a bloody hut. I switched the lights off and then back on again. It was noticeably colder outside, so I shut the door. The sun was

49

lower. It would be dark soon.

If in doubt, make some tea. I'm St Mary's: if hitting someone didn't solve the problem, then drinking tea would. I curled up in the first chair, spread the cloak over my lap, cuddled my tea, and tried to think what to do. It didn't take long to reach the conclusion there was nothing I could do. I could take the panel off and have a look. Then I could shrug my shoulders and replace the panel. There were tea bags with more electronic know-how than me. I could see no way round it. I was fucked.

Strangely, I found the conclusion quite liberating. When you're fucked, you're fucked. Things really can't get much worse.

With that thought, the last sunlight disappeared outside. The sensible thing would be to conserve power and go to bed with the sun. But I don't sleep well anyway and there was no chance tonight, so I thought I would use the time productively. I began opening and closing doors, pulling out drawers, checking my resources, and generally taking stock.

I had rations for about fourteen days. Or more, if I stuck to just two meals a day. Water, ditto. The toilet worked (for the time being). The incinerator worked. I found two old-fashioned scribble pads I could use for my log, something I'd forgotten about until now. I had heavy weather clothing and boots, all too big for me. I had matches, a compass, and water tablets, two sleeping modules, and a spare blanket that smelled a bit iffy. It could be a lot worse.

I shoved an arm into the rations pile and pulled out two trays at random. Chicken curry and stewed apple. Sod that for a game of soldiers. I tossed the stewed apple and pulled out sticky toffee pud. If I was going to die alone and abandoned I was buggered if I was going to do it on stewed apple.

The food actually tasted quite good. Fortunately, I'm a terrible cook, so my expectations of food are never high. I think airline food is great. I pulled the red heating tabs and munched away. Afterwards I washed my face and hands, took down and plaited my hair, undressed, and pulled out one of the sleep modules. It moulded itself around me and sensing I was cold, began to warm up. If ever there was a time and a place to have a bit of a snivel then this was it. But I didn't.

It was a long night; a long, long night. I think I dozed a couple of times but not for very long. I made mental lists of the Kings and Queens of England, then their spouses. I composed an imaginary essay on the causes of the Wars of the Roses. I listed my top ten favourite books, then my ten favourite movies. I played Shoot, Shag, or Marry. It was a long night.

When the screen showed a cold, grey light outside, I got up and made some tea.

I tried talking to the computer again but it wasn't having any of it. I tried hard not to remember that this time yesterday I was having breakfast at St Mary's.

My training said it was important to establish a routine, so I began to map out my day. Tidy the pod and myself and put away the sleeping gear. Have brunch around mid-morning. Spend some time on the roof looking for signs of human habitation – although if I found any, whether I would run to or from was a good question. Walk or run for one hour. The ground was so flat I should be able to run for some time without losing sight of the pod. Sit in the sun and read until it became chilly. Go inside and tidy up. Eat again. Read again. Write up the daily log. Go to bed. Don't lie awake panicking.

That's how it went for two days. It wasn't unpleasant. On the third day I was sitting outside, using a valuable page in the scribble pad to sketch the mountains when something clicked in my head. This was not a bad life. I had everything I needed; good weather, a safe environment, something to read, enough to eat.

Yes, I did, didn't I? I had everything I needed to survive comfortably for a fortnight at least.

Another click. How lucky that this pod was loaded ready for

51

a quick turn over, even though there were other pods available for use.

And then I started to laugh. As if Chief Farrell would ever send out an unreliable pod with a trainee. This was why they sent you alone. It wasn't spending an afternoon in Shrewsbury that was the test. *This* was the real test. To survive, alone, lost, with no hope of rescue or backup. This was why he programmed the co-ordinates himself. This was why it was all on automatic.

I bet if I just sat quietly and waited; the pod would re-activate itself in twelve days' time and get me back to St Mary's as if nothing had happened. Well, I was going to tough it out. Of course, if I was wrong then I was going to look pretty silly in twelve days' time. On the other hand, who would know?

The days slipped slowly by; each one the same as the last in this unchanging landscape. I sat in the sun, thumb in bum, brain in neutral, and let my mind drift. I thought about the chain of events leading to this moment. I thought about my childhood, but not for long. I wondered if I wanted to be alone all my life. I wondered if I didn't want to be alone all my life.

I wrote my log, spending five or six pages on the subject of technical incompetence and embellishing the text with small sketches. I had long chats with myself. I tried new ways of wearing my hair. And really doing my best not to think about what would happen on Day 14. Which came, of course, shortly after Day 13, as is the scheme of things. I didn't leave the pod all day, waiting for the console to light up again.

It didn't.

Noon came and went.

I sat unmoving.

The sun started to go down. Shadows lengthened. Total silence.

Nothing happened.

It began to get dark. Still nothing happened.

I clenched my hands tightly in my lap. I sat in the dark.

Nothing happened. Nothing bloody happened!

The one thought clanking around my head was that this was self-inflicted. Obviously, *obviously,* I should have declared an emergency and returned home at once, when I could, when the bloody system was still working. How could I have pushed my luck like this?

I must have dropped off because I awoke, cold and stiff, early on the morning of Day 15 with some hard thinking to do. Reviewing my resources, I had about three days' food left and a little less water. It was definitely time to go home.

On the other hand … on the other hand … on the other hand … maybe *this* was the test. How traumatic is it to be marooned somewhere safe and quiet with plenty of food? Maybe the test was survival *after* all expectation of rescue was past and supplies had run out.

How did it go? Three minutes without oxygen. Three days without water. Three weeks without food. So, should I leave the pod to find water and miss the chance of possible extraction? Or should I stay put and gamble on being rescued before death by dehydration, which, I'd heard, was not a pleasant way to die? But short of expiring of exhaustion underneath a chocolate-covered someone whose name I wasn't yet ready to admit to myself, what is a pleasant way to die? And should I start rationing myself? Which meant I could last for maybe an extra two or three days? Or just eat and drink the lot and die anyway?

Day 15 ended. I pulled out the scribble pad and thought about leaving details of who I was and why I was here, in case my remains should ever be found. Bugger it. Let them guess.

I had a sudden, heartrending vision of the Chief, sitting alone with a mug of cold tea by his side and really did have to blink back a tear of self-pity. Would my name go up on the Boards? I wasn't technically an historian yet. It might not count. I sat outside with my arms around my knees and thought gloomy thoughts. I'd just closed my eyes when I heard a click, a hum, and the entire console lit up like the Christmas display in Oxford Street. Lights flashed, requiring a response.

I scrambled to my feet, tripped on my skirt, and rushed in to look. The readouts seemed normal, the countdown held at 4, awaiting confirmation to continue.

For a moment, I thought I might faint. I sat heavily and waited for my innards to subside. Pulling myself together, I shut the door; kicked lockers closed, rolled up the sleeping module, and splashed water on my face, all in about thirty seconds. I sat down, ordered my heart to slow down, and activated the countdown. The world went white, a slight bump, and I was home.

Oh God, I was home!

Peering through the screen, I was amazed to see St Mary's carrying on pretty much as normal. Didn't these idiots know what I'd been through? Then I sat back. Of course they did. I'd never been in any sort of danger at all. Well, if they could play it cool then so could I. I activated the decontamination unit and sat back while the cold, blue light worked its magic.

I saw the Chief crossing the floor with a mug of steaming tea. He knocked on the door.

I called, 'Who's there?'

After a pause long enough for the word 'cocky' not actually to be spoken aloud, he said, 'Room service.'

I laughed and opened the door. He handed me the tea and began to shut things down. Outside, I could see his crew plugging in the umbilicals.

'How did it go?'

'It was fine. Ate, read, worked on the tan. Thought about St Mary's best kept secret. I'm impressed, I'm really impressed. I didn't have – none of us had – the slightest idea about this. How has St Mary's kept this quiet over the years?'

'Everyone who thinks about it sees the benefit of keeping it quiet. It's the most valuable test we have; and the most nerve-wracking, for us, as well as for you.'

'This is fantastic tea.'

'How long ago did you run out?'

'Two long days ago.'

'We were spot on then. We have to try to gauge it so you're close to running out of supplies but haven't yet struck out across country to search for help. When were you planning to go?'

'I wasn't. I knew you wouldn't let me starve.'

'No one likes a smart arse.'

'Does this mean I've failed?'

'No, Miss Maxwell, it means you're top of the class.'

Yes! My future stretched happily in front of me; back to the past.

'How about the others? Are they back yet?'

He frowned. 'Grant activated his emergency extraction as soon as he realised he was where he shouldn't be, which is, of course, the correct procedure. And Nagley, too. I'm sorry to say she wasn't very calm and has subsequently left the unit.'

'She's gone?'

'She couldn't wait. She had a fairly tense conversation with Grant and left immediately.'

'Did she leave a message for me?'

'I'm sorry, no.'

I was hurt. We'd been together a long time and she was the only other girl. I'd liked her. And she'd left without even a goodbye.

'Sussman says he worked it out, but demanded emergency extraction after five days, claiming boredom. He exited his pod, thumped the first technician he came across who happened to be Mr Dieter and so spent the rest of the day in Sick Bay recovering consciousness. You're the last back.'

'Is that good or bad?'

'It demonstrates a certain mind-set.'

I chugged back the tea and set out for Sick Bay and the more than scary Dr Foster. If there is an opposite of a good bedside manner then Helen Foster has it.

'Come in, Maxwell.' She activated a data stack, went to sit on the window sill, and rummaged in her pockets, pulling out a pack of cigarettes. She lit one.

'Have you ingested or imbibed anything other than standard rations?'

I looked pointedly at the smoke detector. 'No.'

'I took the battery out years ago.' I got the feeling Chief Farrell was fighting a losing battle with smoke detectors and fire alarms. 'Have you had sexual relations or exchanged bodily fluids with anyone outside this timeline?'

'Sadly, no. Nor anyone in this timeline either.'

'Too much information. Have you received any injuries, wounds, broken your skin, have a rash or skin lesions …?' And on and on. After a while, she flipped her dog-end out of the window. There was a squawk from outside.

'I keep telling you, Peterson, don't stand there. Idiot!'

We established I'd spent sixteen days of unparalleled tedium and that I constituted no threat to life as we knew it and I skipped off to see Mrs Partridge, who made me sign hundreds of documents which mostly said that everything happening to me from now on was entirely my own fault. She sent me off to Wardrobe, who issued me with a full set of the coveted blues and all the rest of my kit and sent me back to Mrs Partridge again, who offered me the choice of a bigger room in the Staff Block or one in the main building. I went with the one in the main building. It had a bath.

I was allocated an attic room on the small, east landing. I had Dr Foster opposite me and Kalinda Black, another historian, on the other side. My room was long and narrow with a small window at the front overlooking the lake and a larger window with a low window seat overlooking a flat roof. Furnishings were the usual St Mary's minimum – a Narnia wardrobe, a bed, a baggy couch, a bookcase, and a data table. But I did have a small bathroom where, for some reason, I had to climb over a vast enamel, claw-footed bath to get to the toilet.

I bought a rug, some posters, and a corkboard where I could pin up my favourite bits and pieces. I blagged an old table from Housekeeping because I needed somewhere for all the painting gear I drag around with me wherever I go, paints and brushes, added a tin of biscuits and a kettle, and had everything I needed.

I loved my room, from the uneven floor to the pock-marked walls. It was the first space I'd ever had that was truly mine and no one could get in. I arranged my books, hung my blues in the wardrobe, and waited in excited anticipation for whatever came next.

Four

What came next was a reality check. We had two deaths in my first two weeks as a historian. Training had been hard work, difficult, strenuous, scary even, but apart from cuts, bruises, and the odd simple fracture, not particularly hazardous. All that would change now we were fully-fledged members of the History Department.

The History Department wasn't anything like as large as it should be. We were established for twelve historians but until we'd graduated, they'd been limping along with just four. Anne-Marie Lower and Tom Baverstock were Senior Historians, and Tim Peterson and Kalinda Black had just recently qualified. Add the three of us, and that made seven.

'More than they've had for years,' said Sussman. But not for long.

With Industrial History as her specialty and as a Mancunian herself, Kalinda Black was all geared up for the next investigation. The Peterloo Massacre was part of an ongoing 'History of Democracy' assignment, which included the Peasant's Revolt and the signing of Magna Carta at Runnymede. Baverstock and Lower got the peasants and Grant, Sussman and I hoped that if we kept quiet and tried to look normal, at least one of us would be included in the Runnymede jump. But the first in the series was Peterloo.

So keen was Kalinda to go that she ignored persistent abdominal pain, dosed herself with a year's worth of laxatives, doubled over at breakfast one day, and despite loudly declaring it was only a spot of indigestion, got carted off to meet her fate in Sick Bay.

I sat contemplating a morning in the Library with no great enthusiasm. Sussman had taken himself off somewhere and I was lingering over a mug of tea before making a move. I jumped a mile as Grant threw himself into a chair beside me, face flushed with excitement, his faint Scottish accent more pronounced than usual. 'Guess what? Black's got appendicitis. They're whipping it out as we speak.'

Really, I suppose, my reaction should have been concerned sympathy, but first things first.

'So who's going to Peterloo, then?'

'Obviously, it's going to be one of us, isn't it?'

We looked at each other. I stood lazily. 'Well, sadly, I'm in the Library all morning. I've got a pile of anthropology papers to read.'

'Me too,' he said casually. 'What a bummer.'

I beat him to the door, but he drew ahead as we galloped across the Hall and he got to the Library first. Much good it did him because Dr Dowson, wise in the ways of historians, had two files already waiting. I felt a little bit guilty.

'What about Sussman?'

He polished his glasses. 'Oh, he picked his up a good hour ago. I'm afraid he's got quite a start on you two.'

Bastard!

Grant and I eyed each other and then by, unspoken consent, split up. I settled down and sorted through the material.

In August 1819, sixty-thousand demonstrators assembled in St Peter's Square, Manchester. They were anti-poverty and pro-democracy which did them no favours at all in the eyes of authority. Despite this, the demonstrators regarded this as a fun day out for the family, dressing in their Sunday best and bringing the kids.

Equally looking forward to the day, but for completely different reasons, were the local Yeomanry, led by a Captain Hugh Birley. Drawn from local mill owners and shop proprietors, they would have had strong views about workers gaining the right to vote and having enough to eat.

Local magistrates read the Riot Act to a very small section of the crowd and then, legal duty done, withdrew to let the drunken Yeomanry get on with it. They charged the crowd, ostensibly to arrest Henry Hunt who was speaking from a cart. The protestors linked arms to prevent this and were struck down by the Yeomanry, who were, apparently, as pissed as newts. The crowd panicked; this was seen as an attack and six hundred Hussars went in. Eighteen people, including one woman and child, were killed. The military received a message from the Prince Regent, congratulating them on their success.

The assignment originated from Thirsk and the brief was simple enough. Observe and authenticate. Bread and butter stuff. I wondered which of us would get it. It wasn't my specialty or any of my secondary areas either. It certainly wasn't any of Sussman's. Grant was the nearest, with the French Revolution. But he was also quiet and easily overlooked. It had to be between me and Sussman.

I reviewed the file twice and then went for lunch. Sussman was there, smirking.

I sat opposite him and unwrapped my sandwich.

'Bastard!'

'Early bird,' he said, smugly. 'No point in knocking yourselves out, I've already volunteered.'

'But you haven't got it yet?'

'Well, there isn't anyone else, is there?'

'Actually, yes. Grant's specialty is closer than Early Byzantine. In fact, everything's closer than Early Byzantine.'

'Except Ancient Civilisations. Face it, Max, you couldn't be any further away if you tried. And you're female.'

'Exactly, teams consist of one male and one female, so neither of you stands a chance. Peterson will take me.'

'They won't send you to a riot.'

'Don't give me any of that crap. I've started a few riots in my time. It's going to be me.'

'Over your dead body. I'm the obvious choice. I graduated top …'

'No, I was two points ahead of you.'

'… I know the period. I've read the brief. I've already registered an interest. There's no doubt it will be me. Oh, and I'm the tallest, as well.'

I opened my mouth but it never got said because suddenly Grant was with us. We only had to look at him to know. He glowed with excitement and pride and his grin could be seen from space.

'No,' protested Sussman. 'Surely not. What are they thinking?'

He was such an insensitive pillock sometimes.

'You're such an insensitive pillock sometimes,' I told him. Swallowing my disappointment, I turned to Grant. 'You lucky devil. So, you'll be the first of us away, then?'

He nodded, still too full of it to speak.

'Well done,' I said. 'I mean it,' and kicked the insensitive pillock under the table.

'Ow! Yes, well done, mate.' He scowled and I kicked him again. 'Will you stop doing that?'

I nodded towards Grant. 'It's his first assignment. It's *our* first assignment. Make an effort.'

He did. 'Yeah, well done, Kev. When do you go?'

'Tomorrow afternoon. Peterson's briefing me in …' he looked at his watch, '… now,' scrambled to his feet and nearly tripped over his chair.

Sussman handed him his untouched sandwiches. 'Here, you should eat before you fall over. Take these.' Just when I'd decided he was a complete arsehole, he surprised me. You could always say that about Sussman – he always surprised you.

We spent the evening going through Grant's brief with him.

'I still can't believe they chose me,' he said on several occasions, causing me to kick Sussman again before he could agree with him.

'You deserve it,' I told him. 'You worked really hard for this.' And he had. He wasn't showy, like Sussman or me, but he'd put in hours of solid, hard, unspectacular work. It meant he'd have seniority over Sussman and me as well. That hadn't occurred to him yet, but it would. It would occur to Sussman as well and that would be a fun moment.

We saw him off the next day. He marched down the hangar beside Peterson, so full of pride and purpose that my heart nearly burst for him. Even Sussman clapped and whistled. They paused in the doorway, waved and disappeared into their pod. After a minute or two, the Chief came out and waved everyone back behind the safety line. Thirty seconds later, they were gone.

We made sure to be in the hangar in good time for their return. Kalinda Black, grumpy but recovering, came with us. I could imagine Grant, tumbling out of the pod, eager to tell us all his adventures, absolutely full of himself.

I nudged Sussman. 'Be nice.'

He looked offended. 'Of course I will.' We looked at each other and grinned. This would be us soon.

Number Five light flickered. We craned forward on the gantry, all prepared to give Grant a hero's welcome. He was the first of our intake to jump. He deserved something special. We'd got a big night planned as soon as he got the all clear from Sick Bay.

The pod materialised. And nothing happened.

I don't know why, but I felt a chill. As clearly as yesterday I remembered Chief Farrell saying, 'You get a feel for it.' I had a feel for it now and I wasn't the only one. Around me, the hangar fell quiet.

Chief Farrell crossed the floor, tapped on the door, and disappeared inside. We waited for the shout of 'Medic,' but nothing happened. Beside me, Black whispered, 'Tim,' and if possible, got even paler. I nudged Sussman and he found her a stool.

After endless moments, the Chief reappeared, supporting a blood-soaked Peterson. He was upright and walking, so I guessed most of the blood wasn't his, which left …

He looked up at the gantry and shook his head. Dr Foster appeared from nowhere, entered the pod, and shut the door. Dieter began to clear the hangar. We helped Black to the bar and waited silently for Peterson, who trudged in an hour later, looking pale and with a stitched gash over one eye. Sussman and I sat huddled together for warmth and support, the stuffing well and truly knocked out of us.

Kalinda said, 'What happened?'

There was a long silence and then he said quietly, 'He was inexperienced. I didn't supervise him properly.' He touched his head gingerly. 'The Yeomanry were drunk. A woman and her two kids went down in the panic. He ran over to them. Picked up the two kids. Tossed them out of the way. Grabbed the woman. Took a sword to the back of his head. His brains fell out. His body got kicked about all over the place. It took ages for me to get to him. I was shouting and cursing. I heaved him over my shoulder, dodged the Hussars, and got back to the pod but it was far too late. He never stood a chance.' He turned to us. 'You two think about today and learn the right lessons.'

We nodded.

In my mind, I saw snapshots: Grant on our first day, filing papers. Grant sitting alongside me in a classroom, his face frowning in concentration as he built his data stack. Grant with his head close to Nagley's as they laughed over something on his scratchpad. I remembered his calm good nature and his willingness to help Stevens. But mostly I membered him bursting with pride at being the first away – the solid workhorse who somehow got to the prize before the flashier Sussman and Maxwell. And much good it had done him. I felt a pricking behind my eyes, but tears wouldn't bring him back.

Peterson reached for his drink. 'Kevin Grant,' he said.

'Kevin Grant,' we said.

That was bad, but the next was worse. A week later, Lower and Baverstock came back from 1389, the Peasant's Revolt. They were Senior Historians and I didn't know them that well. There were only the four of us to meet them now and two of us were certainly a little quieter and more thoughtful than we had been a week ago.

This time, there was no messing. The Chief, alerted by something unknown to us, went straight in and stayed in. A minute later, Dr Foster and two medics flew down the hangar and went in. And stayed in. Thirty minutes later they were all still in there.

'No,' said Peterson softly. 'No, no, no, not again.'

'They're not clearing the hangar,' said Sussman. 'It might not be too bad.'

But it was.

Baverstock was dead. An accident. He'd fallen under a horse in the chaos following the death of Wat Tyler and been trampled, dying shortly afterwards on the floor of his own pod. He and Lower had been together a long time. It was more than a working relationship. His death finished her. She couldn't let him go. She held him while silent tears poured down her cheeks. When they tried to move her she lost control, screaming incessantly, unable to stop. They tried to sedate her but she fought them off and people were slipping in all the blood, so they had to leave it and Dr Foster and the Chief sat with her and Baverstock for nearly two hours before they were able to get them both out quietly. We never saw Lower again. I did ask Dr Foster once and she just said, 'She's taken care of,' and I knew to leave it alone.

Sussman and I were quiet for a few days, but St Mary's carried on around us and after a while, so did we. It wasn't that we were uncaring and I'm sure many other people grieved as well, but we did it in private. We attended the service and Grant's and Baverstock's names went up on the Boards of Honour and then we moved on.

So there we were; only four of us historians in an organisation established for twelve. Normally, Sussman and I would undergo a series of small, unimportant, bread and butter jumps to give us experience and work the excitement out of our systems. Roman Bath was scheduled, together with a jump to eleventh-century London to watch the foundations being laid for Westminster Abbey. We should be supervised by a Senior Historian, except there weren't any left. We got the best they could offer. Sussman and Black disappeared to Bath and Peterson and I got Westminster Abbey. The main purpose of the jump was simply to confirm the co-ordinates for the Time Map, but Peterson said it would be a pity not take a look around; the comment that gets so many historians, past and present, into such trouble.

I liked Tim Peterson. He wasn't nearly as bad as Kalinda Black who was tall, blonde, and terrifying. She looked like a Disney Princess, spoke with a broad Manchester accent, and, rumour had it, drank the blood of newly qualified trainees to keep herself young.

Entering the pod, Peterson threw himself into his seat, put his feet up, and declared me in charge.

'Go on,' he said. 'Get on with it or we won't be back in time for the footie.'

I verified the co-ordinates and, fingers crossed, initiated the jump. We landed without even the slightest bump, completely failing to materialise inside a mountain or at the bottom of the sea, much to my secret relief. Heart thumping, I checked the cameras and announced it was safe to venture outside.

'Excellent work,' said Peterson, opening his eyes. 'Do you know the way?'

'Yes,' I said firmly.

'Come on, then,' he said, and we discreetly exited the pod.

66

He was very good. He stood back and gave me a couple of minutes to take it all in.

I saw more stone buildings than I thought there would be, but this was London after all and Edward the Confessor's England was a peaceful and prosperous place. Having said that though, most of the buildings were still built of wood. Sturdily constructed and with thatched roofs, but wood still seemed to be the material of choice. Many houses had let down fronts that converted to table tops from which a variety of goods and services were being touted. The noise levels were tremendous. Nobody seemed to converse in less than a bellow. A pall of pungent wood smoke hung over everything.

There were plenty of people on the streets. Some were bareheaded and I could see mops of light-coloured hair. These were Saxons for the most part and taller than I expected. I remembered one of my professors at Thirsk telling me that hair colour was not a reliable way of telling Saxon from Norman since the Normans themselves were descended from Northmen as well. The most reliable method, she always insisted, was to measure people's thighs. As a rough guide, if the thighbone was longer than the shinbone then you were Saxon. If it was the other way round then you were Norman. I have Saxon legs. I peered sideways at Peterson's.

'Why are you staring at my legs?' he asked, more amused than annoyed. I hoped.

'You have Norman legs,' I said.

He shook his head. 'I was warned about you. Come on and don't gawp,' which was a sound piece of advice. Nothing makes you stand out more than looking like a tourist, or a foreigner, or an enemy spy; none of these being good looks for inoffensive historians looking for a quiet life.

I led him around muddy London and we found the site easily. Even I couldn't have missed it. Here was the everlasting chink-chink of metal tools on stone as countless masons and their gangs swarmed over the site. I was surprised at the height of the walls. They had no heavy lifting gear as such – just blocks, tackles, ropes, man power, and occasionally horse power. But the work was going well. With wet stones glistening darkly against the grey sky, I could easily see the grandeur to come.

I looked around eagerly to see if maybe the Confessor himself was on-site today. He would be buried here in January 1066; only one week after the church was consecrated. The first and last English king to be buried there.

I drew brief sketches of the mason's marks and Peterson tried to identify the gangs they belonged to. I sketched the shape of the walls. We wandered around the site as we wanted, thanking the god of historians that Health and Safety hadn't been invented yet.

Peterson paused a moment.

'Hang on. I have to water a wall.'

He eased himself between two piles of lumber.

'Come on.'

'What?'

'I'm not letting you out of my sight on this trip.'

'I'm not watching you pee.'

'Well, shut your eyes.'

'I'm not listening to you pee, either.'

'So hum.'

I turned my back and began to hum Handel's Water Music.

'Stop that,' said Peterson, but I wasn't listening.

I was watching two men walking behind another man as he skirted the site. They both had their hands to their belts and their body language caught my attention.

I took a few steps forward so I could see better and many things happened all at once.

Peterson said, 'Where are you going?'

Someone shouted a warning nearby. I couldn't make out the words, but the alarm and urgency were very clear.

And it suddenly got dark.

68

I didn't think at all. I don't know what made me do it. I ran forward two paces, crashed hard into Peterson and my momentum pushed us both back another three or four paces.

Not far, but far enough for us not to be under the frighteningly heavy block of stone that thudded into the soft ground nearby.

We sprawled on the ground, trying to catch up with events. For me it all happened so fast that I was more puzzled than scared.

I could hear people approaching and several men ran round the pile, shouting anxiously. They pulled up short at the sight of me on the ground, still tangled up with Peterson. And him with his todger out, too. They drew the wrong conclusions, subjected us to several builders' witticisms, which although in Old English were perfectly understandable and wandered off again. It seemed no one was going to file a Health and Safety report.

Inside my head, I heard Dr Bairstow say, 'How difficult is it to cause a ten-ton block to drop on a potentially threatening historian …?'

I unwound my stupid skirts and struggled to my feet.

'You peed on me,' I said indignantly, to hide the sickness sweeping over me.

'Get over it. I peed on me as well,' said England's first *mannequin pis*, climbing to his feet. 'Are you all right?'

'Yes. Fine.'

'Are you sure?'

There was an underlying anxiety in his voice and I remembered Kevin Grant had been killed on his watch.

'Well, I'm all wet if that's what you mean.' I shook out my skirts. 'Oh, yuk!'

He put his hand on my shoulder. 'What was that all about?'

'Don't know. Maybe it was just an accident. They do happen. Maybe not everything is about us.'

He thought.

'Where were you going?'

I remembered. 'Two men, following another man. I didn't like the look of them.'

'Maxwell!'

'I wasn't going to do anything. I just wanted to see better.' I took a deep breath and said in a small voice, 'Do you really think …?'

Now I was aware of my thumping heart. It had been a close call. One minute everything was fine and the next minute, bloody great rocks were dropping out of the sky.

'Where did it come from?' said Peterson, looking up. There was no scaffolding or A-frames; just a cat's cradle of rope outlined against the grey sky. He peered thoughtfully across the site.

'I wonder …'

'What?'

'Well, I wonder if whatever was going to happen to that man – had to happen. Some key historical event. Minor, but essential. And if you were about to interfere, young Maxwell, then we got off very lightly. Very lightly indeed.'

'What sort of key event?'

'I don't know; it could be anything. Suppose he's attacked and someone saves him and he goes on to father children whose descendants are important? Or he's attacked and killed. He might have gone on to do something unspeakably evil and now he won't because he's dead. We'll never know.'

My heart had picked up speed as the implications were becoming clear to me.

'I'm amazed we're not dead.'

'Me too,' he said. 'Maybe History's in a good mood today.'

'Maybe we're the good guys,' I said jokingly and there was a strange little pause.

'Doubt it,' said Peterson. 'We'd better take the hint, however, and clear off.'

'Yes, Mr Peterson.'

He grinned. 'The name's Tim. Now, shall we go?'

'Good idea.'

We edged our way past the block and out of the lumber.

'A nice cup of tea, I think,' he said, striding out.

'Um … Tim …' I said, trotting beside him.

'Yes?'

'You might want to put yourself away first.'

On returning to the pod, Peterson apparently fell asleep. I wrote up the logs, did the FOD plod outside and the POD plod inside, tidied up, made a cup of tea, and gently woke my captain.

He yawned, stretched, smiled, checked around without seeming to and accepted the tea. 'Nicely done, young Maxwell.' We were the same age, but I let it go. 'Return jump set up?'

'Yes, ready to go any time you are.'

'Well, there's no rush, is there?' and he settled back in his seat, apparently exhausted by his afternoon exertions and smiled at me again. His hair, as always, stuck out in all directions. Female historians have yards of hair – it's in the rules and regs; all male historians wear a kind of shaggy-sheep look appropriate to any age. Peterson's made him look like an unkempt hearthrug, but his eyes were gentle. I rarely heard him raise his voice and, a welcome relief amongst volatile historians, he always appeared bombproof. He harboured a passion for Doctor Foster (or death wish possibly) and accepted her complete lack of people skills with good-humoured equanimity. I could have felt sorry for him, Helen Foster on one side and Kalinda Black on the other, but when I mentioned it to him once, he just said, 'Yeah,' in a dreamy sort of voice, leaned back, put his hands behind his head, and smiled happily. 'It's a great life.'

Anyway, I survived my first jump, which was more than poor Grant had done.

The next few jumps passed without mishap, they ticked the last box and eventually our rank was confirmed.

Later that year, I got yanked out of my Ancient Civilisation comfort zone Kal, Sussman, and I got World War One. The Somme. For Sussman and me, it was our first Big Job, as they were known. And afterwards, things were never quite the same again.

To begin with, I thought we were going to get the whole initiative, but our assignment turned out to be more specific.

'A Casualty Clearing Centre,' announced Dr Bairstow, dropping a box of reference material onto his desk. 'Situated in an old French chateau and one step behind the Regimental Aid Posts. Reportedly destroyed by shell fire; whether enemy or friendly was never clearly established. Massive loss of life. The whole incident was buried as quickly as possible to prevent damage to morale. There are anniversaries coming up and controversy has surfaced again. So we've been asked to investigate. You'll need to be on your toes for this one because we don't have an exact date.'

'So we're going into a war zone, knowing we're a target, but not knowing exactly when we'll be blown to bits,' said Kal.

'I don't think you'll be blown to bits,' he said calmly. 'After the initial attack most of the hospital went up in flames. And very quickly too. It's probably the fire you'll have to watch out for.'

'Is this for Thirsk, sir?'

'They are acting as intermediary on this one.' The client, as always, would be secret. The thinking was that if we didn't know who they were or why they wanted to know, then it wouldn't affect our findings. Thirsk would offer to undertake 'new research'. We would nip in and out, then hand over our findings for them to present as 'fresh evidence' to the client. They got the credit; we got the money.

'We need to get this right. After Grant and Baverstock, Thirsk are talking again about establishing a permanent supervisory presence here. Something we really need to avoid at all costs. So get the information, get the evidence, get it right, and get out safely.'

'For how long will we be there?' I asked.

'We hope to get you in between five days and two weeks beforehand. Records show the hospital as functioning at the beginning of October. By the 14th it had been destroyed. When you return, of course, depends on events. Miss Black will head the mission.'

'Could it have been an accident, sir?' asked Sussman.

'It's possible. That's the official version anyway.'

'Have they thought this through? If we find out the truth, there'll be a lot of blame and recrimination,' said Kal. 'Isn't this one of the times it's better not to know?'

'That's not our job,' he said sternly. 'We gather the information. It's up to others what they make of it. That is not our concern.'

'How will we know who causes the explosion that blows us up?'

'I am not sending you there to be blown up, Mr Sussman, but to obtain information. And at vast expense too, so please try to refrain from being killed. Or indeed, incurring any sort of injury at all.'

We said, 'Yes, sir,' and backed out of his presence.

'Bloody hell,' said Sussman in the Library. 'How did I get roped into this? Where's Peterson?'

'On leave,' said Kal absently, examining the contents of the box. We were both startled. Leave? What was that, then?

Kal and I were going in as nurses. Sussman was an orderly/ambulance driver. Because of the considerable amount of interaction that would take place, we were thoroughly briefed. History and politics of both sides. An extensive field medic course, based on the treatments available at the time. They seconded us to a nearby army hospital for three weeks as part of the training; one week's theatre training, one week on the wards, and one week in their A & E, which consisted mostly of burns, fractures, crush injuries, drunken brawls, and on one never to be forgotten night, midwifery. I am never doing that again!

We jumped early one Sunday morning. Chief Farrell and Kal carried out the final checks. Dieter, his senior technician, was fussing around outside, thinking no one knew he just wanted to be close to Kalinda.

'Take care,' was all the Chief said, looking at me and away we went.

Landing without a hitch, we peered outside. Even though it was only mid-afternoon, the day was dark and dreary. Rain was coming down hard and the few people around were scurrying along with their heads down. No one paid us any attention in our quiet corner.

The Matron at the Casualty Clearing Centre scarcely looked at our carefully forged papers before deploying us, which was a bit of a bugger because Professor Rapson and Dr Dowson had spent a long time on them. She sat behind her desk, stiff and starched, and pointed a Roman nose in our direction. The Nose looked us up and down. I got the impression we were found wanting.

'Show me your hands,' she said abruptly. Thanking God I'd remembered to clip my nails really short, I held them out, front and back. She stared. She sniffed. Obviously, the hands weren't up to spec, either. I knew what the problem was – too white and soft. Still, a couple of weeks here would change that.

'Where are you from?' She peered at our papers, 'Black?'

'I'm Maxwell,' I said helpfully and got the look I'd had from every teacher at school and from Bitchface Barclay in the not-too-distant past. I don't know why I bother. Matron was no different and the nose really reminded me of Dr Bairstow. Maybe she was an ancestor.

'I'm Black,' said Kalinda, courageously drawing her fire. The Nose turned in her direction. I hid my hands behind my back.

'And you are from …?'

'Manchester,' she said, broadening her accent and showing her hands without being asked. What a creep.

Matron handed us a list of rules and regulations. There were a lot of them.

Dismissed from her presence we stepped outside. I breathed deeply. The smell was distinctive. The tang of wood smoke and horses. Actually, I've never been anywhere in the past that didn't stink of horses. I could smell the latrines, even though they were in the next courtyard. And the hospital stink was everywhere; even outside in the supposedly fresh air.

I looked around. The shabby old chateau must have been disused for some time. Many windows were boarded over. Plaster and rendering were falling away. Tiles were missing from the roof. I couldn't help feeling it might fall down before it burned down. We'd never been put so deliberately in harm's way before. My heart raced in exactly the way it had for my first jump. Just when I thought I was getting the hang of things they threw something like this at us. But every jump is different; every jump has its own set of problems and every jump has its own set of terrors.

There was cold, wet mud everywhere. Too many people; too many vehicles; too many horses; too much rain. They'd laid planks down but they were already disappearing slowly into the ooze.

Over by the gates I could see a number of tents of varying sizes and people scurrying everywhere. Everyone seemed busy; everyone seemed to know what they were doing, and everyone seemed to have a purpose. Well, so did we and we'd better get started.

We put on our uniforms and got stuck in. Sussman had been whisked away almost immediately. He was billeted separately as well. I would often see him in the distance, or waving as he disappeared round a corner, but he was wise enough to be discreet. We confined ourselves to waving at each other. Kal and I slept in a tiny room in the attic of the chateau. We didn't like being away from the pod, but all female staff were bed-checked each night by a Senior Sister, so we had no choice. The attic was cold, damp, and never saw the sun. We shared a bed and there weren't enough covers. We couldn't bring anything from the pod to make ourselves more comfortable in case we had to leave in a hurry. And with such hardship all around us, it didn't seem right, anyhow.

We didn't know where Sussman was sleeping. A group of orderlies slept above the stables so he may have been with them, in which case, we were much better off than him. It was cold when we arrived and it got colder, and wetter.

The casualties poured in from the Regimental Aid Posts. Matron sent me to work in the reception tent, assisting with sorting and prioritising. I was good at it and it freed up a senior nurse but I hated it. It felt like playing God. But, sometimes you could see death in a face and there was nothing you could do except move on to the ones who could be saved. Most I sent to Pre-op to be prepped for surgery. The Operation Tent was the biggest. Kal was in there somewhere. From there, patients were moved to the wards in the main building before being transferred to a bigger hospital away from the lines.

Men came in on stretchers, carried by Sussman's mates; orderlies whom I can never praise highly enough. Some walked in. I checked everyone's labels and directed them accordingly. If I was lucky, I saw Sussman himself at least once a night and even if we only had time to exchange a glance, it was better than nothing.

The days dragged by. We were into the second week of October now. It rained a lot. Heavy rain meant heavy mud. And there were still all those young men coming in through the gates. Limping, or being stretchered, their faces blurred with pain. Limbs reduced to filthy stumps. Some poor mother's son, having been yanked off the wire, screaming and trying to hold his guts in. One lad lay quietly with a gentle smile on his face and, when I looked more closely, half his head was gone.

As the deadline grew closer, Kal and I took turns to keep watch in our room at night. One of us slept while the other wound bandages or tried to read. We never undressed, partly so we would be ready, but mostly because it was too bloody cold to take our clothes off. The days were ticking by and we had to be ready. I watched my breath frost in the cold night air as I wound yards of bandage by the light of a tiny flickering candle on the floor, with a precious blanket pinned over the window to keep the cold out.

Now that the time was near we arranged to meet Sussman at least once a day to reassure each other. We kept in regular contact and tried to be aware of each other's positions at all times. I kept looking around me. I imagined the whine of the shell, the crump of the explosion – and then what?

I came round a corner from the linen rooms and ran slap into someone. The man lifted the top layer of blankets I was carrying and said, 'Hi, it's me!'

I checked around us, but no one else was in sight. 'Hey, how are you?'

'I'm cold. You must be perished. How are you holding up?'

I was touched. He wasn't usually so thoughtful. 'I'm OK. Not much longer now.'

'No. Tonight, tomorrow, or the day after. Any thoughts?'

'No, none. In fact, I think there's a bit of a lull. The weather's so awful that everything seems to have quietened down.'

'Well, don't relax. It could happen at any time. Look, I have to go. If we get through the night I'll see you and Kal tomorrow, just outside here. By the latrines. We'll have a catch-up and plan what to do next.'

'By the latrines!'

77

'It's the romance in my soul. See you.'

By great good luck, we were all able to get away and meet the next day. Sussman was there already, waiting for us. I could see our pod in the distance, over by the stables, anonymous under bits of rusting metal and carefully placed pieces of old wood. We stood out of the rain and discussed what to do next.

'It's got to be tonight or tomorrow, said Kal. 'Sussman, are you working tonight?'

'Not if this weather continues, no.'

'Stay sharp. Max, the reception tent is the furthest from the pod. At the first sign of anything out of the ordinary, go straight back to the pod and get the cameras activated. Stay out of trouble. You too, Sussman. We're here to investigate. There's no way I'm going back without knowing what happens here and we can't do that if we're dead. Is that clearly understood?'

We nodded.

'I mean it. Any sign of heroics and I'll kick your arses from here to Dr Bairstow's office, pausing only to pick up your P45s on the way. Is *that* clearly understood?'

We nodded again. I shivered under my cape and pulled it more closely around me.

Around the corner, a whistle sounded and voices were raised. Engines turned over, coughing in the damp. 'That's me,' said Sussman. 'Bugger, I was supposed to stock up with extra blankets.' He looked over his shoulder and then back at me. 'Max, could you …?'

'Sure, you go on and I'll bring them to you. How many?'

'Three should do it. Thanks a lot. Gotta go.' And he was gone, slipping in the mud in his haste.

'I must go too,' said Kal. 'I'll meet you after your shift finishes. I think we should stick together as much as possible now.'

'Right. See you then.'

She disappeared and I re-entered the building. I hurried

along the corridor to the linen rooms, ignoring the first two doors. Blankets were stored in Number Three. I reached for the door handle and pulled open a heavy, old-fashioned door made of solid wood. That it opened outwards was the only thing that saved me. I just had time to register the hot door handle before I was blown backwards and sideways and the door came down on top of me.

I lay stunned and only slowly became aware of flames licking around the doorframe. The roaring I thought was in my own head turned out to be the fireball in the linen room. It was hot. I had to get up. Wriggling out from under the door took some effort, but I managed it.

Flames ran along the ceiling above me. I couldn't see a thing for the smoke. The whole corridor was filled with it, billowing out from the linen room. If the fire ripped through the hospital this quickly then this would be a major catastrophe. But that's exactly what it was. It was a major catastrophe. Suddenly, without any warning, or shots fired, this was it.

Five

I tried to pull myself together. There would be extensive loss of life. There wasn't anything I could do. There wasn't anything I should do. Well, sod that for a game of soldiers. Maybe I wasn't very important in the scheme of things, but there's always something you can do.

Pulling my cape up over my head, I hitched up my skirt and crawled down the corridor, keeping low to avoid the smoke. If I could get to the door … A hand bell hung beside every door precisely for this purpose. I knew I'd arrived at the door when I banged my head on it. I took a deep, difficult breath and groped my way up the door frame. Got it!

I opened the door carefully, burning my hand again on the hot handle. The roar of the flames increased behind me, as the oxygen fed them and I slipped through as quickly as I could.

Rubbing my eyes, no one was in sight. It was midday and there wasn't a soul anywhere. I took as deep a breath as I could manage, sucked in a great lungful of wonderful, cold, wet air, coughed a little, spat a lot, and croaked 'Fire! Fire! Fire!' Bent nearly double and bracing one hand on my knee, I rang the hand bell as loudly as I could.

For a moment, nothing happened. And then, around me, doors crashed open and people ran in all directions. Men rushed to hoses, stirrup-pumps, and buckets. Huge red-orange flames began to engulf the old buildings faster than anyone would have believed possible; and the rain, which might just for once have done some good, stopped and the sun came out, bathing the whole tragedy in warm October sunshine.

It was chaos. People ran past me in all directions. Whistles sounded, shouts rang out and over all the noise, a hand-cranked siren hindered more than it helped.

I didn't know what to do. Men ran with buckets. No one thought to form a chain. Water slopped everywhere. People slipped in the mud and fell and those behind tripped over them. I saw three orderlies trying to pull out a fire wagon, but there weren't enough of them to shift it through the mud. They shouted for help but no one heard. People flew out of doors into the courtyard but once there had no idea where to go. Or if they did, they'd forgotten in their panic.

I saw terrified faces at the windows; hands beating at the glass panes. Some windows opened. Men hung out, calling for help. Some tried to lower themselves and lost their grip, falling heavily to the ground. Some jumped and didn't get up. And then, above it all, the high note of a bugle cut through the racket. Heads turned. A young major, I think from the Glosters, raised his voice.

'To the main gates. Get the wounded to the main gates. Get away from the buildings. The walls are coming down. Go to the main gates.'

A number of NCOs emerged and physically pushed people in the right direction. I saw a blind man, barefoot in the mud, wearing only pyjamas. His face was badly burned and his dressing had come away and trailed on his shoulder. He staggered around, arms outstretched, shouting for help. Never mind the big picture. I was a little person. Help the other little people.

I stepped forward and took his hand, saying quietly, 'Now then, soldier, you just come with me.' I put his hand on my shoulder and we fought our way along. At least, now most people were going in the same direction. I found another young lad, on his knees, trying to get up. I reached out a hand. 'Come on, lad, up you get. Can you walk?'

'A little,' he replied, teeth chattering. 'Not very fast.'

So that was three of us and we found another one on the way, bent double and coughing up a lung. We carefully picked our way towards the main drive and a mud-covered ambulance drew up. One of Sussman's mates jumped down. 'Get them in the back, miss. Quick as you can.'

We yanked open the doors and willing hands pulled them in. 'You too, miss,' he shouted.

'No,' I yelled back. 'Get this lot to the main gates. I'll go back for any stragglers.'

'You don't want to do that, miss. That whole section's going to come down.'

'I must,' I said, desperately. Our pod was there. I had to get back. 'Go! Get these men to safety and come back for more.' I turned and ran back before he could argue.

It was like a scene from Dante's *Inferno*. The courtyard was full of smoke, from which ghostly figures appeared and disappeared like ghosts. I could see orange and red flickers as the flames rose higher. The shouting seemed more purposeful now. Two columns of men filed out towards the gates. Many were being carried in makeshift stretchers or slung over shoulders. The initial panic was over. People were helping each other.

The young major was still directing the evacuation. I ran to him and said, 'Sir, there's at least one ambulance on its way here. They can take the most seriously wounded if we can get them all together.'

He nodded. 'Stand here, nurse. You can be our collection point.' He ran off, gesturing to two sergeants nearby. In hardly any time at all, I had half a dozen men gathered around me, sitting or lying in the mud and more on their way. A sergeant came back and handed me a whistle.

'Keep blowing, miss. Let them know where you are.' I blew and blew, turning all the time. They brought up another man, but he was already dead. We left him. Eventually, the ambulance came back. We were loading people on board when the major turned up again. He clambered in after the last man and turned to me reaching out his hand. 'On board, nurse, and that's an order.'

I couldn't go with him and if I ran back into the courtyard he'd come after me, so I said, 'Yes, sir. I'll go in front with the driver,' and slammed the doors on him. I slapped the side and it disappeared into the murk.

The two sides of the building were well ablaze now and even I could see the east wall was going to come down any minute. The heat hurt my face. It was like an oven. Terrible noises came from the third side of the courtyard, the stables over which Sussman lived. There was no chance of getting the horses out, none at all. They screamed in fear and panic and I could hear them kicking against their partitions in their desperation to get out. The building was almost engulfed in flames. There was nothing I could do. I turned and ran.

I knew someone was in the pod, because the scrap had been kicked aside, exposing the door. I picked up my skirts and really ran for it, months of physical training paying off at last. I heard a shout behind me. Thank God, it was Kal. Her hair hung down; she was bleeding from a nasty scalp wound, and smeared black with smoke and soot. I reached out, took her hand and we ran to the pod together. Sussman had the door open, ready. We fell, gasping, into the pod and as we did, I saw the east wall sway, lean impossibly, and then come down with a crash and a great shower of sparks and burning debris. The door closed, shutting out the roaring flames, screaming horses, and the sound of people burning alive.

And then there was silence.

Sussman was white-faced. 'Max? Max, my God, I can't believe it. I thought you were dead. Why aren't you dead?' I shook my head and he passed me some water. 'I heard it started in the linen rooms and I knew that's where you were. I can't believe you got out alive.'

'Hey,' said Kal sourly. 'I'm alive too.' I gave her the water and she took a good slug.

For a long time we watched it on the screen. Sussman had all the cameras working. These films, together with our own personal records were our reason for being here.

Slowly, Kal got up. 'Come on, Max, on your feet. Let's have a look at you.'

'I'm fine,' I said, because that's what you always say, even if your head's just fallen off, but clambered to my feet.

'Sussman, get the med kit. So, what hurts the most?'

'Well, the door fell on my head so I think I've got a bit of an egg. I swallowed my own body weight in smoke and my chest hurts a bit and I've burnt my hands. Otherwise it's only a broken fingernail and loss of appetite.'

She sprayed my hands with medical plastic, to cool and protect the burns and I slapped a quick dressing on her forehead. 'There, that should hold us for a while.' We both turned to look at Sussman sitting at the console and monitoring the cameras.

I said, 'How about you? What's the damage?'

He'd split the screen to show all four cameras and was watching closely. 'What? Oh, I'm fine, thanks. No problems here.'

Kal looked him up and down. 'You're not hurt at all? How's that, then?'

'What?' He dragged his eyes from the screen.

'You're awfully clean, given the state of Max and me. How did you manage that?'

'I was with the other drivers when the alarm sounded. We were dispatched to our vehicles to evacuate the tents. I waited until no one was looking and then got back to the pod. I kept an eye out for you two on the way, but missed you, obviously. So I cleared the door and got inside. The cameras had activated automatically, so I made sure they'd got the best angles and waited for you two.'

He became aware of the silence. 'As per your instructions.' The silence lengthened.

'What?' he said, defensively. 'You said, "No heroics. I'll

kick your arses," etc. So I came straight to the pod as instructed by my mission controller, that's you Miss Black, and got on with our mission, which is to investigate and record.'

He was right, but his manner was over-defensive and belligerent. Behind Kal, I made 'Shut up, Shut up' signs to him, but he couldn't or wouldn't see them. He finished with, 'So what's your problem, then?'

She took a long step forward and seized his wrist. 'Look at these hands. Did you even stop to pick up anyone out of the mud? Did you just step over them? Or did you actually knock them down in your mad dash to safety?'

Morally he could have done more and he knew it. He was angry and guilty and defensive and it brought out his worst side. She'd done too much and she knew it – we'd both done too much and she was angry and guilty and defensive as well. They stood glaring at each other. I decided to risk life and limb and stepped between them.

'Guys! Not now. Davey, go and check the disks are recording OK. No, now please.'

He stepped back and muttered something and that did it. She strode forward and pushed his shoulder. 'What did you say?'

'He didn't say anything,' I said, physically getting between them again. 'He's upset. We both are. It's our first big assignment. It's certainly the first time I've seen anyone die, and it's possibly his as well and the noise from the horses didn't help.'

It didn't work at all. Her eyes narrowed. 'Yes, that's a point. From what you said when we got here, you thought your partner was dead. Good to know you're sitting here safely when you think she's burned to death in an explosion; especially since you sent her there in the first place. You really are a total waste of fucking space, Sussman.'

That really did it. There was no going back now. Something ugly flashed briefly in his eyes and he squared up to her, right in her face. She held his gaze. It was a very long moment and then his eyes slipped sideways to mine and guilt was written all over his face. He pulled himself together.

Ignoring Kal, he turned to me and said, shakily, 'Max, I apologise. I never thought for one moment you could still be alive. If I'd thought there was the slightest chance I'd have torn the building down myself to get to you. I'm really sorry.'

My own heart was thumping away, but I nodded at him and turned aside. He misread my action. 'No, Max. Really, I'm sorry. Don't look like that. It's not true. Don't listen to her.'

I nodded again, still not looking at him. Kal said in a quiet voice, 'Let it go, Sussman.' There was a nasty little silence. I wondered if all assignments ended like this.

Sussman took a long breath. 'Let's get back.'

Kal drew herself up again. 'Stand away from those controls, mister. I call the shots here. You see to your partner.'

And indeed, I suddenly felt extremely wobbly. I opened my mouth to say, 'I really don't feel so good,' and instead threw up violently all down his front. He was covered in it.

There was another silence and then Kal grinned wickedly and said, 'Not so clean now, are you?' We all laughed. Not good laughter, but we chose to interpret it that way and everyone's face was saved. We shut things down and jumped back.

We landed with the gentlest bump. Sussman opened the door and left immediately after decon and without a backward glance.

It was at that moment that I realised just why St Mary's was always banging on about interaction. *You are not there to interact. Observe, document, and record. Don't get involved.* It wasn't only the dangers of inadvertently changing history, but the emotional toll as well. How many people had died today? Matron? The blind boy? My job was to watch events unfold. To record and document. To observe. To stand apart. Not to interfere.

I thought about this and came to the same conclusion that

every good historian should reach. Then I thought about it a bit more and came to the other conclusion that every historian not only reaches but implements. You don't walk away from blind men struggling in the mud. You should, but you don't. Well, Kal hadn't and neither had I. Nor Kevin Grant. But Sussman had. Did that make him a better or worse historian than me? Or a better or worse person?

Yes, there was an emotional price to pay for interaction, but was it greater or lesser than doing nothing? And what about a vengeful History, always on the lookout for naughty historians?

Fortunately, Kal interrupted my thoughts. 'We ought to be making a start,' she said.

I sighed. It would be nice to sit here for ever. I loved this bit between two worlds. The cares of the past behind us and not yet in the present long enough to get into any real trouble. No sooner were her words spoken then there was gentle tap at the door.

'It's Farrell. Are you OK in there?'

'Yes,' shouted Kal in her best 'Bugger off' voice and after a long pause it opened and Farrell and Dieter, stood in the doorway.

'Don't come in,' said Kal.

They looked at us.

'It's not personal,' I said. 'We smell a bit.'

Dieter stepped forward.

'Didn't you hear?' said Kal angrily.

'If it's your smell, it's not a problem.' He picked up her bag. She glared at him but he only smiled. Did he not know how close to death he was? Mind, he was built like a large brick shithouse. Two large brick shithouses actually. In fact he was so big it was possible he distorted time and space. He had his own gravitational pull, like a blond planet, and he'd fallen for Kal like a sperm whale failing to clear the Grand Canyon on a bicycle. He thought no one knew. He slung her bag over his shoulder and helped her to her feet. 'Come on.'

Moving like an old woman, she hobbled out.

The Chief smiled at me. 'Your turn.' I reached for my bag but he'd already picked it up. I looked at my burned hands and my stiff, red fingers, swollen from all that time in water. Now it was all over, I doubted I had the strength to put one foot in front of the other.

'Lean on me,' he said and, just for once, I allowed myself to do so.

Chief Farrell visited us in Sick Bay the next day, bringing with him a box of various bits and pieces we'd left behind in the pod. All the records had been uploaded and everyone was waiting on our reports. We nodded.

He said, 'I've already debriefed Sussman and gather it wasn't shellfire after all, but an accidental explosion. Can you give me the details?'

'I think Max is the best person to talk to,' said Kal, 'She was the one on the spot.' To my surprise, she pulled an incomprehensible face and left the room.

'So,' said Farrell, sitting down next to me and smiling. 'How are you?'

'Absolutely fine,' I said, so pleased to see him.

He regarded me warily. 'Is it safe to be this close? I hear you've developed your own defence mechanism.'

'Oh, yes,' I said ruefully. 'I don't think he'll ever forgive me.'

He looked at me carefully for a while and then said, 'So, tell me all about it.'

'There's not much I can tell you. First of all I was behind the door and then I was underneath it. Then the corridor was full of smoke. Then I was outside. I know it spread really quickly.'

'Yes,' he said absently. 'Old building. Did you smell anything?'

Did I? I shut my eyes and walked through it again. And again. And there it was, on the very edge … 'Yes, yes I did.' I actually sniffed, tasting it with my nostrils. 'Yes … chemicals … like the lab sometimes.'

He sat back. 'I think probably not gunfire at all. I think sabotage.'

'Someone sabotaged a *hospital*?'

He shrugged. 'Looks like it. There's no source of combustion, only the hot pipes from the boilers running through the rooms to air the linen. So I think someone very carefully mixed a chemical cocktail. I think it smouldered for a while, generating some heat and actually opening the door provided additional oxygen and created the fireball.' He was watching me carefully. 'Does that sound likely?'

I wasn't listening properly. 'Oh my God, did I do it? Did I set fire to the hospital?'

'No, no, no. Absolutely not, Miss Maxwell, I didn't mean that at all. Please don't think … The person who mixed the chemicals set fire to the hospital. It wasn't you.'

'You can't know that.'

I spent the rest of the day going over and over things in my mind.

He was right. It wasn't me who had started the fire. And if I hadn't opened that door then sooner or later, someone else would have. Someone who might not have been fortunate enough to escape as I had.

We were both restless all day. Sussman had been discharged. By unspoken consent we left the lights on. Nurse Hunter irritated us by constantly sticking her head round the door and going away again. After an hour, I couldn't stand it any longer. I sat up and, for something to do, rummaged around the box the Chief had brought. There was something knobbly at the bottom. I pulled out a paper-wrapped bundle. Six pieces of chunky charcoal. The big stuff, not the little girlie willow sticks.

I looked at them.

I looked at the big wall to my left.

The big, blank wall.

The nice, big, blank wall.

I swung my legs out of bed. 'Give me a hand to shift this table.'

'Why?'

'I want to stand on it.'

'You're not going to hang yourself, are you?'

We shoved the table into place and I clambered up. Once I got started, I couldn't stop. Using wide arm movements, I sketched in a black sky, lit with starburst shells. Stark figures raced and fell across a lunar landscape. I drew faster and faster, unable to stop, taking the pictures in my head and transposing them on to the wall. I drew the explosions, the cold, the terror, the heart-breaking waste. I drew limbs, heads, and blood. I drew men dying on the wire, drowning in the mud, eyes wide, mouths gaping, hands clawing. It poured out. Beside me, Kal added her own contributions. At some point, Dr Foster came in, watched, and surprisingly said nothing. We moved the table out and I drew the reception tent. I drew rows of soldiers, wrapped in blankets and coats, all stiff and heavy with mud and blood. I drew cold, grey, vacant faces; contorted faces; screaming and crying faces. The last piece of charcoal crumbled and flaked with the pressure. A hand touched my shoulder and Dr Foster said, 'Enough.'

I looked round. A crowd of people had gathered behind us; the entire medical team, Farrell, Dieter, Doctor Dowson, and some more. I waited for the trouble coming my way but it didn't happen.

We washed our hands and Nurse Hunter brought us a cup of tea. Then we switched out the lights and fell asleep.

We got over it, of course. You have to. We wrote our reports and submitted them to Dr Bairstow. We spent an afternoon with him and Chief Farrell, talking them through everything before they made the final report to Thirsk for them to present to the client. And then it was nearly done.

The three of us accompanied Dr Bairstow to the Remembrance Day ceremony in Rushford that year. We were smartly turned out as he always insisted we were in public, wearing the full, formal uniform, hair up, shiny shoes, and make-up. We paid our private respects while he laid a wreath on behalf of St Mary's, as he did every year. In my mind I saw the tents, the rows of wounded, saw the faces, heard the guns that never went away.

The Last Post sounded, thin in the cold air and the echoes took a long time to die away in more ways than one. I thought of the blind soldier and of that young major from the Glosters whose presence of mind had saved so many lives and wondered if they had survived the conflict. I dragged myself back to the present. We joined in the prayer.

They shall not grow old, as we that are left grow old
Age shall not weary them, not the years condemn
At the going down of the sun and in the morning
We will remember them.

There was a curious postscript. A small event that had enormous consequences. I had a birthday soon after. Left outside my door, I found a small box, neatly wrapped in coloured paper. This must be from Sussman. Typically, he'd never talked about the explosion and fire at all, just carrying on as if nothing had happened and expecting everyone else to do the same. I wondered if he was trying to make amends with a present. If so, he'd certainly succeeded.

Inside the box nestled a small statue. A model of the Trojan Horse. About six inches tall and exquisitely made. From its delicate features to the trapdoor in its belly, it was absolutely perfect.

That evening, however, Sussman handed me a box of chocolates. I was surprised but did remember to thank him, although this didn't solve my problem. Who left the horse for me? I pondered this as I ran downstairs and collided with Chief Farrell who was going up. We're supposed to keep to the right.

'You're supposed to keep to the right,' he said, mildly.

'Sorry, Chief. You OK?' And then I got it. I don't know how I could ever have thought Sussman could have come up with anything so exquisite. Whatever had I been thinking? Sudden realisation swept over me. He'd given me a gift, a perfect gift, a wonderful gift. I was so happy. An inner voice said, 'Don't read too much into this,' but how could I not?

I said, without missing a beat, 'Thanks very much.'

He smiled back at me. 'Keep it safe.'

I felt a little offended he thought I might lose or break it. I don't have so many possessions I can afford to be careless with any of them and certainly not this one.

'No,' he said seriously. 'I mean it, Miss Maxwell. Keep it safe and keep it accessible. It's important.' Then he was gone again, leaving me, happiness subsiding, bewildered and just a little bit uneasy.

We had the usual big noisy party that evening – all our parties are big and noisy – and everyone attended, but not all the music, dancing, and drinking in the world could mask the underlying tension. I don't know if anyone said anything to Dr Bairstow, but Sussman and Kal never went on another assignment together again.

Six

Another all-staff briefing from Dr Bairstow.

'And finally, I have been asked by Mrs Partridge to raise this issue. As some of you may struggle to remember, next month is your annual appraisal and I'm advised by Mrs Partridge that some of the forms you were asked to complete as a preliminary need … more work.

'Your personal details update form … Mr Sussman; you are not a Jedi Knight. Kindly amend the details in Box 3 – Religion. Ditto Mr Markham, Mr Peterson, Miss Maxwell, Mr Dieter, and Miss Black.

'Miss Maxwell, Box 5. You are not five feet seven inches tall and never will be. Live with it and correct your paperwork.

'Mr Markham, the box marked "Sex" is not an invitation. Please amend the details and apologise to Mrs Partridge.

'Mr Dieter, the claims made in the box marked "Other Interests" are physically impossible and, in most of the civilised world, illegal. You also render yourself liable to prosecution for misuse of government property. Amend.

'Miss Black, there are two P s in oppressed and only one N in minority. You are neither. Delete.

'I would also take this opportunity to remind you that Doctor Foster will be circulating similar medical paperwork for your completion and does not share my enlightened attitude towards employee relations. As I'm sure at least some of you are aware, she enjoys a robust, thorough and above all, penetrative approach to your annual medical examinations. Mess her about at your peril.

'Miss Maxwell, please report to my office in thirty minutes and persuade Mr Sussman to take time out from his religious conversion to accompany you. That is all. Dismissed.'

Grumbling and shuffling our paperwork, we watched him limp away to his lair. I looked round for Sussman but he'd disappeared already. Kalinda joined me and gave me a look.

'What?'

'He'll get you killed one day.'

'No,' I said. 'He's just a bit … unreliable sometimes.'

'No, he's trouble. If you don't watch it, Max, you'll lose your chance at the next Big Job because of him. The Boss does not like him and I don't either. Nobody does but you.'

'He's my partner,' I said defensively, getting tired of this. 'He's not that bad.'

'Exactly, Max. He's your partner and the best you can say of him is that he's not that bad. Doesn't that tell you anything?'

'He's OK with me. It's you he doesn't like and he winds you up deliberately. It's not a problem, believe me.'

Exactly thirty minutes later we stood outside the door. Time is important in our organisation. If you can't even get to an appointment in your own building on time, they argue, you're not going to have much luck trying to find the Battle of Hastings.

Sussman pushed me in first. Mrs Partridge gave us an unloving glare. You could see the words 'feckless' and 'irresponsible' hacking their way through her thought processes. I looked in vain for some human emotion. She made the Boss look like a humanitarian aid worker. She was, as always, impeccably dressed in a black suit and white shirt, with her dark hair in a French pleat. As always, she reminded me of someone. She handed us each a mission folder and nodded us in. I began to feel excited. This could be a Big Job.

The Boss was waiting for us at his briefing table. Files, cubes, and data sticks littered the surface. He motioned us to sit. Without speaking, he began to bring up data. He was such a showman. Data began to twist and spiral, culminating in Thirsk's logo and two short paragraphs.

I sat stunned. Beside me, Sussman's mouth hung open. For the first time ever, the pair of us were speechless. We stared at the screen. I looked away, blinked and looked back again.

There were only the two paragraphs but I couldn't take them in at all. So I read them again. And again. I took my scratch pad out of my knee pocket, laid it on the table in front of me, clasped my hands, and looked expectantly at the Boss.

'Well?' he said. 'Are you interested?' I could almost hear my own excitement. I looked at Sussman's flushed face. He grinned at me.

'Sir,' I said. 'We will climb over the cold, dead bodies of our colleagues for this one.'

He smiled grimly. 'Shouldn't you inquire if it's safe? Or even possible?'

'If you think it's do-able, sir, then that's good enough for me.'

He sat forward and handed us the files and data.

'You should find everything you need here. Certainly enough to get you started. I want to see a mission plan here in my office at 0930 on Friday. You may allocate mission responsibilities as you think fit. I estimate a preparation period of about three months, three months on-site and around two weeks to work up your data and present your findings. Miss Maxwell will head the mission. Are there any questions at this moment?'

We both shook our heads. I was still gobsmacked and Sussman knew better than to talk in front of the Boss. We withdrew.

We filed sedately through Mrs Partridge's office, feeling her stare on our backs. We walked quietly along the corridor and slowly down the stairs. We entered the Library, nodded politely to Dr Dowson, who was peering into a microfiche reader and again to Professor Rapson, muttering to himself in the Early Mesopotamian section. We dropped our files on one of the big data tables to establish ownership, climbed out of the window, walked casually down the path, and into the sunken rock garden, where we finally took a breath.

I jumped onto a bench, lifted my head to the grey sky and shouted 'Yes! Yes! Yes!' and began to sing, 'We are the champions' and play air guitar. Sussman cartwheeled off down the path and back again, whooping incoherently. I jumped off the bench, met him as he straightened up, and the two of us hugged, jumping up and down together until we got tangled up and fell over. I was on the bottom, still shouting 'Yes! Yes! Yes!' as Chief Farrell came around the corner. The ground never opens up and swallows you when you need it to.

There was a fairly crowded silence and then he said politely, 'Good morning, Miss Maxwell and whoever that is. May I be of any assistance?'

Sussman was shaking with laughter and deliberately keeping his face hidden, so I looked over his shoulder and said, 'Good morning, Chief. No, everything's fine, thank you. We're just having a small celebration.'

'What do you do for large celebrations?'

'Oh, we really let rip for those, Chief. This is only a 2.5 on the Richter Scale.'

Eventually, we calmed down, climbed back in through the window, and got down to it. We were laying out our files when Kalinda and Peterson turned up. Word had already got around.

'What have you got?' demanded Kal. 'Come on, is it a Big Job?'

I grinned at Sussman. 'You have no idea.'

'What? What have you got? Don't make me come over there!'

I took a deep breath, savouring the moment. Once I told Kal and Peterson it would be all around the unit in minutes. Or less.

'It's a big one,' I admitted. 'In fact, it's *the* Big Job. Three months full study, climate, geology, flora, fauna, even a star map. The works.'

She grinned at me and I could see my own excitement

reflected in her eyes. 'Flora? Fauna? When? Where? What have you got? Jesus I'm going to kill the pair of you in a minute.'

'Guess,' said Sussman.

'Oh God, I don't know. Flora, fauna … something biological. The *Beagle*! You're going to the Galapagos.'

Sussman snorted with derision. 'Oh, come on Kal, look at our specialties. I'm early Byzantine and Max doesn't even get out of bed for anything after the Peloponnesian Wars.'

'Well, not Troy. The two of you would be screaming from the rooftops. Egypt? Mesopotamia? Oh, I know. The Great Rift Valley. You're going to study the early migrations.'

'You don't know the half of it. Way further back than that.

'Jeez, I don't know. What?'

I drew deep breath, feeling it all bubbling up again. 'The Cretaceous Period. Sixty-seven million years ago, give or take. We're going to live with the dinosaurs!'

And then again, the two of us were jigging about like a pair of idiots, chanting, 'We're going to see a T-rex, a T-rex, a T-rex,' until Dr Dowson frowned gently at us.

They stared. I could see the conflict. Envy competing with shock. I didn't blame them. Something similar was going through my mind. Peterson, the sensible one (and imagine a group where Peterson is the sensible one), said quietly, 'But have you thought? It's so far back.'

I knew what he meant. The further back you go, the fewer reference points there are. How do you know if you've gone back twenty, thirty, sixty, one hundred million years without a handy newspaper or dress shop opposite? And, although this was ridiculous, I think we all instinctively felt the invisible cord, our trail of breadcrumbs, our route home stretched thinner and thinner the further back we went. Sixty-seven million years ago (give or take) would stretch it very thin indeed, possibly to breaking point.

Kal had been too quiet too long. 'Max, it's so far. Far further back than anything we've ever done before. Aren't you just a bit worried?'

'It shouldn't make any difference. Yesterday, or sixty-seven million years, they're the same; you know that. Look on the bright side; we're far more likely to be eaten by the indigenous fauna than lost in time.'

She sighed. 'Do you guys need a hand?'

'Not at the moment. We need to look through the parameters now, but we'll almost certainly need you at some point.'

'How long's your lead-in?'

'Three months.'

She blinked. 'Yes, it would be, I suppose. We've got late nineteenth-century Vienna and we'll be there and back before you've even set off.'

'I hope you'll be here when we go,' I said and Sussman nodded.

'Of course we will. Give us a shout if you need us.' And they wandered off, presumably to spread the word.

We got stuck in again and set up the categories.

The star map; they wanted to map the night sky. Conditions would be ideal with no light pollution. I had no idea how different the stars would be all that time ago, but now was a good time to find out, I suppose. However, we'd need horizon-to-horizon vision, so we wouldn't want to be in the middle of a forest. Ideally, we could set up on the pod roof and just leave the equipment to do its thing. I made a note to talk to the Chief about co-ordinates and how much control we would have. None, I guessed. We would almost certainly land in some boggy swamp, or under water. Don't think about that. We colour-coded that black and moved on.

We looked at climate next, dividing that down into sub-sections, temperature, wind, rain, etc. Oxygen levels would be important. I'd heard CO_2 levels were higher then. Too high and moving all our kit around would be difficult. I made another note to talk to Helen about high-altitude medication. Climate was allocated blue.

Geology would be interesting. I wanted that one for myself, although I wouldn't be telling Sussman that. There would be a certain amount of horse-trading and almost certainly tears before bedtime. We couldn't bring anything back, so all samples must be photographed, catalogued, and analysed on-site. That meant even more equipment. And from what I could remember, the period was seismically active, so we could add being enveloped in pyroclastic flows to our list of fun ways to die. Geology was imaginatively coded brown.

Flora: again no samples; only photos, images, and on the spot analysis. No grass, if I remembered rightly, and lots of coniferous forests, though broad-leafed trees did exist. And flowers had evolved too, so we could expect big, stingy insects. Yay! Flora got green.

And so to the biggie – fauna; a field so big we decided to spend a week or so on research before coming up with a plan. Fauna was orange.

'Like techies,' said Sussman. 'Big and clumsy with small brains.'

I frowned at him. 'Don't do that, Davey.'

'Oh, I forgot, you actually talk to them, don't you?'

'Davey …'

'Well, I'm just saying, I wouldn't want my sister to marry one.'

'You haven't got a sister and if you did she'd slap you senseless if you tried any of that crap on her, so give it a rest.'

He sat back in his chair. 'You're the boss; so who gets what, then?'

This was where he could be difficult if not carefully managed. 'What do you want? Make a case. And don't cherry-pick all the good stuff for yourself.'

'I'd like the star map. I could do a good job there. You know I could. I'll talk to Barclay about it. She's red-hot at this sort of thing. She tells me what she wants and I set the equipment accordingly. Then I can liaise again when we get back. We'll input the data and project a moving star map. It could be spectacular, Max and I'd like to do it.'

I thought. He was right. He certainly got on better with Barclay. They could produce something really exceptional. I nodded. 'Yes, agreed. I'll leave it with you, but I want daily updates and full training. If anything happens to you then I'm your back-up.'

His face lit up. 'That's great, Max. It'll be the dog's bollocks. You just wait.' He paused and I knew. This was it. This was what he really wanted.

'The dinosaurs ... I'm thinking we could do something similar.'

I started to shake my head.

'No, listen Max. We could do something along the lines of "A Day in the Life of ..." We've done statics for junior schools – "A Day in the Life of a Medieval Peasant" or a Roman soldier or an Egyptian stone mason, you know the sort of thing. We can set up near a waterhole or some centre of activity. We'll have everything coming down to drink, or bathe, or whatever they do. And there'll be fights and kills and sex and cute babies. Max, just think, if we could pull it off, we can do a 3D holo for this. People could actually look up at some thumping great reptile as it passes twenty feet above them. We'll have sound as well and the computer can add vibrations, even the smell of dinosaur shit. Barclay can work all that out. Come on Max, it'll be awesome!'

It would too; images of actual dinosaurs, living, walking; a dinosaur experience. It was a brilliant idea, but he wasn't going to get it easily.

I leaned forward. 'OK, here's the thing. I agree, but it's huge. It's adding huge to an already huge workload. Thirsk have paid for this and they'll want what they paid for, which is just unspectacular, boring, raw data; otherwise the shit will really hit the fan. I don't want you spending all your time on this while I'm disappearing up my own arse like the backward-flying bird of fable trying to get all the other stuff done.' I leaned back. He nodded.

'Look,' I said. 'I'll do climate and geology,' as if conferring a huge favour. 'You do the star map, which you want anyway. You can do flora, which I don't fancy. We'll both have to do fauna because it's big.'

'And the holo?'

I pretended to consider, turning the corners of my mouth down.

'Oh, Max, come on. I tell you what, you let me do the holo and I'll do all the housekeeping. All of it. And I'll talk to Barclay about the star map specs so you don't have to and then you can talk to the Chief about the pod, equipment, layout, etc., so I don't have to. It's perfect.'

It bloody was, too. Game, set, and match.

We shook hands on it and went for a late lunch.

We were, of course, the centre of attention. Sussman loved every minute of it. Professor Rapson dropped an extensive research programme on the table that would mean us not sleeping from now until the end of the next millennium. Major Guthrie produced a massive survival training schedule. I decided to forge a sick note. The Chief congratulated us with a handshake and a request that at least one of us attend sessions on pod and equipment familiarisation.

The next day I settled myself in a study carrel and began to review the material I would want uploaded to subliminal reference tapes. There was a lot; tons of it actually. I called up Gorecki's Third Symphony and as Dawn Upshaw let rip, I got stuck in.

I was roused, hours later by Doctor Dowson, part of whose job was to ensure historians didn't lose all track of time and become welded to the furniture. Stumbling stiffly off for a drink, I met Chief Farrell and we took our tea outside into the sunshine.

Gradually a routine developed. I spent the mornings researching, broke for lunch, usually with Chief Farrell, took my data to Barclay's team for uploading, spent an hour or so discussing equipment operation with the technical section and rounded off the afternoon with Professor Rapson, setting up the next few days' research programmes. After which, I collected my tapes from Barclay, had a working dinner with Sussman when we updated each other, grabbed a drink with him or Kal and Peterson, went to my room and wallowed in a long bath while playing the tapes (during which I usually fell asleep), before toppling into bed, entangled in my earpieces.

In between all this, I assisted Kal and Peterson setting themselves up for late nineteenth-century Vienna, debriefed them when they got back and saved Sussman's life when he told Kal her bum looked big in a bustle. We updated our field medic skills and I began to talk to the furniture.

Having got what he wanted, Sussman knuckled down and got with the programme. He also got Barclay off my back for which I was grateful. I repaid him by ensuring Farrell dealt mainly with me which was no problem at all for either of us. The Chief and I usually lunched together and, when weather permitted, we sat outside against a sunny wall scoffing sandwiches. By unspoken agreement we didn't talk work during lunch hours, preferring to take half an hour or so just to think about something else. Sometimes we didn't talk at all, sitting with our faces turned towards the sun. 'Like daffodils,' I said on one occasion.

'What?' he said, laughing. 'Daffodils?'

At that moment, Dieter said, 'Hold it,' and a camera flashed. He looked down and tinkered a little. 'Yes, it's working fine now.'

'Let's have a look,' said Farrell. 'Not bad. Do you want a copy?'

'Yes please,' I said. There were very few photos of me in this world and even fewer in which I didn't look either drunk or criminally insane and this one had him in it as well. A couple of days later it appeared in my pigeon hole in a neat frame. I put it next to the Horse.

It was a lovely day. I spent a little longer than usual over lunch and most of the techies had disappeared for the regular Friday afternoon football match. I leaned back against the wall in the sun and closed my eyes, savouring the peace and quiet. No one was around and I was half asleep when someone sat down on the ground next to me. I knew who it would be without opening my eyes.

'Hi.'

'Hi yourself,' he said, offering me half his sandwiches. 'Have you eaten?'

'Yes, thanks.'

He wrapped them back up again and put them down. 'This is peaceful.'

'Mm ...'

The far-off sounds of violence receded in the afternoon sunshine. I enjoyed a pleasant feeling of isolation.

'Miss Maxwell. Max ...'

'Mm ...' I said again.

'Are you awake?'

'Mm ...'

'I've been looking for an opportunity to talk to you; sometime when you're not drunk, or obsessing about something. Sometime when you're *listening*.'

'I'm listening,' I said, a little indignantly, because really, I hadn't been.

The long silence made me open my eyes. 'Chief, I'm here, awake, listening. Is there a problem?'

'It's not always all about work, you know.'

'What is it all about, then?'

'You're happy here, aren't you?'

'Yes,' I said, surprised. 'Why do you ask?' I sat up

suddenly. 'Are they cancelling the mission? Are we looking at redundancies?'

'No, no,' he said quickly. 'For heaven's sake, don't panic.'

'It's an historian thing. And it's not just any old panic. It's highly trained panic. It's taken years of hard work and practice. Please don't mock.'

'My apologies. Speaking as your primary trainer, it's gratifying to see my poor efforts bearing fruit.'

'So when historians are rioting in the streets, you must be absolutely over the moon.'

'To drag the conversation back on track …'

'Yes, sorry Chief. You wanted me.'

He looked taken aback for a moment before pulling himself together. 'Do you remember when we met?'

'Yes, on my first day here. You were coming down the stairs.'

He said, 'You've come a long way since then. You stood in front of me, radiating attitude and defiance and now look at you, heading up the most important assignment we've ever had. I'm very proud of you.'

No one had ever been proud of me before. No happy, smiling family at my graduation. He stared out over the gardens. I wondered what on earth was going on.

'Chief, is there a problem with the assignment?'

'No, everything's fine with the assignment. Are you all right?'

'Yes, we're getting there slowly. Not long now. I can hardly believe it.'

'The experience of a lifetime?'

'No, that will be Troy.'

'Apart from Troy, do you have any plans for the future?'

'Oh, yes. Thermopylae. Agincourt. Ramses the Great. Don't get me started.'

'No, I mean plans that do not actually involve St Mary's.'

'Well, no, not really.'

'Do you see yourself doing this for ever, then?'

'That's a bit unlikely. I mean, none of us make old bones, do we? Look at poor old Kevin Grant.'

'And yet you still ...'

'Well, as either Achilles or Kurt Cobain would probably have said, "A short life but a merry one."'

'Do you really mean that? Don't you see yourself moving into a more – conventional line of work? Or what about a family?'

'Oh God, no. Families are the invention of the devil. I'm never doing that.'

'They're not all bad, you know.'

Something in his tone of voice stopped me pursuing this line of conversation. And it was true, for some people families could be a source of strength and security. Just not for me.

'My family is at St Mary's.'

'You mean Sussman?'

'What? No!' Where did that come from? Suddenly, it was vitally important to get this straight. 'He's my partner. That's all.'

He nodded and shifted round to face me. 'The thing is, Max ... I wanted to say ...' and stopped again.

Good God Almighty, he was worse than me. I had no idea what he wanted to say. A corner of my mind remembered the conversation I'd overheard in the paint store. A treasured memory I'd tucked carefully away and took out occasionally to relive and hug close to me. And the Trojan Horse. And the photo. But looking at him now, I had no clue. I knew what I wanted to hear, but he was shy, I was wary, he was a senior officer – seriously, what were the chances? And how much of this was just wishful thinking on my part? Imagine if I said something and he didn't ...

I turned towards him and caught him smiling down at me with such a look of – and then the sodding, bloody football thudded against the wall beside us and I nearly jumped out of my skin. A voice shouted, 'Can we have our ball back please?'

I threw it back to Dieter. When I looked back he was eating his sandwiches with one hand and typing on his scratchpad with the other. Thank God I hadn't said anything.

I felt really stupid. 'I have to get back,' I said, getting up.

He nodded. 'Max …' I looked back at him. 'After this assignment …'

I nodded and walked away before I became even more confused.

I met Kal at breakfast one day soon after.

She handed me her newspaper and grinned. 'What do you think?'

I peered at an ad for a local hotel and their next event.

'Look,' she said. 'Spa, beauty treatments, massage, Jacuzzi, and ta-dah, the big finish: dinner, cabaret, and disco. They've got that illusionist off the TV. We book in for one night, spend the day making ourselves even more beautiful (always supposing that's possible), drink too much, dance till dawn, have a bit of a lie-in, a very careful late breakfast, and be back here before anyone notices we're gone. What do you think? It's just what we need. Come on, when did you last get away from this place?'

Suddenly, it sounded absolutely fabulous. 'Oh God, yes,' I said with mounting excitement. 'Look, they've got an indoor pool. We can lie around sipping cocktails and looking sophisticated.'

'Well, I can,' said Kal. 'One sniff of the glass and you'll be unconscious; but it's a good thought. And here's another; let's ask Helen if she wants to come.'

'OK. Here she is now. Ask her.'

'Ask her what?' said Helen, seating herself alongside. We showed her the article. Surprisingly, she was enthusiastic. 'Count me in. I'm sick of this place. And you two *must* go. Given your occupation, I'm aware of the irony, but the pair of you should definitely get out more.'

'I have to go; the Professor wants me,' said Kal. 'I'll book it this afternoon and let you know.' She exchanged a glance with Helen. 'Separate rooms?'

'I'm not sleeping with either of you two,' said Helen. 'You both snore and Max makes funny whiffly noises as well.'

'I do not!' I cried, indignant.

'You do,' they said in unison and exchanged another look. 'Separate rooms.' Was something happening here? I don't snore that badly; although the bit about the whiffly noises might be true. I'm told they're hilarious.

They pushed off together and I sat sipping my second cup and savouring the pleasure of not thinking about the Cretaceous for a moment.

I looked up and saw Izzie Barclay pulling out a chair at the next table. 'Hey, Izzie, how are you?'

I got the pained look she always gave when people didn't call her Miss Barclay, or (more laughably) ma'am.

'I'm very well, thank you,' she said crisply and began to spread her toast. Low fat spread. No marmalade. It figured. That was why she was thin and I wasn't. Or would ever be. On the other hand, who eats toast without butter or marmalade? No wonder she was such a misery. I had a sudden thought and looked at her. We should invite her too. It would be a nice thing to do. She must be lonely. Nobody liked her much. She looked up from her toast.

'What?'

I took a breath, 'Izzie ...'

Mrs Partridge appeared abruptly at my shoulder, clutching an armful of papers. 'Miss Maxwell, Dr Bairstow would like to see you at once.'

'Two minutes,' I said.

'No, I'm sorry, now please.'

I sighed and got up. 'I'll be back,' I said to Barclay and followed Mrs Partridge upstairs. It took longer than I expected and unsurprisingly she'd gone when I got back. I set off to Hawking after her, but got distracted by something and it went out of my head. If it hadn't, if I'd asked her, if she'd come, how much would have been different?

Seven

On the Saturday morning I packed a bag and met Kal and Helen outside. We wanted to slip away as discreetly as possible, having no desire to explain our plans to anyone. We tussled briefly over whose car to take and eventually settled on Helen's.

Determined to get our money's worth, we made full use of all the facilities, including the hairdresser. I let them cut my hair. Not short, obviously, but an amazing amount lay on the floor when they'd finished. And it looked so much better, sleek and shiny and giving the impression I could control it. Yes, like that was ever going to happen. Monday morning and it was back in the sock bun – like it or not.

Back in my room, I dressed slowly – impractical but pretty underwear, an oriental style gold and black tight-fitting dress and my precious butterfly shoes. They were actually the only girlie shoes I owned. I'd bought them on a rare shopping trip in Rushford, years ago, shortly after I came to St Mary's, just to remind myself I was a girl. I loved them and rarely got the opportunity to wear them. Tonight, however, the shoes and I were hitting the town! They seemed quite excited.

I put on a little make-up and it looked OK, but everyone knows that if a little is good then more must be even better, so I added more. In my defence, I can only say I would be making an entrance with two tall, slim women, each in their own way quite stunning and the odds were that no one would notice me anyway. Kal was going for her snow princess look in glittering white and silver with Helen doing dominatrix in severely cut dark red.

'Bloody hell,' we all said, looking at each other.

I've got to say, our entrance was a triumph. Just for once,

when the conversation paused briefly, it was for all the right reasons. We were escorted to our table by the head waiter himself, who ruthlessly elbowed his subordinates aside for the privilege.

The table was laid for six.

'This is the wrong table,' I said. 'This is for six people.'

I'm not bright.

Kal perused the wine menu and ignored me.

Helen looked round the room and ignored me.

'Guys,' I said, but someone put a margarita in front of me, so I didn't care anymore; it was a good table, right up front, so I just sat back and was grateful.

'Can we order?' I said. 'Because I'm famished and I need to soak up all the alcohol.'

'In a minute,' said Kal vaguely. She looked round the room too. Since everyone else was doing it, I joined in. The first people I saw were Dieter and Peterson. Followed by, of all people, Chief Farrell, looking a total knockout in a black suit, black shirt, and silver-grey tie. Wow!

'Look!' I said, cheerfully. I know, but the margaritas were beginning to kick in. 'There's some of our guys.'

I'm not bright.

'Oh. What a surprise,' said Helen. 'So there are.'

'Oh. Goodness me, you are right,' said Kalinda. 'Shall we ask them to join us?'

'Why not?' I said. 'There's plenty of room.'

Have I said I'm not bright?

Kal waved. They came over.

'Good evening,' said Dieter. 'You all look very nice.'

'Yes,' said Farrell. 'Very nice.'

Peterson rolled his eyes. 'Oh, for God's sake. Orange people stand aside for a minute. Watch and learn, guys.' He pulled out three long-stemmed roses from behind his back.

'First, a red rose for the love of my life, the beautiful Helen. A white rose for my partner, the Ice Princess, Kalinda. And a

112

golden rose for my golden friend, the lovely Max.' Five people stared at him. 'And that, my orange friends, is how it's done.' He seated himself next to Helen and smiled at her. She blushed. Never thought I'd see the day.

Kal stood up. 'Would you like to sit here, Chief? Then I can sit here.' Nobody ruthlessly gets their way like Kalinda. In a flash, everyone was sitting down in their new places. I stared at my rose, which matched my dress. As did Helen's. As did Kal's. A solitary non-alcohol soaked neuron began to fire.

We ordered and ate. The cabaret started. I was very conscious of him sitting next to me. We watched the show and then the disco started, so after shouting pointlessly at each other for a few minutes, we got up to dance. The usual thing happened. Just as we arrived on the dance floor the good music stopped and they started with the smooch stuff.

We suffered the usual embarrassed indecision. What do you do? I got no clues from him, so I smiled and stepped forward. We could do distance dancing. It didn't happen. I stepped forward into his arms. He took my hand and wrapped the other firmly around my waist. We danced. I stepped a little closer. He tightened his grip. Normally, I don't like this sort of thing. I get panicky if held tightly, but this was – nice. He danced well. He smelled good too. He didn't hum with the music. I rested my head on his shoulder. The music stopped. I looked up. And he kissed me.

My whole world stopped. Along with my breathing, my heart, my thought processes, and Time itself. And hundreds of fragments of glorious colour and light swirled and swept across the room. Oh no, sorry, that was the glitter ball.

I'm not completely without experience. There was a very nice boy in my last year at Thirsk, whose name I can't remember; and another during my time in Europe, whose name I can't remember either. Nothing serious. If truth be told, it was mainly curiosity – after my childhood, would I be able to – would I even want to? I felt nothing; nothing at all. Sex is a bit like scratching a rash – it's nice when you stop.

I rested my forehead against his shoulder and tried to remember my name. He leaned forward and spoke into my ear. 'I really, really need to speak to you. Tonight. In fact, now.' He slid an arm around my waist and we left the room. I wondered what the protocol was for asking a senior officer to one's room.

'Would you feel safer in my room or yours?' he asked.

'Mine,' I said firmly. 'Three oh five,' in case we got separated on the way. We headed for the lift.

My room was warm and dim – a bit like me really and he settled himself on the couch. I wandered aimlessly. Drink, confusion, high heels, all making significant contributions to my lack of grasp on current events. He said nothing and eventually I came to rest alongside him and assumed an attentive expression. I wondered again how two people who normally had no problems communicating when they wore blue and orange could become so tongue-tied when wearing black and gold. Wasn't there some work done on using colours to induce certain states of mind? Like painting the home team's dressing room a vigorous red and the visitors' dressing room boring beige?

I re-focused to find him staring at me. 'Where do you go?' he demanded in exasperation. 'I'm about to make the biggest speech of my life and you're just not here!'

'I'm sorry,' I said defensively. 'I was thinking about colour-induced moods.'

'I'm not even going to ask. Focus!'

'Sorry.' I wriggled round to face him and waited expectantly. He said nothing, just stared at me, and I began to feel a little alarmed. Several times I thought he seemed about to speak but nothing happened.

Eventually I said, 'Look, I'm well and truly focused now, but I'm not sure how long I can keep this up. If you don't get a move on then I'm going to be wandering off again. What's the problem?'

He took my hand and held it gently and I knew this was going to be bad.

'Do you trust me?'

'Yes,' I said, because I did, but with a little twist of unease.

'Well, you shouldn't. Nothing is what it seems, least of all me.'

Shit. He was married. No, he was a woman. No, he was gay. I thought I felt something tear inside me.

'Well, what are you then?'

He took a deep breath and exhaled, not looking at me. 'I'm from the future.'

'You're … from the future?'

I don't know why I should be so surprised. I know I'm an historian and we tend to think in the past, but, after all, our now was someone else's past. Really, the only surprise should be that it hadn't happened before.

He nodded fractionally. Now I could see it – the typical historian's instinct to give away as little as possible. I could relate to that. Don't contaminate the timeline.

'Why are you here? Are you on assignment?' Bloody long one if so. 'Are you a fugitive? Are you on the run?'

'No, no, nothing so exciting.' He got up and began to wander around the room. I recognised that behaviour. I hate being bombarded with questions, so I left him. After a while he stopped by the window and turned to face me.

I said, 'Why not start at the beginning, go on to the end and then stop.'

He smiled his small smile. 'Yes, Lucy.'

'Shouldn't that be Alice?'

'No, you're my Lucy; the girl in the song – the one with kaleidoscope eyes.'

I was breathless again.

'Leon Farrell is not my real name. I was born in France. My mother was English and a teacher. I never knew my father. We didn't have a lot. My mother took extra jobs. So did I. Anything to get by. I got a full army scholarship to – well, a place in France. I graduated with honours and served three years at various land bases around Europe. I got transferred to a carrier, served there for two years, met a pilot named Monique, and married her.'

I sat very, very still.

'Things were great for a couple of years. She got pregnant. We had a boy. Alexander. Alex. Then another, Stevie. Then she left me, citing career, demands of the military, not enough excitement. I tried to be both parents and carry on working but it was hard. My mother joined us to take care of the boys. Life got better for all of us and it was a pleasure to make things easier for her after all she'd done for me. Those were good years.' The way he said it made me think there hadn't been many of those. 'I came home whenever I could and then I got posted to a research establishment just outside – well, somewhere in England. We all moved. We were happy. Alex started school.'

He stopped, drew back the curtains and stared out into the dark.

'There was – will be – an outbreak of flu. There's one nearly every year, I know, but this one was a killer. And cruel. It took the old and the young. Anyone from twenty to fifty only seemed to get it mildly. Other people, the ones outside that age group, just dropped and died. It was that quick.

'My mother got it first. I'm glad, actually, that she went first. So she never knew … All public establishments closed. The country was at a standstill. I sat with my mother at the hospital until she died, quite quietly and without a fuss. Typical of her. Next day, the boys got it. There was nothing anyone could do. Alex went first. Like his grandmother, he went quietly. Just closed his eyes and drifted away. Stevie … suffered. He didn't know me. I held him and tried to keep him cool. He cried for his grandmamma. He cried for me. It was … very bad. He died in the small hours. It was the end of my world. I started the week with a happy, healthy family and at the end of it I was the only one left.'

He took a very long, deep breath. 'They were working on a cure by that time; a vaccine. They took samples of the boys' blood. And mine, because sometimes … When the doctors asked to see me I thought there was a chance they could … and then they told me they couldn't … because the boys weren't mine. They didn't even have the same father. There was no chance for them. I buried all three on the same day. Their mother didn't come.'

What can you say? What can you do? He cleared his throat, closed the curtains, and continued with bitter amusement.

'I was blind drunk for a month. I hit anyone and everyone who spoke to me or who even came near me. I nearly tore France apart looking for my ex-wife, but fortunately never found her. I've never seen her since. I don't even know if she knows the boys are dead. I got suspended from my job and was all set to drink myself to death in six months when St Mary's found me.'

He turned and started looking out of the window again.

'Edward found me – in a bar, obviously. He picked a fight; we took it outside, and he hammered seven bells out of me. I woke up in St Mary's. They offered me a special job.'

He came and sat next to me. 'Forget all that other stuff. This is what's important. In my time, St Mary's is in big trouble. There are, or will be, people who think History can be manipulated, made more profitable. There were more of them than anyone knew. They stole a pod, jumped back and – acquired – two more.' He watched to see if I would make the connection.

'Four and Seven! You never found the pods. I thought that was strange. How can you lose a pod?'

'Exactly. There was no malfunction. We think they killed the historians and stole the pods. And now they have three at least.'

117

He got up and switched on the kettle.

'We know that now is a vulnerable time for St Mary's. Expenditure is massive, there's no financial return, and losses are high.'

'They want us closed down?'

'No, we think they want us – diverted. Or subverted is a better word. St Mary's must continue now so that it exists in the future. There must be at least one pod for them to steal. So our problem is on two fronts. We don't want to be closed down by the current authorities and these guys are whizzing up and down the timeline causing havoc. It's dangerous but profitable so they don't care. The future St Mary's is weak and vulnerable, so it made sense to send Edward and me back to fight the good fight here, before they become too powerful.'

I considered this for a while. The kettle boiled and he made some tea. When he sat down, I said, 'You and the Boss – are here to strengthen St Mary's?'

'That's partly the reason, yes.'

'But it was the Boss who founded St Mary's.'

'Yes, he brought a pod back with him, pretended to "discover" time travel, and used it as the foundation for all the others.'

'So the Boss brings a pod from the future to now. And that pod is the template for all future pods?'

He knew where I was going with this and smiled.

'So who actually discovers or invents time travel? Who builds the first pod?'

He smiled and shrugged his shoulders. 'You do not want to go there. Trust me, that way madness lays.' I could believe it.

'OK, back to you. You came back with the Boss to sort things out?'

'No, there are two distinct assignments here. Edward and I jumped separately. He jumped back to found St Mary's. I arrived later.'

I thought of me and Kal. 'What's it like to see your friend

118

suddenly so much older than you?'

'It was nearly an emotional moment, but we took it like men.'

'So, St Mary's is up and running. The Boss has done the grunt work and then you turn up.'

'Drink your tea. Yes. I'm here to safeguard St Mary's. Guide us through various technological breakthroughs. And to keep an eye on you.'

'Am I strategically important?'

'Actually yes, very important, but also I just like looking at you.'

I ignored this for the time being. 'So you know the future.'

'No, absolutely not. We need to be very clear about this. I was recruited and trained by the future St Mary's. I have a detailed knowledge of you and St Mary's up until the day I arrived here. After that – nothing, for obvious reasons.'

'Bloody hell.'

He was sympathetic. 'I know. It's a lot to take in. I've been looking for an opportunity to talk to you for quite some time, but you're always either drunk, injured, stressed, or not actually in this time at all. It's not been easy.'

'So, do you have any instructions for me? Do I have to do anything?'

'Just stay safe. I know, what am I thinking? But seriously, Max, watch yourself. Just be aware, will you?'

I nodded and sat back to think about all this. I looked at him. He was different. I was different. I'd walked into this room one person and I'd walk out another.

'How far in the future is this?'

'I can't tell you, Max. Please don't ask.'

'But surely, one day your assignment will be finished. You'll be recalled. Your pod is here. One day, you'll leave.' I tried to keep my voice level.

'My pod is here to give me flexibility to track down these people. There are no plans to recall us. Edward and I are here

119

for the duration.'

I thought about how he'd left everything behind to do this. I wondered if he had leapt at the chance to escape his past. I think I would have. No, I already had.

The radiator ticked in the quiet room. I wondered what would happen next. Things had changed. I was stone-cold sober for a start. He looked tired. I looked at the clock. It was so late it was early. And not that early either. The night had nearly gone. He got up and went to the window again. What now? Again, he came and sat down and took my hand. Amongst this torrent of revelation I had forgotten …

'I wondered if I might talk to you for a moment.'

'Yes, of course,' I said, wondering what we'd been doing up till now.

'The thing is … the thing is … I wanted to tell you I like you.'

I felt oddly disappointed. 'I like you too, Chief. We work well together.'

'That's not what I meant. What I wanted to say is that … is that I have feelings for you.'

My heart kicked up a gear. 'What sort of feelings?'

'Respect, admiration.' A long pause. 'Love.'

My little heart was going like a hammer. He mistook my silence.

'I'm sorry; this must be a bit of a shock for you. I've tried very hard to … not to … I have to ask and I know you'll be honest with me. Is there any chance you could ever … I mean, could you see yourself …?'

'Yes.'

He stared very hard at his hand, the one with the scar, which still held mine painfully tightly. I don't think he realised how strong he was.

'Oh, OK. In that case, I'll leave you. I'm sorry to have … Of course, this won't affect …' and he trailed off again. The guy had real articulacy issues. He wasn't that good at listening, either. He got up, crossed the room, and quietly let himself out. I sat, stunned and exhausted and happy and elated. And slightly exasperated. There was a knock at the door. I got up and opened it.

'What did you say?'

'I said yes.'

He smiled, hugely. 'Yes, you did, didn't you?' He bent his head and kissed me again, very gently. 'After this mission …'

And before I could even get myself together and reply, he was gone.

I went to bed and for the first time in months, my thoughts were not Cretaceous-based.

Eight

Seven days later, we were as ready as we would ever be, with both pods fully loaded. Sussman was taking Three and I had Eight. We had decided to work from Three and sleep and eat in Eight, or maybe the other way around. We'd see when we arrived. As far as possible we were programmed to aim for higher ground. We didn't want to land in three feet of water. 'It's not an exact science,' said Farrell, looking, for him, worried. 'Keep your fingers crossed.' He looked tired and worn, just like everyone who had anything to do with this assignment. And we hadn't actually started yet.

Sussman appeared. 'All set?'

'Yes, let's crank them up and get going.' We looked up. Kal and Peterson waved. Dr Bairstow stood quietly with Professor Rapson and many others. The gantry was packed.

'Let's go.'

We entered our separate pods. My second solo jump. What a long time ago the other one seemed. I stowed my bag carefully in the locker. I'd left the Horse behind, but I'd hidden my precious photo in my pack. I certainly wasn't going to put it out for Sussman to mock, but just knowing I had it with me was a comfort. As if I'd brought him along.

Farrell stood in the doorway, scratchpad in hand, but it wasn't needed. We'd been over everything twice already. We looked at each other. It was time. He said, 'Try and stay safe, Max. I have plans for your return.'

My heart did a little twist. I nodded. 'You take care, too.'

He smiled, stepped back, and the door shut. I opened the com.

'Counting down.'

123

The computer said, 'Jump initiated,' and the world went white.

And green. Everything was green. Green was everywhere. I was so entranced I forgot to give my usual thanks to the god of historians that I hadn't materialised inside a mountain or at the bottom of a sea, or in this case a swamp. I craned my head to see out of the screen. Nothing but green.

'Davey! Are you there?'

'I'm behind you. I can see you, about one hundred yards away. Bloody hell, it's bright!'

'Activate your monitors. Let's have a good look before we go outside.'

He started the read-outs. 'Temperatures are high, but not bad. Humidity is off the charts. Hope you've got your rot-proof knickers on. Oxygen levels are acceptable if we don't run about too much. No proximity alerts.'

I checked my own readings. 'I concur. I'm coming over.'

'I'll put the kettle on.'

I slipped on vest and helmet and activated the mike. 'Com test.'

'Loud and clear.'

Hefting a blaster from the locker, I clamped a stun gun to the sticky patch on one thigh and hooked an industrial strength pepper spray to my belt. Closing my eyes I sprayed myself liberally with Professor Rapson's Special Spray. Theoretically I now smelled vegetable rather than animal. In reality I smelled like a giant rotting cabbage. Checking the proximities one last time, I stood by the door, took a couple of deep breaths, jumped up and down, shrugged my shoulders twice, and said, 'Door.'

Bloody hell, it was hot; like opening an oven.

And wet. I felt the sweat break out all over my body. Experience told me the inside of both pods would be unspeakable within a week.

And noisy; mostly chirping insects, but distant bellows and grunts hinted at larger stuff.

And green; with thick, lush growth everywhere. All the colours blazed bright and fresh and new as if the world hadn't yet had time to wear them out.

And smelly; even the smell was green. Wet earth, wet foliage, wet shit; like the strongest farmyard smells ever, sized up a hundred times.

And eggs; faintly, I could smell bad eggs. I knew what that would be and sure enough, on the horizon, I could see smudgy shapes with suspicious clouds above them. Volcanoes and all the fun things they bring to the party; eruptions, molten lava, earthquakes, and pyroclastic flows. Yay! But all with luck a nice safe distance away. I turned around, looked up and nearly had a heart attack. All right, we weren't at the bottom of the sea, which was good, but we did appear to have landed on the lower slopes of Krakatoa's great-grandmother. The smoking summit looked a long way off, but it wasn't really where we wanted to be in terms of Health and Safety. Still, Health and Safety is something that happens to other people and there was no time to stand and stare. Move!

'To your right and downhill,' said Sussman in my ear. Turning my head, I could see him, correctly dressed for once, standing in his own doorway.

'On my way.'

The ground seemed firm enough. I set off downhill. After twenty paces I turned and looked back at my own pod so I could find it again, nestling just below the treeline on a small plateau. To my left, a thick wood sloped upwards. To my right, the slope continued down to a wide, flat, treeless area which served as a coastal plain for either a large lake or possibly a small inland sea.

I remembered to drop to one knee and not let go of the blaster, but that's about as far as Guthrie's careful training got me. Oh, and I remembered to shut my mouth. Otherwise, I just stared like a trainee. It was shameful. Good job there were no senior staff around to see it. A movement beside me made me jump a mile, but it was only Sussman.

'Got fed up with waiting,' he said crossly. 'Fuck me!'

Now I knew why I did this job.

Below us, a small herd of what I recognised as Maiasaurae, the Good Mothers, plodded across the plain. They herded tightly together, nervously protecting their young from predators. I looked round to see if any Troodons were trailing the herd. They would be around somewhere. The procession continued out of view.

'Ankylosaurus,' whispered Sussman, pointing to his left and proving he hadn't been wasting his time these last months. 'The last armour-plated dinosaur. Just look at him.' Hard not to – he was as big as a bloody tank.

'Come on,' I said, getting up. 'Time for this later. Let's do a recce.' Even then, it took a few minutes to drag ourselves away. We were the first humans, the only humans, ever to see all this, but we had to have to sharpen up or we wouldn't last ten minutes. Anything could have crept up behind us while we gawped like tourists.

'Watch your step here,' he warned, as we made our way to Three. 'It's a bit dodgy underfoot.'

It was a bit loose, but so long as we took things slowly and didn't try it in the dark, we should be OK.

We grinned at each other in excitement. 'Let's do this thing!'

We were on Day 74 of a near-perfect mission.

The day everything blew up in my face.

We were so tired even I was sleeping like the dead. Sussman had been as good as his word about the housekeeping – well, most of it anyway – and each morning woke me with a cup of tea.

I don't know why, maybe some deep-seated instinct kicked in, I don't know, but I opened my eyes that morning to find Sussman kneeling over me with an erection the size of a telegraph pole and a not very nice expression on his face.

Instinct kicked in. Literally. I brought my knees up, slammed both feet into his chest and straightened my legs. He flew backwards.

What the fuck did he think he was playing at? *Now* I remembered Kal's previous warnings. *Now* I realised I was sixty-seven million years from home with someone I couldn't trust at all. Not a good feeling. I grabbed my pepper spray and made it personal.

He fled around the pod, sneezing, crying, coughing, and trying to grab his clothing. I wedged myself into a corner to protect my back and stopped. The aircon had packed up or maybe it was me, but the sweat poured off me, running down into my eyes. I shouted at him, shaking with rage and adrenalin, unsure what to do next.

It's always been a question of trust. You take two people of the opposite sex and throw them together in a small pod thousands or millions or hundreds of years from anywhere and trust to luck. And, as far as I knew, it had never been a problem. Kal and Peterson, Lower and Baverstock, all my predecessors, I'd never heard even a rumour of any problems. I mean, obviously you do see each other naked from time to time, but it's not an issue. It's brisk and business-like and let's get on with it because it's our job. Of course, most of the unit was at it like rabbits anyway; but not me and not with my partner. And then the built-in female guilt kicked in. Had I somehow given him the impression …? Was it all my own fault?

No, it wasn't. I refused to go down that road. I wiped the sweat out of my eyes and said, 'Get out.'

He started to stammer something.

I said, 'No, don't even bother. Get out. Get back to Number Three and stay there until I call you.'

'But …'

I pulled down a blaster from the locker. I'd meant just to cover him as he made his way back, but he misinterpreted the

127

gesture, shouted, 'Door!', and was gone. I stood in the doorway and watched him run. He lost his footing on the narrow bit, but picked himself up and got to Three intact. Back in Eight, I closed the door, put the blaster away, sat down heavily, and considered my options.

I could send him home. This would mean finishing the assignment alone which would be hard work, but it could be done. No, the Boss would have me recalled. This was no place for a solo mission.

I could take us both back, maybe returning with Kal or Peterson. But we wouldn't have records for ninety consecutive days. We'd have to start again, maybe. But we don't come cheap and Thirsk wouldn't pay for the extra time. They'd want reasons and it would make us look so bloody unprofessional. Not only would they want a permanent presence at St Mary's, but they might even want to accompany us on future jumps.

Or I could continue and complete the assignment. No matter how little sharing any sort of time and space with that bastard appealed to me, this had to be my favourite option. I could banish him to Three and we could just meet outside during daylight hours. Our relationship would be on a purely professional basis. It would be awkward and embarrassing, but that was his problem. My problem would be deciding what course of action to take back at St Mary's. He was my partner. And I had no proof. And nothing had actually happened. It would be my word against his. The age-old female dilemma. I sighed. I'd think about that later.

Of course, I could just shoot him.

I showered the sweat off, dressed, and tidied the pod. Keep the hands busy while the brain ticks over. I was laying out stuff for the day's programme, when my com crackled. 'Max? Are you there? Can I speak to you?'

If he thought he could smarm his way out of this one, he was mistaken. Having no idea what I would say to him, I said crisply, 'I'm busy at the moment. Remain where you are. I'll speak to you later.' It only occurred to me afterwards that he might jump to the conclusion I was logging the incident.

I looked at that day's programme. Nothing unusual, collect the meteorological disks and enter the info, ditto for the geological records, and insert new disks for the star map. We were scheduled to explore and map the northern end of the valley. Priority work. We'd spent so much time filming dinosaurs for the holo we'd got behind on other things. Time to catch up. Maybe I could work him to death and that would solve all my problems.

I knew, deep down, I'd decided to continue the mission. Returning to St Mary's with Sussman's tail between his legs was not an option. But I could take reasonable precautions and at the same time send out an unmistakable message.

I said, 'Computer, restrict access to this pod. Access Maxwell only. Authorisation: Maxwell five zero alpha nine eight zero four bravo. Confirm.'

'Restrict access to this pod. Maxwell only. Confirmed.'

I opened my com. 'Report to me, please. At once.'

I watched him scurry up the path. That narrow bit was really beginning to look a bit dodgy. I made a note to look for a new route. He was correctly dressed in woodland camouflage, swollen-eyed and pale, his hair still wet. Arriving at the pod, he said, 'Door,' and nothing happened. He waited a few seconds then repeated himself more loudly. The door stayed shut. He got the message. Raising his arm, he knocked quietly. I let him in.

I didn't ask him to sit down, nor did I sit myself. The dinosaur-strength pepper spray stood ostentatiously to hand. I opened my mouth to speak but he held up his hand.

'No, please Max, just let me say something. I'm sorry. I'm truly sorry. I don't know what happened. Well, I do, obviously, but I don't know why. If it's any help, I'm as horrified as you are and deeply ashamed. I'm begging you, please don't end this mission now. We've come so far. There's only sixteen days left and all we're scheduled for now is data gathering. I see you've put a lock on your pod. That's fine, I understand, but let's finish the assignment. Please Max, I ...'

I cut across him. 'I've already decided. This mission will continue. But there will be different rules. Unless instructed otherwise, you will remain in your pod. You will eat and sleep there. You will keep a reasonable distance at all times. You will not touch me. Any and all conversation is to be of a professional nature only. If you do not agree to this then this mission is terminated now with all the subsequent unpleasantness that will entail.'

He swallowed and nodded.

'Right, the northern end of the valley. We've not been there yet. We'll do another contour map. Note any new species of dinosaur we might come across, but today I mostly want to get to grips with flora, which is your area. Is your weapon charged?'

He nodded again, looking paler than ever. 'May I speak? I only want to suggest we concentrate on equipment today and do the northern end tomorrow, when we feel more ...'

'No. Today.'

He looked unhappy but I didn't care.

I shouldered my pack. 'Let's get started.'

We set off down the path.

'Wait a minute,' he said. 'This next bit's not good.' He remembered, swallowed and said formally, 'Perhaps you would like to go first. If you take off your pack then I can throw it across to you and then do the same for mine. If you agree, that is.'

God help me, I took all this meekness at face value. I slipped off my pack and started across the narrow bit.

'Watch your feet,' he said.

They warned us over and over at St Mary's, but until it actually happens to you, you can have no idea of the speed and silence of a raptor attack. I saw and heard nothing. The first I

130

knew was when something solid caught me across my back and shoulders. I staggered heavily, the path gave way, and I lost my balance and went over the edge.

I rolled, fell, and bounced for what felt like a lifetime. Other things hit me; hard things, rocks, boulders, branches. I had a mouth full of shale. It went up my nose. I had no idea which way was up. I tried grabbing at things to slow my fall, but everything was falling with me. I hit something solid and stopped. I could feel debris piling up around me. I tried to bring my arms up to protect my face and give myself a little breathing space. And then, I think, I passed out.

I only became aware of things very slowly. It was raining and the moisture felt pleasant on my face. I lay under a great weight. Turning my head carefully, I could see I was partly wedged under a fallen tree trunk and partly buried by what felt like half a mountain. I spat gravel and took stock. My back hurt, but I suspected that came from the initial attack. My helmet and vest had done a good job of protecting me on the way down, but every exposed piece of skin burned with Cretaceous road rash. My first instinct was to try and wriggle free, but second thoughts told me to stay put. I had no idea how long I'd been out, seconds or hours. There might still be raptors around and if they heard or saw me moving they'd be down here in a flash. And I was in a very precarious position here. This tree trunk was the only thing keeping me from falling any further and I would like it to continue doing so. It looked a long way down.

It was a bloody long way up, too. Not only that, but the ground looked treacherous and unstable. If I did manage to get free then I would have to work my way over to the left, to solid bedrock and try to get up that way. Some dinosaur deity somewhere was smiling on me though, because the rain felt soft and warm and refreshing. If it turned into a typical Cretaceous downpour I'd either be washed away or maybe drown. How can you possibly drown half way up a mountain? Maybe I should be looking at office jobs again.

131

Activating my com, I whispered, 'Sussman, can you hear me? Davey, are you there? Report.'

No reply. Nothing but static. Trapped as I was, I dared not try again.

I decided to go at this slowly. I was lying more or less the right way up and on my back, so I gently wriggled my left foot. It came free. Good start. My other leg was wedged under the tree so I left it for a while and tried my left arm. Inch by painful inch, I got that free. But as soon as I tried my right arm, the shale started moving again. I rolled over onto my side as best I could and gently began to ease my arm free. The problem was my leg. I couldn't afford to dislodge the tree trunk which was the only thing preventing me from tumbling down the lower skirts of the volcano into the dinosaur's feeding ground below. Finally, my brain started to work and I hit on the idea of digging under my leg and easing it out that way. Many, many ruined fingernails later, I struggled free.

Free, but not safe. I can't say how long it took me to work my way across the scree; one step across, two steps down. But once there, the actual climb up was quite easy. I took my time getting over the top, lifting a careful eye above the edge and scanning the area. I waited perhaps ten minutes until my arms started to tremble, hoisted myself over, rolled to my feet, got my bearings, and set off for Eight.

Activating my com again, I said quietly, 'Sussman, are you there? Sussman, answer me.'

Nothing.

'Sussman, report.'

Nothing.

Shaking like a leaf now, I inched my way cautiously along that path and then I saw why he wasn't answering. Pools of black, sticky blood lay all around. Away, off to one side, I saw a boot. His foot was still in it. Something brittle snapped inside me. I grabbed it, ran as fast as I could on trembling legs, shouted, 'Door,' crashed headlong into Eight, and lay gasping and shaking on the floor.

I gave myself twenty minutes. No more, otherwise I'd never get up. I double bagged the foot and went to put it in the chiller. I saw a bottle in there and was sorely tempted. I made tea instead and moving like a robot, showered carefully, cleaned my wounds, plaited my hair, and exhausted, pulled out my sleeping module and closed my eyes.

And climbed back out again and found my photo. Getting back into bed I hugged it tightly and curled myself around it. I missed him. I could go back, feel the comfort of his arms around me. No one would blame me.

I would blame me.

After another minute, I gave up the idea of sleep completely and let my mind do what it wanted, which was to think of Sussman being Sussman; alternately loved and loathed. I remembered his kindnesses, especially to me. I found it so hard to believe that this time yesterday he'd been snoring away beside me. And now he was dead. I wished to God I could have this day again and do things differently. Do them better. Suppose he'd tried to get back to my pod. I'd put a lock on it. He wouldn't have been able to get back in. Common sense told me that was rubbish. Once the raptors closed in he wouldn't have been able to go anywhere.

We'd been together for some time now, bickering, laughing, competing, always trying to get the edge, but not anymore. Never again. This was my mission. How could I have let this happen? I couldn't believe I'd never see him again. And so on and so on, all that long night, recrimination, grief, and regret surging around inside until, finally, I fell into an exhausted sleep just before dawn.

The next day I dressed stiffly, stuffed some food in another backpack, took what I needed, hefted my blaster, and stood by the door. I took two or three deep breaths. I'd checked all the proximity alerts. Nothing lurked nearby. Get back on the horse,

Maxwell.

I opened the door. I don't know why I was surprised to see everything exactly as it had been. I set off, but not for the northern end of the valley. That was too far on my own, but I could do useful work further along towards the lake, on the eastern side.

I found a crack in the cliff face where I could safely wedge myself and started work. I filmed, measured, and noted the vegetation. Conifers on the high slopes, and *pinus* and *metasequoia* and broad-leaved trees lower down. All trees were here, from oaks to palms.

Around mid-afternoon, I trudged back; keeping a careful watch, weapon ready, but all was quiet. I'd worried the raptors might return, looking for more of the unusually flavoured mammals, but I guess they'd moved on. I checked all our equipment, collected the used disks, and replaced them with new ones. I'd left it all out overnight and none of it seemed to have suffered at all, so I decided to leave it in situ. It was heavy and I didn't want to break anything by trying to lug it around by myself.

It was difficult going into Three. Sussman's stuff lay all over the place. I tidied it all carefully away, concentrating only on what I was doing and not allowing my mind to wander. I watched my hands fold his clothes and stow his kit neatly. I took the readings, turned off the lights, and left without looking back.

Approaching my pod from a different route, I found myself looking down on the clearing and path. The stains were still there. I didn't want to attract predators so I went down, kicked dust and gravel over the blood, and picked up what I could find of our packs.

I climbed on to the pod roof, checked the scanner alignments, changed the disks, and climbed down again. Inside, I showered, ate, wrote careful logs for that day and the day before, and did my data entry. I filed the disks and still slightly surprised at this calm, efficient me, went to bed.

And that was pretty well the pattern for the next fifteen days. It was hard work alone, but I needed it. I drew strength from my photo, now set up on the console where I could see it. I felt sad and shocked and lonely and for the first time in my life I missed someone, but this work had to be done and only I could do it. Each day I went out, did what had to be done, and came back. I talked to the photo. I talked to myself. I think I even chatted briefly once with a rock.

Whether all the drama had been used up on that awful day, I don't know, but everything remained relatively trauma-free. On the other hand, I had sprayed so much cabbage spray all over me and my kit that everything probably thought I was a walking bush. My wounds seemed to be healing without infection and I told myself the worst was over.

I spent the last two days heaving all the kit back to Three. That bloke who said, 'Give me a lever and a place to stand and I can move the world,' obviously never stood up to his knees in a Cretaceous swamp, trying to manoeuvre a refrigerator-sized packing crate uphill.

I spent half a day in Three, prepping for the jump and setting the countdown. I shut the door and watched it go, then stared for a while at the flattened area where it had been – no idea why I did that – before making my way back to my own pod, carefully, because I didn't want to get into trouble now.

I sorted my pod, dictated my final notes, updated the logs, and checked all the disks were present and correct. I looked at the small mountain of boxes in the corner. Data. Unique, priceless, hard-won data. I got the sky scanners off the roof and packed them away. There really was nothing left to do.

I made a cup of tea and sat in the doorway. This had been my home for three months. Sussman had died here. I felt reluctant to leave. I watched the activity around the lake. A solitary Torosaurus trundled down to drink alongside a pair of Parasaurolophus with their banana-shaped crests and still no clues as to their purpose. Resonating chamber? Sexual display? Enhanced sense of smell? Someone else would study the data and decide. My favourite, Andrew Ankylosaurus, shuffled around with his great tail. And the bastard raptors, doing what raptors do. Who could blame them? And the infamous velociraptors. They were smaller than I had expected, but clever. I hoped someone would pursue the link between meat-eating and intelligence. And a group of Proceratops; we had some great shots of their nests with their eggs laid in those fascinating spiral patterns.

I had a huge affection for these creatures; old friends now, all of them. And dead. All dead. Long dead.

Oh, for God's sake. I threw away the remainder of my tea, did the FOD plod, the POD plod, and had no reason to stay any longer. I let the computer initiate the jump – and it was done.

Nine

Finally, I was home. The blue decon light flickered and I felt the hairs on my arms stir. I took a breath and savoured the moment. I was home. Craning my neck slightly, I could see Number Three down at the other end of the hangar. Techies swarmed around it, doing techie things. I sighed. Suddenly, I felt very tired.

Someone tapped at the door. I had to open it. He would have seen that Three was empty and come straight across to Eight, expecting us both to be here. I was going to have to open the door and let the world in. I hit manual. He stood on the threshold and took in the lack of Sussman.

His face said everything. He didn't ask what happened, which was just as well, because for a moment, I couldn't speak.

'Are you all right?'

I nodded. It was enough simply to hear his voice after all this time.

'Take your time.'

I took him at his word, leaned back and closed my eyes. I heard the door close and when I looked, he stood just inside. He said, 'Come here.'

I stood shakily, took a step towards him, and put my arms around his solid warmth. He held me tightly. He really was the best of men. He said nothing, rubbing my back gently. I went to pull away but he tightened his grip and said, 'No,' very softly, so I laid my head on his chest and listened to his strong, steady heartbeat.

Time rolled on and if I stood any longer, I would be there for ever. I started to pull my bag towards me but he stopped me. 'I'll take it. Come on, let's get you to Sick Bay. Can you manage?'

Nodding, I opened the door. A small orange crowd waited outside. Someone said, 'Welcome home.' I could see them looking over my shoulder for Sussman. Behind me, I guessed the Chief was making signals because they all moved back. I looked up to Kal and Peterson on the gantry and shook my head.

We took the lift to Sick Bay. After three months in the Cretaceous I couldn't remember what stairs were for. Helen and her crew waited as the doors opened.

Farrell handed over my bag and said, 'We'll make a start with the tapes and upload to you as soon as possible. Dr Bairstow will be along later, I expect. Get some rest.' He walked away and I felt disappointed and alone.

Helen treated me quickly and gently. I was scanned and had my wounds dressed. There was no infection. I crawled into bed and slept.

Next morning I showered and found my blues in the wardrobe. Helen came in. 'Yes, you can go,' she said, sarcastically.

Nurse Hunter came in with a printout which they both scanned. 'It all seems fine. Battered and bruised, Max, but nothing permanent. Report here tomorrow morning for a final check-up. Now, let's go and get some breakfast in you.'

I walked into the dining room to a round of applause. Not wild applause, because of Sussman, but congratulations were in order nonetheless. Mrs Mack beamed and handed me eggs, bacon, and hash browns. And fruit to follow. Helen nodded. 'At least two pieces of fruit a day, Max, that's an order. You've been on rations for three months. You'll be like a log jam on the St Lawrence.'

We sat with Kal and Peterson, both of whom were quieter than usual. Just as I finished, the Chief turned up. He looked serious and didn't smile. Dr Bairstow wanted me. Of course he did.

138

Dr Bairstow was surprisingly brisk. I thought out of respect for Sussman he might tone it down a bit, but he got straight to it. 'We were surprised, Miss Maxwell, to find a lock on Number Eight. Apparently only you had access to that pod.'

Shit, shit, shit, I'd forgotten to take the lock off. Sometimes I think I'm too stupid to live. I wasn't looking forward to explaining this at all, but I didn't have to. He said into his com, 'Mrs Partridge, would you come in now, please?'

Normally she sat beside or just behind the Boss, but today the Chief put a chair for her next to me. She wore Paris. I'd never noticed before.

The Chief activated the screen. For five seconds or so, it remained dark. Shockingly suddenly, Sussman's face appeared, close up, slightly distorted, fiddling with the controls. Apparently having adjusted the camera to his satisfaction, he stepped back and I could see what it was pointing at. Me, asleep in an untidy heap in my sleeping module. I lay on my back, a light sheet over me with one leg stuck out the side.

The Boss said, 'We'll go and organise some tea,' and to my astonishment, he and the Chief left. I stared at the door and then at Mrs Partridge and she gestured back towards the screen. On it, Sussman knelt beside me. He reached out and, oh so very gently, began to lift the sheet off me. I wore T-shirt and shorts and even as I watched, he began, an inch at a time, to lift my T-shirt. He turned to the camera and grinned.

I felt physically sick. With a nasty heave of my stomach, I remembered all the times I'd woken with the sheet on the floor.

Back on the screen he'd got my T-shirt nearly to my breasts and the other hand was bashing the bishop as fast as he could go. And any second now … Yep, there I was. One minute dead to the world and the next minute I'd got my feet on his chest and pushed him backwards. And here I was with the pepper spray. He got a mouthful. And I sprayed his penis as well, on the grounds that if he hadn't had it out and been waving it around then it wouldn't have come to any harm. Watching myself on the screen, I stopped feeling sick and began to feel a little better. There's nothing like good, healthy anger. Mrs Partridge turned to me. 'Good move with the spray.'

'Thank you.' My voice came out more wobbly and hoarse than I was happy with.

Back on the screen, I'm giving Sussman the bollocking of a lifetime. He's scrabbling round the pod, grabbing his clothes and whatever of his stuff he can carry. I grab the blaster and he makes a bolt for the door.

Mrs Partridge blanked the screen. 'The tape runs out about thirty minutes later, just after you put the lock on,' she said calmly. She paused. 'We found three more tapes. In them he is not so – bold, but there is no doubt he was escalating.' The sick came back. And the anger.

Little Jenny Fields from the kitchen came in with a tea trolley, followed by the Boss and Chief Farrell. I saw Mrs Partridge nod slightly. Suddenly, I didn't want her to leave. I turned to her and she sat down again. Farrell poured the tea.

The Boss seated himself at the head of the table. 'This tape and any others of a similar nature will be destroyed immediately on conclusion of this meeting.'

I nodded.

'You appear to have dealt with the situation with your usual aplomb.'

I nodded.

'Should I perhaps be reviewing our customary pairings of one male and one female, do you think?'

I shook my head (for a change). 'Hard to see how you can, sir. Firstly, there are only three of us now until the next intake qualifies and that's not for at least another six months. Secondly, and this should have been firstly, Peterson would die at the stake rather than pull a stunt like that and, thirdly, one male one female works best. There are always places women can go and men can't and vice versa. We would be shooting ourselves in the foot, I think.'

'Very well, we will continue as we are for the time being.' He paused. 'No one outside this room has seen these tapes and no one will. I understand the unique bond between our three historians, but I would appreciate you not discussing this with anyone else, Miss Maxwell; unless you feel the need for professional counselling, of course.'

Yes, sir. And no, sir.'

'To spare you any undue speculation from others, the usual procedures for Mr Sussman will be followed; the service and so on. Please do not feel under any obligation to attend.'

'Thank you, sir.'

'Is there anything you wish to say? Or any questions to ask?'

'I don't think so, sir.'

'You are surrounded by friends here. If you find yourself in difficulties you have only to ask.'

I nodded.

In the outer office, I said, 'Thank you, Mrs Partridge.' She smiled slightly. It changed her face. I couldn't help smiling back.

'I think a change of scene would be good for you today, Miss Maxwell. If offered the chance, take it.'

I was staring out of the window in my room when the Chief turned up with my kit as promised. He dumped a box on the table then dug a disk from his pocket. 'Where's your laptop?' I lugged it out from under the couch and switched it on. He sat beside me and inserted a disk.

'What's this?'

He looked at me with an odd mixture of concern and sympathy that alarmed me more than I would care to admit. 'More unpleasantness.'

'What's going on?'

'You need to see this. Just watch please.'

I sat back, curled my legs under me and watched a clearing in the Cretaceous come to life. 'This is …' I paused. The angle wasn't right. 'Where did you get this?'

'This is from my pod. I've just been back to the Cretaceous. You need to see this. And I'm sorry. I'm very sorry.'

Again, that chill. I uncurled my legs and sat forward.

Number Eight's door opened and I stuck out my head. Obviously all was clear because I stepped out, followed by Sussman. I looked at the Chief. Why was he making me watch this? He nodded back to the screen.

I watched the two of us cross the clearing. I watched us walk single file where the path narrowed. I watched Sussman pick up a piece of wood from behind a rock and hit me hard across the back and shoulders. I watched myself stagger forwards and sideways. I watched the path crumble away beneath my feet. I watched my struggle for balance. I watched myself fall. I watched Sussman toss the branch aside, walk to the edge, peer over, shout, 'Up yours, you fucking, jerk-off bitch!', and spit.

My throat closed. I had to make a conscious effort to breathe. I'd liked this guy. I'd worked with him, played with him, and lied for him. Massive betrayal sat like lead in my stomach. But more was to come. Other figures walked into the clearing and joined him. What? Who? Where did they come from? Who else was there? There was me. And Sussman. And Farrell. And now this lot. It was like the Cretaceous equivalent of bloody Piccadilly Circus. They all spent some time carefully looking over the edge of the path. I got the feeling they weren't a rescue party. I tried to think.

Farrell said gently, 'Tell me what's happening to you at that moment.'

'I'm wedged under a fallen tree, quite a long way down. I'm covered in loose shale and stuff that came down on top of me. I'm probably quite invisible from above. Being semi-conscious helped.' My voice was hoarse and I had difficulty making my lips move.

Finally, the figures turned away and returned to the clearing. Sussman talked to a man in a long leather coat. He had no weapon so I guessed he was in charge. They were too far away for audio, but the body language spoke for itself. They were arguing.

'I think,' said Farrell quietly, 'you weren't meant to go over the cliff. It was supposed to be a quick, clean kill. There was supposed to be a body. For Sussman to take back.'

'Why? To what end?

'I think, and I'm guessing here, but that would have meant the end of the mission. This big, important, prestigious mission. This would be the final nail in the coffin. You may be unaware of how hard the Boss is working to keep us going in the face of what's being deemed unacceptable losses. He would be removed and the unit would be taken over by – someone else.'

'Who?'

He shrugged. 'The government. The military. No idea. But certainly St Mary's would go in a different direction, with different goals, different targets, and maybe instructions to turn a profit. There would be less research, more interaction. It certainly wouldn't be our endearingly crackpot little organisation any longer. But, and again I'm only guessing here, setting the unit on a path leading straight to the state St Mary's finds itself in in my time.

I pointed at the screen. 'Who is he?'

'His name is Ronan. He's angry because Sussman made it personal. Can we talk about him another time?'

'Why did Sussman wait so long before …?'

'So you could do most of the work and he could get the credit.'

Unbidden, there came to my mind a picture of Sussman in France. The hospital engulfed in flames. Kal and I burst into the pod. Sussman turned from the controls and said – what did he say? He said, 'Max, my God, I can't believe it. I thought you were dead. Why aren't you dead?'

Not, 'Thank God you're not dead,' but *'Why aren't you dead?'* And who arranged for us to meet by the linen rooms?

And who sent me in for blankets? And who had I met the day before coming *from* the linen rooms?

Somehow, I got it together. A coincidence. It had to be. I was being paranoid. He was dead and we'd never know now. What I saw next pushed it out of my head completely.

On the screen, Sussman stormed back to his pod. At a signal from Ronan, he was grabbed, held by two men and dragged, struggling, away from his pod. Ronan stepped forward, crouched low in front of him, and slashed, stepping back quickly. I watched the blood spurt and heard the scream in my head.

Everyone vanished very quickly. They wouldn't want to hang about with that amount of blood around. They say sharks can smell blood in the water from miles away. Sharks had nothing on the local wildlife here. Sussman tried to walk but blood gushed from wounds in his upper leg where Ronan had slashed his femoral artery. No power on earth could save him now. He tried to press both hands against the wound and walk at the same time, failing to do both.

'Davey,' I whispered. But even as I spoke a shadow flitted across the bottom of the screen. Fast and low. Then another.

'Davey, get back to your pod.' I leaped to my feet and the Chief stood with me. He reached down to switch off the laptop but I pulled his arm away.

I watched as the raptors gathered. I watched them circle their victim; classic predator behaviour. He crouched low on the ground, screaming with fear, bloody arms over his head.

Farrell said, 'Max …' but I had to watch. Whatever he'd done, he'd once been my partner and my friend. I owed it to him and to me.

I watched as the first two leaped in a pincer movement. Deinonychus. And it's true; they don't wait until their prey is dead before eating. I watched them rip and tear. I watched two of them fight over an arm. I watched his head roll away and felt glad because it was over for him. I watched them snarl and gobble. I watched them disperse afterwards. I watched the empty clearing until the Chief gently closed my laptop.

'You didn't have to see that,' he said quietly.

'Yes, yes, I did. I did this. I locked my pod. He couldn't get to safety.' My voice was hoarse. I swallowed once or twice. He wrapped his arms around me from behind, warm and comforting. The silence in the room sounded very loud. I could hear my own harsh breathing. I stood tense and still, willing it to slow, to regain control. Gradually, I unclenched one muscle at a time. As I relaxed, so did he. I laid my head back against his shoulder and closed my eyes briefly, then let my head hang forward.

'Getting back into the pod would not have saved him. He was bleeding to death. Nothing could have saved him.'

'He was my friend. The first one I made here. We've been friends for years. We were partners. We trained together. We cheated together. I wrote papers for him. He held my hair when I threw up. We were friends …' I hadn't realised I was speaking aloud.

'Really? I saw someone who pinched your work and took the credit. Holding your hair was the least he could do. I saw someone who never hesitated to use you for his own gain. How many times have you covered for him with the Boss? And that last business in the pod? He met a bad end and I'm sorry for that, but I'm sorrier to see you blaming yourself for this. It's nothing you did. It's not your fault.'

I shook my head. 'He couldn't get into the pod to save himself. I killed him.'

'No, you didn't.' His voice sounded crisp and authoritative. 'You need to be very clear about this, Miss Maxwell. His death was the result of his own actions. And if his plans had not gone wrong it would have been you in that clearing, not him.'

'But why did you go back? You couldn't interfere. What was the point?'

'After we saw the tapes, the Boss sent me back to do some

checking. Initially, we thought Sussman was just being … well, Sussman. We were wrong. We think it's starting.'

I shook my head again, too distressed by all this to speak.

'I don't want to leave you alone here, especially when anyone can barge in. Would you like to come with me?'

'Where to?'

'To the place I go when I need a little peace and quiet. Come on.'

I remembered what Mrs Partridge had said.

Unsure, but not up to argument, I followed him along corridors and down stairways, through the paint store to his pod. I sat quietly in his seat while he punched in some co-ordinates and then the world went white.

I don't know why I expected rest and relaxation. I suppose I thought I was entitled to a little gentle cherishing. Was I buggery!

It started well. The door opened on to a sparkling turquoise sea and cloudless blue sky. Fragrant pines marched down to the shoreline and cast dark pools of shadowy purple. Their apple-green foliage clashed beautifully with the brick red rock. I'd never seen such colour and light.

'Where is this? When are we?'

'A small island in the eastern Med, about five thousand years ago.'

I hesitated, still in the doorway. Old Cretaceous habits die hard.

'It's quite safe. There won't be people here for a thousand years or so yet. What's the problem?'

I stuck my chin in the air. 'No problem,' and stepped outside. The light on the sea dazzled and I was allowed to admire it for very nearly a whole second.

'Can you get some wood?'

'What sort of wood?'

'What do you mean, what sort of wood? Why do historians

always have to overthink everything? Wood wood.'

'I mean dry wood? Wet wood? Firewood? Building wood?'

'Building wood?'

'Well, it's you. Are you going to knock together a hotel? Build a suspension bridge? Install a spa? Will there be grouting?'

'What?'

'Isn't that what men do? You know, grouting, sawing, sitting in sheds. Men things.'

'Just wood for a fire.'

'A fire? It's warm. Even I'm warm.'

'To cook lunch.'

'We have to cook lunch?'

'No, first we have to catch lunch.'

I shifted uneasily.

'Is there another problem?'

'I've just come from a time when lunch catches me.'

'Well, this is your chance for revenge.'

'Don't we have rations?'

'Yes, but you've eaten rations for the last three months. Don't you want fresh food?'

'Well, the way I look at it there's some poor little fish out there having a nice lazy day and making plans to meet its mates down the pub tonight and I don't want to be the one getting the reproachful stare as I knock it on the head.'

He stared at me.

'I'm just saying,' I said defensively. 'I don't like killing things.'

'You eat fish. And meat. And eggs.'

'I know, but I don't actually go out and club a baby lamb when there's already a pack of chops in the freezer, do I?'

'All right, point made. Go and get wood.'

'But we don't need a fire now.'

'But we will later.'

'Why?'

147

'Because it's cool at night.'

'We're sleeping outside?'

'Is there yet another problem, Miss Maxwell?'

'No,' I said in the voice which means '*yes*'.

He sighed even more heavily than usual. 'We've been here ten minutes. No wood, no fire, no lunch. Remind me again how you survived three months in the Cretaceous.'

'No fires, no cooking, and no sleeping outside.'

There was a long, long silence.

'What?'

'Just go and get some wood!'

The reason I can't deal with sympathy is because I never bloody get any.

I sat beside him on a blanket, leaning back against the warm rock. Ahead of me, the sea flashed and sparkled like a giant glitter ball. I closed my eyes and heard a glass clink.

'Here.'

'What's this?'

'Slivovitz.'

'What?'

'Plum brandy to you.'

'What?'

'Think of it as a kind of fruit drink.'

'Great. I'll put it towards my five a day.'

I sipped, got my breath back, and listened to the enamel on my teeth erode. Actually, it wasn't that bad. I said so.

'Just don't get it near any metal; and for God's sake don't spill it on the console.'

We sat sipping and silent.

'How are you feeling?'

This required some thought. The standard 'I'm fine,' wasn't going to cut it, but I still couldn't talk about things in a non-wobbly voice. However, he'd brought me here to get myself together, so at least I should make an effort. I gave him an honest answer.

'I'm better. I was … sad … when he died. Then angry with him, but now I'm back to sad again.' I smiled. 'It's because I'm shallow. I can only do one emotion at a time and even that not for very long.'

He didn't smile back. 'You're more generous than I think I would be.'

'Yes, well, he's dead and I'm not. If it was the other way around I'd probably be a bit miffed.'

'So, what will you do now?'

'I've got my presentation to Thirsk coming up so I'm concentrating on that for the time being.'

He drew a pattern in the dust. 'No, I mean, will you stay?'

'At St Mary's? Yes, of course.'

He nodded.

'Kal and I will probably share Peterson for a while and the new intake will be fully qualified before too long. So, not a problem, I hope. I certainly don't want to be anywhere else. This is my dream job.'

The pattern became more intricate. 'Is that your only dream?'

'I did warn you I'm shallow.' Time to deflect attention from my dreams. 'What about you? What's your dream?'

'Actually I'm living one of my favourites now.'

It was very quiet in the hot afternoon sun, just the chirp of insects and the distant sounds of the sea. 'Only it hasn't turned out quite as I intended.'

I chugged back more fruit drink and found some Dutch courage.

'So what did you intend?'

'I did think your first time here would be under happier circumstances. I thought we could watch the sun set.'

We both looked up at the sun, which remained obstinately high in the sky.

'We would drink champagne.'

149

We both looked down at the gloop in our glasses.

'And I thought maybe you would be cleaner.'

He leaned down, looked into my face and smiled gently. 'And sober.'

'Don't worry. I think it's perfect. And,' said the slivovitz, 'there will be other dreams and other times.'

He took my hand. I rested my slivovitzy head on his shoulder and fell asleep.

After we'd eaten I said, 'So tell me about this Ronan. The one who ...' I found I couldn't actually say, '... who killed Sussman,' and changed it to '... back in the Cretaceous.'

He moved away from me slightly.

'It happened before my time,' he said and stopped. I sat quietly and waited. You couldn't rush him. Eventually, he said, 'I was brought in – afterwards.'

'After what?'

Just when I began to think he might never speak again, he said, 'There were three of them: Edward Bairstow, Annie Bessant, and Clive Ronan. People said they were the dream team, but it was more like a triangle. Do you understand what I'm saying?'

'Yes.'

'The assignment was James VI. Annie got caught. You know James and his witches. Suspicion everywhere. Maybe she was careless – used her com perhaps and someone saw her, maybe some little modern mannerism. They rescued her eventually but she'd been knocked about a bit. Broken arm – concussion.' He sighed heavily. 'And she'd picked something up. It came on fast. She said she was fine, but the rules are very clear about this sort of thing.'

I nodded. They were. They were very, very clear. It was our nightmare, letting loose some God-awful infection on an unprotected world. The Boss was paranoid about it. I began to see why.

'She was coughing and had a fever, which meant she couldn't return immediately for treatment. They should have stayed put, done the broad-spectrum antibiotics thing, kept her warm, you know the drill. Ronan grew frantic. He insisted on returning so she could get treatment for her injuries, especially the concussion. Edward argued. Annie tried to argue, started to cough, couldn't stop, and that was it for Ronan.'

He stopped again.

'What happened?'

'He shot Edward in the leg and pitched him out of the pod, returning to St Mary's with Annie, who was by now unconscious.'

I sat appalled. He'd left the Boss to die! I tried to imagine Kal or Peterson doing such a thing. Or me, even. What would we do? I'd like to think we'd do the right thing but I suppose you never know until it actually happens to you. And after Sussman, I was beginning to think I didn't know anyone very well.

After a long while he continued. 'He brought Annie back. Edward, he said, was dead; killed in the rescue. Obviously, they got her to Sick Bay as soon as possible. When they realised she was contaminated, they moved her into isolation. Well, you know us – we're St Mary's. We never leave our people behind. A search team went back for Edward and found him in a bad way, lying under someone's cart. They brought him back, operated, and he's limped ever since.'

'And Ronan?'

'They tried to arrest him for breach of medical protocol and attempted murder. Knowing St Mary's, probably in that order. He didn't wait around. He took Annie from Sick Bay and attempted to reach Hawking with her. Shot two techies. One died. She put up a fight. He tried to force her into a pod. She wouldn't go. They struggled. Security turned up. She was caught in the crossfire. He stole Number Nine – and vanished.'

'Did she recover?'

'No.'

'She died?'

'Yes.'

'Does he know she's dead?'

'Yes.'

'And he blames himself?'

'No. He blames Edward and St Mary's and just about everyone but himself.'

'So it's – revenge?'

He shrugged.

'And the Boss?'

'Never mentions it. Go and get the blankets. It's getting chilly.'

His voice was final. There would be no discussion.

We did sleep outside. I wrapped myself in a blanket and stared up at the stars. Something moved nearby. I sat up and stared into the darkness. A muffled voice said, 'What's wrong?'

'Nothing. I thought I heard something.'

On the other side of the fire, his breathing deepened.

I got up, picked up my blanket, and walked round the fire. 'Move over.' He shunted over. I lay down beside him and he covered us with the blankets. I lay with my back to his front and pulled his arm over me like a cover.

He said, 'Rumour has it you snore.'

'You don't know the half of it.'

I fell asleep listening to his heartbeat.

We stayed for two days and he never stopped winding me up. He gave way on the rations but I became chief wood-gatherer, water-getter, tea-maker, and anything else he could think of. We bickered our way through the days. I felt my thoughts sharpening again and climbed out of my pit of self-pity.

Ronan was never mentioned.

We snuck back to St Mary's. I had a sunburned nose. No

one noticed.

I found Kal and Peterson sitting on the stairs. I tried to remember that although it was two days for me, for them it had only been a couple of hours. The routine of St Mary's closed around me.

They helped me organise my material while I gave them the details. I expected all sorts of 'I told you so,' especially from Kal, but she only rubbed my arm briefly, expressed regret she'd been unable to tear him apart herself, and changed the subject. I described everything. We always do this. It helps us get our heads together for our report and presentation – the next big event on my horizon.

After lunch, I got down to it. Fortunately, I'd done so much work on-site there wasn't a huge amount still to do, which was just as well because I'd had an idea.

I went to see the Boss. Mrs Partridge waved me through.

'Good afternoon, sir. Can I talk to you for a moment please?'

'Of course. Please sit down. What can I do for you today, Miss Maxwell?'

'I've had an idea, sir.'

He nodded, but said nothing.

'Do you remember, a long time ago when we met, I said it was a good idea there was no such thing as public-access time travel?'

He nodded.

'Because of the damage that could be done to the public themselves, to the timeline, and to History?'

He nodded.

'You know we made a holo?'

'Yes, Miss Maxwell. I hear it's something a little above and beyond our normal records.'

'Well, I've been thinking, sir, maybe that's a way we could make time travel available to the general public without them actually knowing. We can continue to film and record as we usually do. But, instead of simply filing it all away in the archive for future reference, IT could fiddle about with it; we could put in a commentary, and then hire our films out to show in holo theatres around the country. People would know that they were watching dinosaurs for instance, but not that they were watching actual dinosaurs. They could watch the Battle of Hastings, Stephenson's Rocket, the pyramids being built, or the Crystal Palace Exhibition. Being produced by us sir, under Thirsk's umbrella of course, will ensure its credibility.'

I remembered to take a breath. 'And we can charge, sir. The public, academics, educational establishments, theatres, they'll all pay to see what we produce. It will be accurate, informative, educational, and entertaining. They'll just never know *how* accurate, informative etc. I think we'll never have a better opportunity than now. Everyone loves dinosaurs. With your permission, I would like to take it with me to Thirsk and see what their reaction is. If they like it they can contribute to the costs of future films and take a cut. If they don't want to then we keep it all for ourselves. We offer it as a loss leader. If we could regularly bring them material of this calibre, sir, they might change their minds about wanting a permanent presence here, or God forbid, actually wanting a representative along on each assignment. We tell them there's no need for them to risk life and limb. We can do that and they could reap the benefits.

'And, on a more personal note, the eyes of the world are fixed on Mars at the moment, sir. Everywhere I look the arts are being shunted aside for technology. It's not necessarily a bad thing but maybe in some small way this could redress the balance a little. History – the new sex. Sir.'

He stood looking out of the window, face quite expressionless. No clues there. I sat quietly and let the silence gather. I'd made my point; there was no use boring on. I wasn't Barclay.

He turned back into the room and picked up his pen again. 'Take it to Thirsk. See how they react. I'll talk to the

Chancellor, tell her what to expect so she can put the word around and make sure you have an audience worthy of the occasion. We'll see how it goes, shall we?'

Barclay sent for me at 1600 to discuss the holo. The Chief had sent her the material and I'd given her a list of the highlights I wanted included, but left the rest to her. Half of me looked forward to seeing what she had done; half of me didn't want to go out and mix with people just yet and half of me (presumably the half that can't add up) didn't want to see her because I knew she would blame me for Sussman.

As it turned out, she was reasonably OK. The Chief attended in his role as buffer zone and this helped. She showed me what they'd put together so far. She'd changed two of my suggestions (for the better) and added some new ideas. I was pleased.

'Only two things, Izzie,' I said. She bridled immediately. 'Can you make sure our logo and copyright appear on the title page? This is going to be big and I'm sure the Boss will want to make sure St Mary's is shown somewhere. Otherwise Thirsk will be all over it.'

She nodded. 'And the second thing?'

'The dedication to Sussman.' She started to speak. I cut across her. 'Put it at the beginning. This is so good they'll be in no fit state to notice at the end, so put it up first, while they're all still able to pay attention.'

I looked at the Chief. 'His idea and his work. He should get the credit.'

I got one of his full-on smiles. The crinkly-eyed one. It made me feel better and it pissed Barclay off no end, so no downside there, then.

'Chief, before we show it at Thirsk, I thought we could give it its world premiere here in Hawking tomorrow. Let everyone at St Mary's get to see it. After all, everyone contributed. If the Boss agrees, of course. '

'I'll talk to him. I can't see a problem.'

'Oh, and Izzie?'

'What?'

'Make sure your name and your team's names are on it somewhere. It's a cracking piece of work.' And walked out before she could speak. Ha!

The world premiere in Hawking was a huge success. The IT section, thrilled at the thought of producing something creative instead of the daily uphill struggle to instruct the computer illiterate, really put their backs into it. Everyone in the entire unit assembled in Hawking and waited to be impressed. I couldn't stand still. I went from Barclay's last-minute tweaking to the Chief setting up the streamers around the designated area. They both, in their own ways, told me to go away. Eventually, I ground to a halt near Kal. She rubbed my arm encouragingly. 'It'll be OK.'

'It's got to be better than OK. It's got to be bloody fantastic.'

'It will be. Stand still. Breathe.'

The lights dimmed, to simulate dawn and we were off. Poets bang on a lot about rosy-fingered dawn and that's just what we got, beautifully reflected in the still water. Tendrils of mist floated above the ground. The quality was amazing. The Cretaceous period was all around us, three hundred and sixty degrees. And solid – this was no cheap, wobbly, see-through simulation. I looked down at my feet, watching them sink into holo mud.

Far away, just on the edge of hearing, I could feel a deep rumbling in my chest. Looking around, I could see people looking at each other, hands on their own chests and laughing, but nervously.

The rumbling increased and out of the mist emerged the long, grey neck of an Alamosaurus, then another and another, then a whole group of them. Necks swayed sinuously and the noises increased. They were greeting each other and the day. One long neck snaked down towards the camera, revealing a small head and cow-like eyes. The bovine resemblance increased when it emitted a long, low mooing noise. The camera trembled. Satisfied we were no threat, the head moved away.

The mist cleared away and the neighbourhood came down to drink. We had some beautiful shots of a group of Ankylosaurus moving around the waterline, struggling to drink and protect their young at the same time. A familiar green smell rose up around us. Industrial-strength farts. Even a T-rex thought twice about biting into one of these. A miracle the cameras hadn't melted. A large herd of slow-moving Proceratops, manoeuvring their bulky bodies through the swamps gave them a wide berth. Ankylosaurus tails could shatter bones and teeth.

The Proceratops were shadowed by a small group of fast-moving Oviraptors flitting in and out of the dappled shade, looking for nests.

The quality of the shots was excellent. Colours, skin patterns, markings, all the frills, horns, cheek plates, crests, sclerotic rings, everything the well-dressed dinosaur wore those days – all crystal clear as Barclay's team had steadied wobbly camera work, re-focused close-ups and generally sharpened up the whole thing.

The day wore on, we were past noon now. She'd managed to get our very few Triceratops shots incorporated. And a fleeting glimpse of a herd of Deinonychus (I looked away); enough to give an impression of their deadly speed and co-ordination.

The now much fewer numbers of animals at the shoreline dwindled even further. You could see everyone thinking it must be siesta time. We'd done that deliberately, so when the T-rex exploded into camera view everyone nearly wet themselves. Its prey, a half-grown, limping, exhausted Edmontosaurus turned to face the end. When we'd picked this up, we'd hardly been able to contain our excitement, but the best was yet to come. The T-rex leaped, finishing its prey with a skull-crushing bite. The Edmontosaurus's skull cracked and it went down like a tree. Red gore splashed the T-rex's face, jaws, and chest. The shot clearly showed its little forelegs opening and closing spasmodically. I wondered again if this was a display of excitement, supporting the argument that these little forelegs, too small even to touch each other, were for sexual tickling. Alternatively, maybe just a reflex action. Others would decide.

The successful T-rex however, made the mistake of bellowing his triumph in a half shriek, half roar that reverberated off the surrounding hills. A red cloud of blood and flesh fragments belched from his massive jaws. Everyone stepped back. Hardly had the echoes died away when another, much bigger, T-rex erupted into shot; possibly a female this time. At this point, even Sussman had been in two minds whether to run or not.

Earsplittingly, they screamed their rage as they circled each other. Dust flew in clouds as they stamped their feet. They lashed their tails. They battered each other with their enormous heads. The bigger one, by virtue of her size, seized the smaller by the scruff of his neck. Instead of pulling away, he closed and ducking his head even lower, clamped his jaws on one of her tiny forearms. She screamed, shook him like a rat, and hurled him away from her. He cartwheeled over and over and, before he could stand, she leaped on him. She raked a hind claw across his belly and as he raised his head to get up, she went for the exposed throat. No messing. He gurgled and was dead in seconds. She strutted, roared her victory to the skies, and settled down to feed on his kill.

Professor Rapson beamed. 'It's not a chicken after all! Not a feather in sight! Well done, Max.' Although how I could take the credit for disproving the theory that T-rex was nothing more than a giant, scavenging chicken was hard to see. Still, it was good to know the image of the world's favourite predator remained intact.

We faded from that and before anyone had time to draw breath, the hangar began to vibrate. Dust fell from the roof.

158

Tools rattled and clattered to the floor. And from the far end of the hangar, slowly and with majesty, came a herd of Alamosaurus. The first one was colossal – fifty feet high and seventy feet long easily, with a body the size of a swimming pool. Unarmoured – they didn't need to be. Size matters. Don't let anyone tell you otherwise. Others emerged from behind the leader.

Izzie gave us maybe thirty seconds worth of establishing shots. Enough to appreciate their size and proportions and then cut to shots from me and Sussman, ducking and diving like the idiots we were that afternoon. In and out, weaving around giant, slow-moving legs, getting close-ups of bellies, armpits, feet, orifices, you name it – we filmed it. Bloody great haystack-sized dollops of Alamosaurus shit splatted to the ground around us. We could see the different textures of the skin, the calluses on the joints, thick skin, thin skin, the creases and folds.

People gasped. Even over the deafening thud of their feet hitting the ground, we could hear their ghastly gurgling digestive noises. They were so much larger than anyone had thought. Previous estimates of size must have been based on immature bones. They were magnificent. They plodded endlessly on. Finally, the last of the herd passed through the hangar, to eventual dinosaur oblivion, leaving total silence behind. The hangar drew a collective breath, but we had one last spectacular shot to come.

As the sun set, orange and smoky blood-red behind the distant volcanoes, a solitary flying shadow came out of the clouds and the only Pteranodon we ever saw dipped low across the water. Slowly and serenely, he spread his wings and glided over the surface, racing his shadow. A long snake neck whipped out of the water, seized his wing, and dragged him under without a sound and barely a ripple. The sun sank. The day was over.

Ten

I spent the next two days incessantly going over the data. I wrote a commentary for the holo. I checked all the data cubes, disks, sticks, and stacks were loaded and correct. I collated all the documentation and labelled everything. I couldn't leave it alone. Peterson took me for a drink but I couldn't settle, so I guess they thought it would be easier just to let me be.

The Chief and I set off early – the Boss had loaned us his Bentley; a rare favour. The boot and back seat were stacked with archive boxes filled with the fruits of our labours. With Sussman gone, the Chief was coming along to handle the technical side of things.

'You'll be all right once we get started,' he said, accurately reading my mind.

I sat and stared out of the window and fretted. Had I mentioned iliac crests? Did I mention the Proceratops eggs laid in spiral patterns? And the flap of skin covering Saurolophus nostrils? Yes, yes, and yes. Calm down and focus, Maxwell.

We were met by the welcoming committee, the Chancellor and her gang, all of whom seemed very pleasant. I don't know why the Boss always carried on as if they were the Antichrist. Although I suspected if this presentation failed and they weren't happy with our data then I would soon be finding out. The Chief disappeared off in the direction of their main lecture hall and I went alone into the lion's den to meet the Senior Faculty.

In the privacy of the Chancellor's office I introduced myself, listed my qualifications and experience, and detailed the mission parameters. I always start that way. It gives my brain a chance to catch up with my mouth.

I followed the same format for all the categories. I outlined the requirements, described the methodology, and congratulated them on the reliability of their equipment. I brought up a few stills from the star map, just enough to whet their appetite, then moved tantalisingly on to geology and climate. Again, just as they became interested I switched to flora and fauna. I showed them how to access the raw data. Nothing had been worked up and no conclusions drawn. Not our job.

I gestured to the piles of disks, cubes, and tapes on the table beside me and formally handed them over to the appropriate heads of departments who had been slathering impatiently for the last twenty minutes. Out of compassion for them I'd kept it as brief as I could and I appreciated they wanted to get at it, but I wanted to be sure St Mary's got the credit it deserved.

I asked 'Any questions?'

Someone stood up (primed by the Chancellor, I suspected) and said, 'Yes, but what was it actually *like*?'

There would never be a better opportunity. Before I could respond, the Chancellor rose to her feet and said, 'This way please, everyone.' Muttering and looking longingly back over their shoulders to the piles of data on her table, they complied.

The lecture hall was massive. On the downside, of course, given the seating capacity, I could be embarrassing myself in front of millions. The Chief had already erected and aligned the streamers, three down one side and three down the other. Every chair was taken. Standing room at the back was packed. They contravened fire regs. and sat on the floor in the aisles. If this place caught fire, not only were they all doomed, but two of St Mary's finest were going up in flames as well. Better than going down in flames, I suppose. I swallowed and wondered again whether I'd suit an office job.

The Chancellor introduced us, to a polite smattering of applause. We had a minute's silence for Sussman. She sat down. Here we go.

The lights went out, the blinds automatically covered the

windows, and the streamers came on line.

I said, 'Ladies and Gentlemen, utilising the very latest technology developed at St Mary's, I present to you: *A Typical Day in the Cretaceous Period.*'

The opening scenes came up and to gratifying gasps of amazement the Alamosaurus head snaked down and looked the Chancellor directly in the eye. All credit to her, she took it well.

They'd forgotten all about me, so I sat down and watched them watch the holo. My commentary went down well although, honestly, I'm not sure how much they actually heard. They shouted with surprise as each species made its debut appearance and after that it was chaos. I watched them scramble over each other and the furniture trying to get better views. A hundred arguments broke out around the hall as cherished theories were mercilessly amended, embellished, or discarded.

I watched in amused horror as a great dinosaur dollop apparently enveloped a group of venerable academics arguing in the corner.

'Oh, I say,' murmured the Chancellor. 'All over the Senior Faculty!'

'Oh dear,' I said.

'No, no, they've been trying to do that to me for years. Jolly well done.'

'Always happy to oblige, ma'am.'

'My compliments to Dr Bairstow. Tell him the cheque's in the post.'

They loved it and us, as they bloody well should. We'd scored a huge PR success for St Mary's. The Boss had asked me to be polite, so I talked to everyone, gave out my card, and promised St Mary's would be on hand to answer any queries that might arise concerning data collection. Finally, we found ourselves in the car park.

We chucked our jackets on the now empty back seat and I settled myself in the front as we drove slowly away.

163

I stared out of the window, still on a high. They'd liked it. It had gone well. I hadn't embarrassed myself or St Mary's. I couldn't ask for more. Now I could draw a line under recent events and legitimately take a bit of time off. I would go for long rides, eat chocolate, do some painting, catch up on my reading, and generally laze around a bit. The assignment was all over and I could relax. I decided to start by just looking out of the window, admiring the scenery and enjoying the ride home.

After two miles I was bored.

I looked around the car for something to do and obviously, the first thing I saw was Chief Farrell. I let my gaze wander a little. He'd rolled up his sleeves over his forearms. Heaving huge lumps of pod around every day had given him great arms. Great hands too. Even as I looked, he turned. 'Everything OK?'

'Yes,' I said happily.

He yawned.

'Would you like me to drive for a bit?'

'No. I choose life.'

'That's a little bit unkind, Chief.'

'Miss Maxwell, I have every respect for your many abilities. You are a talented and passionate historian, a skilful artist, and a fierce and loyal friend. You are warm, compassionate, smart, funny, and incredibly sexy. You are also the world's worst driver. Ever. God knows how you passed your driving test. I can only assume the examiner was so dazzled by your beauty that he ticked the "pass" box before you even put the keys in the ignition.'

A couple of heart-thumping seconds passed before I was able to say, 'Thank you.'

He nodded, his eyes on the road.

'And if you pull over now, I'll give you the blow-job of a lifetime.'

We hit a tree.

The only sound was the ticking engine. I got out to survey the damage. 'Well, for crying out loud, Chief!'

He clambered out and buried his head in his arms on the car roof. I looked at him anxiously. 'Are you hurt?'

He lifted his head, sighed, and pulled out his phone. 'Dieter! Yes, crank up the low-loader will you? We've had an accident. No, we're fine. About three miles out, on the Whittington road, just before the crossroads. Yes, at the top of the hill. About half an hour, then. OK.' He snapped the phone shut and walked round the car undoing his trousers.

'You. No more messing about. Across the bonnet of this car. Right here, right now.'

Before I could move he lifted me bodily and tossed me across the bonnet. It was hard and hot. So was he. He pushed my skirt up around my hips and tore off my knickers. I really didn't know that could happen. I don't know where they went. I never saw them again. He slipped two fingers inside and, satisfied, pushed himself into me – hard. It should have been brutal, but it wasn't. I arched up to meet him, wanting every inch, wrapping my stockinged legs around his waist and pushing hard against him. We crashed together and I felt heat building in and around me. His hands were all over me, rough and urgent. I moaned and this galvanised him further, thrusting harder and faster. It hurt, but it was glorious, and I couldn't have stopped to save my life. I pulled up his shirt and raked my fingernails across his back. He gasped and groaned, but didn't stop. I bit his neck and he took my head between his hands and kissed me, tongue pushing its way into my mouth, matching the rhythm of our bodies. I could hear a wailing noise, rising in crescendo and volume. Oh God, it was me. I twisted my hands in his hair and pushed back, matching him all the way. He whispered, 'Lucy,' and as soon as he said it, I was away, heaving and shuddering and gasping as wave after wave broke over me, increasing in frequency and strength. I couldn't stop, all control gone, totally abandoned, lost in a sea of sensation and pleasure, until my body convulsed, a scream ripping from between my clenched teeth. He pushed again and again, prolonging the moment endlessly until, with a series of harsh, inarticulate cries, he shuddered and collapsed across me. I could feel him inside, pulsing over and over, as he finally released himself and we both slowly came down together.

Eventually, he lifted himself up and looked down at me. I sprawled across the bonnet, breasts exposed, skirt around my waist, legs spread wide. My hair had come down and hung over my face.

He rested his weight on his hands and tried to catch his breath. Slowly, he withdrew and straightened up. 'Dear God.'

I struggled to breathe. I pushed my hair off my face and looked up through the green and gold dappled sunshine to the blue sky above.

'Wait,' he said. 'Let me help you,' and he did, helping me sit up. He pulled down my bra and tucked in my shirt. He was slow and careful and very gentle. His hands shook so badly I had to button his shirt for him, so we took care of each other. Finally, we were presentable. Not decent. We would never be decent again.

I slid down off the bonnet and cast a quick glance around, wanting to make sure my knickers weren't hanging off a nearby tree. He caught and steadied me. Still experiencing aftershocks, I was almost unable to stand.

We sat together on a nearby log, his arm around me. He gently kissed my hair as I twisted it back into shape.

'Do I look all right?'

'Not in any way. You look wanton and dishevelled and knickerless and outrageously desirable. I'm a lost man.'

I put my hand on his cheek and he leaned into it, turned his head and kissed my palm.

'Can we do that again?'

'Well, I think I can hear the low-loader, so you might want to hold off until we get back home, but I warn you, I'm not finished with you. I want you again. And again.'

I drew a sharp breath and for a moment, lost my place in the world.

Dieter arrived. He jumped down and we went to meet him.

'Are you two OK?' he asked. 'Because you don't look it. Bloody hell, Max, sit down will you. You too, Chief. I think you're both in shock.'

'No, we're fine.'

'You crashed the Boss's Bentley, Max. I'd develop shock if I were you; and severe internal injuries. It's the only thing that will save you.'

'Actually,' said the Chief. 'I was driving.'

Dieter winced. '*You* crashed the car? What happened?'

'Deer,' I said quickly. They both looked at me. 'A deer ran across the road. We swerved. Missed the deer. Hit the tree. We could have been killed. Neat bit of driving. Good job it wasn't me. We'd be a ball of flame by now.'

The Chief rolled his eyes and folded his arms.

Dieter said, 'A deer? At four o'clock in the afternoon?'

'It was confused,' I offered.

'It's not the only one. Did you bang your head?'

'Not my head, no.'

'Get your stuff,' said Dieter, 'I'll start the winch.'

'Do you want a hand?'

'No thanks, Chief. Perhaps you'd better get Max on board.' He grinned. 'You both look pretty shagged out to me.'

So we did as we were told and climbed into the cab.

We were all quiet on the way back. Word of the accident had got round and a small, jeering crowd met us at the hangar doors. No sign of the Boss. He would be off somewhere organising our P45s.

'Stay where you are,' said Dieter, walking round the front of the vehicle. He opened the passenger door and helped me down.

'Doctor Foster says to go straight up,' said Polly and I groaned. God Almighty, was there no respite?

Helen, thank God, didn't mess about. 'No blood, no pain, no fractures. Chief, as the marginally more sensible one here,

167

watch out for pallor, shaking, decreased physical co-ordination, and loss of consciousness.'

'Already had that!' I muttered and got a nudge.

'Of course, Doctor, pallor, shaking, unconsciousness – got it.'

'Go away now. I think the Boss wants you. Before you go, Maxwell, a word.'

'I'll wait outside.' He closed the door behind him.

'What's up, doc?'

She looked unusually serious. 'I need you to answer this question honestly and completely. It's important. This has serious implications.'

I felt uneasy. 'What?'

She looked at me sternly. 'Have you just had intercourse?'

I threw caution to the winds. 'Not so much intercourse as such. More like full-blown, in your face, head-banging, shrieking, shuddering, mind-blowing sex that's probably illegal in many parts of the known world. Why? Are there medical implications?'

'Oh, no, nothing to do with that. It's just there's an awful lot of money changing hands in this building even as we speak and I want to be sure I get mine off Peterson.'

I opened my mouth to speak, couldn't think of anything to say, shut it, blushed, swallowed, and opened it again.

'You're speechless, aren't you?'

I nodded.

'Good, that's an extra tenner Peterson owes me. You can go now.'

We left. Emerging from the lift I went to turn left, back to the main building but he caught my arm and pushed me across the foyer. To the paint store! We were going to the paint store! We were almost running when we hit his pod door and then we were inside and safe.

'Take off your clothes,' he said hoarsely. 'Get them off now.' I was pulling off my jacket when the world went white. I knew where we were; somewhere quiet and private five thousand years ago where noise didn't matter.

We didn't make it outside. Up against a wall inside the pod, outside on a blanket, outside off the blanket, outside up against a tree; the man was a machine. They say the quiet ones are the worst. Take it from me, the quiet ones are the best.

Hours later, night fell. I knew how it felt. We wound down to a halt.

'No more,' he gasped. 'For God's sake, woman, leave me alone.'

I put my head on his chest and felt his heart race. We were in a sorry state, sweaty, covered in dust, bruised, and scratched. I'd never felt better. He got to his feet and came back with a bottle of wine and a mug. We shared. I was parched and grateful.

'Should we be getting back?'

'I can't take you back looking like that. You look like a fallen angel.'

'I didn't fall – I was pushed.'

He tightened his arm and bent to kiss me. 'Please, no.' I whispered. 'I can barely walk as it is.'

'Not one for the road?'

I looked down. 'For heaven's sake, don't you have an off switch?'

'Not since I can remember. You have no idea how often I've thanked God for baggy jumpsuits!'

'Really?' I didn't know I could do that!

'Right from the moment I met you. You stood on the stairs with the sun in your hair and smiled at me and I was lost from that moment.'

I stretched up and kissed him. 'Can I trust you in a shower?'

'You'll be warm, wet, and slippery. There will be soapy hands. What do you think?'

It took hours to get out of the shower. We'd probably be there still if the tank hadn't emptied. Slowly, we got ourselves ready for the here and now and finally, suited and booted, we returned, no more than half an hour after we left, and made our way to the Boss's office.

He congratulated me on my presentation. Thirsk had obviously contacted him, telling him all about it and singing our praises. 'Satisfactory,' was the exact word used, so he was obviously pleased. He didn't mention the car.

'Saved your bacon there,' I said as we left. 'Fancy a drink?'

'So much. Give me a minute. I'll see you in the bar.'

Pushing open the heavy vestibule door I could hear the racket immediately. Either they were re-enacting the battle at Marathon or there was another massive punch up in the bar.

This happens occasionally.

Every section, rightly or wrongly, regards itself as the most important at St Mary's. I don't know why, since it's obviously the History Department that runs the show, but techies and Security, and occasionally R & D always fail to recognise this and someone says something unfortunate, sometimes accidentally, but usually not, and away we all go.

From the doorway I could see this was no ordinary bar fight. This was a riot. Orange, black, green, and occasionally blue bodies struggled, locked together, rolling on the floor, cursing, shouting, and flailing wildly at each other. Glasses shattered and furniture overturned. The bar staff were yelling for order.

I pushed my way through the watchers and eggers-on and looked for an opening. Dieter and Markham rolled free, struggled to their feet and squared up to each other. Given their respective sizes, it was rather like a chipmunk hurling itself at Mount Everest.

Without thinking, (there's a first!) I tried to get between them and push them apart and Dieter, already swinging a fist the size of a small armchair, caught me just below the eye and knocked me to the ground. He did pull it at the last moment, but, even so, it still hurt.

But at least the fighting stopped while everyone waited to see what would happen next. Typical. The least they could have done was carry on trying to kill each other and given me the time to get myself together again.

I wobbled to my feet and tried to pull my skirt down.

'You're not supposed to hit girls,' said Markham provocatively. 'It's not polite.'

'Oh, my God, Max,' said Dieter, horrified (as well he might be). 'I'm sorry.'

My instinct was to deck him and blacken at least one of his eyes so we could have a matching set. His and Hers. I used the anger.

'What the fuck do you fuckwits think you're playing at?'

No one answered but no one looked particularly contrite either. This was going to re-ignite at any minute and at any minute the Boss could walk in and after Bentley Trauma he wouldn't be in the best of moods. Taking a deep breath, I moved between the opposing groups; a buffer zone with a black eye.

'Well, let's just have a guess what's going on here, shall we? Some prat told the "How do you raise the intelligence level of a pod? Take out the historian," joke. And then some smart arse said, "How many techies does it take to change a light bulb? Only one, but you need a lot of light bulbs!" and someone else didn't find that funny and then some other joker showed his ID to the dog rather than the security guy because everyone knows the dog's the one with the brains and the next thing is you're all kicking seven shades of shit out of each other.'

There were some murmurings from the group and someone said, 'Hey.'

'Don't "hey" me. I'm ashamed of all of you. I'll tell you this now. This "My section's the best and only we've got any brains in this outfit," attitude is really beginning to piss me off. Everyone makes a contribution here. The techies provide the wherewithal for us to do our job. Security keeps us all safe. Mrs

Mack feeds us. How far would any of us get without her Toad in the Hole on Wednesdays? Wardrobe makes our costumes and equipment. Mrs Partridge's gang make sure we all get paid on time. How important do you think they are?' I paused. 'And historians are the ones out there bleeding in the mud. Anyone here want our job?'

I took a deep, ragged breath and spoke more quietly. 'We're all special and we're all the best there is, but sometimes we're such a pain in the arse.'

Silence. It hadn't worked. Most people looked sulky; the technicians looked smug and Security was thinking about whom to hit next. We were one deep breath away from meltdown. And my face hurt.

Suddenly, I was so tired of all this. This was no way to behave. I had, what seemed at the time, to be a brainwave. Turning to Dieter I said, 'Come with me tomorrow.'

He stared at me.

'No, seriously, come with me tomorrow,' I said, making it all up as I went along. 'I have to return to the Cretaceous to check out something that arose out of today's presentation. I'll need a wingman, so why don't you come along and see what it's all about. Come on, Dieter, come and say hello to a T-rex!'

I'd put him in an impossible position. He didn't want to go. They all knew what happened to people who went out with me. I saw Kalinda stir and Peterson caught her arm.

'What do you say, Dieter? Are you going to put your money where your mouth is? Or would you prefer to stay quietly at home? I'll quite understand if you do.'

Looking at him, I could see he wanted to say no. He was just looking for a face-saving way to do it. Well, I wasn't going to help. Everyone watched in silence.

'It's OK, Dieter, I understand.' I patted his arm gently. 'It's no big deal. But I think you would have enjoyed it. What a shame.'

Just to add a little pressure, I touched my face gently and

winced.

He shook my hand off. 'Of course I'll go. Someone has to keep you historians out of trouble.'

'Great. I'll see you after breakfast for a quick briefing. It's not a long jump, just a couple of hours, but enough to give you an idea. Greens by the way, definitely not orange. Some of them hunt by sight. And no more alcohol – that goes without saying.'

He nodded, obviously wondering what he'd let himself in for. I moved off before he had time to change his mind and joined Kalinda and Peterson.

'You'd better bring this one back,' said Kalinda darkly. 'And all of him, too; living and breathing.' Just in case I hadn't got the message.

'It'll be fine. It's only a couple of hours. You'll be shagging each other senseless again this time tomorrow.'

'Oh, please,' said Peterson. 'Max, you can't take a techie on a jump.'

'Why not? I took a techie on the presentation, which went very well, thank you for asking.'

I wanted to distract them with the presentation and historians are easily distracted. Attention span of a – what was I saying?

I saw Chief Farrell standing in the doorway surveying the destruction. He looked at me and the look clearly said, 'Seriously? I leave you for ten minutes and you have a black eye?'

Belatedly, I remembered protocol. I gestured to Dieter to join me.

'Chief Farrell, as you know, I need to return to the Cretaceous tomorrow and with your permission, I'd like Mr Dieter to accompany me on a short jump. I need a wingman and he has expressed an interest. If you have no objections, of course.'

He glanced around the room slowly being put to rights. I felt a little guilty. I'd really sprung this on him. Dieter knew it and

173

stood waiting for permission to be refused. I moved my hand slightly to where the Chief could see it and crossed my fingers.

He smiled slightly. 'A new experience for you, Mr Dieter. Well volunteered. Enjoy yourself.'

Dieter took a deep breath. 'Yes, sir. Thank you, sir,' shot me a look, and disappeared.

'Leon …'

'I know,' he sighed. 'The night before a jump is traditionally spent in a solitary and sober fashion.'

'Well, I've got a passenger tomorrow. You'll want me to take care of him.'

'I would be grateful if you could.'

'I'll bring him back without a mark on him.'

I made the promise in all good faith.

We parted in the Hall.

'Never mind,' he said. 'There's always tomorrow night.'

But there wasn't. It only goes to show – take your eye off the ball and Fate, Destiny, History, call it what you will, steps up and just pisses all over your chips.

Eleven

I put together a short briefing for Dieter and met him at breakfast. He'd remembered his greens and looked sober and calm, albeit apprehensive.

We looked through things. He asked questions, good ones and I began to feel quite optimistic. I planned to show him around the lakeside where, hopefully, there would be enough wildlife to make it interesting without being life-threatening in any way. So long as it was far enough away, I quite hoped for a T-rex.

Loads of nosey people had found things to do in Hawking that morning. I waved to Kal and Tim up on the gantry. They gestured back. So rude!

We settled into the pod, good old Number Eight, and the Chief carried out the last minute checks. Dieter was very quiet. At last we were done. I started flicking switches. The Chief leaned over Dieter.

'Just one last thing. Miss Maxwell is in charge of this pod, this mission, and you. You do exactly as she tells you, when she tells you, because that will save your life. Is that understood?'

He swallowed. 'Yes, sir.'

'Good luck, both of you.'

'Thanks Chief. Put the kettle on.'

I locked the door. The world went white.

Again, Fate, Destiny, whatever, took a hand. We were near the lake, but higher up on the slope, at the unexplored northern end. We bumped as we landed and one of the hydraulic legs unfolded automatically to keep us level. I checked all the read-outs very carefully. This mission would be by the book. There was no way I could take back a damaged Dieter and ever hear the last of it. But everything seemed quiet. Nothing large appeared within biting distance.

I checked over my passenger – helmet, vest, com, and blaster; everything the well-dressed historian carries. We jumped up and down. Nothing jingled and nothing fell off. We activated the cameras and set off.

I remembered my first time and gave him a couple of minutes to get his head around it. The warm blue sky, the forest noises, the heat, the smell, the sheer exhilaration. He spun around and around. 'Wow! I'm sixty-seven million years ago! Max, this is absolutely, bloody amazing!'

'You just wait,' I said. 'We'll go this way and then down a bit.'

He pulled himself together and we headed towards a gap in the trees which should give us good views of the lake and the flat areas around. I stayed vigilant because although I wasn't expecting any trouble, this was the Cretaceous period after all. And I was quite fond of Dieter.

Vigilant and alert I may have been, but I was totally unprepared for the brain-numbing, gobsmacking shock I got when we emerged from the small copse and got a good view of down below. I stood transfixed, then grabbed Dieter by the arm and pulled him down to the ground. We wriggled forwards on our bellies and tried to make sense of what we were seeing below.

It was like a small town down there. I could see tents, people, cages, vehicles. Pop music played over a PA system. I could smell cooking. What the fuck was going on?

'Dieter, make sure you're getting all this.' I started to dictate into my com. I could hear him doing the same. He estimated numbers of people and described them, counted the pods, and noted their positions. I counted the cages and identified the occupants as best I could, all the time turning my head so the camera could get the full sweep.

A large cage stood slightly apart – its occupant a young, half-grown T-rex. Even though not fully grown, he was still too big for the cage and he roared and bellowed trying to swing his head around and batter his way out. As I watched, a group of men wandered past on their way to somewhere else. One pulled out what looked like a stun gun and casually zapped him as they passed. He bellowed and lunged against the bars and they all laughed. I felt my blood turn hot and beside me, Dieter growled.

Further towards the tree line, another group of men were pulling a Hadrosaur from her cage. She was fitted with restraints but they still shouted and poked and prodded her forwards. Not understanding what was happening to her, upset and confused at being separated from her herd, she wailed in distress and fear. Even as we looked, she reared. They jerked the restraint viciously and she twisted awkwardly in mid-air. I heard the crack of a broken bone from all the way up where we were. She crashed heavily to the ground and lay, crying in pain. Someone stepped forward and put a bullet in her brain. Dieter gasped. Suddenly, I liked him a lot. A forklift bustled forward to remove the carcass. Obviously, this had happened before. And still they did it.

Both the T-rex and the dead Hadrosaur had a splodge of green paint on their sides and a red one on their forehead. I looked around and saw some caged animals had the same markings. Was it some sort of classification?

Dieter was describing vehicles and plant, together with lists of power provisions and generators. I set up a live feed back to the pod and tried to identify their security arrangements. There didn't seem to be any apart from an electrified perimeter fence and a lookout tower by the gate. The whole camp seemed to be built around some large central structure, but the view was obscured.

I was speculating on the origins and purpose of the camp below when Dieter nudged me. 'Look at that, over there. Does that look like a kind of arena to you? And that's a funnel. Have you ever seen a salmon run? The fish swim forwards into the funnel and then can't turn round. This is a dinosaur run. These guys are hunters. They're going to drive the animals in and shoot them. That's what those paint marks are. They're targets. They're painting targets on dinosaurs; so many points for a red hit and so many for a green. Maybe they even shoot them in the cages. Max, we can't let this happen. This is so wrong.'

He was right. I could easily imagine the scene; panicking and confused dinosaurs milling around an enclosed space. Depending on the species, some would vainly seek to escape. Others, (the ones for whom I had a sneaky soft spot), would not understand the threat and would make a stand, roaring their challenge and all of them screaming in pain and terror as high-impact bullets or armour-piercing shells tore into them, shredding flesh and bones, as they crashed to the ground in blood and dust while these – tossers – stood in perfect safety, cheered each other on, and called it sport. I remembered that night at the hotel and the Chief telling me about problems from the future. This was why he came back. Suddenly it really was balls to the wall time. Trouble had arrived and it was up to us to deal with it, even if we had only stumbled upon it by accident. I wondered what would have happened if I hadn't decided to take a techie to work today?

And another thought – was this what Sussman had been protecting? We were at the unexplored northern end. Maybe it was no coincidence he attacked me on that very day. What was his role in all this?

I was so busy thinking this through that it took some seconds to register the five or six muffled explosions at the head of the valley.

'What the fuck now?' said Dieter, taking the words out of my mouth. The ground began to shake. I heard a noise like thunder. We both looked up at the cloudless sky, but this was continuous, never-ending thunder, drawing closer all the time.

Tens, scores, possibly even hundreds of animals were coming our way. I could hear trees splintering and crashing to the ground. Flying reptiles erupted into the air, screaming and shrieking. Small rocks tumbled past. The dinosaur run had begun.

'Come on Dieter, we have to go. Now! Come on!'

We ran together. The ground shook and we were continually pulling each other to our feet. I was really worried about the pod. Even with its bracing leg extended, it wasn't as stable as I'd like it to be.

'A bit like its owner, then,' panted Dieter and I began to think we might make a historian of him yet.

Number Eight was still there and upright, but the loose shale on which it balanced was beginning to slide downhill and taking the pod with it. The thunder grew louder and over the crest of the hill came the stampede, invisible in a huge cloud of dust. No time to look – we had only seconds.

Dieter's strength got us across the shale. He had the sense to head slightly down hill, which made things easier for us and we met the pod as it slithered past. The door opened and we leaped in. No time to buckle up. The leg snapped off and we tilted. The next moment the stampede was upon us.

Something big and heavy hit the roof. The ceiling sagged badly, tiles fell and wires dangled, spitting and twisting. The lights flickered wildly. Something else kicked us and we tipped over, rolling down the slope. Locker doors swung open and their contents crashed down on top of us. We were hurled around the inside of the pod, bouncing painfully off the walls.

With a bellow, something really big fell on top of us, the walls bulged outwards and frighteningly, with a noise like a pistol shot, the screen cracked. I think Dieter was yelling. I know I was.

I shouted, 'Computer, emergency extraction …' and it all went horribly quiet. Through the distorted screen I could see the ground – a long way down. We'd gone over the bloody cliff!

'… Now!' hoping desperately we would jump before we hit the ground, which was getting closer and closer. And then the world went black.

Much later, I saw the tapes of our landing. Every alarm in the unit went off. The hangar was still full of nosey sods awaiting our return. As our pod appeared about eight feet above the plinth, people scattered. Techies threw aside their umbilicals and ran for their lives. The pod landed on the plinth with a thunderous crash. Dust and debris dropped from the hangar roof. The whole hangar shook. They felt the impact all through the main building. Apparently, the shock was such that one of our decorative stone pineapples fell from its plinth and crashed onto the front steps beneath, narrowly missing our caretaker, Mr Strong, who had stepped outside for a crafty fag.

The pod bounced down the hangar like something dreamed up by Barnes Wallis, inventor of the famous bouncing bomb, scattering people as it went and finally came to a stop, door side down naturally, in front of Plinth Three at the other end of the hangar.

On the tapes there was a long, shocked silence. Red and blue lights bounced off stunned faces. Chief Farrell moved first.

'Emergency evacuation! All non-essential personnel out. Now. Crash teams to me. Move.'

Karl and Peterson got people off the gantry while contriving to stay put themselves. They were joined by the Boss, who had turned up to see who was trying to wreck his unit.

Major Guthrie and a security team appeared from the back of the hangar, closely followed by Helen and her team of medics. All in all, the hangar cleared and key personnel assembled in around two minutes. Quite impressive. When they discovered the pod had landed on its door, the Chief kicked the pod in frustration, snapped an order, and Polly Perkins dashed off out of the picture.

Inside the pod, where the important people were, Dieter and

I were still wondering who we were and what the hell was going on. Amazingly, we were still conscious and gave thanks for our vests and helmets.

'Jesus,' whispered Dieter, 'I am never going anywhere with you again, Max. Ever. I'm not even using the dining room if you're there. You're a fucking disaster!'

'I think that's a little unkind,' I said, weakly. 'You're surely not blaming me for this.'

There followed some argument which it would not be useful to repeat, but he seemed better afterwards,

'How are you?' I asked.

'Well, I'm lying on the door which means we can't get out and they can't get in, with the contents of seven lockers on top of me and there are live wires everywhere. What about you, Max. You OK?'

'Yes, I think so. Listen, Dieter, this is important. If I pass out you must make them download the tapes first. I know we've got live cables everywhere, but if they switch the power off then we might lose all our data. I'm sorry, kiddo, but it's more important than we are.' Silence. 'Dieter, I'm sorry, but you've just become an honorary historian, which means you rank somewhere between blue-green algae and the duck-billed platypus in the scheme of things. The Boss must see those tapes.'

More silence. I didn't know what to say to him. I'd brought him with me in a stupid attempt to promote equality and co-operation and I'd nearly got him killed.

'Dieter, are you still awake?'

'Honorary historian, eh?'

'Could be.'

'So how does this work? Do I have one orange leg and one blue leg?'

My com crackled. Farrell said, 'Max, can you hear me?'

'Good afternoon, Chief.'

'Is Dieter OK?'

'Yes, we're just redesigning his uniform.'

'Are either of you injured?'

'We may be a little shaken.'

'We'll get you out in a jiffy.'

'Is the Boss there? Can I have a word?'

'Just a minute.'

He came on immediately. 'Miss Maxwell. That was quite an entrance.'

'Sir, I apologise for disturbing your afternoon. We've got some data here and it's important you see this. It's more important than we are. Please sir; under no circumstances allow them to disconnect the power in this pod. You must preserve the data. You'll understand when you see it.'

To his credit, he didn't argue or delay.

'Miss Barclay, upload these tapes immediately and advise me when you have done so. Now, please!'

Back on the outside, Polly Perkins arrived with a forklift truck. The plan was to use the prongs to ram open the cracked and weakened screen and get us out that way.

Back inside, I sniffed. 'We've wrecked the toilet. Can't you smell it?'

'Ah, no, sorry. That would be me.'

Polly lined up carefully, revved the engine and hit the pod with a crash. It took her four goes before they could batter their way in. Shouts of 'Cover your eyes in there!' would possibly have been more helpful if they had been uttered before impact. Still, let's not be picky.

The Chief clambered in first, went straight to the trip switch, and pushed it up, ignoring my warning whimpers.

'We've got the data,' he said. 'Relax and we'll get you out.'

They got Dieter out first, manhandling him through the shattered screen. He reached out to me and I grasped his hand.

'So, Mr Dieter, apart from that, how was it for you?'

'Awesome, Max; the earth moved.' They took him away.

The Boss waited quietly. As they stretchered me away, I

grasped his sleeve and croaked, 'The tapes?'

'Safe and sound, Miss Maxwell, I shall be reviewing them in a few minutes.'

Satisfied, I closed my eyes and let go for a bit.

I woke up in Sick Bay. Actually that happens so often I'm going to put it on a hotkey. I was asked to prepare a briefing. I spent two days getting down as much as I could and preparing a large-scale map of the area, including the previous site where Sussman and I had worked before. I took my time because I wanted to get it right. That's the beauty of this game; we could take whatever time needed and still go back to about ten minutes after we left.

Guilt-stricken, I persuaded them to let me visit Dieter who lay heavily bruised in the next room.

'What's the damage? I said, trying not to wince in sympathy.

'Broken arm, broken wrist, sprained ankle, cuts, bruises, in-growing toenail, and mild concussion.'

He moved his arm fractionally and caught my sleeve. I gently patted his hand.

'Don't worry,' I said. 'We'll get the bastards. And the pods they came in on.'

He nodded, yawned, and when I looked again he was fast asleep. Typical techie.

The day after I was able to start hobbling around again, Chief Farrell came and collected me from Sick Bay and we walked to the Boss's office.

As I limped down the Long Corridor he said, 'We got it wrong. Well, I got it wrong. We assumed the point of killing you was to bring back a body that would lead to mission shutdown. However, I think their plans were further advanced than we thought. The point may have been to keep you away from the northern end of the valley where Ronan and his team were carrying out their very illegal, but highly lucrative temporal tourism. Sussman's bank account shows a rather large recent deposit.'

I looked at him.

'He was always jealous of you, Max. Didn't you know?'

I shook my head.

He didn't mention this could be the reason for Sussman's behaviour as well; a quick bit of rough sex before tossing me to the raptors. I looked up to find him watching me. He'd followed my thought processes. He put his hand on my shoulder. 'The bastard deserved what he got. Don't think about it. How's your leg?'

'A bit bruised. Twisted knee and a banged-up shoulder. A few cuts and bruises but everything's fine.'

I limped thoughtfully down the corridor. With all the vastness of the Cretaceous period, what were the odds two expeditions would end up within a few miles of each other and at the same time? Did they use our co-ordinates? Did we somehow use theirs? Was it just coincidence?

I asked him, 'Who did the co-ordinates?'

'IT provided them and we laid them in.'

Barclay. Barclay and Sussman. No, I was just allowing my prejudice to get the better of me.

The Boss sat at the head of his briefing table. Mrs Partridge sat behind him. The Chief took a seat at his right hand and Major Guthrie was opposite him. I sat at the end.

'Miss Maxwell, it's good to see you up and about. We've spent some time reviewing the tapes made by you and Mr Dieter. Have you seen them?'

I shook my head and he brought them up. We watched in silence. It seemed worse the second time around. I dragged out my scratchpad from my knee pocket and made one or two notes.

At his request, I brought up the detailed and comprehensive contour map I had made, showing the location of Site A, the position of the lake, the coastal plain, the forest, the volcanoes, and the slopes.

Then I moved it up a few miles north, showing Site B, where Dieter and I landed. I showed them the shale slope and cliff, warning them to avoid this area. I showed them the route Dieter and I had taken and the position of the compound and we went back to the tapes and superimposed the buildings, cages, pods, fence, generators, and power sources. We speculated about the big structure in the middle. I showed them the direction from which the stampede had come, estimated where we'd gone over the cliff, and we added the dinosaur run and arena. At the end, we had a reasonable facsimile of the layout.

Major Guthrie asked me to describe conditions.

'It's hot and wet. The rainfall is like vertical water. The humidity is very, very high. It stinks. The smell will make our eyes water. We will sweat continually. It doesn't get much cooler at night and it's certainly no safer. Most of the predators seem to operate on a twenty-four hour basis. Their night vision is far superior to ours. Their sense of smell is acute. I recommend a thorough dowsing of cabbage spray and insect repellent.

'It's rough underfoot. As well as loose shale higher up, there are swamps lower down. Things live in the swamps. Rotting tree trunks, branches, tree roots, and boulders are everywhere. The few paths made by animals going down to drink are monitored by predators. What seems the easiest way will not be the safest. We need to watch our footing. Progress will be very slow. I advise operating in pairs at least. No one should go anywhere alone. We should watch our backs at all times. A T-rex standing motionless among dappled trees is completely invisible until it's too late. Raptors move faster than you can possibly imagine and they come at you from all directions, including above. We must always remember this is their world. We are their prey. They won't know the difference between us and the other lot and they certainly won't care. The inadvisability of underestimating any dinosaur cannot be emphasised enough. And we need to do it quickly. The longer we're there the less chance we have of getting out successfully.'

I didn't like the pause.

'We?' said the Boss.

I couldn't believe they were thinking of leaving me behind. I drew a breath. 'I think that undertaking this – enterprise without the only person in this unit who has spent three months on-site would be inadvisable, sir.'

'You can barely walk. What would you bring to this – enterprise?'

'Knowledge, experience, expertise, you name it, sir, I've got it. I'm the third most experienced historian in this unit. Even if I just pilot the pod, I'm freeing up another body.'

Another pause.

'Thank you, Miss Maxwell. That will be all for now.'

To say I fretted for the rest of the day would be an understatement. I didn't bother going back to Sick Bay, but spent the day in my room, walking off my stiffness and frustration. At 1800, I attended the briefing in the Hall.

Present were us three historians, most of the security section, and a few techies. The Boss attended, but Major Guthrie presided. We were divided into three teams with three pods, piloted by Kal, Peterson, and me. My main anxiety relieved, I began to pay attention. I got Murdoch, Whissell, Evans, and the irrepressible Markham. He grinned at me. I grinned back. Always nice to see someone who's even more of a disaster magnet than I am.

'Maybe we'll cancel each other out,' he whispered. 'Like white noise.'

Fat chance! He was the only person in the unit to have more yellow disciplinary sheets in his file than me. Despite eating like a horse, he remained small and slight and his hair stuck up in spikes around his crown. He'd been involved in the disastrous Icarus experiment last year, tumbling off the stable roof with his wings well ablaze. He'd thudded heavily into the paddock, panicking the horses who took exception to small, burning humans dropping on them from a great height. Running for his life and looking anxiously over his shoulder, he'd run slap bang into a horse's bottom and knocked himself senseless. The entire unit lay face down on the ground laughing. Even the Boss barked out something between a snort and a cough. The security section clubbed together and sent a Get Well Soon card to the horse, who promptly ate it. That's St Mary's for you.

The Boss stepped forward. 'You will all have seen the disturbing images brought back by Miss Maxwell and Mr Dieter. The purpose of this mission, therefore, is to return to the Cretaceous and disrupt, with extreme prejudice, whatever is occurring there. To this end, I want chaos; I want noise, confusion, and maximum damage. I don't want them to know what's come out of the dark and hit them. We go through the place, destroy everything in our path, and get out. After twenty minutes, we're gone. You may shoot to defend yourselves but otherwise just scare the living daylights out of them. I want survivors returning to the future with such tales of blood, terror, and carnage that no one will ever want to try this sort of stupidity again. Major.'

Guthrie pointed to the contour map. 'We land here in a V formation, about twenty yards apart. Pod Three will be at the apex and will contain an EMP device. On landing and on a given signal, a directed pulse will be fired at the compound. It's non-lethal, but highly destructive. At a low level, it will jam any electronic systems. A stronger pulse will corrupt computer data and a powerful pulse will fry any electronics within range. It will immobilise vehicles; knock out communications, electronic doors – the lot.'

He continued. 'Because of this, Pods Five and Six will be slightly behind Three. Pods are Faraday cages, but, to be on the safe side, will power down immediately. Peterson, Black, and Maxwell, you will shut down your pods on landing; all coms, everything. As soon as the compound goes dark – and it will –

187

power up again, get to the doors and wait. Maxwell, you will not set foot outside. Guard your pods, have them in a state of readiness, and wait for your teams to return. We will not be hanging around.

'Security section, as soon as the pulse is fired, you're up. You go through their main gate here. Chief, you and I go to the left, along here. Murdoch, your team to the right, along the perimeter here, and Ritter, your team goes straight down the middle. Stay in your groups. They will be blind, confused, and helpless. We come at them from all directions. Don't get yourselves shot. That's an order.

'Right, study the layout; get it straight in your heads. You'll have night visors, but do it anyway. If you can't get back to your own pod then get back to someone else's and advise your team leader. Does anyone have any questions?'

I raised a hand. 'What about the captured animals?'

Barclay said, 'Weren't you listening, Maxwell? The EMP device will lock any electronic door systems. You don't need to be afraid.'

I swear I'll swing for that woman one day. 'You misunderstand me, Izzie. Do we free them, sir? Or leave them in their cages?'

The long silence answered that question. I wasn't happy and nor were Kal and Peterson. We shifted our feet and prepared to argue. The Boss intervened. 'Should it be necessary, we will do what we can afterwards. While the attack is in progress they are probably safer in their cages and we certainly are. I appreciate your concern arises out of your training.' (Ha, Barclay, swivel on that!) 'The matter will be addressed.'

We spent three hours studying the available data and talking it through.

We drew our bits and pieces of kit and rehearsed our moves to get the timings right. I made sure I got a painkilling shot for my knee. We had a bit of a meal, a final briefing, and then we were ready to go.

This was my first combat mission ever. I was acutely aware of my own heartbeat. Even though I wouldn't be leaving the pod – and now the actual moment had come I was grateful for that – I still had nerves. I looked at Kal and Peterson alongside me – a little quiet maybe, but quite calm. Well, if they could do it, then so could I.

We marched down the long corridor, now brightly lit. I could see Guthrie and Farrell ahead and Murdoch and his team stumped along behind. I could hear Weasel and Markham bickering about something. All the colours seemed very bright and all the sounds very loud.

We split up in Hawking and I got to Number Six. Murdoch and his team filed in behind me. I started the usual checks, glad to have something to think about. On the other side of Hawking the Boss and Farrell had their heads together over a scratchpad. They exchanged a few quiet words, heads close together. They stepped back, paused, and then shook hands. Possibly only I knew how important this moment was for both of them. Not long now.

I jumped up and down in my unfamiliar night gear, flexing my arms and checking my weapon.

And then we waited.

I counted my team again: Murdoch, Whissell, Evans, and Markham. They were checking themselves, their equipment, and each other.

I said, 'Are you guys going to be OK on your own, or would you like me to come with you to hold your lunch money?'

Murdoch looked at me. 'You?'

'Yes, me. Is there a problem?'

'Just have the kettle on for when we get back like a good little wifey.' He looked at the pod. 'You might want to run a hoover around as well.'

'Just to be clear; you're winding up the person who's in charge of the getaway car? So it is true what they say about

Security.'

He refused to rise to that one. A voice in my ear said, 'Stand by.' They lined up by the door. The voice said, 'Jump.' And the world went white.

It wasn't as dark as I thought it would be. The light and noise coming from the compound lit up the whole area. These guys were morons. They couldn't hear over the music and had no night vision built up should anything nasty emerge out of the dark. Like us, for instance.

I set my watch. Barclay set about preparing the EMP. It took her less than four minutes but seemed far longer.

I said, 'Good luck, guys,' and opened the door ready for them. They disappeared into the night.

I limped to the trip switch, pushed it up, and the console went dark. I heard nothing at all when the pulse fired, but everything went very black very suddenly. For long seconds there was silence. Over in the compound, a few voices were raised, more in exasperation than anger. They still had no idea we were here. And then, very loud in the still night, an unexpected series of metallic clicks and clangs. I stared out of the door. Now what?

And then the screaming started.

Shit, shit, shit. Suddenly, I knew what this was. Bloody Barclay and her high-tech gizmos. The pulse had caused the cages to open, not lock. There was now no question of completing the mission. Everyone's priority would be to get back to the safety of their pods as quickly as possible. How could things go so wrong so quickly?

I crossed my fingers and pulled the power switch down and just as it had done on my first jump, everything lit up again. I could hear the chatter over the com system. I switched to the night light.

Someone started shooting. Someone else shot back and then trigger-happy tourists were letting off at everything in sight including each other. Voices were raised, shouting to cease fire, but no one listened. Terrified out of their wits, they blasted away wildly into the night. I prayed our people were on their way back, leaving this lot either to shoot themselves, or fall prey to whatever was roaring and bellowing in the darkness around them. It seemed very possible we would all be killed by idiots rather than villains, which would be typical.

Someone shouted an alarm. I suspected we had been discovered, but they still weren't sure what was happening and in the unexpected darkness they were their own worst enemies. Over the general din I could hear the unmistakable sounds of large animals moving through the night. God help everyone and everything out there.

The shooting had stopped. Everyone was running. Our guys would be trying to get back, but in the confusion I couldn't work out who was who. I stood in the doorway, armed and ready to repel anyone or anything that wasn't St Mary's.

Close by, I could hear heavy breathing. Very heavy breathing. I took a silent step backwards into the pod and whatever it was pounded away into the night.

The screaming redoubled. You put dinosaurs and people together, you always get screaming. For the dinosaurs, of course, it was a feeding frenzy. They roared, pounced, and ripped. Lumps of things that were no longer human were flung around the landscape. The top half of a man, still screaming, hit the side of the pod and bounced off into the night.

I could see green figures running back towards my pod. As they came closer I opened up the med kits so I could start giving treatment as soon as possible. The roaring and shrieking got closer. Come on guys! Then, finally, I could hear Murdoch shouting and they fell into the pod.

'Report,' I said.

'All here except Markham. Two casualties but nothing serious. Evans ran into a building in the dark and knocked himself silly, although it's hard to tell.'

Evans, lowering himself to the floor and clutching a blood

191

soaked dressing over his right eye, grinned at me. 'Did you see those fuckers run?'

'Any news?' asked Murdoch.

'The livestock's free.'

'Yeah, we noticed. It's bloody chaos out there,' he said, slapping another dressing on top of the blood-stained original. Evans yelped. 'Wuss! Those things are crazy for blood. It's going to take more than cabbage spray to keep us safe tonight.'

I went back to the door. 'We're missing Markham and we may get stragglers from the other pods. I'll stand guard. Who's the other casualty?'

'Me,' said Weasel, thickly. His nose was broken and bloody.

'What happened to you? You fall over your own feet?'

I swear he blushed. 'Go on,' said Murdoch. 'Tell her.' Weasel shook his head. 'He was hit by a flying body part. A bloody leg flew through the air and caught him right between the eyes.'

I know I opened my mouth to make some sarky comment and I know I never got to say it. A white-hot flash seared my vision, leaving purple and green after-shadows. The ground heaved beneath my feet. I swear the pod bounced and a shock wave knocked me backwards. I fell heavily on my injured shoulder. Everything flickered wildly. Fractionally later, I heard the massive boom. It seemed to go on for a very long time. The pod trembled. Shakily, I got up on to my knees and groped for my gun because the door was still open. Beside me, Murdoch, also on his knees, shook his head.

I said, 'What was that?' and my voice seemed miles away. I crawled to the console to check the systems. Maybe one of the volcanoes had erupted. I wasn't steady on my feet and my ears rang. The screen broke up, showed nothing but static and then cleared again.

I said to Murdoch, 'Any ideas?' My voice sounded strange inside my own head.

He shook his head, carefully. 'At a guess I'd say a fuel

dump, given the heat and ferocity of the explosion. Bloody hell.' He shook his head again.

I scanned the outside. Fires had broken out everywhere. There were a lot of figures on the ground. Huge shapes were swooping on the few still desperately trying to get away. I looked back into my pod. Evans and Weasel had managed to cover everything in blood. The place looked like a slaughter house. I was uneasy at having the door open, but had no choice. The two or three seconds it took to open could be the difference between living and dying a particularly unpleasant death. We heard a bellowing roar close by. Murdoch picked up his gun. 'I've got it.' he said. 'Can you see to Whissell?'

I mopped up the still gushing Whissell. 'I'm OK,' he said wonkily, determined to be the tough man, so I switched the coms to speaker, to listen to the chatter and find out what was happening.

It wasn't good. I could hear Kalinda's voice raised over the racket in her pod. From what I could gather they had taken heavy casualties and the Boss was down. Her team was all present. I heard her ordered to return.

I said, 'Wait ...' But she had already gone. Faintly I heard Barclay say, 'Maxwell, return to St Mary's at once.'

I said, 'Izzie ...' but she said, 'At once, Maxwell. That's an order.'

'She must have Markham,' said Murdoch. 'Silly pillock.' Not quite sure who he was referring to there.

I closed the door on the snarling and screaming. Sudden silence fell; no sound but Whissell's bubbly breathing. I took one last look at the screen just in case Markham could be seen somewhere, and we jumped.

I had the decon light on even before we got back. Helen waited with medical teams at the ready. I got my people sorted and away and then pushed my way towards Kal, shouting for Markham as I went. No one had seen him. Kal and Helen were bent over the Boss. His front was soaked with blood and his face looked very white. I couldn't see if he was conscious.

Kal gripped my arm. 'I'll go with the Boss and see what's happening upstairs. You get this lot sorted.' I nodded and moved away, bumping into Perkins.

'Come on, Polly; let's get them all back behind the line.'

Shoving, persuading, cursing, we got everyone out of harm's way and behind the safety line. I stood on a crate.

'Markham? Has anyone seen Markham?' People shook their heads and looked around.

Someone said, 'He'll have gone back to the wrong pod. You know what he's like. Barclay will be bollocking him rigid at this very minute.'

I sent up a prayer to any deity who might be taking a temporary interest in St Mary's and at that moment, Number Three turned up. There was an audible sigh of relief and a minor surge forward.

'Stay back, all of you,' I shouted and went forward. As I got there, the door opened and Barclay stepped out. She looked awful; so bad that I visually checked her for injuries. She leaned forward and put her hands on her knees, gasping for breath. I rubbed her back gently. She was IT and not on the active list. It was her first mission. She had the right to a wobbly moment. I stepped past her into the pod. I don't know what I expected. Worst case scenario: dead and dying men, blood, pain, trauma, the works.

The pod was empty.

I couldn't grasp it. I kept looking round and round. It just didn't go in. I stepped back outside. 'Where are they?'

'They're dead. All of them. All four of them. Oh, God.' She threw up on her own boots. I ignored my sympathetically heaving insides and stepped back into the pod again. Still no Farrell, Guthrie, Markham, or Peterson, no weapons, no trace, not even a blood stain. I felt my own head spin. I took two or three very deep breaths and closed my eyes for a moment. Then I stepped back out of the pod and ran my eyes over those left.

'Murdoch, Ritter – to me.'

She straightened up, wiping her mouth. 'What are you doing?'

'Rescue mission. You two; get your weapons charged up and back here to me.'

'No.'

'What?'

'They're dead. I told you.'

I said very gently, 'Be that as it may, Izzie, we still go back for the bodies. You get yourself upstairs and I'll see to this.'

'No, I told you, they're dead. There's no point.'

I was hanging on by my fingertips here. I wished to God she'd stop saying, 'They're dead.'

'We don't leave our people behind, Izzie, you know that. Don't worry, no one's expecting you to go back; you've more than done your bit tonight. I'll go. Are you ready, guys?'

'Stand down, you men. Back in line.' They looked at me, which pissed her off no end, but she had the seniority, so I kept my face neutral. They slowly backed off, not looking happy at all.

I tried again. 'Look, Izzie, we have to go back for them. We can't …'

'For fuck's sake, Maxwell!'

Her voice rose to a scream. She never swore. I was startled into silence. 'I know you never listen to anyone else, but do you ever stop to listen to yourself? How many more people do you want to kill tonight? This whole cluster-fuck is your fault. You're a disaster. Everything you touch, everywhere you go, people die. You brought Dieter back in pieces. You didn't bring Sussman back at all. The Boss is down. Half the unit is injured. Farrell, Guthrie, Peterson, Markham – dead. All thanks to you. There will be no rescue mission. No more lives will be risked over this. Now get your report written up and see me in the morning so I can decide what to do with you.'

'Fine, yes, whatever. But for God's sake, you've got to send someone. If not me, then –'

'Jesus fucking Christ, Maxwell, what do I have to do to get through to you?' She really was screaming now. I could hear people breathing in the silence.

I struggled for the calm I wasn't feeling. 'Izzie, I know you don't understand how important this is, but …' I could not have said anything worse but I was hurt, frightened, and fighting rising panic.

'No, Maxwell, what is important is the safety of every person in this unit, not your own over-inflated ego. You will – where are you going?' I had stepped into the pod.

'I told you. Rescue mission. I'll go alone. No risk to anyone.'

'Murdoch, Ritter, get her out of there.'

I've never known the unit so quiet. There was nothing, no sound, no background noises, just the total absence of any sound at all except for the blood thudding in my head. I tried again.

'Izzie, I'll go alone if that's what's concerning you. Just let me get a weapon.'

'No!' She was verging on the hysterical.

'Then I'll go without one.'

'You will not go at all.'

She turned and began to walk away. I reached out, grabbed her arm and yanked her back, harder than I intended. 'Izzie …' and realised what I had done. Everything went very still. She looked down at my hand. I let go and stepped back. Her eyes glittered and she looked half mad.

'Maxwell, with immediate effect you are dismissed from this unit.' She turned to Murdoch. 'She is to be gone within one hour. She may take personal items only. She turned back to me. 'No books, no printed material of any kind. No electronics. Your computer will be sterilised and returned to you after a security check. You will not now or ever discus anything pertaining to this unit with anyone. You will not contact any member of this unit. Ever. For you, St Mary's no longer exists. Now get out. If you are still here in one hour, I will have you arrested. Murdoch, she is to speak to no one and no one is to speak to her. Is that clear?' She raised her head and glared around the hangar.

No response. They were in shock. I was in shock. She nodded to Murdoch. 'Get her out of this building. Everyone else remain here for one hour.'

I couldn't have moved to save my life. Murdoch, who looked pretty distressed himself, took my arm, probably more gently than she would have liked, and we began the long walk back to my room. Ritter fell in behind.

As we passed the kitchen, I saw Mrs Mack directing operations. She came out. 'Where is everyone?'

I waited for Murdoch to speak but he said nothing. Neither did Ritter. I remembered I wasn't the only person who'd lost someone tonight.

Mrs Mack said, 'Max?' and looked at each of us in turn.

Finally, in a tiny, dead voice I found from somewhere, I said, 'They're … confined to Hawking for an hour. They'll be gagging for a drink … Can you get that lot on trolleys and take it down to them, please?'

She nodded and looked in puzzlement at Murdoch and Ritter who were looking at the floor. Neither of them looked happy at all and for a moment I wondered … but Guthrie trained his people well. They would follow their orders.

I stumbled up the stairs to my room. My home for the last five years. But not any longer. I stood blankly by the bed and it was Murdoch who reached my sports bag down off the wardrobe. He unzipped it, checked it was empty, and put it on the bed.

'Come on, Max. Time's passing.'

As if anyone knew that better than me.

What I wanted to do was curl up in a corner, turn my face to the wall, and just let go. What I had to do was pull myself together, pack what I needed, abandon the rest, and find somewhere to go,

And not think. Don't think. Don't think about anything. I'd been trained to deal with catastrophe. First rule. Deal with the now. Deal with everything else later. It's not as if any of it was important. Nothing was important any more. Nothing mattered.

I picked up the Chief's photo and pushed it into an outside pocket. Murdoch pulled it back out again. 'No, Max. Sorry.'

'It's a personal possession.'

'It's a picture of a member of this unit.'

My voice wobbled. 'Not any more it's not.'

'Can't allow it. Sorry.' And his voice wasn't steady either.

I wouldn't let go. He tried to pry my fingers away.

'Max, please don't make me hurt you.'

I remembered this was Big Dave Murdoch and no matter how many times he'd fallen over for me in self defence classes, at the end of the day, he could hurt me badly. He wouldn't want to, but he would.

He wouldn't let me take the Trojan Horse, either.

'Dave,' I pleaded and my voice cracked. He shook his head, not looking at me.

Nor my little book about Agincourt, the only thing left from my childhood; nor any of my other books; nor any of my artwork. Just underwear, a set of sweats, jeans, a couple of hoodies, and some tees. I had to leave behind my beautiful, golden dress with the beautiful, golden memories. I wore my boots and riding mac. I took toiletries from the bathroom and a towel. And that was it. Five years of my life and I was leaving with even less than I started.

Mrs Partridge arrived with some paperwork to sign. While she was laying it out on the table I covered the Horse and photo with the towel, meaning to pick the whole lot up together and just casually drop in my bag. Murdoch and Ritter waited outside while I re-signed all the secure paperwork again. She handed me a month's pay. When I looked across, the towel was neatly folded and the Horse and photo were gone. It seemed so unnecessarily cruel. Shock and disbelief were wearing off and the full awfulness finally dawning on me. Where would I go? What would I do? I opened my wallet and slowly handed over my ID card.

I looked outside. It was dark. It was raining. It was half past ten at night. I didn't even know what day of the week it was. Who was Prime Minister? What was happening in the world? Too late now to remember the Boss's advice about maintaining a grip on the here and now. Mrs Partridge collected her papers, regarded me expressionlessly for a moment, and then swept out. There was no reason to stay. I was no longer a member of the unit.

Flanked by Murdoch and Ritter, I walked slowly down the stairs. No one spoke. The building was completely silent. No one was around. I thought Kal might manage a small appearance somehow, but there was no sign of her or anyone. No one came to say goodbye. I was officially a non-person. I never thought I would leave like this. I turned up my collar, huddled into my clothes, and crept across the Hall like the ghost I already was.

A troubled-looking Mr Strong unbolted the front doors and I passed through them for the last time. No one spoke. Bending my head against the rain, I trudged down the drive. The gates opened silently in front of me and closed as silently behind me.

There I was, just gone eleven at night in the pouring rain with the gates of St Mary's locked behind me and no idea what to do next or where to go. I turned and looked back one last time. Lights blazed everywhere. Sick Bay was lit up like a Christmas tree. Peterson would never stand underneath the windows again, waiting for his love to shower him with dog ends. A door opened somewhere and light streamed out briefly, then disappeared as quickly as it had come. Somewhere in there, Kal was grieving for Peterson. The Boss was fighting for his life. Murdoch would be mourning Guthrie …

And the man I loved had been dead for sixty-seven million years. I dropped my bag onto the wet road, leaned forward, and put my hands on my knees. Huge, thick, rasping sobs tore at my throat. I fell to my knees, curled into a ball and wrapped my arms around my head. The rain drummed on my back. Wet soaked through my clothes.

I'd always said my life began the day I walked through the gates of St Mary's and now I'd walked back out again and it was ended.

I have no memory of how I got to Rushford, or why, but having got there, I lacked the strength or the will to go any further. Every time I tried to get to grips with things, my mind just slithered away.

The bit in my head that had kept me safe through childhood found me a two-room flat in an old building somewhere at the back of St Stephen's Street. It was cold, damp, and dirty and I could barely afford it. I applied for jobs but rarely received even an acknowledgment. With no employment history, no previous employers, and no references, I had no chance.

It was an alien world. I'd been nearly five years at St Mary's and everything had moved on and left me behind. It would have been a difficult readjustment if I'd left the unit normally, but this sudden displacement left me bewildered and lost. I had no place here. I was more at home in the Cretaceous period than in modern-day Rushford. Grief and shock kicked down my defences and left me vulnerable and exposed in a world I couldn't comprehend.

I had one small electric cooking ring and lived off baked beans and packet soup but even so, my meagre savings melted away like ice in the sun.

The cold didn't help. There were days when I barely moved, let alone went out. I was filled with a dreadful lethargy that could not be shaken off. I cut my hair. I couldn't keep it clean and drying it was impossible in my damp, mildewy rooms.

Besides, I didn't need it any more. It stuck out in spikes everywhere. It scared me – God knows what it did to everyone else.

One day passed so much like another that I was shocked to find three months had passed. Small signs of spring began to appear. Then I began to cough.

I ignored it to begin with. I've been injured a lot; some of it friendly fire, but I'm rarely ill and waited for it to go away. It didn't. I drank copious amounts of water and sweated it all back out again half an hour later. My temperature was so high I wondered if I could hook myself up to the broken water heater. My chest grew tight and hurt. Then my back hurt. Breathing in was one pain and breathing out was another.

And then, one morning, I had a different pain.

Fortunately, I lived in St Stephen's Street with the Free Clinic just around the corner. I got myself there somehow, expecting antibiotics and maybe painkillers if their budget was reasonably healthy. I sat in a cubicle and tried to explain. I saw people's lips move, but fortunately, none of this was anything to do with me, so I curled into a ball, closed my eyes, and let someone else sort it all out.

Twelve

Knowing you are pregnant for only twenty minutes is not the same as being pregnant for only twenty minutes. I wish it was.

I stared up at the ceiling above me and tried not to think about anything. In my head, Izzie Barclay said, 'Everything you touch, everywhere you go, people die,' over and over again, relentless and unstoppable. She was right. How many more lives would be lost because of me? How much more damage could I do? The last piece of Leon Farrell had gone. Now he really was dead. Now I really was alone.

They chucked me out after four days.

I stood outside in the sleety rain and tried to think. Even my bones were cold and that had nothing to do with the temperature. A passing van splashed me with cold water and I realised I'd been standing there for over half an hour.

My future looked bleak and consisted of a cold, damp, mould-filled flat and very little money. There was nothing left for me. I'd lost the man I loved and I'd lost his child too. Suddenly I was so tired, tired of everything, tired of trying to get by, tired of struggling with love and loss. I felt as if the strings of my life had been cut with a pair of scissors. This was the end for me. I'd had enough.

This is how it ends. One minute you have a job, somewhere to live, friends, and no provision for a future you never expected to have. Take away the job and the friends and the home disappear all by themselves. Then the last money is gone, benefits that were inadequate anyway are never paid, the rent is due, and suddenly a whole life just crashes to the ground, never to get back up again.

I wandered slowly down the High Street, stopping outside

The Copper Kettle. Today's special was roast beef and I had just enough money. I could stick two fingers up at the universe and go with a full stomach. It seemed like a plan.

It was warm and steamy inside. I ordered the beef, with a pot of tea to follow. I cleared my plate and by eating slowly, managed to make it last over an hour. The pot of tea lasted another half an hour and I read all their newspapers as well. I was in no hurry, but they would be closing soon. It was time to go.

As I began to get my things together, there was a bustle of movement; someone pulled out a chair and said 'Hello, Madeleine, how are you?'

It was Mrs De Winter. I stared at her. Apart from a few glimpses at St Mary's over the years, I hadn't seen her since she handed me over to the Boss.

I managed to say, 'I'm fine, thank you. How are you?'

She said, 'Oh, fine,' and touched the pot. 'Let's have a refill, shall we?' She signalled to the waitress and ordered more tea. I started to get up and then wondered where I was going to go and sat back down again.

She chattered aimlessly while we were served, but as soon as the waitress left she leaned closer and said in a low voice, 'Where have you been? I've been looking everywhere for you.'

'Have you? Why?'

'Dr Bairstow wanted you found as soon as possible. He's been really worried about you. We all have been. And rightly so, I think. You look terrible. What's been happening?'

'I've been here in Rushford since I left St Mary's,' I said carefully. 'But these last few days I've been in the clinic.'

'Nothing serious, I hope?'

I lost my baby.

'No, I had a bit of a chest infection, but I'm all clear now. And I must be going.' I really don't know what stupidity was pulling me out of the warm café and back to my spore-ridden ice-cube. Pride probably, but pride doesn't keep you warm.

She put her hand on my arm. 'Wait a minute. I need to speak to you. But not here.' She looked at me carefully. 'I have a proposition for you. I'd like you to come back to my house.' I started to speak. 'No, just for a few days. I have some of your things with me. My sister gave them to me for safe keeping.'

'Your sister?'

'Cleo Partridge – my sister.'

Cleo? Sister? *Now* I knew who Mrs Partridge reminded me of.

I considered this, trying hard to close my ears to the siren song of a warm house, maybe another meal. I opened my mouth to say no and it came out yes. I felt ashamed. I felt even more ashamed when she paid the bill. We argued. I lost, but told myself I could leave the money at her house later. She insisted we drive to my rooms, where, under her gentle bullying, I packed my stuff. It still all fitted in one small sports bag. I looked around. I knew, for one reason or another, I'd never come back here. I slammed my door behind me and left the keys on the table by the front door and never looked back.

She had a very large house on the outskirts of town. 'I sometimes do B & B,' she said. 'Life is boring since I retired. I get to meet some interesting people. But the house is empty at the moment.'

We went up to the big double room at the front. It was warm and nicely furnished. I loved it. 'Make yourself comfortable. I'll get your stuff and see you downstairs.'

I thought about unpacking, but it seemed presumptuous, so I left it. I met her downstairs in her big kitchen and we sat at the table. She pushed over a small box. Inside, I found the photo of the Chief and me, together with my Trojan Horse.

I looked at them both and then slowly reached out to the photo. The sense of loss cut through me like a knife. I stood it on the table in front of me. Him and me, laughing together about daffodils, of all things. I touched the frame with one finger. Then I fished out the little Horse. Still as exquisite as the day he made it for me. Other memories rolled over me in waves.

I could have shown the photo to my son and said, 'Look, this is your father.'

I could have shown the Trojan Horse to my son and said, 'Look, your father made this.'

I said hoarsely, 'These mean a great deal to me. Please convey my thanks to Mrs Partridge when you next see her.'

'I will. May I?' She picked up the Horse. 'Is this a model of the Wooden Horse of Troy?'

'Yes. The Chief made it for me. He always used to say he would have given a lot to see Odysseus and his men dropping out from under the Horse's tail. He didn't believe the trapdoor was in the belly because he said that would have weakened the structure, but he was just winding me up.'

She turned the Horse over. 'Well, he's put the trapdoor in the belly, nonetheless.'

I took the Horse from her. She was right. I shrugged. 'He was just teasing me,' and put it down.

She poured another cup of tea. 'So tell me what's been happening to you?'

I countered, 'If you'll tell me what's been happening at St Mary's.'

'Nothing's been happening. That's the point.' she said angrily. 'That stupid woman has everything nailed down. No one's going anywhere. Well, they can't. She has no historians left.'

'Wait,' I said, alarmed. 'Dr Bairstow? He's not dead, is he?'

'No, you can't kill Edward, but he's still on "sick leave", and she's doing her best to keep him out.'

'And she has no historians?'

'Well, no, how can she? You're gone, Peterson's dead, and Kalinda ...'

A cold hand touched me. 'What about Kalinda?'

'It's rather funny, actually. Barclay started throwing her tiny weight around, introducing inspections and paperwork and bureaucracy and I got the impression that spurred on by the redoubtable Miss Black, they all rather enjoyed a spell of civil disobedience. It all got a bit out of hand though when she tried to put Dieter on a charge for the damage to Pod Eight. Apparently, words were exchanged and Miss Black and Mr Dieter left the building to cheers and applause.'

I had to laugh. Good old Kalinda. I couldn't help wondering just how civil the disobedience had been. I knew, none better, how very creative St Mary's could be in their disobedience while actually doing exactly as they'd been told.

'But, of course, the key people are now all gone. There's only Andrew Rapson left and he's keeping his head down. And Doctor Foster, but they tell me the fight's gone out of her. I don't think she realised how deeply attached she was to Peterson. Barclay's running a historical research organisation without any historical researchers. Nothing's moving and people are leaving in their droves.

'So, tell me about you.' She was relentless. She had been a schoolteacher after all. In the end, I just gave her the bare facts. Sacked. No employment history. Unable to get work. No money. Cold flat. Chest infection.

I managed to get it all out in about six brief sentences. She patted my hand gently but said nothing, which I appreciated. I never know what to do with sympathy. But she kept patting.

'What? I said.

'I'm so angry. And so is Edward. This should not have happened. We don't just throw our people out into the streets, Max. Do you think this hasn't happened before? There's an exit procedure. You should have been offered alternative employment at Thirsk for a year, to give you some sort of employment history and ease you back into outside life. Remember Stevens? And Rutherford? Do you think we just cast them adrift? She knew this. She's a spiteful, jealous cow!'

She brooded a while and then said with determination, 'You

207

must stay here. No, don't say anything, Max. I watched you through the café window and I don't know what you were thinking, or maybe I do, but I'd like you to think of my house as a haven, at least for a few days while you recover your strength. I hope you'll stay. This is a big house, you know, and sometimes …' She trailed away to give me time to appreciate her loneliness. The redoubtable Mrs De Winter had never had a lonely moment in her life, but was making me a face-saving offer I couldn't refuse.

I smiled a little and said, 'Well, if you're sure I won't be in the way …' She laughed and after a while, so did I.

To relieve the embarrassment I picked up the Horse again. It felt good in my hand and it comforted me a little. Strange about the trapdoor though. He'd always been so definite about them wriggling out from under the Horse's tail like so many heroic tapeworms. I looked under the tail and saw a tiny hole, exactly where …

I said, 'Do you have a paperclip?' She looked surprised but rummaged in a drawer and produced a box. I took one, un-bent it, and inserted it into the tiny hole. There was a click, the trapdoor in the Horse's belly sprang open and a little box clattered onto the table. The remote control for his pod.

Something inside me woke up.

I tried to think clearly. I could use this. I could return, now, to the Cretaceous, as near as I could get to that awful night and bring them back. If they were still alive. And if they weren't … well, that wasn't important. The point was that I could go. Now. I started to get up.

'No, wait,' she said. Being a teacher she obviously did mind reading as well. 'No, I don't mean you can't go. Obviously you must go, but you'll only get one chance and you have to do it properly. Now, the first thing is to bring the pod here so we can check supplies, equipment, and suchlike. Once we've ascertained our resources, we can make a proper plan.'

One surprise after another. She knew not only what the

device was, but what it related to. I was beginning to have a great deal of curiosity about these sisters.

'Do you have a back garden?'

She flung the curtain aside to display a back garden the size of half Rushfordshire. I'd never used this gizmo before, or seen it used, but it seemed relatively simple, even for me. There was only one button. Presumably you pressed it. Walking out into the garden, I selected a spot and, hoping it had a built in safety margin and wouldn't materialise on top of me, I pressed it. Ten feet away from me, one of those rotary washing-line thingies crumpled flat under the weight of an invisible pod.

'Sorry,' I said. 'Learner driver.' Thank God, she seemed more relaxed about this sort of thing than her sister Mrs Partridge did. I stood at where I thought the front would be and said, hopefully, 'Door.' It opened and I stepped inside.

Nothing had changed since I was last here. I inhaled the familiar smell. This was my world. This was where I belonged. I wondered when he had programmed me into the controls. Why had he given me a remote but not told me? He always maintained he knew nothing of the future after the day he arrived in my timeline, but I sometimes wondered. And if he didn't know, I bet the Boss did. I couldn't imagine the Boss not knowing anything.

I became aware of Mrs De Winter standing on the threshold. 'Come in. Please.' She began opening lockers and I activated the console.

'Can you do it?' she asked. I was flicking through past co-ordinates.

'Theoretically, yes. His last jump but two was to the Cretaceous. I should recognise the coordinates.'

I heard my own voice saying to him, 'But why did he send you? You couldn't interfere – what was the point?' Was the point to get the co-ordinates into the memory so I could use them later? Forget it. Deal with the now.

'Yes, here they are. I need to sit down and work out how

many days elapsed between these and our mission to the Cretaceous. Then I should maybe add a day for safety's sake – I don't want two of me there – and if they're alive then I should be able to get them out. I hope.'

I wasn't anywhere near as confident as I sounded. This was not my pod. I had no idea how it handled. It might not even accept commands from me.

'Do you have a calculator?' She nodded and slipped out, returning a few minutes later with that, two pens, and a pile of paper. I thanked her absently and began to fire things up.

I sat and worked it all out very slowly and carefully, showing my calculations in a way I hadn't done since basic training. I checked everything. It seemed OK. I worked it backwards and the co-ordinates matched.

Mrs De Winter came back. I realised I'd been working for two hours. She asked me how I was getting on. I showed her and asked her to check. She said, 'But I can't do that!'

'No,' I said. 'But you can check the maths, which is my weak spot.'

She did so and twenty minutes later said, 'Your calculations are correct,' which was encouraging. I just hoped they were the right calculations. She stocked the chiller with beer. I hadn't thought of that.

And then, just as everything was going so well, I started to lay in the figures and the bastard computer wouldn't accept them. Initially, I didn't know if it was me or my figures it disliked, but it accepted commands for the door and lights happily enough, so it had to be the figures. I added one day, increasing the interval between our night attack and my proposed new jump, and it spat that back at me as well. I added another day and another and with increasing dismay, another. All the time, Mrs De Winter stood quietly beside me, whispering, 'Keep trying, Max. Keep trying.'

Finally, it accepted the co-ordinates for no less than eleven days after that disastrous night. Eleven days! How could they survive that long? No one knew better than me how long eleven days could be in the Cretaceous period. And these were four men, possibly badly hurt, bleeding, and low on ammunition, no shelter, no food, and no clean water; not prepped in any way.

'Stop that!' said Mrs De Winter, accurately guessing what was going on in my head. 'They'll be fine. They'll be tucked away, keeping themselves safe, ready for rescue, you'll see. There might even be other survivors there. They may not be alone.'

I shook my head. 'I doubt it. Eleven days. It will be a miracle if anyone's left alive.'

'It's Guthrie, Farrell, Peterson, and the indestructible Markham. Do you want to put money on it? Now, in addition to essential beer supplies, there is bottled water, and some sandwiches for you. There are two torches with working batteries. Eight flares in that locker over there – fizzers I think you call them. As for weapons, there's a wide-angle blaster, charged. There's a stun gun showing a small charge and a jumbo-sized pepper spray, half-full. There are matches, fire-lighters, and toilet paper. What else could you need?'

What else indeed?

I took a deep breath and looked at Mrs De Winter. She said, 'I could come too,' but I shook my head.

'If I don't come back, someone will need to tell the Boss where I've gone and why. Don't let him waste anyone coming after me.'

'You'll be back. I know it.'

I had a sudden thought, just as she stepped out of the door. 'What day is it today?'

'Friday.'

Oh. Bugger.

She stepped outside and I closed the door behind her. Alone now, the familiar pod smell wrapped itself around me. Hot electrics, wet carpet, the toilet, the incinerator, a faint whiff of cabbage; awakening memories as painful as lemon juice in a paper cut. Eau de pod; the most evocative smell in the world.

I eased myself into the seat and checked the console. Everything seemed OK.

'Initiate jump.' And the world went white.

And stayed white. What? It was foggy. It was bloody foggy! God Almighty, does nothing ever go right? This meant the eight fizzers were useless. Ditto a fire – the smoke would be invisible in all this murk. Could the universe never cut me a break? I had a think and then started rummaging through the lockers. There was bound to be something somewhere. There was. I found four or five discs including *Sergeant Pepper* – an omen if ever I saw one. Now all I had to do was switch from internal to external speakers and even I could do that.

Five minutes later I was ready to rock and roll. Literally. I'd checked the proximity readings and nothing was moving anywhere. But I reckoned it was only just past dawn which gave me all day. At night, if the fog had cleared then I could use the fizzers. Or light a fire. Of course, all this sound and light would attract the attention of everything within a five-mile radius, but that was OK. So long as my guys knew I was here, we could work out how to dodge the wildlife later. The important thing was them knowing I was here. If they were still alive. Eleven days was a lifetime. I threw that thought out of my head and cautiously opened the door. I couldn't see my hand in front of my face. Everything was strangely silent. Well, I'd soon put a stop to that.

I de-activated the camouflage device because I wanted to be highly visible and muttering, 'Balls to the wall, guys,' flipped a switch and a second later The Beatles were asking a startled prehistoric world to picture themselves in a boat on a river. With tangerine trees and marmalade skies. I shut the door and fortified myself with some fruit drink.

There's a protocol for this sort of thing. Certain information should be broadcast calmly and clearly, giving location, routes, warnings, number and disposition of rescuers – all that sort of thing. I'd done it scores of times in simulations and now, now that it really mattered, now that lives depended on it, I couldn't remember a bloody word.

Worried that my voice would let me down as badly as my memory, I switched off the music and opened my mouth.

'Gooooooood morning, St Mary's! This is your early morning wake-up call.

'Will all passengers returning to St Mary's today please immediately make their way to approximately one hundred yards south of Ground Zero, just under the tree line.

'Please have your boarding cards ready for inspection and your passports open at the photograph page.

'Please be aware that anyone pissing off the pilot will not be allowed to board and since the pilot's already both pissed and pissed off, there's a very good chance some of you won't make the cut.

'All passengers for the red-eye to Rushford please make your way to the boarding gate immediately. Hands off cocks and on with socks, boys, you're going home.'

I shut down the mike, glugged a little more slivovitz, and checked outside again. As the sun rose, the fog lifted. The good news was that I was almost exactly where I wanted to be. The bad news was that it was a scene of total devastation. Trees and branches were snapped off and strewn around at crazy angles. Tangled and twisted debris lay everywhere in piles. Presumably the result of the blast; or maybe stampeding dinosaurs. Across the badly churned up ground, not far away, I saw that old cliché, the smoking crater. This was the site of the big bang, obviously. A pall of greasy smoke still hung over everything, even after all this time. It had to have been one hell of an explosion. Worst of all, reptilian bones and body parts were everywhere. These were the remains of the animals (and maybe people) who hadn't made it through that night. I'd try and have a closer look later on.

I picked up the big blaster and the heavy-duty pepper spray. Climbing up onto the roof, I fired off my first fizzer. It wobbled a bit but went screaming up into the bright sky where it hung, a big, red, fizzing ball and a beacon for miles around. I had enough for eight hours – one an hour. After that I'd have to light a fire. After that I'd stay until the food ran out. After that – I had no plans.

I laid the blaster on the roof beside me and hung the pepper spray on my belt, just in case. Pulling out binoculars I slowly scanned three hundred and sixty degrees; round and round and round, along the tree line, behind boulders, along the streambed, checking for any sort of movement, anywhere.

There was nothing, but give them time. If carnivores had been scavenging the site then they might have moved a mile or so away, looking for water and shelter and staying out of trouble. I launched another fizzer and continued rotating. Several times something big crashed in the forest but I saw nothing. Each fizzer produced another cacophony of sound but I reckoned this was good. Everything alive must know I was here. So if they didn't come, they weren't alive. I tried not to think about that, but it kept thudding away in my brain. I kept going. Round and round. Fire another fizzer. Round and round. Lives could depend on my vigilance.

Noon passed. I'd used half my supply of fizzers and still nothing and no one. I jumped down, took off my jacket, and used it to collect pine cones and small pieces of wood. I made sure some of it was damp. I would light a fire and use the smoke to mark my position when the flares ran out. Tying the jacket arms to hold it all together, I dropped the bundle by the door and went to get a drink. I hadn't realised how thirsty I was. I had another swift slug of something slivovitzy with a glass of water and went back outside.

By mid-afternoon, I felt so weary. My chest hurt and breathing was difficult, but I had to stick with it. I would not let myself believe they were dead. If anyone could survive, it would be these guys.

I lit the fire and watched the smoke rise lazily. There was no wind.

Then, as the shadows lengthened, I caught a flash of movement, just at the edge of the forest, a couple of hundred yards away. And again. With a thumping heart and suddenly unsteady hands, I focused the binoculars and saw four men moving as a group, slowly, along the tree line. I counted again. Four. They were all there.

And at exactly the same moment, with the kind of dreadful inevitability that is so ... dreadfully inevitable ... a T-rex emerged from the other end of the clearing heading on an intercept course. It wasn't huge, so maybe a male or young female. Unaware of our presence, it turned things over and investigated bones. Evidence, had I been in the mood, that T-rex was both a predator and a scavenger. But whichever it was, it would eventually finish between me and them. More balls, more walls!

It could have been worse. One big lizard is easier to deal with than a pack of smaller raptors. I remembered how they'd taken Sussman down.

I jumped down, staggered, and ran to a nearby rock outcrop, away from the pod and shouted, 'Hey! Hey! Over here!' Heads appeared from between the trees. I held up the blaster so they could see it and left it propped against the rocks for them and then took off, running like hell across the rough ground, away from the pod. Get it away from the pod. Give them a chance.

I never think things through. It gave an enthusiastic bellow and thundered after me. However, more by good luck than good judgment, I'd chosen really rough ground, strewn with debris and broken trees, which hampered it more than me. It shouldered its way through the smaller stuff, but its big tail dragged at it every time it had to swerve. I dodged and jinked around tree stumps, boulders and unknown detritus until I was too breathless to move. For a moment's respite, I wedged myself in a crack in a rock and tried to get my breath back. This was a good place to be – it couldn't get to me here.

Too bloody good. It sniffed around for a while and then, baulked of its prey, turned and saw the running figures heading towards the pod. As it took a few paces towards them I squeezed out of the crack and shouted again, waving my arms.

And then the bloody thing stopped, turned, lowered its huge head to my height, and looked at me. Its head was absolutely fucking enormous. It was only about twenty feet away – just one giant stride. It was the most frightening moment of my life. The world receded and all sound died away.

If you see a T-rex in a movie or a holo, they're always so clean, with perfect dental work and nice markings. In the real world they're not like that at all. This one's lower legs and belly were thick with dried mud. Scarred and battered, it had a really gruesome gash down its left flank. Several teeth were missing and its entire snout was caked with dried blood and bits of rotting flesh. Its breath was the most fearsome thing in existence. Saucepan-lid sized nostrils flared in and out, assimilating my unfamiliar scent. The insides were a pale red. I could see its eyes. I don't know why I'd ever thought it wasn't fully grown. It was absolutely colossal. And it was looking at me. Instinct told it to attack. Experience told it to avoid humans. This indecision was saving my life, but not for much longer. Instinct would kick in soon enough.

Sound came back slowly. I could hear its massive breaths whistling in and out of its nostrils. I'd long since stopped breathing myself and slowly, very slowly, I eased the pepper spray from my belt. It lunged. I closed my eyes, held my breath, and squeezed the trigger. It bellowed, enveloping me in a blast of fetid air. I threw myself backwards off the rocks, landing on something hard and uneven. I rolled behind a rock and risked a look. It was shaking its head and shifting its weight from leg to leg, obviously in some discomfort, but not enough to slow it down. In fact, I'd just made it mad. Way to go, Maxwell!

I heard a shout from off to one side and the ground exploded about mid-way between it and me. Nice shot! They'd got the blaster. I waited no longer, turned, and ran as fast as I could for the pod. I could feel the ground shaking under me but dared not look back. Another warning shot. It wheeled away and then came at me again from another angle.

The pod was closer now, but my breath was failing. The legs were still pumping but I was going nowhere. Wreckage lay everywhere and I needed to watch where I was going. Falling now would be the last thing I ever did.

And then I saw something that stopped me dead. Just off to my left was a largish piece of metal, dark green with the letters RD T stencilled in yellow paint.

A voice bellowed, 'Don't bloody stop, you muppet!' Another small explosion behind me. I started forward again, almost finished, and a long arm grabbed me and pulled.

'I've got her. Shoot the bloody thing!'

Now there was a volley of fire. Earth and small rocks rained down upon me. I tried to shout not to kill it, but had no breath left. Another hand grabbed my other arm. One last, lung-bursting effort, we all fell through the door together and the mission ended in the traditional St Mary's manner with a panic-stricken tangle of limbs on the floor and everyone yelling for the door.

Thirteen

For a long time I heard only the sound of panting and the occasional groan. Farrell said, 'Max, are you all right?'

'Of course she's all right,' said Peterson, crossly. 'She fell on me.' Someone rolled off me. I rolled off Peterson and we all got our breath back.

I took stock. The door was safely shut. Something huge and disappointed prowled outside, but I didn't care any more. They were all here. They were safe. For the first time in months, the sun came out. Guthrie stowed their useless weapons. Markham sat against the wall with his elbows resting on his knees and his scorched hands held out in front of him. He had a coating of medical plastic on them, but after eleven days it was peeling away. I reached up and got the med kit. 'Now then, young Markey. How're you doing?'

'I'm OK. It's been a bit of a bugger keeping all these senior staff safe, but yeah, I'm fine. You?'

'Oh, you know, struggling on.'

I turned and found myself face to face with Peterson. Stepping forward, I gave him a hug. He held me tightly.

'Oh God, Max.' He couldn't say any more.

I was a bit choked myself. 'Tim, my dear old friend.' I kissed his cheek. He turned away. Ian Guthrie shook my hand in a grip of iron and in a rare show of affection, clapped me on the shoulder. Obviously an emotional moment for him. This left Leon Farrell.

We looked at each other. I felt awkward. It was Markham who solved the problem. 'Oh, for God's sake, Chief, give the girl a kiss!' So he did. A bone-crushing hug lifted me off my feet. I felt a butterfly-light kiss in my hair. He – they all –

smelled absolutely awful; the cabbage-smelling masking spray, sweat, mud, and they'd all coated themselves liberally in dinosaur shit in an effort to mask their own smell. Having the four of them in such a small space was making the paint bubble.

I opened the chiller and pulled out a six-pack. I think it's fair to say they were impressed.

'Bloody hell!' said Markham. 'You truly are the perfect woman. Will you marry me?'

'I'd love to,' I said. 'Sadly, at the moment I'm unemployed, so I need someone who can support my expensive chocolate habit.'

'No, I'm sorry, absolutely out of the question,' said Peterson. 'There's no way the two of you should ever be joined in matrimony. This world is not yet ready for your offspring.'

I pretended to be insulted, but actually I was quite happy to continue this conversation. I could see Peterson looking around. He would know this was no regular pod. I glanced at the Chief and then looked meaningfully at the seat where he should sit. He shook his head very slightly, so I took it for myself, placing my foot where I could give Peterson a discreet kick when he started asking awkward questions.

He looked me up and down. 'You're looking charmingly informal today. What happened to the dress code and what have you done to your hair?'

'Get used to it. This is not just a hairstyle. This is a way of life.'

'Why are you alone? Where's your wingman?'

'I told you, I've been sacked. I haven't got a wingman. I'm here on my own.'

'Are you saying Kalinda's not involved in this?'

'Kal's no longer at St Mary's. She resigned.'

'What? But if she's gone and we're here then that means there's no historians at St Mary's!'

'Correct. And Dieter's gone too. That's why I'm taking you to Rushford.'

'Didn't you contact Kal when she left?'

'I didn't know she'd gone. I'm forbidden by law to have any sort of contact with any St Mary's personnel, in any timeline. So, if any of you guys grass me up then its fifteen years' hard labour for me.'

'So where did you get the pod from?'

'I stole it,' I said, not without some pride.

He looked around. 'Yes, but …' I pressed his foot. He looked at me, raised an eyebrow and drank his beer. 'Are you drunk?'

'As a newt,' I said happily. 'You think anyone would ever have done this sober?'

'Good point.'

Guthrie was spraying Markham with plastic. Peterson was swilling his beer which left one other. I knew he would be happy to let others talk and then zero in on the detail which wasn't always what I wanted!

He said quietly, 'Why were you sacked?'

'Oh, I got into it with Barclay and was invited to vacate the premises.'

'Why?'

I played stupid. 'Why what?'

'You've lived reasonably peacefully with Miss Barclay for the last five years. Why now, suddenly do you fall out with her?'

I drank some water and looked down at my feet. I really hadn't wanted to do this. But it was better they hear it now, from me, in private.

'I couldn't persuade her to send a rescue team for you.'

It didn't go in for a moment and then Peterson said, 'You mean no one's been looking for us? We thought we just kept missing the search teams. That's why we didn't go far away. We thought …'

Silence. This was what I hadn't wanted to tell them. Each of them had withdrawn into his own thoughts, but their

221

expressions were the same. Each face, already grey-shadowed and haggard grew more so. We're St Mary's – we don't leave our people behind. But they'd been left. If I hadn't come, they would have died here and quite soon too. It was a miracle they'd lasted so long. They would have died waiting for a rescue that would never happen. It hurt me to look at their faces. Disregarding the pain from his hands, Markham crushed his can and tossed it into the bag. Peterson said softly, 'I'm going to have a quiet word with our Miss Barclay.'

'No, you're not,' I said. 'She's mine.'

No one argued.

It was the Chief who asked the question. Only he and I knew how important it was to him. 'What about the Boss? I heard on the chatter he was wounded. If Barclay is in charge then presumably he didn't make it?'

'As far as I know,' I replied, 'he's still recovering from his injuries. He's not yet back at St Mary's anyway.' I took another chug of water. 'So I'm not taking you back there.'

'Oh? And where are we going back to?'

'I'm taking you back to Rushford.'

'Rushford? Why can't we go back to St Mary's?' demanded Markham. 'What's at Rushford?'

'Well, for a start, spicy lamb casserole followed by treacle tart and custard, hot showers, warm beds, more beer than you can handle, and probably a bottle of something potent. But of course, if you're not interested then I'll just release you back into the wild, shall I?'

Typically from Markham, 'So, no women then?'

'Tim,' I said. 'Open the door and throw him out, will you?'

I wanted to hear their stories, but it was important I got them back. I initiated the jump, the world went white, and we were back in Rushford in the dark. Immediately, the back door swung open and a long tongue of light flooded across the dark grass. I opened the door and helped them to their feet.

'Head towards the light.' Not a phrase I ever thought I would get to say. They filed out, heading towards the back door where Mrs De Winter waited for them.

I shut things down and made to follow when Leon stopped me, simply by pulling the back of my jacket. I turned and was in his arms again.

'I knew you would come.'

I hugged him as hard as I could and we took a couple of moments just to be together.

'You'd better go after them,' I said, eventually, 'Markham's quite capable of getting into trouble between here and the back door!' He gave a short laugh and left. I finished with the pod and followed him out, locking the door behind me.

The kitchen was full of light and warmth and noise. The first person I saw was the Boss. Of course, Mrs De Winter would have contacted him as soon as I left. I wondered how long I had been away. About four hours as far as I could see; long enough for fabulous smells to permeate the room. There was no messing about. These guys looked ready to eat the furniture.

We seated ourselves. The Boss stood up. 'A toast, I think. Gentlemen, welcome back.' We all drank to that.

Farrell stood up. 'With your permission, sir. Max, on behalf of all of us, thank you.'

They all said, 'Thank you,' and raised their glasses. Markham winked at me.

I said, 'An honour and a privilege, guys,' and glowed inside.

A huge pot steamed in the middle of the table and we served ourselves with the best lamb stew I've ever eaten. I cut up Markham's meat for him.

Beer flowed and the talk got louder. Obviously we were desperate to know what had happened to them and they needed no encouragement.

As I expected, things were fairly straightforward until the explosion. People were thrown around all over the place. Reptiles and tourists bounced off each other to the detriment of the tourists. Fighting their way through the smoke, dazed and disoriented, Guthrie and Farrell lost each other. Peterson, dispatched by Barclay to find them, got lost himself, fell over Markham, and nearly got himself shot. No one saw any glimpse of Barclay.

I mulled this over as they ate. There was something …

The four of them were hoovering up everything on the table, laughing with each other, making private jokes and winding each other up and then it happened. One minute I was chuckling at Markham and then all at once a wave of exhaustion swept over me as the events of the last months suddenly presented their bill. Things blurred. The large meal and alcohol hadn't helped at all. I got to my feet.

'If you'll all excuse me,' I said. 'Suddenly I'm very tired and can't keep my eyes open. I'll see you all tomorrow.'

They surprised me. They all stood up. Guthrie opened the door for me and the Boss offered me his arm and walked me to the door. 'Goodnight, Miss Maxwell, and thank you again.'

'An honour and a privilege, sir.'

I meant to put my clothes out for washing as Mrs De Winter had requested, but only remembered after I'd climbed into bed and it was too much effort to get back out again. I also meant to take a few minutes to savour the luxury of a warm bed and clean sheets (indeed, any sheets at all) but I fell asleep as soon as my head hit the pillow.

I woke later, vaguely aware of someone climbing in beside me. I hoped it was Leon but was too far gone to care. If this was one of *those* books, there would now be three pages of head-banging sex. The reality was that he pulled me close, whispered, 'Mfhbnnntx,' and I pulled his arm over me like a cover and muttered, 'Trout,' and that was pretty much it.

I woke reasonably early the next morning and slowly took stock. I could see a mop of dark hair on the pillow beside me. I lifted the sheet just to check I was in bed with the right man.

Typical – our first night ever in a proper bed and both of us too knackered to do anything about it.

I listened carefully and could just faintly hear crockery being bashed about. Mrs De Winter was up and in the kitchen. I slipped out of bed, splashed water on my face, dressed, and padded downstairs.

Pushing open the kitchen door, I was astonished to see the Boss limping around, laying the table for breakfast. He looked up. 'Good morning, Miss Maxwell. Would you like some tea? The kettle has just boiled.'

'Um …'

'I didn't get a chance last night to say how pleasant it is to see you again. Please, come in and sit a moment.'

I didn't work for him anymore and for a brief, suicidal moment considered asserting my independence and remaining standing. Good sense and cowardice prevailed.

'You left abruptly last night.'

'Yes,' I lied. 'I was tired.'

'Really?'

Time to put the record straight. 'I've been dismissed, sir. I was chucked out. Hurled out, actually. On top of that, I'm guilty of stealing government property from a secure establishment, consorting with St Mary's personnel after having been expressly forbidden to do so and contravening … Well, I'm always guilty of contravening something, so just fill in the blank space with the contravention of your choice.'

'Miss Maxwell, you have been, still are, and always will be a member of St Mary's. I regard you as one of the key members of my unit and it would cause me considerable concern (and surprise) if, at any point, you weren't contravening something, somewhere.'

I couldn't look at him. He watched me for a while and then said quietly, 'I understand.' I snatched a glance. He was Dr Bairstow and because he was Dr Bairstow he really did understand. He leaned forward. 'Return to St Mary's and I'll give you what you want.'

'And that would be?'

'Isabella Barclay.'

I used the long pause to pull myself together. Then I nodded. He refilled my mug, poured out a second one for the Chief, and said, 'Breakfast in one hour.'

I said, 'Yes, sir,' but also, because he was Dr Bairstow, he had to have the last word.

'Miss Maxwell.'

'Yes, sir?'

'Grow your hair.'

'Already on it, sir!' and whisked myself out of the door before he could say anything else. Normal service had been resumed.

Back in my room he was just pulling himself into a sitting position and thumping his pillows. I handed him his tea and said, 'Hi, how are you feeling?'

'I was a little worried it was a dream, but no, here you are and with tea. Do you have to work at being so perfect?'

'No, it's effortless.'

I got settled and looked at him. He still looked thin and exhausted, but the awful grey look had gone.

'I like the beard.'

He rubbed his raspy chin. 'Oh, that's going as soon as I can lay my hands on a razor.'

I rubbed my spiky hair. 'I know the feeling,' and he laughed which was good to hear, but there was some awkwardness.

He said, 'You don't look so good.'

Now was the moment to say. Now was the moment to tell him. Say something. Now. I bottled out. 'Chest infection, but all gone now,' and sipped my tea.

To break the silence, he said, 'I know what happened to me. What happened to you?'

I cuddled my tea. 'Oh, you know ... bitchfight with Barclay,

226

chucked out, flat in Rushford, Mrs De Winter, found the remote, stole the pod, came to rescue my boys. Same old same old.'

He grinned at me from under his tousled hair. His eyes looked very bright. 'I've got to know – tell me about the bitchfight. Were you wearing leather? Was there mud?'

I couldn't help laughing. 'You wish! It was quite dull actually. Nowhere near fantasy standards.'

'I don't understand why you went to Rushford. Why on earth didn't you go to Thirsk like good ex-employees are supposed to do?'

I snapped in justifiable exasperation. 'Well and so I would have done if I had known, but since I got marched out of the place with less than an hour's notice and with barely the clothes I stood up in, there wasn't time to say goodbye to anyone, let alone conduct an exit interview.'

No sooner were the words out than I realised I had said too much. I'm hopeless.

'Wait! You didn't get the month's notice?'

'No.'

'The twelve months' employment at Thirsk?'

'No.'

'The references? The employment history?'

'Again, no.'

He was angry now. I could see it in his eyes.

'So now tell me what really happened.'

My natural instinct is to keep secrets. Not to make things any worse. On the other hand, he'd told me his secrets. Now I should tell him mine. To make it easier for me, I didn't look at him. He got nearly everything, although I did try to play it down a little. In this quiet, warm room it didn't seem real. I described the black mould, trying to make that funnier than it was, too. Some vain attempt to divert the conversation, I suppose.

He said nothing the whole time and even though I knew

better, I kept talking to fill the silence.

'So the mould got bigger and annexed the bedroom, but that was OK because I was into one-room living by then anyway, so I could lie in bed and watch TV. And I thought it was working, because I woke one night feeling quite hot and although I had a bit of a temperature, I was quite pleased because I was warm. Which was really stupid, because it was a chest infection and it got worse and my chest hurt a bit and I got hotter so I thought I'd better go and maybe get some antibiotics. So I went to the Free Clinic and I thought they'd just give me something and chuck me out again, but they didn't and I was in there four days, I suppose because of all the upheaval and not eating much which wasn't really my fault and I was too fat anyway. They kept me as long as they could, but they wanted the bed, so I went into town because it didn't matter any more and met Mrs De Winter, who offered me a room here for a little while. I felt a bit guilty, but she insisted and I was glad not to have to go back and face the mould again. And she gave me the photo and your Trojan Horse, which I'd had to leave behind and I was so happy to have them and then the remote fell out onto the table, so I worked out the co-ordinates while Mrs De Winter got the supplies together. But I couldn't get any closer than eleven days, no matter how hard I tried, because the computer just wouldn't accept it. So I whopped in the closest co-ordinates I could get, crossed all my fingers, and punched it and when I saw the devastation outside I really thought I was too late; but I'm not good enough to override your computer's safety protocols and I just couldn't get any nearer than eleven days and I'm really sorry.'

I stopped then because I was going blue.

There was the most appalling silence. I mean, really awful. It wasn't just him not saying anything; it was things not being said, if that makes sense. And it went on for ages. I wondered what, out of my pathetic catalogue of catastrophe, he would pull out first. I put my fist to my chest and tried not to cough.

'What do you mean, "Because it didn't matter anymore"?'

Of everything, I hadn't expected that. 'What?'

'You said, "I went into town because it didn't matter" What was that all about?'

All that gabble and he picked on that one little phrase. Tell him. Tell him now.

I drew a ragged breath and said, 'Because you were gone. St Mary's was gone. Everything was gone. I had no money, no job and no way of getting one. I was cold and ill. I was head sick and heartsick and nothing really mattered any more. You said, "I knew you would come," as if I'd done something marvellous, but I got it all wrong. You guys are alive through your own efforts, not mine.'

'So, you get discharged from hospital, still not recovered from a serious illness at … what … eleven a.m.? You stop for a quick lunch, meet a friend, steal a pod from a top-security establishment, do a series of complex equations, and an hour later you're skipping around the Cretaceous, rescuing four men and facing down the world's greatest predator with a can of pepper spray and a hard look. I think you're pretty amazing.'

I smiled, shook my head, had a good cough, and finished my tea. We weren't talking about what we really should be.

'So Max, how are you? Really?'

Now was the moment to tell him. I bottled out – again.

'Really, really glad to see you again.'

The moment passed. He leaned over and took the photo from the bedside table. 'I remember this.'

I took it from him and traced my finger around the frame again, then gave it back to him.

'Is this all you brought from St Mary's?'

'No, they wouldn't let me take it away.' We both knew by 'they', I meant Bitchface Barclay. 'I only saw it again yesterday.'

He smiled, looking down at the photo. 'That day seems such a long time ago now. I never forgot your face. I saw it every time I closed my eyes. Whatever you say, I knew you would come. I told the others you would come. You may not think so, but you were saving us long before you arrived with just a bad attitude and a photo to remind you of what I look like.'

'I don't need a photo to know how you look. I know how you look. I know how you sound. I know when you enter a room without lifting my head. I know how I feel when you touch me. I don't need a photo for any of that. I love the photo and I love the horse because you gave them to me.'

In the silence I thought, Shit, shit, shit. There must be women on this planet who know when to shut up. Why can't I be one of them?

'Max, look at me. Look at me.' There was something wrong with his voice. I looked at him. There was something wrong with my eyes.

And I still didn't tell him.

Breakfast was a lively meal. I listened with one ear to the banter, helped Markham as he scattered his food over the table, caught Leon's eye occasionally, and all the time I was thinking.

Finally, after about an hour and just as the toaster began to overheat, we got down to talking about how to get back to St Mary's. I had something tickling at the back of my mind. It had been in there for months and I'd been too apathetic to chase it out. I knew though, that if I dived in after it then it would vanish in a puff of smoke, so I left it and drifted into my own world.

I was jolted back by a shout of laughter and Peterson saying, '... so after that, the four of us went south again ...' And I suddenly knew what it was and it was far, far worse than anything I could have imagined.

I sat quietly while I worked it out in my head, not wanting to speak before I was sure. I really thought I kept my face fairly neutral, but silence made me look up. Everyone was staring at me.

'Sir, can I speak to you for a moment please?'

'Yes, of course,' he said, rising from his chair. 'Shall we get some fresh air?'

'Back in a minute,' I said vaguely, following him out.

We walked slowly around the garden. It was cold but sunny. We reached the end of the path and stared at the compost heap. It seemed appropriate.

I took my time and let it out slowly. No gabbling this time. And I moderated my language. This was business and it was important. I described what happened after he was carted off to Sick Bay. He didn't seem much surprised so I guessed he'd heard most of it before.

I talked about Barclay's appearance, her throwing up, her refusal to send a search party, her insistence they were dead.

He shifted his weight. 'What's your point, Miss Maxwell?'

I was reluctant to make it. 'Well, sir, as far as I can remember her exact words were, 'They're dead. All four of them.''

'Yes?'

'Well, the thing is, how did she know there were four of them? Markham was one of mine. I reported him missing before she arrived back. I'm reluctant to say this, sir, because I loathe the woman, but I think at some point during that night, she *must* somehow have seen them, the four of them out there in the chaos, heard you were down, seized the opportunity, and jumped back alone. In one stroke she cleared you, Farrell, and Guthrie out of her way. She appointed herself Caretaker Director knowing full well there was no one else and it would be made permanent. The only impediment was me and she'd sacked me less than twenty minutes after her return. She had to. I'd have been back to the Cretaceous as soon as her back was turned and she knew it. And as for Miss Black, I'm guessing she just wound her up until she snapped and left, taking Mr Dieter with her. You've got to admit sir, it's flawless. Ruthless but flawless.'

231

He stared at me. 'One moment please.'

He took out his phone, moved away from me, and talked quietly for a few minutes. I turned tactfully away and watched a robin jumping about. He put his phone away and came back, his face empty.

'Are you aware Miss Barclay has filed a report claiming she saw the bodies?'

'Has she indeed? Then we've got her.'

'As per our previous conversation, Miss Maxwell, I would like you to deal with this matter. In public and with prejudice.'

'Happy to oblige, sir, and with extreme prejudice.'

We spent the rest of the day talking things over and making a plan. We could, of course, just march through the front door but that wouldn't be half so much fun. We were going to do things the St Mary's way.

Ian Guthrie took me to one side. 'If you have any trouble with Security,' he said quietly, 'just say, "Hawthorn".'

'Why? What does it mean?'

'Just say it and they'll leave you alone. Don't ask any more questions or I'll have to kill you.'

'Hawthorn!'

'Very funny!'

The next day we all crowded into the pod, even Mrs De Winter, who refused point blank to be left behind, and who could blame her. We arrived in the paint store and silently dispersed to our various positions.

This part of the building was deserted as everyone finished breakfast and assembled for the now daily staff briefings, during which, presumably, they discussed all the things they wouldn't be doing that day. She did like the sound of her own voice.

I made my way up to the attic floors and across to the other side of the building. Quietly opening a door, I could hear a single voice, three floors down. She'd just got started. I checked my watch. Perfect.

I stepped off the threadbare carpet and began to walk slowly down the wooden stairs, knowing from personal experience just how noisy they could be. I walked very slowly, partly to buy time and partly to build suspense.

Reaching the landing, I turned and started down the next flight. My slow unhurried footsteps echoed ahead of me. Downstairs, I heard her voice pause for a moment and then resume on a slightly sharper note. People's attention was wandering, which was probably punishable by death under the new regime.

Now I walked along the gallery, keeping close to the wall so I was still invisible from the Hall. Another half dozen steps and I would be at the top of the stairs.

I took a deep breath, pushed my hands deep into my coat pockets for that Clint Eastwood look, stuck my chin in the air, and started down the stairs.

Showtime!

Fourteen

'You left them, you cowardly bitch! You ran away and left them. You murdered them as surely as if you pulled a gun and shot them dead yourself.'

She whirled around, jaw dropping and just for an instant, I saw the panic and fear in her eyes and I knew I was right. I felt my heart-rate drop and I got very cold. This bitch was going down.

'Maxwell! How did you get in here?'

I spoke very quietly because the more quietly you speak, the more people listen. Convinced it was about to hear something good, St Mary's collectively leaned forward.

'I regret that due to circumstances beyond my control, I have been unable to present my final report on what has turned out to be St Mary's last mission.'

I moved to her lectern, picked up her pile of notes, and dropped them contemptuously on the floor without looking at them. Dr Bairstow never needed a lectern.

'Allow me to rectify this omission.'

She made a sudden movement and then stepped back. She'd obviously decided to allow me enough rope to hang myself.

I took a long, deep breath and forced myself to speak slowly and deliberately, as if I really was presenting my report.

'At approximately 22.00 hours local time, three pods, Numbers Three, Five, and Six touched down at a pre-programmed location in the Cretaceous period, some sixty-seven million years ago.

'Acting on instructions, Miss Barclay, now Director Barclay, of course, assembled and fired an EMP device and once our opponents were rendered electronically helpless, security teams were despatched to inflict as much damage as possible during the twenty-minute length of the mission.

'An unforeseen result of the firing of this pulse (although possibly not unforeseen by Director Barclay), was that it caused the cages containing the captured dinosaurs to unlock, thus releasing some twenty to thirty dangerous predators into the scene of operations.

'As you can imagine, St Mary's personnel began to make their way back to their pods with all possible speed.

'However …' I paused. You could have heard an earthworm sneeze. I had everybody's rapt attention.

'However, this retreat was further hindered by a massive and completely unexpected explosion, which threw everything into confusion and, according to Director Barclay here, resulted in the deaths of Chief Farrell, Major Guthrie, Mr Peterson, and Mr Markham.

'On her return to this unit, Director Barclay reported the deaths of her colleagues, forbade any rescue attempts, appointed herself Caretaker Director, and has, ever since, been presiding over the gradual decline of this unit.'

I paused, looked around at her and pitched my voice so that it rang around the Hall.

'You now have a choice to make … Director. You can, with immediate effect, remove yourself from my sight, thus effectively saving your life. You have ten minutes to leave this building. You may take absolutely nothing with you except your life. And you will be grateful. Or …'

I left it hanging.

She put her fists on her hips and stared me out. 'Or what?'

She'd pulled herself together and was going to make a fight of it.

Good.

'Or … Director … I will drag you down to Hawking by your hair. I will take you back to the Cretaceous Period. I will hurl you out into the night and slam the door behind you and I will

236

leave you there, alone for ever, screaming for help that will never, ever come. I tell you now … Director … if I do this, no one here will lift a finger to save you. Your choice.'

'I choose neither. Security – arrest this woman and hold her until I can arrange her incarceration.'

Behind her, Murdoch, now presumably Head of Security, and two or three others rose slowly to their feet.

I looked him in the eye. 'Hawthorn.'

He froze, did nothing for long seconds, and then gestured to the others to sit down again. He himself moved quietly to the end of the row and stood, waiting to see what would happen next.

I turned back to Barclay. 'That was your version of events. Now let's hear the truth.'

She said, through gritted teeth, 'That was the truth. They died. All four of them.'

I spoke directly to her, standing so that to face me, she had her back to the room.

'Let's talk about what actually did happen, shall we?'

'I've told you already. Security –'

I cut across her.

'At approximately 22.05, the security teams left the pods. At approximately 22.12, the explosion occurred. Of these facts, there is no doubt.

'At 22.15, Director Barclay despatched Mr Peterson to locate Chief Farrell and Major Guthrie, leaving her alone in the pod. At 22.20, she ordered Miss Black to return to base, taking an injured Dr Bairstow with her. Two minutes later, she ordered me to return to St Mary's; before I had time to report a missing Mr Markham.'

A stir ran through the hall. Murdoch lifted an arm and they fell silent.

'Well?' she said. 'All this is on record. Tell me something I don't know.'

'I'll tell you something I don't know,' I said, quietly. 'I

don't know how you were so sure four of them were missing.'

'I don't understand.'

But she did. She'd gone so white I could see the freckles under her makeup. My heart-rate picked up.

'Mr Markham was on my team, not yours. I reported him missing before you got back. I repeat – how did you know there were four men dead?'

Silence.

'I'll tell you what happened, *Director*.' I made the very word an insult. 'They came out of the smoke and explosions, running towards your pod, running for their lives, and you slammed and locked the door in their faces. You left those men there to die. Did you even hear them banging on the door? Did they scream your name? Beg to be let in? Do you ever hear them in your head, kicking at the door, hammering with their empty weapons? How long did you wait? You couldn't jump too soon, could you? You had to be the last back. So you waited and waited and they screamed and screamed and then *you* pressed the button and *you* jumped to safety and *you* left those men. In the middle of a feeding frenzy; in the middle of a battleground, with no food, no water, and no shelter; *you left them!*'

Someone, I think it was Helen, drew a shuddering breath.

Barclay said, 'It wasn't like that; I swear it wasn't like that.'

Which was true, but I wanted her to dig herself in even deeper.

Never knowing when to shut up, she obliged me.

'I …' She paused and swallowed hard, tearfully brave. My fingers itched. 'I went outside to check. I know it was against Dr Bairstow's orders, but I had to know for myself. There … there wasn't much of them left, but it was certainly them.'

She suddenly remembered she'd despatched Peterson after the explosion. 'Peterson lay a little distance away. He'd been shot.'

She uttered these blatant lies without hesitation, knowing

there was no way they could be disproved. No one ever went back to check.

Except me.

'You're telling me you saw *four* dead bodies?' I let uncertainty bleed into my voice, just to draw her in a little further.

She lifted her chin and said clearly and without hesitation, 'Yes. I saw four bodies. They were damaged, but recognisable.'

'So you knew them?'

'I did.'

'These four dead bodies you saw – would these be the same four people standing behind you now?'

She didn't move. A small, disbelieving smile crossed her face.

I said softly and with complete contempt, 'You still don't get it, do you? And that's why you'll never be one of us. We're St. Mary's. We never, ever, *ever* leave our people behind.'

And finally, she got it. She turned slowly. They stood quietly at the back of the Hall, headed by Chief Farrell. I had, like everyone else, always seen the gentle, likeable man, but I swear the look on his face chilled my blood.

In the silence, someone swore softly.

Helen rose shakily to her feet, hanging onto the back of a chair. 'Peterson?'

He shouted 'Helen!' and started climbing over chairs and people to get to her. It broke the spell and people surged forward, laughing, cheering, and shouting. We're a noisy bunch.

I remembered where I was and turned around to face Bitchface Barclay. She stared at the Chief, her mouth still open.

I said softly, 'Hey!' and she jerked her head around. Suddenly, we were face to face, our eyes only inches apart. I could feel the hatred coming off me in waves. For two pins, I could have ripped her head off there and then. The Hall was packed with shouting, cheering people, but for me, there was

239

only her.

I watched a thousand emotions chase across her face. It took several efforts, but eventually, she got the words out.

'You stole my life.'

In a million years, I hadn't expected that.

'All this.' She jerked her head backwards, whether at Leon Farrell, the noisy horde behind her or St Mary's in general, I never knew.

'You took my life. I was the one with the golden future. I worked so hard … He would have seen me eventually. Seen what I could offer. All this – it should have been mine. It could have been mine.' Her eyes narrowed. 'One day it will be.' Spit flew from her lips. She quivered with suppressed fury. 'One day, Maxwell, I will finish you. I swear it.'

I should have let it go but I thought of what I'd lost already and something, somewhere, demanded revenge.

My fist, travelling at the combined speeds of rage and retribution impacted hard on her nose. There was a glorious cracking and squelching noise and a great big gout of blood darkened the front of her beautifully pressed uniform. She went over backwards, fell onto her stupid lectern, and the whole lot crashed to the floor.

I looked up at the gallery. 'Was that how you wanted it done, sir?'

The Boss came slowly down the stairway, to huge applause. Such a showman! Standing beside me, we both surveyed the wreckage of the lectern, which had bits of Izzie Barclay sticking out of it.

'Very satisfactory,' he said, and went to speak to Mrs Partridge.

I was joined by the Chief. He stood looking down into my eyes, smiling his slow smile. We had one of those conversations where you don't need words.

After a while, he said, 'Broke your hand, didn't you?'

'Yep.'

'Forgot to un-tuck your thumb?'

'Yep.'

'Hurts like buggery?'

'Yep.'

The Boss cleared his throat. 'To clear up a few minor points: I am Dr Edward Bairstow and I am the Director of St Mary's Institute of Historical Research.'

His unit cheered. He bent over the vaguely stirring Barclay.

'Madam, you are relieved!'

We were all shunted off to Sick Bay, even Barclay. Apparently, there's something in the Geneva Convention or the Human Rights Thingy about leaving people lying around bleeding. I was going to require some convincing.

I got shoved into the scanner thing and, as I knew she would, Nurse Hunter took one look at the printout and went out. I sighed and tried one-handed to unlace my boots. Hunter came back and helped. I sat in the stupid white gown and waited for the storm to break. They were bringing someone into the next cubicle. It struck me that directly or indirectly, I was responsible for everyone currently in Sick Bay. That had to be some sort of record. Hunter finished putting the Flexi Glove on my hand. It began to cool and gently flex and the pain retreated.

Helen bustled in. 'OK, Max. I want to listen to your chest.' I did a bit of breathing; in and out – the traditional way. 'And hold it please. And out again.' I leaned forward and she tapped my back a lot. I breathed in and out again. I coughed a bit. Then I coughed a bit more.

'Can you lie down, please? Knees up.'

'Is this legal?'

She just looked, so I did it.

'I'm impressed, Helen. This is just the sort of thing real doctors do.'

She ignored me, stripping off her gloves. 'Hunter, could you organise some tea, please?'

It got very quiet in the cubicle after Hunter had gone. Helen sighed heavily. 'You're really not fit to be allowed out on your own, are you?'

'So, what's the damage?'

'How do you want it? From head to toe? Alphabetically? Chronologically?'

'Surprise me.'

'Well, your feet are holding up well.'

'Glad to hear it. I'll be on my way then.'

'So tell me what's been happening here.'

'Exactly what your scan tells you.'

'No, I want to hear it from you and you will remain here until I do.'

So I trotted it all out again. Hunter brought in some tea. Helen handed her the chart and she disappeared again.

Helen lit a cigarette and took her usual place at the window. 'OK, you are malnourished. You will eat at least four meals a day. You will eat portions of fruit and vegetables at every meal. You will drink plenty of fluids. You will not drink alcohol. I'm prescribing more antibiotics for the infection and you will complete the course. You are anaemic. You will eat iron-rich foods. I'll give Mrs Mack a list. You will go to bed for eight hours a day, even if you don't sleep. You may read, but no TV, holos, or computers. You will take one week's sick leave during which you will not work – at all. You will take a little gentle exercise in the grounds every day. You will not ride. You will not run.'

I looked at the cubicle floor.

'You will not argue or you will spend the next seven days here in Sick Bay. I will release you under your own recognisance if you agree to the above. Either way, Max, you will comply.'

'Bloody hell, I knew it. You're Borg, aren't you?'
Silence.

'OK. Sleep, read, eat, shit, got it.'

'Are you going to tell him?'

And that, as they say, was the sixty-four thousand dollar question. I honestly didn't know. 'Probably not.'

'Why not?'

'Because I don't want to. Because it's my problem. Because either it will hurt him badly, or he won't care at all, which will hurt me. Because I don't want to add to his total of dead children. Choose any or all.'

'I understand your motives, but he has a right to know.'

I couldn't think of anything to say.

'How would you feel if it was the other way around?'

'He need never know.'

'Losing a child is nothing to be ashamed of.'

'I only knew I was pregnant for about twenty minutes and he never knew at all. I don't think it qualifies.' Even to me that sounded hollow.

'What if he finds out?'

'How can he?' I looked at her hard.

'Think this over very carefully, Max. It's not just you who's involved here.'

She stood up and then hesitated. I waited. She was hopeless at this sort of thing. Without looking at me, she said awkwardly, 'Thanks for bringing Peterson back.'

'You're welcome, Helen,'

She changed the subject. 'Your clothes are here. We'll wash them if you like and you can go back in a dressing gown.'

'No thanks. This is literally all I have in the world.'

'Mrs Partridge and I saved some of your stuff. She'll be along to see you later. So what's it to be; your custody or mine?'

'Mine,' I said, and reached for my clothes.

Back in my old room I put the Trojan Horse on the empty shelf and the photo next to the bed. I was home again. I was back where I belonged. Around me I could hear St Mary's getting on with the day. Doors opened and closed; people called out to each other. The floorboards in my room creaked as the radiator warmed up. I sniffed – they'd had curry for lunch. This time last week, being back at St Mary's was all I had wanted. A lot had happened in the last week. Why wasn't I happier?

I lay on my couch and everyone turned up at once. Peterson, liberated from Sick Bay, arrived first with two cardboard boxes. 'Some of your books,' he said. 'How do you organise them?'

'By order of enjoyment.'

'Yes, that's helpful.'

'Fiction goes on the top shelf, alphabetically, and everything else underneath in chronological order.'

'Apparently various people grabbed bits of your stuff before Barclay got in here. Helen got your books and Kal got some of your clothes. It's all slowly on its way back to you.'

Mrs Partridge was hard on his heels, clutching folders and trailing a printout.

'Miss Maxwell, there is some paperwork to work through here.' She sniffed and looked around the room. 'I really think you should do your laundry.'

'Before we start,' I interrupted. 'I want to thank you for saving those two items for me. They mean a great deal to me. Thank you very much.'

'You're welcome, Miss Maxwell. Shall we make a start? Now then, Dr Bairstow has approved the following expenditure. Firstly, unfair dismissal; you were inappropriately dismissed and the correct procedures were not adhered to. Secondly, there are subsistence payments for your period outside the unit. Thirdly, there is compensation for your illegally seized belongings and computer. I'm sorry we couldn't save your artwork; it was all destroyed. Your computer has been sterilised and even the operating system is gone, I'm afraid. Fourthly, back pay from your day of dismissal to today, the date of your reinstatement.'

I said, 'Um, isn't there a bit of a discrepancy here? You

can't compensate me for dismissal and at the same time say I was on the payroll. Surely, it's one or the other? And you've paid me at the wrong rate as well.'

Listen to me telling Mrs Partridge she'd made a mistake. Death-wish Maxwell, they call me.

She said evenly, 'No, I believe Dr Bairstow's figures are correct.'

'But …'

'They are quite correct, Miss Maxwell.'

'But …'

'Just sign, Max,' said Peterson. 'I've got a similar deal. Not as generous as yours but good enough. You've lost more than anyone else. Just smile and sign.'

This was the Boss. This was the Boss doing what he could to put things right. I looked at the column of figures. The total was huge; too huge. I shook my head and said, 'But, Mrs Partridge …'

The door crashed back into my already pock-marked wall and Chief Farrell was suddenly in the room. He looked terrible. Even worse than when I'd left him a couple of hours ago. His face was haggard with purple-green shadows under his eyes, which were dark and glittery. I took a breath to speak but never got the words out. I realised with a sick lurch to my stomach that he knew. Somehow he knew and he was angry. No, beyond angry. I'd made a big, big mistake.

He interrupted me. His voice shook and I realised with a twist of fear that he was losing control and this was going to be ugly. It came out in an Exorcist-style rasp. My chest tightened.

'When were you going to tell me? I thought we'd got past all this, but obviously we haven't. You're never going to change, are you? I've just been wasting my time with you. Why didn't you tell me?'

I should say something. He paused to draw breath and there was an infinitesimal window of opportunity, but no words came. Peterson and Mrs Partridge seemed paralysed.

'You weren't ever going to tell me, were you? You can't even talk to me now. What is it with you? Anyone would think – oh, I see, of course. How stupid do you think I am? I see it now. It wasn't mine. Whose was it? What about you, Peterson? Was it yours? You two are pretty close. Oh, no, of course not. It was fucking Sussman's wasn't it? You never had eyes for anyone but that worthless piece of shit. And you were going to pass it off as mine, but luckily you lost it, so you didn't need to mention it at all. And no one else was going to tell me. I had to hear it from Barclay. You called her a bitch. Well, it takes one to know one.'

He spun on his heel and was gone, taking all the air in the room with him. My world crashed around my head. Somehow, I got myself together and took a deep breath. The centre held. I could function.

I turned to Mrs Partridge and said lightly, 'I'm so sorry, I've forgotten where you wanted me to sign. Can you show me again please?'

She silently pointed and I moved the pen blindly. Half the signature ended up on the table-top, but she made no comment. She gathered up her papers, caught my eye, said quietly, 'Do your laundry, Miss Maxwell,' and left, closing the door behind her. I turned to look at Peterson who sat among my books, looking like Lot's wife.

'Tim, what's the matter?'

He had the thousand-yard stare that never bodes well. 'Tim, look at me. Look at me.' I took his cold hands. Finally, to my relief, his eyes focused on me, but he still looked half-blind. I knew what this was; one shock too many.

'It's OK, Tim. Just sit for a moment and I'll make some tea. Or would you like me to fetch Helen?' Who was going to have some explaining to do.

'I never thought it would be you two. I thought you two were rock solid. I never thought he would ... he could ... When we were lost, before you came, he kept saying, "She will come.

246

She will come." He never doubted for one moment you would come. Sometimes, he said, "If she can't come, she'll send." He believed. And I believed his belief.'

He swallowed. 'I used to look at the four of us and think about who would go first. Obviously, Markham, because of his hands and then I thought the Chief would be next because he would die defending him because that's what he does and then Guthrie who would fight alongside the Chief and I would be the last one left and how would I feel? To be alone in that place? But he never lost his faith in you and when we heard your voice over the speakers he sat down on a rock and the tears just ran down his face and he said to me, "I knew she would come," and knowing you both I would have bet my life that the two of you would be together for ever. And now, not forty-eight hours afterwards, to think … to say those things about you, to say them to you, in front of …' He shook his head.

I gripped his hand more tightly. 'It's nothing, Tim. I don't know what he was talking about …'

He shook his head again. 'Yes you do. So do I.'

Yes, he did. As did Barclay, apparently. How? Why was Barclay talking to Farrell? Well, that was easy – she'd be making trouble. More to the point, why would he be talking to her? I was too tired to think about it.

We sat for a long time. I held his hand and gently rubbed his back. He sighed. 'This is not about me.'

'Nor me,' I said cheerfully. 'Are you hungry?'

'No,' he said. 'But shall we go and have one of our prescribed four meals a day?'

'Why not? Give me ten minutes to wash my face and hands.' I didn't need ten minutes, but he did.

'I'll see you there,' he said, getting stiffly to his feet. He paused for a moment. I grinned at him. 'Get out of here.'

I tried to tidy myself up bit and clattered down the attic stairs to the landing. I was just passing Wardrobe when Whissell the Weasel stepped out and made me jump. I remembered he'd been part of my team in the Cretaceous – the one with the broken nose. It hadn't improved his appearance any. And I remembered him from my training days as well. I'd never liked him and he knew it. A man who could legitimately describe his occupation as brain donor. I stopped and the small hairs on my neck began to rise. Instinct told me this was not good. Shit, shit, shit.

He stepped up close. 'Slut!'

Oh God, did everyone in the unit know? How had this got round so quickly? Was this how it was going to be from now on?

'Moron!'

'What?' he said, taken aback.

'Sorry. *Deaf* moron!'

'Bitch!' Ah, we'd moved on. 'All these years you acted like Little Miss Perfect. You were too good for the rest of us and now it turns out anyone can have you, Little Miss Slut.'

He grabbed my arm and pulled me into Wardrobe. My face bounced off the wall.

I'd been at St Mary's for five years now. They'd never taught me to handle difficult personal relationships, but on the subject of attempted assault in any century you care to name – they'd bored on about that for ever.

I waited until he caught hold of my jacket then stretched my arms behind me and pulled away. He found himself holding my empty jacket. I couldn't match him for strength but I saw a sweeping brush within reach and that, I could do! I seized the broom handle and waded in. They say, 'A red mist descended ...' Well, it bloody well does. I was so angry. Boiling, red-hot, gut-churning angry. Something burst inside me like an angry sun. I just wanted to hurt somebody and here he was. Legitimate prey!

Eventually, breathless, I stepped back. He was swaying, but still on his feet. I stepped forward and punched him with my other hand, remembering to un-tuck my thumb this time. It still hurt though. He crashed to the ground. I nursed the pain and waited for him to get up.

Part of me was in shock and disbelief. This was St Mary's for God's sake. How could this happen? We were falling apart. The damage Barclay had done to this unit ran deep.

Abruptly, Peterson appeared beside me and he really looked like someone ready to do some damage. 'What the hell …?'

All of a sudden, I'd had enough. I couldn't stay here. These were people whose good opinion I valued and it had gone. All I'd wanted was to get back to St Mary's. I would have sworn St Mary's was in my bones, but now it was spoiled for ever. I was out of here. I reached over to a work table. There was a coffee mug full of pens and markers. I selected something indelible, knelt beside Weasel and wrote, I RESIGN, across his forehead and signed and dated it.

Peterson chuckled, stepped forward and took the marker from me. He wrote, ME TOO, on one cheek and signed and dated the other one, picked up my jacket, and we walked out. We were half way down the stairs when he said, 'Are you going to put that broom down anytime soon?'

'Probably not,' I said. 'I'm not hungry. I'm going to the bar and I'm going to spend my last night at St Mary's getting right, royally rat-arsed! Would you care to accompany me, Mr Peterson?'

'An honour and a privilege, Miss Maxwell,' he said. 'Let's see if we can't set some sort of record for alcohol abuse, disreputable behaviour, and generally pissing people off.'

'Well,' I observed. 'We've made a good start.'

'Yes, but we can do even better. We just have to try harder.'

We entered the bar, radiating defiance and attitude and typically there was no one there apart from the bar staff. They eyed us uneasily. You'd think they'd never seen a woman clutching a broom before.

'Now then,' said Peterson to them. 'We don't work here any more, so you're going to need to run a tab and we'll settle up at the end of the evening, or more probably, the beginning of tomorrow morning. Margaritas for the lady and single malt for me. Keep them coming and I'll sign the tabs.'

I protested.

'Yeah, like you can even hold a pen. Come on.'

We found a table and got stuck in. I drank to drown the anger and betrayal. My own unit had rounded on me. More drinks arrived. Peterson signed, looked at me, and ordered another round.

It was either late afternoon or early evening, depending on how you approached things. Given that Weasel must be in Sick Bay by now, the lack of senior staff coming to investigate was surprising. Still, give them time. They did have a knack for turning up just as St Mary's was on the verge of meltdown. I took another long drink and felt it start to do me good.

'Tim, you don't have to do this, you know. This is my fight.'

'What?' He pretended horror. 'You're surely not leaving me here alone with all these big, rough boys?'

I looked at him. 'Seriously.'

'Yes,' he said. 'I do have to do this. Firstly, I haven't forgotten what I owe you, even if others have. Fourthly, we've given ourselves to this bloody unit and asked for nothing in return. You needed someone today and where are they?' He gestured round the empty room with the hand not holding a glass. 'Thirdly, I've had a brilliant idea for making our fortunes and secondly, let's see them run this place with no historians. Barclay tried it and look what happened to her. On a related subject I have to say, Max, I've never seen anyone knock two people senseless in one day. I swear it's a pleasure to drink with you. Hey, drink-slingers, another two over here please!'

'What's Kal going to do when she arrives back and we're gone?'

'She will pause only to torch the place on her way out.'

'But what about you and Helen?'

He shrugged. 'I'll explain and give her an address. If she

wants me she can find me.'

'And Kal and Dieter?'

'Max, you're not responsible for all these people. We can all sort ourselves out. You concentrate on you. Drink up!'

So I drank up, sucked the salt off my bottom lip, and the corners of the room blurred.

Others started to trickle in. They stared across at us, as well they might. I looked down at my blood-splattered T-shirt. 'It's official. I now have nothing to wear.' I sniffed and mopped my tender nose with my sleeve.

'You're such a class date,' complained Peterson. 'It's a little late in the day, but should you be drinking with antibiotics?'

'Relax,' I said. 'I stopped taking them to make room for the booze.'

'Fine grasp of priorities, that woman.'

'So what's this fantastic money-making scheme, then?'

'Oh, yes, you'll like this. We play to our strengths.'

'I'm not sure I've got any at the moment.'

'Max, your presentations are legendary. That one you did on Agincourt for those school kids was epic.'

'I taught them the origins of flicking the V-sign. Did you see their teacher's face?'

'They loved it. They hung on your every word. You tailored it for your audience. It was just right – mud, blood, battles, violence, and a big finish. They loved it. As they say now, "They were engaged", which I always thought to mean something else completely, but maybe I'm getting old.' He started to brood about getting old. I nudged him back to reality.

'Oh, yes, look, what I'm saying is, let's do this professionally. Get hold of the school curriculum and tailor presentations around it; fun and light-hearted for the youngsters, bloody and violent for teenagers, serious and scholarly for exam students. We'll dress them in armour; we're bound to be able to pick some up off eBay or "Rmour is us" or something. We show them some weapons, teach them some moves. We'll make

251

some of them up to look as if they've got the plague, boils, buboes, pustules, you know. We've got a bit of cash between us; enough to get started, so we needn't charge too much to begin with and then, when people see how good we are, we can put our prices up a bit. And let's face it, between the pair of us, we have more qualifications than you could throw a short peasant at. In fact, if you didn't know us at all, you'd think we were quite respectable.'

He was really enthusiastic now. And actually, I quite liked the idea too. He carried on. 'I can give archery demonstrations. We could cook medieval meals or provide a Roman menu for dinner parties. And not only schools, but private groups, societies, evening classes as well. Max, it'll be fun. And we'll be our own bosses. And we might even make a bit of money. Just think – history for profit.'

I kept my face very still and my hand very steady as I put down my glass. Inside my head my thoughts were racing. History for profit – was this how it started? Was I responsible for this 'offshoot' of St Mary's that wreaked such havoc in the future? Did it start this innocuously? Two people forming an organisation that would grow to threaten both St Mary's and the timeline itself and all because Tim and I had had a bad day and a good idea.

And what did I say to him? 'Yes, it's a fabulous idea, Tim, let's do it,' and trust myself to guide future events away from dangerous areas?

Or, 'No Tim, let's not,' and then worry that he went it alone; or worse, started with someone else who didn't have my foreknowledge? Or would it all happen regardless of any action I could take? Were we back to Calvin and predestination? Bloody hell, I was drunk!

We got in another round and Mrs Partridge wafted in. 'Dr Bairstow's compliments and could Miss Maxwell please join him at her earliest convenience?'

'Miss Maxwell's compliments,' I slurred. 'Owing to the

copious amounts of alcohol consumed, it's not only not convenient but probably well-nigh impossible, given the location of his office at the top of an outrageous number of stairs. Probably Miss Maxwell's apologies would be more appropriate. How about tomorrow morning?'

'Dr Bairstow is currently downstairs in the Library,' she informed me with considerable relish. Well, that solved that problem.

I helped Peterson to his feet and we set off at an angle. Mrs Partridge frowned at him. 'For the purposes of this exercise,' he said carefully, 'you may regard Miss Maxwell and me as joined at the hip.' We followed her disapproving back.

Not only was Dr Bairstow present, but Major Guthrie and Professor Rapson were there as well. They didn't look good. We sat down and the Boss opened the batting.

'On behalf of the senior staff at St Mary's I want to apologise to you, Miss Maxwell. This afternoon's incident was inexcusable and that it should happen to you, today, is mortifying in the extreme. I hope you will accept our apologies.'

I murmured something.

'You are very generous,' he said, choosing to interpret that as acceptance. 'I can assure you that after suitable treatment at the hands of Dr Foster (another one in Sick Bay, thanks to me. I was on a roll today!), Mr Whissell has been removed from the premises. I hope you will soon be able to put this matter behind you. You have my unequivocal assurance that, should you go or should you stay, nothing of a similar nature will ever happen to you again on this campus.'

He paused and sipped his drink. I didn't dare look at Guthrie. If the Boss was mortified, God knows how he felt. Beside me, Peterson stirred.

'I agree, Mr Peterson. But there were several reasons why I did not wish to intervene. Firstly, you both are capable of looking after yourselves. And you needed to get some things out of your systems. You see, you can't just order people to get along. You're not children,' he said, in the teeth of all the evidence.

'Now, concerning your resignations, I understand completely the reason why you feel compelled to leave, Miss Maxwell and why you, Mr Peterson, feel the need to support her. I am not, at the moment, going to try to dissuade either of you. No one should be making important decisions today. However, this unit needs to start pulling together again and for that I need you both. And Miss Black too, if I can induce her to return. I am, therefore, not accepting your resignations at this time. Should you feel the same way in say, three days, then if I cannot change your minds, I will accept them with regret. Do you agree?'

Cunning old bugger!

'I think I speak for both of us,' said Peterson slowly. 'We can agree to those conditions. I think it only fair to tell you though, that Max and I have spent the evening discussing our future, to which, I have to say, we are both greatly looking forward. We both feel it's time for new beginnings. We only tell you this, sir, so you're not unprepared for our departure.'

Cunning young bugger! The words, 'considerable pay rise,' though unspoken, were up there in neon lights. To support him, I did my best to look less battered and more like someone with a rosy future.

The Boss wasn't having any of it. 'In three days you may feel differently. We'll discuss it then.' he said, slowly getting to his feet. 'In the meantime, I suggest you take yourselves out of harm's way. And get that hand looked at tomorrow, Miss Maxwell.' He limped off to his coffin.

Behind him, Professor Rapson stretched and got to his feet. 'Not our finest hour,' he muttered. 'I do hope the two of you decide to stay,' and wandered off. This left Ian Guthrie, who looked exactly as you would expect Weasel's boss to look.

I said, 'It's OK, Major.'

'No,' said Peterson angrily. 'It's not.'

'No,' Guthrie agreed. 'It's not and I'm very sorry, Max.' He left too. We watched him go.

'I'm knackered,' I said.

'And me. I'm for my bed.'

And the day still wasn't over.

We helped each other up the stairs. We had to stop twice to re-coordinate various limbs and stop giggling. We were rendering 'Stairway to Heaven', giving it everything we'd got and, as we turned the corner, we tripped over the Chief, sitting at the bottom of the attic stairs, forearms on his knees, head bowed.

'Aha!' said Peterson, obviously itching to thump someone.

Farrell got to his feet. 'I wonder if I might have a word, Miss Maxwell.'

'Fat chance,' said Peterson, belligerently. 'Look at her. That's what happened last time you had a word.'

How much longer could this day go on?

The Chief did something he rarely had to do. He gave a direct order. 'Dismissed, Mr Peterson.'

Peterson snorted. 'You're behind the times, mate. We don't work here any more. You're the one who's leaving, so just fuck off out of it, will you?'

'You've resigned?'

'In three days,' I said, 'Tim and I are out of here.'

'But you can't go.'

'Yes, we can.'

'I really must speak to you.'

'You're not listening,' said Peterson. 'Do I have to thump you?'

'There's no need for that. I've come to tell you I'm leaving too, so you don't have to go if you don't want to. I'm applying to join the Space Programme.' I spared a thought for the Boss, who wasn't having the best day staff-wise. 'I just wanted to …' he tailed off. He didn't know what he'd just wanted to.

Peterson turned to me. 'This is up to you.'

'I'll be OK. He looks as if one good puff of wind would have him over.'

'You're sure?'

'What else can happen today?' I said, getting that wrong too.

He looked mutinous, but nodded. I said, 'Why don't you go and find Helen?'

He nodded and sighed. 'Goodnight.'

'Tim – thanks.'

He glowered at the Chief. 'Don't take any crap from him,' and wandered unsteadily away.

I managed to get myself up the stairs and into my room. It was still a bit of a shock to see how bare it looked. I'd made the bed and my smelly sports bag lay in the corner. I heard Mrs Partridge. 'Do your laundry, Miss Maxwell!' My books still littered the floor where Peterson had left them.

I didn't sit down. I stood in the middle of the room so he would make it quick, folded my arms and said, 'How can I help you?'

He leaned a hip against the couch for support and seemed unsure what to say. I hated this. I didn't want any more messy emotions or feelings. Just get it over with. But he didn't, so I said, 'Chief, I can understand why you want to go. I want to leave myself. We both need a new beginning. It was fun, but it was a mistake and I can see now why the Boss discourages workplace relationships. Surely we don't have to make this any more difficult than it is. I'm sorry you feel you have to go. St Mary's loss is the Space Programme's gain. I hope, not too far into the future, you'll be able to look back at – everything – and find a few happy memories.'

OK, not my best, but I was drunk, battered, stressed, and distressed. Full house again! He jerked upright, stared at me a moment, and then said, in a voice that cracked so much I hardly recognised it, 'I don't want to be only a memory. I know you can't … you don't … it's not easy for you, but it's not easy for me either. I don't want much. I just want you to tell me you love me sometimes.'

I shook my head. 'Yes, you see, I can't do that.' He turned his head away. 'I love you all the time.'

He made to speak, but suddenly his chest heaved and he collapsed onto the arm of the couch, coughing out terrible, racking, dry sobs. He covered his face with his hands. I didn't know what to do. I just didn't know what to do. I walked up to him, put my arms around him, and rested my cheek on top of his head and made a discovery.

Some behaviour is contagious. Yawn in front of me and I'm at it for the rest of the day. And vomiting. If I so much as hear someone heave I'm barfing up everything I've eaten in the past ten years. Now I discovered a third behaviour. Crying. Even as I stood with him, something forced its way up through my chest. And again. And again. It was uncontrollable. I couldn't stop. He put his arms around me and we cried together.

It wasn't romantic. This was no gentle mingling of tears. This was painful and raw and wet. My tears ran down into his hair, his were soaking the front of my T-shirt, which was pretty well covered in body fluids anyway. After a while, we slowed down, but he didn't let go. He really was in a bit of a state and he hadn't been in good condition when he came in. I couldn't let anyone see him like this.

I persuaded him to let go, went into the bathroom, and wet a flannel with warm water. I gently washed his face and hands, got his boots off, and put him to bed. He went out like a light.

Things were a bit more difficult for me. I'd never cried like that before and it was every bit as unpleasant as I'd always thought it would be. My head throbbed (although that may have been the drink), my sinuses were blocked, and my throat raw. I looked terrible and my chest and hands hurt. I wasn't going to be doing that again anytime soon. I made a quiet cup of tea and sat down to pack up my books again. Half an hour later I'd finished and there was still no way I was going to be able to

257

sleep and, besides, my bed was occupied. I looked round for something else to do.

My sports bag. I pulled it over and began to sort out the stinky mess inside. The bag itself went out on to the roof to air. I clumsily turned out all my pockets and stuffed everything into my laundry bag. That left my jacket; burnt and ripped, but still the only one I had. I started to feel the pockets, but something had gone down a hole in the lining. I fished around, finally locating it in an armpit, yanked it out and everything in the world changed. For ever.

Fifteen

I honestly thought I was going to faint.

What a day this was turning out to be.

I held on to the back of the couch and tried to breathe deeply. It didn't help. I sat down and leaned forward, putting my head between my knees. It works better if you put your head between someone else's knees, but after a while my head cleared. I sat up and opened my hand. You would not have thought such a tiny thing could change the world.

I was looking at a fir cone. Not a big one; about three or four inches long and having easily as bad a day as me. It was almost completely burned away on one side and quite badly charred on the other. I put it gently down on the table, rubbed my face with my hands, and tried to think. A few minutes later, I got up and quietly put the kettle on again. My thoughts were all over the place so I sat back and let my mind wander as it wanted.

About twenty minutes later, I got up and found pen and paper. I jotted words at random. I drew lines to connect them. It took an hour because I was slow and clumsy. My hands hurt too much to type so I fired up my data table and dictated quietly. It was the middle of the night. I sat in a little pool of light and changed the world.

I took what I had, awkwardly built my data stack, indexed, and colour coded. My thoughts were on fire and the words just presented themselves as I needed them. I read it through, drew a couple of organisational charts, wrote the introduction and a conclusion and sat back. Only now was I conscious of how cold and tired and stiff I felt. I read it through again and couldn't think how to improve it any more. I headed the file, *Boss – this will rock your world!* – obviously not completely sober yet then – and sent it off to him.

Dawn was not far away and I was far to strung-up to sleep. I made another cup of tea and took it into the bathroom. I lay in hot water for an hour, wondering if I'd missed anything, got out and dressed in the old sweats which were all I had left. Farrell still hadn't moved, so I checked he wasn't dead, grabbed my battered old jacket, and quietly let myself out.

Sitting on the stairs I activated my com and called the long-suffering Peterson. It took a while but eventually his voice said, 'What?'

'Where are you?'

'Strangely, I'm in bed.'

'Get up, I need you.'

'What's happened?'

'Something important and I need to speak to you as soon as possible.'

'Dining room. Five minutes. Have coffee.'

He looked awful. Wet hair standing on end and still in last night's rumpled clothes. I handed him coffee.

Jenny Fields, the kitchen assistant, was on earlies. I said, 'Bacon sandwiches please, Jenny. Quick as you can.'

I took him to a table.

'Tim, are you with me? I need you to concentrate. This is vital.'

Something in my voice must have got through to him because he took a good swig of coffee, closed his eyes briefly, and then said, 'Go ahead.'

'Cast your mind back to the Cretaceous.' He nodded. 'OK, you're at the tree line, looking towards the pod. I'm holding up the blaster.' I mimed holding up a blaster. He nodded. 'I'm racing off away from the pod. There's a bloody big lizard chasing me and the Chief and Guthrie are chasing the lizard. You get Markham into the pod. Are you with me so far?'

He nodded.

I leaned forward. 'What happened next? Tell me everything.

In as much detail as you can.'

He was such a good friend. He asked no questions. Closing his eyes, he said, 'I got him into the pod and sat him down. I went back to the door which I'd left open because you'd be coming back in a hurry but I didn't want anything else getting in. I could just see you ducking and diving. You were in a hollow and –'

'Never mind me. What did *you* do?'

'I stood by the door and watched. I smelled burning. Your jacket was beginning to smoulder. I stamped on it.' He stopped.

'Go on.'

'I heard shouting. I looked over and everything was running back towards the pod. I grabbed your jacket off the ground, shook out the all the wood and cones, and checked around quickly to make sure everything was inside – worst FOD plod ever. I threw your jacket into the pod and jumped in after it. The three of you appeared – you fell in through the door. I went down and you landed on top of me and Guthrie fell on top of you. Someone got the door closed and said –'

'No, never mind. That's the bit I wanted.'

The bacon sandwiches arrived and we both realised we were famished. He cut my sarnie up for me. He had more coffee. I had more tea. He went back for more sarnies. When he sat down he asked, 'Any chance of knowing what this is all about?'

'Yes,' I said and opened my hand to show him the burned pine cone. For a long while he just stared – as I had done. I watched the blood drain from his face – as mine had done. 'Oh my God,' he gasped. 'Oh my God. Oh my God.'

'Shh!' I said looking over my shoulder as people started coming in for the early shift.

'How did this happen?'

'Well, I have a theory. This is what I wanted to talk to you about. Come into the Library.' We found a quiet corner. The place was deserted anyway, but I was feeling cautious. I think that's the first time I've ever said that. I spoke for about half an

261

hour, just giving him the outline. At the end I asked 'What do you think?'

'Bloody hell, Max, what do I think? I think this changes everything. I think … I think we won't be leaving in three days.'

'No,' I agreed.

'When are you going to tell the Boss?'

'I already have. I was up all night writing a proposal, outlining future developments, and restructuring his unit. He's going to have a hell of a shock when he opens his emails this morning.'

'Wish I could see his face.'

'You will. This is all your doing.'

'What?'

'Well, you're the one who somehow got this little fellow caught in my jacket lining, thus bringing something out of its own timeline for the first time ever. You did this, Tim. All I did was get in the way.

'Just think. It gets caught in my jacket. I bring it back to Rushford. I'm too lazy to give my jacket to Mrs De Winter to clean as she asked me to. We might have lost it then. I'm wearing it when I go to Sick Bay. If I'd changed there, as they wanted, we might have lost it again. I'm still wearing the jacket when Weasel has a go at me and it gets kicked across the room. Suppose someone had trodden on it. And finally, I can't sleep. I'm looking for things to do and I hear Mrs Partridge, clear as day, say, 'Do your laundry Miss Maxwell,' and then and only then do I find this little chap – on his last legs but hanging in there, safe in St Mary's at last.'

We regarded the little chap fondly. 'Yes,' said Peterson, 'but that's just it, isn't it? It's the fact that he's on his last legs that made it possible.'

He'd got it!

'I'm going to take some coffee upstairs,' I said, casually. 'I'll be back in a minute.'

'You don't drink coffee,' he said suspiciously.

'No, can't stand the stuff.'

I picked up a flask of coffee and two more bacon butties from the kitchen and took them upstairs. He was still sleeping like the dead. I checked him again and left them on my bedside table.

I'd just rejoined Peterson when Mrs Partridge appeared again; clearly another woman who never slept.

'I did my laundry,' I said, before she could speak. I meant it as a joke, but the most extraordinary expression of relief spread across her face. Interesting. I would think about that later. In the meantime apparently, the Boss was requesting the pleasure of our company again.

'Here we go,' said Peterson as we bounced up the stairs.

He regarded us from behind his desk.

'I can't remember a time when you two weren't standing in front of me.' I couldn't think of a response so I grinned at him, just to annoy him some more.

'Sit down,' he said. 'I want to go through this with you both. Step by step, line by line. Firstly, I want to be absolutely certain this – object – originated from the Cretaceous period and not from the local municipal park. May I see it, please? And the jacket?'

I spread the jacket on the desk and showed him the tear in the lining. I described how I'd bought it, lining intact, from a charity shop about a month ago. I laid the fir cone on the desk. I told him how I'd collected the cones and wrapped them in my jacket. Peterson described throwing it into the pod.

The Boss said, 'I'd like the Professor to take a look at this. I know there's not a lot to work with but maybe he can identify the species, hopefully to something that hasn't existed in the last million years or so. That would really nail it. Now, let's get to work.'

For two hours we went over my proposals. He challenged every line. I had to justify every word. He pushed. I pushed back. I made my case from every angle possible, advanced every argument I could think of. It was tough – the Boss takes no prisoners.

Peterson, bless him, stuck with me every inch of the way as we slogged through it. I watched the shadows move across the carpet. Lunchtime approached. My mouth got dry and Peterson grew hoarse. I wouldn't give an inch. I stopped defending and went on the offensive. I questioned St Mary's established practices and challenged existing thinking. I was in mid-rant when he raised his hand.

'Enough.'

He stared out of the window for a while. 'I will speak to my senior staff this afternoon. Please report to me at six this evening. Thank you for your time.' And that was it.

'What do you think?' I asked Peterson as we headed for food and drink.

'I think I'm hungry.'

'But is he going to do it?'

'Of course he is. It's genius. He was just testing your commitment. Try telling him we're leaving now!'

Mrs Mack handed me a plate of leaves.

'What's this?'

'Mushroom omelette and salad. Doctor's orders.'

'But it's green.'

'Green food is good for you'

'Can't I have mint choc-chip ice-cream instead?'

'And this is a glass of orange juice.'

'What?'

'And you too, Mr Peterson.'

'What?'

'And if you eat it all up, there's a gooseberry crumble with your name on it.' I knew she wouldn't let us down.

'I'm off to see Helen,' he said, when we'd finished. I looked at him. He blushed slightly. 'We have more catching up to do.'

'You'll go blind,' I said and we parted.

He was sitting up in bed drinking coffee from the flask I'd brought. The bacon butties had vanished. He looked much better, as people tend to do when they've got fat, calories, salt, sugar, and cholesterol inside them. Bleary and unshaven, but better. I dragged up a chair and put my feet up on the bed. We looked at each other and proceeded to tread carefully.

He raised his mug. 'Thanks.'

'You're welcome.' I took a deep breath. 'How did you know?'

He sighed. 'I went to debrief her. There's something we need to know. Whissell was guarding her. I thought there might be a problem getting her to talk. As it turned out, I couldn't shut her up. She couldn't wait to tell me. I don't know what you ever did to her, but she really doesn't like you.'

'How did she know?'

'She was in the next cubicle receiving treatment. Whissell was with her. They heard every word you said.'

'Where is she now?'

I thought I might pay her a little visit.

He was evasive. 'Not here.'

Actually, did I care?

'So,' he said, changing the subject. 'What's happening in the world?'

'I've submitted a proposal to the Boss and he's considering it. He wants to see his senior staff this afternoon.'

'I'll finish this and take myself off.'

'No rush.'

A pause.

'So, how are you?'

I started to say, 'Absolutely fi–' and then realised my mistake. I took a deep breath. 'I'm tired. Really, really tired. Tired to the bone. I'm lost. I don't know where I am in the world. I don't know if I'm a hero or a villain. I do know my world is full of grief and loss and pain and that nothing will ever be the same again.'

He nodded.

'And how do you feel?'

His eyes went dark again. 'Ashamed. I broke the thing I loved most in the world. I can never get that back.

I remembered again the anger and fear I'd felt with Weasel, the red urge to destroy everything in my path. To assuage my own pain and hurt by lashing out at those around me.

I said, 'Yes you can. It never went away,' and sat next to him on the bed. He put his arm round me and laid his head on my hair.

He said quietly, 'I'm very sorry.'

'You weren't yourself. None of us were. I think everyone went a little crazy.'

'Please, tell me. Tell me what really happened to you, Lucy.'

I took a long, deep breath. 'I'm not sure. By the time I could understand what they were telling me, it was too late.'

I closed my eyes and talked and talked and pretended not to notice his tears plopping down into my hair.

When I woke, he was gone. I showered and shot off to see the Boss.

Peterson was waiting for me with Mrs Partridge. We went straight in. The Boss sat with Major Guthrie, Professor Rapson, and Chief Farrell. The table was covered with disks, cubes, sticks, scratchpads, papers, files. They had the look of people who'd been at it all afternoon.

'Good evening,' said the Boss. 'As you can see we've discussed everything very thoroughly. Gentlemen, does anyone have anything to add? No? Miss Maxwell, there will be an all-staffer at eleven tomorrow morning, at which you will present your proposals. Then we'll take things from there.'

I was surprised. 'I think it will be better coming from you, sir,' I said.

'No, I want you to do it.'

'Very well,' I said.

Bloody hell!

Kal and Dieter came back that night. She thumped on my door. Until I saw her again I hadn't realised how much I'd missed her. She brought wine and we got stuck in. Unlike everyone else, Kal got everything. Everything from the moment she escorted the Boss to Sick Bay, up until the present. We laughed together over St Mary's creative disobedience. I told her about the fir cone and we talked far into the night. Finally, I took a deep breath and told her about the clinic. She said nothing but put her arm round me. I rested my head on her shoulder and we both fell asleep.

'Good morning, everyone, it's good to see my unit together again. Welcome back to Miss Black and Mr Dieter; a special welcome to our colleagues who have returned from their extended stay in the Cretaceous period; and a very special welcome to Miss Maxwell who has returned from civilian life with the impact of a small asteroid.

'These last months have been traumatic for everyone, but I do feel we have gained more than we lost. A line has been drawn underneath this period and we are preparing now to move in a different direction. Exciting times are ahead for all of us –'

'And it's been so dull up till now,' muttered Peterson

'– and I would like Miss Maxwell to outline the proposals for our future role. Miss Maxwell.'

I took my place on the half-landing with trepidation. This was way worse than my presentation at Thirsk.

'Good morning. I'd like to introduce you to this little chap.' I placed the fir cone, now safe in a specimen jar, on the table. People craned to see so I brought it up on the screen. 'This is a small pine cone, some four inches long, badly burned, species

267

as yet unknown and up until about three or four days ago, he was happily living with his friends in the Cretaceous period.' It went quiet while people worked this out. I made it easy for them.

'You are looking at the first, the very first object ever to be transported from its own timeline into ours. In short, people, we have done the impossible and without even trying. Imagine what we could do if we put our minds to it.'

'But how?' said a voice I didn't recognise. 'We've always been told this can't happen.' There was a buzz of agreement.

'You're right,' I said. 'But the first thing you notice about this specimen is how badly damaged it is. Another couple of minutes and it would have been completely destroyed.' I stopped and watched them to see who would get it first.

Dieter stood up. 'You were able to bring it back *because* it was about to be destroyed. It had no future; therefore it couldn't influence the timeline because it wouldn't exist any more. That's it, isn't it? '

I beamed at him. What a good boy!

'I think that the reason all previous attempts failed is because those objects still had an existence in the future; they had a role to play and therefore History wouldn't allow it. Take, for example, the Mona Lisa. Consider all the events in which she has been involved over the centuries. Now consider what would happen if we had stolen the portrait from Leonardo before the paint dried and brought it back here to the future. Those events would not take place. We would be changing History and that would not be good. But if we think in terms of search and rescue, then all sorts of possibilities open up.'

Some were looking interested, some were not.

'Let me give you an example,' I said. 'Mr Murdoch, would you step up please?' I chose him because if I'd used Peterson or Dieter then everyone would have thought they were ringers.

'Congratulations, Mr Murdoch,' I said, as he stood uneasily beside me. 'You are now King Tarquinius Superbus, last king of Rome.'

'You're making that up. No one's called Superbus.'

'No, I'm not. Ladies and gentlemen, may I introduce King Tarquinius Superbus, benevolent and enlightened ruler of Rome.' There were jeers and catcalls from the republicans in the audience. Dave, however, drew himself up and dispensed a regal wave.

At the back of the Hall, Sibyl De Winter unfolded her arms and gave me a strange look.

'King Tarquinius is going about his daily business, dispensing justice, raising taxes, and carrying out general ruling when he's told that a scruffy, elderly crone – no, not me, Mr Markham – wishes for an audience. Somewhat surprised, he overrules his officials and they bring in the old lady. She's filthy, dressed in rags, and has obviously escaped from a Care in the Community scheme. She lays nine books in front of the king. In those days, obviously, they would have been scrolls and she places them carefully, one by one, at his feet. And then she proceeds to offer them to him, but he's not allowed to open them. Amused, he asks the price. She names a sum that is his country's entire budget for the year. Everyone laughs, including the king.'

'Ho, ho, ho,' said Murdoch, padding his part.

'He asks her why he should buy these books at such a price. What's so important about these particular scrolls? She doesn't answer. She simply says, 'Yes or no?' Of course, the king says no.'

'No,' boomed Murdoch, regally.

'The old woman says nothing. She picks up the scrolls and leaves the audience chamber. On an impulse, the king sends one of his officers after her,' – Murdoch waved his arm and nearly took my head off – 'to find out what she does next. The man returns and tells him she went to the courtyard, took three of the books, and burned them. Then she left the palace.

'Everyone agrees the woman's a nutter and thinks no more

of it. The next day, however, much to everyone's surprise, she's back and with just the six books this time. Again she lays the books in front of the king. Again, she asks the same price: the country's entire budget for one year and now for only six books. This time, no one laughs. Well, Mr Murdoch, what would you do?'

Too late, I realised he would say kill the crone and take the books anyway! But he didn't. He was perfect and when I think what happened to him later, it just breaks my heart.

He stood for a while then said, 'What's in the books?'

'No one knows. Maybe nothing; maybe the secrets of the universe. But it will cost you all the money in your country to find out. What do you do?'

'Yes,' shouted someone from the back of the room.

'No,' shouted several other voices.

He frowned, turned to me and said, 'There's no way of knowing what's in them?'

'No way.'

'Then, no. I won't waste the money. If I don't buy the books then I'm no worse off.'

'Are you sure?'

'I'm not, no.'

'Neither was the king. The story says he thought long and hard, but in the end, he too said no. Again, in silence, she picked up the books and departed.'

Unprompted by me, King Murdoch regally dispatched an officer to follow her and report back. I gave him a look. He grinned back at me. Now I knew how the Boss felt sometimes.

Mrs De Winter was smiling and shaking her head.

I took up the tale.

'Again, the soldier returned to say that once outside, she burned three of the books and now only three remained. The king,' I said, pointedly, 'said nothing.

'On the third day, she comes back with just the three remaining books, which again she lays at the king's feet and offers to sell them to him. 'How much?' says the king, knowing the answer. She tells him the price. The king looks at the three remaining books. This time, the chamber is completely silent. As always, the old woman says nothing. She doesn't need to. If he refuses she'll burn the last three books and no one will ever see her again. Well, Mr Murdoch. *This is the only chance you will ever have.*'

The words resonated strangely. I turned to look at Mrs De Winter. She smiled slightly. I dragged my attention back to King Dave. 'What will you do?'

We all looked at him. He rubbed the back of his neck and looked doubtfully at me. You'd have thought there really were three books on the floor and the future of his kingdom depended on his answer.

'Yes,' he said loudly. 'I'll buy them.' We were all so caught up in the drama he actually got a round of applause. I clapped him on the shoulder. 'Thanks, Dave. You were brilliant. It's OK to sit down now.'

'Oh no, no, no, I want to know what's in the books. After all, I paid for them.'

'Well, the three books were taken to the deepest part of the vault beneath the Temple of Jupiter and there examined by the wisest men in the kingdom. They contained not prophecies as many have thought, but the religious observances necessary to avert great catastrophes. They were so important to the Romans that ten and later fifteen citizens were appointed to safeguard them and these citizens had no other purpose than to ensure no harm came to these books.

'Rome, as we know, conquered Italy and then spread out across the known world. The books were known as the Sibylline Books after their former owner, the old woman, the Sibyl. It was said that whatever crisis faced Rome, help and advice could be found within the three books of the Sibylline. They were one of the Empire's greatest treasures – guarded night and day to prevent them falling into the wrong hands. In

271

the end, the books were only lost because Stilicho ordered their destruction when Alaric and his barbarians were at the gates. You can't help but think – if that's what three books could do, what could they have achieved with all nine?'

Polly Perkins stood up. 'Are you saying we could go back and rescue the six Sibylline Books?'

'We could indeed, Miss Perkins, but wouldn't it be better to go back and rescue all nine of them?'

'But they kept the last three.'

'But they were still destroyed in the end. It's just a case of choosing the right moment.'

An electric current ran round the hall.

Mrs De Winter was laughing.

'And not just that. If you stop and think for a moment there are many examples of lost treasures down the ages. The Great Library at Alexandria, which supposedly held a copy of every book in the known world, went up in flames no less than three times. Who can imagine what was lost? Rome itself burned under the Emperor Nero. St Paul's in the Great Fire of London in 1666. The possibilities are almost endless.'

Someone said, 'But, how could we do all this? With respect, Max, there's only the three of you. Is this instead of, or as well as our Thirsk work?'

This was the opportunity I had been waiting for. I glanced at the Boss and he nodded slightly.

'Well, think about it for a moment. There aren't just the three of us, are there? There are at least eleven historians in this unit.' They didn't get it to begin with and then heads began to turn towards the back rows where our eight trainees were sitting with the traditional trainee expressions of exhaustion, confusion, and terror.

I jumped in with both feet.

'It is proposed to divide this unit into three sections. The first will continue and build on the work already started. Members of this section will be known as Pathfinders. Your job,' I said, speaking directly to the back rows, 'will be just that: to find the path. You will establish, visit, and confirm co-ordinates for key historical events. In many instances, you will be the first on the scene. It will be your job to structure and maintain our Time Map. You will be called upon, as you become more experienced, to assist in other operations. You will also participate in the training of other Pathfinders. Congratulations to you all – you just got promoted.

'The second section will be responsible for policing the timeline and identifying any anomalies. There will be high levels of interaction and it's not a place for the faint hearted. In addition to the normal hazards of the job, there will almost certainly be hostile interference from the future. You will all remember our recent successful efforts in the Cretaceous period. Make no mistake people, we were lucky. No permanent damage was done, at least not to us. In future, we will have to be more careful. We are not the only people out there and they don't give a rat's arse about the time continuum so long as there's a profit in it somewhere. This stupidity endangers us all. This section will not be permanent, but will be established as needed. It goes without saying that this section's requirements will always take priority over any existing commitments.

'The third section, as I previously mentioned, will devote itself to search and rescue. This will be our main role in the future and it concerns the whole unit. Let's take, for example, the Library at Alexandria. Imagine us jumping to try and save the contents of the Great Library there. Personnel for this assignment would consist of at least one historian to make the tea, security staff trained in fire fighting techniques, together with members of our research team to advise on what to save. And it won't stop there. We'll need medical staff with us, archivists who can advise on the best ways to conserve this material and someone with archaeological experience to advise where to hide it. Think about it, we can't bring stuff back here and risk any modern contamination. It all has to be dealt with in situ, stored and hidden away until, and this is the genius bit, we tip off Thirsk. They mount an expedition based on the info we pass them and make the archaeological find of the decade. Maybe even the century. And once we've done that a couple of times our reputation will be such that they'll go wherever we direct them, instead of vice versa and we'll never, ever have to worry about funding again.'

I paused for breath. I'd never known them so quiet. I know no one ever dared interrupt the Boss in mid-flow, but I'd expected a bit of heckling at this point.

'Now I know this is not what some of you signed up for. You've seen this unit go through historians like laxatives through a short grandmother. Let me say now, there is no compulsion here; if you don't want to do this then that's fine. I personally guarantee there will be no comeback. All of you have a think about it. Talk to your section heads and –'

'I'll go,' said Dieter, standing up.

'Well, you've got a short memory,' I grinned. 'The last time we spoke you swore you wouldn't even use the dining room if I was there!'

'Yeah, well, if you're not driving I should be OK,' he said. 'But yes, I want to do this. Put my name down.'

Others stood up. This was encouraging. It got better. Professor Rapson waved a printout.

'I've put together ideas for future rescues,' he said. 'Some big, some small and I'd certainly welcome suggestions from anyone else.' Excited chatter broke out.

'The lost bit of the Bayeux Tapestry.'

'Aristarchus's book on heliocentric theory'

'What?'

'That bloke who said the earth went round the sun.'

'Oh.'

'Tons of stuff by William Blake got lost.'

'Or what about Homer's *Margites*?' I said, becoming temporarily distracted; always a hazard for historians.

274

And then to one side, I saw Jenny Fields. Her lips were moving, but she was such a quiet thing I couldn't make it out. 'Shut up, you lot,' I shouted. 'What is it, Jenny?'

'Dodos. We could bring back dodos.'

And that was the moment. That was the moment when the true potential of all we could achieve became apparent. That was the moment when everyone's imagination took flight and we became unstoppable.

Sixteen

Dieter frowned. 'If we did go to Alexandria then we'd need something bigger than a normal pod. Something that could sleep up to say, ten people and provide a practical working space.'

'And carry equipment,' added someone.

'And storage,' said someone else from R & D. 'Suitable containers for storing scrolls long term. And either some sort of resin or gum to seal them, or the wherewithal to make some.'

'Tar. How about tar? The Dead Sea Scrolls were sealed in earth jars with tar.'

'But it can't be too large. It still has to be relatively inconspicuous. We don't want something the size of the Town Hall. We're not talking Thunderbird 2 here.'

The Chief joined in. 'We could still have something larger, but it could be serviced by normal pods bringing supplies, equipment and relief personnel in and out; like a shuttle service.'

'It would have to be big enough for fire-fighting equipment,' contributed Guthrie.

'We could have various containers with the right equipment for fire fighting, or underwater salvage or excavating and just load whichever one is required and go.'

'How would we know what to take?'

Kal and Peterson jumped in. 'We would need to set up reconnaissance jumps. Survey the library. Find out what's where. What the building's made of. Where's the nearest source of water. The Pathfinders could do that.'

'I think my team can help here,' offered Guthrie. 'I've got two ex-firemen on my strength.' He walked off, shouting for

Weller and Evans and a small crowd began to gather around them.

Peterson forged on. 'We also need a team to suss out appropriate storage methods and containers. Everything will have to be obtained on site. It must all be contemporary. Anything anomalous will be a disaster.'

'Dr Dowson is the best person for that,' said Professor Rapson. 'He should also supply us with a list of desirable scrolls, just in case we have time to pick and choose, rather than the approved St Mary's method of just grabbing anything and running like hell.'

Dieter had his scratchpad out and was tapping away for dear life. 'Say ten people aboard, food and water for ten days – Mrs Mack, how many …?' He plunged off towards the kitchen staff.

Everywhere I looked, people were dragging tables together. Scratchpads were produced. Knots of people began to form. People rushed from one group to another, dragging long printouts behind them. Data stacks began to appear, glistening and ghostly.

'Good God, we've created a monster,' said the Boss, calmly, appearing behind me. 'Peterson, stop writing on the walls. Don't you know this is a listed building?'

Whiteboards were dragged in and set up. The noise level was enormous. It was all out of my hands. I turned to the Boss and he shrugged. 'Welcome to my world.'

I wandered over to the Chief and his crew who were hunched over a table-top holo. A voice was saying, 'And if we put doors at each end then the plant, equipment, whatever, rolls on and then rolls off. No reversing. We get the equipment out and the empty space doubles as a working area. Then we can put living quarters on a second floor, or a mezzanine, out of the way. That way, the tanks can go over here …' There was a storm of protest.

I left them arguing and went over to Guthrie.

'I'm saying we can't use foam – too modern. We can't use

water, either – there's no point in saving the books from burning by drowning them. We need fire mats – get Professor Rapson to see what they should be made from. And poles with hooks on. And wooden ladders, but we should be able to treat those with some sort of flame retardant …'

'But what about protective gear? What do we wear? Do we have to fight the fire in sandals and tunics? Will there be contemporaries there? How authentic will we need to be? Professor …?'

'And Field Medics. Everyone will need burns and crush-injuries training. Maybe at least one doctor should be part of the team. Dr Foster …?'

I left them arguing and made my way over to Mrs Mack.

'Ten people, say three meals a day for ten days. That's thirty times ten … Will they have any sort of cooking facilities? Or will they be entirely dependent on supplies shuttled in? And water? They're going to be hot and thirsty. What's the weight of a cubic foot of water? '

She looked up and saw me. 'Well, Miss Maxwell, you've put the cat amongst the pigeons and no mistake. And to think two days ago we were nearly at meltdown.'

I smiled. 'I don't want to interrupt you, but I want to keep this going as long as possible. There's some good stuff happening. Can you feed and water us in here?'

'Already taken care of. Soup and sandwiches in ten minutes.'

'I should have guessed. And what about you and your team, Mrs Mack? Can I tempt you to step outside St Mary's?'

She grinned at me and I caught a glimpse of the girl who'd stood back to back with her husband the night they threw the Fascists out of Cardiff. She'd be there.

Lunch didn't even slow us down. Two hours later the Hall looked like a war zone. Discarded printouts littered the floor, along with plastic cups and plates. Practically every surface was covered in scratchpads, disks, sticks, cubes, papers, file covers, and assorted debris. Three or four half-finished data stacks rotated slowly in unfinished limbo. Whiteboards were full. The noise had died down considerably. People were now grappling with the details.

I sat on the stairs with Kal and Peterson. Together we'd knocked out a tentative schedule and a pile of enquiries for other crews.

A shout went up. 'Max! Over here a minute!' I heaved myself up and trudged over to Dieter's table. Hundreds of pieces of paper littered the surface. Equations, diagrams, sketches, scribbled lists – they'd really been going at it here.

'Look,' said Dieter, spreading out a large sheet of paper on top of everything. 'This is a sketch of how we think it could look from the outside.' He anchored the corners with a mug of cold coffee, two cubes and someone's scratchpad. We crowded round.

It was rectangular and flat roofed. 'We can use the roof as another working area. We have a door at each end of the pod. Here and here. The doors let down to be ramps,' he said, 'and here we have …'

The Boss gently touched my shoulder. 'Start putting it together, Miss Maxwell. You have one month.'

And just like that, we were off to Alexandria.

I paused outside the door, striving for calm. I had worked really hard on this. Actually, we'd all worked really hard on this, but mine was the final voice. And I was the one presenting. My month was up. It was time to deliver.

Sticking my chin in the air, I pushed open the door. Mrs Partridge looked up. 'Go on in, Miss Maxwell; they're all waiting for you.'

I clutched my briefing notes even more tightly and walked in. She was right; they were all waiting for me. The Boss sat in his usual position at the head of his briefing table, Chief Farrell at his right hand, Major Guthrie on his left. Next to him sat

Helen Foster, then Mrs Mack and Mrs Enderby from Wardrobe. On the other side, Professor Rapson and Doctor Dowson should probably not have been allowed to sit together.

They were all here. I'd argued that all departments should be represented, but at the time, I never thought it would be me taking the briefing.

Mrs Partridge joined Kal, Peterson, Dieter, and Jamie Cameron from R & D, all of whom were sitting along one wall. Everyone had their scratchpads open and everyone stared at me with bright anticipation. The Boss nodded for me to start. I very nearly turned and ran.

'Good afternoon, everyone. This is a three-part briefing: a quick background, an update from all the teams and a provisional schedule.

'We'll start with the background briefing.

Ptolemy II of Egypt founded the Library at Alexandria at the beginning of the third-century BC. Estimates of the contents vary between 400,000 and 700,000 scrolls although the actual total may have been very much more or very much less. We just don't know. Don't look so dismayed; we won't be in any position to save even a fraction of that number.

'Because there are some doubts about the content of the main Library by this date, we're going for the well-documented destruction of the Serapeum – the daughter library.

'In 391 AD, Theophilus, Patriarch of Alexandria, instigates an anti-paganism campaign in the city. He incites the Christians, urging them to destroy the Serapeum and other pagan sites. The mob, doing what mobs do, is very happy to comply. So, when the library is burning around us and fighting breaking out everywhere, that's when we move in.

'Thanks to the Pathfinders we now know the exact location of the Serapeum. We also know the internal layout. There are a number of areas, each devoted to a single subject – mathematics, astronomy, natural sciences, anatomy, early history, scientific discourse, and so on.

'Detailed layouts are in your folders. You'll see the landing points marked in yellow with the pod number alongside. It's a big place, but not that big. We don't want anyone landing inside a wall, so Chief Farrell will personally lay in all co-ordinates.

'What we do need to worry about, however, is the wholesale destruction occurring around us. But, if we take reasonable precautions we'll all be fine.'

Someone snorted.

'Are there any questions so far?'

Apparently not.

'Chief Farrell, if you could update us on the progress with our new pod, please.'

He looked up. 'Everything is on schedule. There are some logistical difficulties with the internal layout, but nothing that can't be resolved. We won't have time for the outside shell, but we can fix that later. No one will see it but us. I'd like to take this opportunity to remind everyone that Hawking will be out of bounds to all personnel except Mr Dieter and me for three days, starting the day after tomorrow. Please make it clear to your teams that there will be no access for any reason whatsoever during this period until we give the all clear.'

God knows what they were doing in there. There was no point in asking. I'd tried and he'd just grinned at me. So irritating.

I continued. 'Dr Foster, you're responsible for all things medical. How is the training going?'

'We've worked our way through first, second, third, and fourth degree burns and the effects of smoke inhalation. We've now moved on to the treatment of crush injuries. Everyone going on the assignment has to re-take their Field Medic exam. But, we're all on schedule.'

I nodded. 'Dr Dowson?'

'I've located a suitable site where we can hide whatever we do manage to salvage. It's reasonably near Alexandria and yet should remain completely undisturbed for nearly 2,000 years.

You do understand that I can give no guarantees?'

'We understand, Doctor. And this site is in Egypt, obviously. An unbreakable rule for the future, everyone. Whatever we rescue remains in that country. This is an Egyptian treasure. It stays in Egypt.

'Professor Rapson, I believe you've been to Alexandria.'

He had too, cunningly disguised as an absent-minded academic. Not much disguise needed really. We'd just wrapped him in a sheet, wound him up, and pointed him at Alexandria.

'I've managed to locate a source of earthenware jars I think will be appropriate, Max. I can nip back and conclude the deal whenever you're ready.'

'How are you paying?' Payment had to be with contemporary material.

'We have … induced … the Egyptology department at Thirsk to part with one or two small treasures.'

'Excellent. Mrs Mack.'

'Yes, Max.' She sat with her scratchpad, all attention.

'We need you to keep us fed and watered. Dr Dowson tells me Site B has no water supply of any kind. Because we don't know how much material we're going to be able to save, or how long it will take us to pack it all away in the desert heat, we have no idea for how long we need to be provisioned.'

The Chief said, 'This shouldn't be a problem. We can run a shuttle-pod service ferrying supplies and people as required.'

'Good,' I said. 'Please can you two work out the details and let me know.'

I was being really unkind here. She was bouncing with excitement beside me. I put her out of her misery and grinned at her. 'Mrs Enderby.'

She glowed.

'We'll need Wardrobe to provide fireproof clothing, canvas shelters to keep the sun off, and something appropriately sterile to wear when we work.

'This is most important. Any archaeological find is subject

to rigorous scrutiny. This goes double for what we're about to do. People are going to be screaming, "fake," if even the slightest detail is wrong. And if we screw this up then we'll never be trusted again. It will finish us. We have to get this exactly right. So, it's important to minimise contact with the scrolls as much as possible. All heads must be covered. Nothing to do with religion – or sun, come to that – we can't afford to have people shedding hair all over these scrolls. Especially if that hair is covered in modern hair product. I don't know what would survive over two millennia but I'm not taking the risk. We don't need scientists wondering if the ancients really did use anti-dandruff shampoo. So, Mrs Enderby, Wardrobe's most rigorous checks please. And no sun cream when handling the scrolls. Cotton gloves. We don't know how the chemicals will react with the papyrus over such a long time.

'Any questions before we move on to the schedule?'

They shook their heads, shifted their papers, cleared their scratchpads, and we moved on.

'Professor Rapson, you and your team jump to Alexandria, Site A, to acquire the pots, tar-making materials, provisions, etc., taking them on to Doctor Dowson at Site B. You and your team are in Number Three. Mr Dieter will accompany you.

'Dr Dowson, your team is in TB2 and you jump straight to Site B, the re-burial site, to set things up and wait for the Professor. Chief Farrell will accompany you.

'The scroll-retrieval team, that's my gang, are in Number One because it's small. There are three teams – mine, with Markham and Van Owen; Mr Peterson's with Schiller and Evans; and Miss Black's, with Weller and Clarke. One historian, one Pathfinder, and one security guard to each team.

'The medical team are in Number Two and the fire-fighting and security teams are in Numbers Five and Six. We all jump to Site A together and get cracking inside the library.

'Once we've done the biz in the Serapeum, we take everything we've got to Site B. The medical team returns to St

Mary's with any seriously wounded.

'We start unloading the scrolls and under instructions from Dr Dowson and the Professor, pack them into the pots, and seal them up. As I said, near sterile conditions to apply. We then bury them, wall them up, or drop them down a chasm; whatever Dr Dowson has decided is appropriate, to be found by the joint Thirsk/Egypt expedition being organised as we speak. We do the world's most rigorous FOD plod and return home to wild acclaim.

'Any questions or comments?

Professor Rapson said thoughtfully. 'The Dead Sea Scrolls were sealed with tar, but I'm not so sure. Maybe pitch would be better.'

Doctor Dowson snorted. 'How will you hold it together?'

'What about droppings of some kind? Plant fibre is a wonderful binding agent. I'll try with horse dung. Or rabbits. Or maybe human excrement. An organic and a renewable source.'

Yes, good luck with that. If they were relying on me then the jars would be unsealed for ever. After years living off rations, I only go about twice a year, usually at the summer and winter solstice. I like to have a bit of a ceremony …

We discussed things for over an hour and a few things were changed, but, basically, that was the plan.

I had the final mission plan on the Boss's desk within a month as requested. He nodded and said, 'This seems satisfactory.' So he was very happy with it. 'I assume you have contingency plans?'

'Well, yes and no, sir. Sod's Law decrees if a thing can go wrong it will. We've done our best but something will happen that we haven't foreseen and then we'll just have to wing it.'

'Ah,' he said. 'The History Department's motto.' He smiled thinly. 'Almost, I envy you.'

I stopped gathering things together. 'Would you like to come with us?'

He stood quite still and we looked at each other.

'Why not, sir?'

After a long pause, he said softly, 'Yes, why not? Although not to the library. I shan't be able to contribute anything there, but I might drop in to Site B.'

'I'll leave it up to you, sir, but you'll be very welcome.'

Outside, Mrs Partridge gripped my arm. 'Is he going to Alexandria?'

I was really surprised. She was hurting me. 'If he wants to.'

'He shouldn't go.'

'It's up to him.'

'You are the mission controller. You should use your veto.'

'Why?'

But the moment had passed. Her face smoothed. She released my arm and stepped back. 'Do you have anything for me, Miss Maxwell?'

If I was back to Miss Maxwell again, I must really be in her bad books. I handed her the data cubes, schedules, and distribution lists. She nodded, took them back to her desk, and began to hammer her keyboard.

I slipped out of the door.

There was a terrible smell on the second floor. I went to see what was happening. I'm not sure why I bothered. I could hear what was happening.

'Rabbit shit? You're cooking rabbit shit in here? Are you insane? Dear gods, man, you can't cook rabbit shit. Are you seriously telling me ...?'

'Dr Dowson,' I said soothingly. 'What's the problem?'

He pointed a trembling finger. 'This madman ... this idiot is cooking rabbit shit. Can you believe such stupidity? Rabbit shit, for God's sake ...' He gasped for breath.

'Calm down, Octavius,' said a completely unrepentant Professor Rapson, emerging from the murk and removing the handkerchief tied across the lower part of his face. 'You're going to have a seizure at this rate. Jamie, can you open the windows, please?'

The awful fug began to dissipate a little. The fire alarms hadn't gone off. I climbed on a table and pulled off the cover to investigate. No battery.

'Professor ...'

'I had no choice, Max; the stupid things keep going off. It's very annoying.'

'Rabbit shit,' raged Doctor Dowson, displaying a focus not often seen at St Mary's. 'Of all the idiotic, moronic ...'

'For God's sake, Occy, show a bit of gratitude. We're working on a recipe for pitch here and I need some sort of fibrous binding agent. I have to say, before you self-combust, this batch seems to be working very well. Show a little gratitude, please.'

Dr Dowson swelled and his colour deepened. 'Gratitude? For what? I knew I'd end up doing R & D's job for them. Tell me this, Andrew, exactly how much rabbit shit do you think is going to be available in a city? In Egypt? In the heat? In the desert? I'll tell you now, you're wasting your time. Cow, camel, or donkey dung is the way to go. Plentiful supplies and bigger dollops. Have you seriously thought how many little rabbit pellets you would need to equal the average cow pat?'

'Well, it should be easy to calculate,' said Professor Rapson, more easily diverted, thank goodness. 'Say between seventy to one hundred pellets to one pat – although we could do it by weight, of course ... Jamie, my boy, can you get me some cowpats, please. We'll need to poke them about a bit to check for plant material, so can you ask Mrs Mack for some forks as well. Now, Occy, we need to consider our source of resin ...'

The two of them plunged back into the murk.

Major Guthrie's final briefing laid it on the line.

'Listen up, everyone. I shall say this only once. As soon as we land, even before we step outside, you will – all of you –

answer to me. Everyone from historians upwards should be aware of this. If you can't accept this then you don't go. It's that simple. So, no one leaves their pods until I give the word. And when I say, "Pull out," you pull out. You don't stop to grab just a few more scrolls or investigate what's round the corner; you go. You drop whatever you are doing and return to your pods. Is that clear?

We murmured a response.

'Right, I've already briefed my team on this and now I'm telling you. We are not there to fight the fire. We'll try and contain it while you work but our main job is to protect you while you seize what you can. We'll give you every opportunity to get the job done, but your safety is our priority. And don't weigh my people down with piles of scrolls because that's not what they're there for.

'A couple of us will be in full fire-fighter's gear. Everyone else will be wearing protective fire suits. And there's no point in the History Department shaking its head and muttering. I don't give a rat's arse about historical inaccuracy. Live with it.

'Those of us not on fire-fighting duties are on crowd control – guarding against hostile contemporaries. Again, don't rope them into scroll-rescuing activities. Their purpose is to protect you long enough for an ordered retreat back to the pods.

'Number Two is converted to a medical purpose and Dr Foster and her team will be located in and around. If any injuries are incurred, *all* members of the team should report to her. You must remain in your teams at all times. No one wanders around on their own.

'Whatever happens, we spend no more than two hours on site. However well it's going. Number Six will have a designated driver who will monitor oxygen levels, act as timekeeper, and advise me when it's time to pull the plug. This brings me back to where I started, people. When I say we go – we're gone. Any questions?'

Helen's final medical briefing was even worse. She gave us a depressingly long list of the circumstances and/or injuries which would result in us being deemed not fit for purpose. It seemed anything more serious than a slight headache would result in us being returned to sender.

I shifted restlessly in my seat. Beside me, Peterson whispered, 'Bloody hell, Max, we've got to stop including these amateurs. We'll never get anything done at this rate.'

Unfortunately, at that moment, Helen stopped talking and his voice was heard around the Hall with disastrous clarity.

'You can say this about historians, we may be the tea-drenched disaster-magnets of St Mary's but bloody hell, can we think quickly when we have to?' He turned in his seat, fixed a startled Ian Guthrie with a glare, and said, 'Shh!'

It didn't save him. I did what I could, but she separated him from the herd and when she'd finished with him, a vengeful Ian Guthrie was waiting.

Afterwards, I took him for a drink and said fondly, 'Idiot.'

'Yes,' he said, downing it in one go. 'But there's always make-up sex afterwards.'

'True,' I said. 'Tell me, I've always wanted to know – what's he like in bed?'

Chief Farrell delivered sets of co-ordinates. The big pod, now known for ever as TB2, was completed and loaded only two days after its scheduled date. All the other pods were serviced and ready to go. He did not manage to set fire to himself in any way. No screaming was involved. No alarms went off.

'Well,' I said. 'That was dull.'

And then, suddenly there was nothing more to do and we were ready.

We assembled in Hawking, unfamiliar in our stiff new fire suits.

Doctor Dowson and Chief Farrell had loaded up TB2 and stood on the ramp ticking off the inventory. Helen and her team waited outside Number Two. Guthrie's teams, already in fire-fighting gear, lined up outside Numbers Five and Six. Peterson, Kal and I assembled our teams and marshalled them into Number One. Professor Rapson quivered with excitement outside Number Three. The gantry was packed. Every single member of the unit had assembled in Hawking for this. This was it. This was The Really Big One. Our future was on the line. Every pod would be in use and over half the unit on the active list for this one. Thirsk was on stand-by. If this went wrong then St Mary's was finished.

What had I done?

We stood in silence. There was no point hanging around. I gave the word and the world went white.

Seventeen

Everything went wrong. Right from the off, everything went wrong.

We landed an hour later than planned and a good half of the library was well ablaze. Fortunately, we were at the other end. The Christians, showing a level of intelligence not normally associated with the religiously fervent, had pushed off. We exited the pod to a red-hot wall of heat and noise. It was like stepping into hell. We had no time to waste. We got stuck in.

Two paces from the pod and I was drenched in sweat. The heat was suffocating. I could hear my laboured breathing inside my own head. From the corner of my eye I could see leaping flames. It was impossible to describe the library; all details were lost in the smoky haze. My world was limited to the few square feet in front of me.

Our teams deployed to their given positions. I had Markham and young Van Owen. We nodded to each other for luck and got started. We'd rehearsed for this, but it was far tougher than I thought it would be. The slightest exertion made me sweat even harder. My head pounded. I couldn't catch my breath.

We established a routine. Markham forced the armarium door. Van Owen and I stepped forward. Markham held the torch. We scooped the contents of the top shelf into the tub, then the next one down, then the next and so on. Pass the tub down the line. Grab a new one. Move on to the next armarium. Markham forced the doors … and so on.

Occasionally, someone passed us some water. Dark figures criss-crossed the room, shouting over the noise of the fire. I ignored them, whoever they were, trusting Guthrie to keep us safe. Concentrate on the job in hand. Deal with the now.

Breathe. Ignore the increasing heat, the pounding headache, and the blurred vision. Just get on with it.

We shuffled up to the next armarium. Markham splintered the doors. These bloody scrolls were never ending. We were reaching for the top shelf when, over the clamour, I heard a new noise.

Something went over with a crash. I saw flames running across the floor towards us. The floor was marble. How could it burn? It must be oil – maybe a lamp had gone over. No, it wasn't a lamp. The bloody Christians were back. Through the smoke, I could hear shouting. They must have seen or heard us. We were making no efforts at concealment. Markham stepped away from us to give himself room.

The security team swung into action. Their instructions were very clear. No violence of any kind. Absolutely no contemporaries were to be harmed. Moving as one, they charged towards the mob, sinister in their fire-fighting gear, uttering blood-curdling cries and waving their arms. Moving as one, the Christians turned and fled. Maybe they thought we were pagan demons come to defend our temple. They would regroup around the corner, find their courage and religious zeal, and be back. It would get bloody. Time to go.

I felt a sudden change in pressure and heard Guthrie's voice raised in warning. In my ear, someone shouted, 'Get down. Get down. Get down.'

None of us had wasted our time over the last months. We hurled ourselves to the floor.

Too late. A hot wind picked us up and I slammed backwards into an armarium, which toppled. It and a million scrolls fell down on top of me. The heat intensified to unbearable temperatures. Was I on fire? I screamed and rolled, scrabbling to get out from under the crushing weight of the cupboard.

When I opened my eyes, Markham was bending over me, backlit by orange flames. 'Max. Can you hear me?'

I nodded. He seized an arm and Van Owen got hold of the

other one.

I shouted, 'Wait,' tore myself free, and grabbed the half-filled tub. There might be anything in there – the exact location of Alexander's tomb, the true story of Cambyses' lost army, even a note from Plato saying to disregard all that Atlantis stuff – he'd had too much cheese late at night. I wasn't leaving anything behind if I could help it.

All around, figures were grabbing what they could and flying back to the pods. Above us, I heard a crack and something massive dropped from the roof to crash and splinter on the marble floor. Flames billowed and roared hungrily.

Guthrie was yelling. 'Evacuate. Now. Everyone out. Move. Move.'

I got seized again and we raced back to Number One as blocks of masonry, tiles, and burning wood dropped around us. The roof was coming down. The library was finished. I turned back at the door. I wanted a final look at the greatest library in the world, but it was already gone. Just fire, smoke, and destruction. I could only guess at what was being lost. Someone yanked me into the pod as a flaming beam fell across the doorway.

I heard Peterson initiate the jump and then the world went white.

The god of historians was watching out for us. We arrived at the desert site at night. We were crowded and suffocating inside the pod. Peterson ripped open the door and we all tumbled out into the crisp, cold night air, desperate for relief. I tore frantically at my smouldering fire suit. I was so hot I couldn't bear it another second. If I didn't get out I would scream. My gloved hands couldn't grasp the fastenings and I panicked. Dimly, I heard Chief Farrell's voice. He pulled my hands away and others came to help. I've never been undressed by so many people. My boots came off and I was down to my tee and shorts when someone wrapped me in an exquisitely cold, wet towel. I groaned with relief. Someone tipped water onto my head and neck. I sagged to the ground and took a minute off. Someone else passed me a drink and I grabbed it, suddenly realising just how desperately thirsty I was.

'Steady,' said Leon, crouching nearby. 'Just sip it slowly.'

He took the bottle away, wiped my chin, let me sip a little more, and then helped me sit up.

He smiled. 'It went OK then?'

'How can you tell?'

'You're all here. No one's on fire. The pods are intact. There's no screaming. An intelligent and perceptive man can read these small signs.'

I nodded. 'Do you think I'll ever meet one?'

He wiped my face with something cool. 'I'm sure I saw you in a dress once. You were clean. And smelled good. Sometimes it seems like just a dream.' He rubbed my arm and then went away to deal with the others.

I lay for a while looking up at more stars than I'd seen since the Cretaceous. Occasionally, I grinned to myself. We'd done it. We'd managed to save a part of the Great Library of Alexandria. Not a big part, admittedly, more like a tiny fraction, but that was better than nothing. We'd done it. And no one was dead. History, it would seem, had either been looking the other way; or had possibly given up where St Mary's was concerned.

And this was just the beginning! If this assignment went well …

We were being tended to in a rough square area, formed by TB2 on one side, Number Three at right angles, and now Five, Six and One completed the set. All doors opened onto the square, making it defensible should the need arise. They'd laid rough mats over the sand to give us a reasonable surface and in a vain effort to keep sand out of the pods. Canvas awnings were stretched overhead and around the pods to give shade during the day.

We were camped in a small ravine, closed at one end and

approachable only by a narrow, enclosed, rocky path. Somewhere among these rocky crags lay the hidden cave where we would store the scrolls.

The ravine would trap the heat. The scorching, baking, sweltering heat. We came straight from the inferno into the cauldron. It would be almost unbearable during the day. I could smell dust, stale air, and the memory of hot rock. The canvas awnings would keep us shaded but nothing could keep us cool.

I struggled to my feet as the Boss approached.

'Excellent work,' he said softly.

Time I earned my pay. I raised my voice. 'Report.'

'Mostly present,' croaked Guthrie. 'And mostly correct. Evans and Ritter have been med-evacced. Nothing serious, but a sandy desert is no place for weeping burns. We've all been lightly toasted but no one actually managed to immolate themselves.'

'What did we get?'

Peterson coughed and spat. 'What we came for. At a rough guess, between fifteen hundred and seventeen hundred scrolls. No idea of the contents. We grabbed from all over the Library so it should be a nice mixed bag. Of course, with our luck, it'll be just multiple copies of the furniture inventory,'

But he was grinning. They all were. I was too. Fifteen hundred scrolls. Fifteen hundred scrolls containing the secrets of the Ancient World.

'Thank you, everyone,' said Dr Bairstow. 'Extremely satisfactory work.'

Professor Rapson and Dr Dowson wrung my hand, incoherent in their excitement. We dissuaded our two fanatics from investigating the contents of Number One right at that moment.

'OK, people,' I said. 'Let's get some rest. Tomorrow, we make a start.'

Guthrie set the watch. We switched out the lights, stretched out on the ground, and fell asleep.

They came in the night. They'd chosen their time well. Most of us were spark-out after our crowded day.

I opened my eyes to the crackle of gunfire and sat bolt upright, disoriented and groggy. Guthrie was bellowing over the din. Someone tossed me a handgun and two clips. The Boss was giving urgent instructions to secure the pods.

I sent Van Owen, Schiller, and the other Pathfinders, together with all R & D staff to the pods with instructions not to come out again. Under any circumstances. Ignoring orders to get inside myself, I grabbed my boots and joined those hidden at the narrow entrance, peering out into the darkness, trying to make out what the hell was going on. Whoever it was, there was no way they were getting those scrolls.

There were no more shots. I could hear only the breathing of those around me.

Tactically, Guthrie had us in a very sound position, controlling the only entrance into our ravine with the pods clustered behind us. Always try and hold the narrow ground. Leonidas did it at Thermopylae, delaying the Persian army for three valuable days, giving the rest of Greece time to get its act together. Henry V did it at Agincourt, positioning his army in the narrow waist between heavily wooded areas and watching the French knights ride over each other and drown in the mud. Leonidas and Henry V. Two men who'd have a lot to say to each other should they ever meet. And where were they when we needed them?

I had no idea what was going on. Neither did anyone else. Guthrie made it simple for us.

'We're here. The rest of St Mary's are safe inside the pods. Therefore shoot anyone you see trying to get up this path. They're not contemporaries. They have modern weapons. Legitimate targets. Shoot their arses.'

Well, that made it easy. We're historians. We need things kept simple.

I checked and loaded my weapon, clashed my boots together

to dislodge any scorpions, laced them up, and wished for body armour. Murdoch updated me. Someone heard a noise in the rocks and challenged an indistinct figure. The resulting fusillade of gunfire woke everyone up. After that initial burst, however, everything was silent. And continued so. We waited, but nothing happened.

We were just beginning to wonder if it was all a false alarm when they came at us out of the darkness. Guthrie gave the order. 'Here they come. Fire at will. Good luck, everyone.'

I crouched behind a rock and fired at the muzzle flashes. The noise was overwhelming and the stink of cordite everywhere. Casings, mine and others, flew around me. A small part of my mind was thinking what a bitch of a FOD plod we were going to have. There wasn't much kickback from my small weapon but still my hands, wrists and forearms ached with the strain of keeping it steady. It all seemed to go on for a very long time. I kept firing until empty, reloaded and fired again. Gunshots reverberated around the canyon. The noise was deafening. My gun grew hot in my sweaty hands and the acrid smell made me thirsty again. A voice shouted in the night and they retreated. Silence fell.

'Sound off,' said Guthrie and we did. In our group was Murdoch, Peterson, Markham and me. Guthrie and another, larger group were a little above us and to the left. The Boss commanded a team on the other side of the path. Really, we had pretty well everything locked down. Nothing was getting past us.

Wrong.

I blame myself. I'd actually made the comparisons between us and Leonidas and Henry. I just hadn't taken it far enough. They both employed similar tactics. They both encountered the same problems. Everything's fine so long as no one comes up behind you. Because then, in a narrow space – you're trapped.

In Henry's case, it was because the French POWs, sent to the rear of the army for safekeeping and future ransom, forgot themselves and cheated. They tried to attack Henry from the rear, which just wasn't done, but that's the French for you. They killed the baggage boys left in charge and for Henry, the position was so perilous that he forgot the rules as well and had them all killed. Problem solved.

Leonidas was betrayed by that bastard Ephialtes, who led a Persian contingent through the mountains to fall upon the Spartans from the rear. That didn't end well but Leonidas and his boys went down fighting.

They came again, a full frontal assault. Lots of sound and fury. I was peppered with painful pieces of flying rock. We were pinned down. We couldn't get out, but they couldn't get past us either, whoever they were. We were well placed; the pods were secure and we were in no great danger.

Wrong again.

All firing ceased and in the ringing silence, I heard the distinctive whine of a couple of heavy-duty blasters, cocked and locked. Behind us. The bastards were behind us. That's what they'd been doing under cover of heavy fire – creeping around behind us. I heard Guthrie curse fearsomely under his breath. We could have slugged it out, but really, there was no chance.

A voice called out of the darkness for us to lay down our weapons. I was all for battling on to the end, but the Boss gave the only order he could. In the silence of disbelief, Guthrie's voice came out of the darkness, saying quietly, 'No one opens a pod except on Dr Bairstow's instructions. That is an order.' Indistinct figures emerged out of the darkness and we were marched, at gunpoint, back into our little basin.

The sky began to lighten. Dawn was happening behind the mountains. And with the sun would come the heat again.

There were fewer of them than us, but they were better armed and equipped. And they had the advantage of surprise.

They lined us up on the sand, in front of the pods, in two rows facing each other. We were on our knees, hands behind our heads. They weren't gentle. The next half hour or so was not going to be much fun. Commands were shouted and a few of them peeled off to check the surrounding rocks and the rest took up positions behind us.

I looked around. Opposite me I could see Farrell, Peterson, the Boss, Markham, and Dieter. I couldn't see any Pathfinders at all. I hoped they were safe in Number One with the scrolls. I'm an historian. I thought they'd come for the scrolls. I was wrong about that, as well.

Jamie Cameron from R & D was here, but Doctor Dowson and the Professor were not. They would be in TB2. I was a little worried that they *would* open the door. Three, Five, and Six, I suspected, were empty and locked. Yes, the bulk of us were here in the sand. Helpless.

Our opponents meant business. Clearly now, in the early morning light I could see they wore desert camouflage, body armour, headsets, and carried enough weaponry to effect a regime change. No words were spoken. They looked tough and professional. Just how tough and professional we were about to find out.

One stepped forward and pulled off his helmet.

Ronan.

The man who had killed Sussman.

We'd ambushed him and now he'd done it to us. I tried not to sag. This wasn't good. I'd seen what he was capable of.

Close up, he was surprisingly nondescript. No savage scars, no sinister sneer. His dark hair was thinning and his lined face made him look older than I suspect he actually was, but having said that, he looked in surprisingly good condition.

You see, people think it's easy, living in the past. You turn up with a big bag of gold and enough foreknowledge to ensure you back the right horse, or the right king, or the right dot com companies, and retire to count your money.

It's not that simple.

Try it in the last hundred years or so and you'll find the lack of National Insurance number, ID card, or credit rating means you're officially a non-person and after America closed its borders last year, all sorts of security alarm bells start ringing.

Or, you think you'll go back a little further before all these tiresome records were invented, but that doesn't work either. Society is rigid. Everyone knows everyone else in their world. Everyone has their place in the scheme of things. If you don't belong to a family, a tribe, a village, a guild, whatever, you don't exist then, either. And you can't just pitch up somewhere without mutual acquaintances, recommendations, or letters of introduction. Life on the fringes of society, any society in any time is tough. I should know. The four months I spent alone in Rushford had not gone well.

If that was how these people lived then they should look like shit. And so should their pods. Pods need regular aligning or they start to drift. And yet these people looked in reasonably good nick. Better than us at the moment. They had a base somewhere. They had to have. Someone, somewhere, was giving them shelter.

I dragged myself from that problem to the more pressing issues of the moment.

Ronan scanned the rows of kneeling figures. As usual, he showed no more emotion than a corpse. If he felt anything at all, it was all kept within, locked down, stifled. I'm used to St Mary's, where no one is at all backward in expressing whatever emotions they happen to be experiencing at the time and this quiet, deadly calm filled me with fear.

He pointed, apparently at random. A single shot echoed off the walls and Jamie Cameron fell forward into the sand with part of his face blown away.

The shock of it stopped my heart. Young Jamie Cameron. With his mop of dark hair and perpetually singed eyebrows. One minute alive and the next minute – not. I swallowed down real hysteria and dragged my eyes away. Who would be next? Because there would be a next. There would keep being a next until Ronan told us what he wanted and the Boss refused to give

300

it to him.

They dragged Markham to his feet.

'Open the pods.'

I held my breath. He'd just seen Jamie die. There was no saying what our uncoordinated little troglodyte would do.

I underestimated him. That boy was gold. Grubby gold, but gold nonetheless.

He drew himself up to his unimpressive height and said quietly, 'I take my orders from Dr Bairstow.'

Ronan smiled unpleasantly and raised his weapon.

'Not any more you don't. Open the pods.'

It was Chief Farrell, of all people, who broke. He jumped to his feet. 'No. Stop. Don't do this.' Two men seized him.

I stared at him in shock. What was he doing?

Ronan regarded him impassively for a moment, then turned back to Markham and fired. Another shot echoed off the rocks and Markham crumpled to the ground, blood seeping into the sand beneath him.

The Boss's face was bleak and, if he ever got out of this, I wouldn't give much for Ronan's chances. Or Farrell's either.

'What do you want, Clive?'

'What do I want, Edward? I want it all. I want your pods, including the nice, big, shiny one over there. I want the contents. Those scrolls will fetch a fortune hundreds of times over. I want you to know that this disaster will end your command of this pathetic little unit. But most of all Edward, I want to leave you here, last man standing, with all your bright young people bleeding to death in the dirt around you. I want you to know I've won and everything you have struggled to achieve has just led to me getting exactly what I want.'

Hatred crackled between them. I could feel it twisting the air. They had no thought for those around them. This was up close and personal. We were looking at the end of our St Mary's. He shouldn't have come. I'd been wrong to include him. If he'd stayed safely at home then whatever happened to us here would not be the end. He could have rebuilt, somehow. Was this what had thrown Mrs Partridge into such an untypical panic?

'No.'

Short and to the point. No arguing, no pleading, no messing. Just 'no.'

Ronan smiled again. 'We've done this before, Edward, and look how that turned out. How is the leg?'

'How many is it now, Clive? What's your tally? How many people have you killed since Annie?'

'I didn't kill Annie. St Mary's killed Annie.'

'If she was here now, what would you do?'

'If she was here now and knowing how you felt about her, Edward, she would be the first to go. But I think we have a very acceptable alternative here, somewhere, don't we? Ah yes. Good morning, Miss Maxwell.'

Shit, shit, shit.

I heard someone move behind me. Footfalls in the sand and the rustle of clothing. That unmistakeable click as the safety came off.

I straightened my back, stuck my chin in the air, and really, really, *really* wished I had an office job. This was it. I closed my eyes.

The wait seemed endless. I felt the sweat pour down my face and back. I swayed, whether through heat or fear or both – I don't know. Would I know anything about it? Was it better to be the first to go? To be spared the sight of my friends being gunned down around me? Would it hurt? I'd just convinced myself I was ready to die when –

'No!'

The sudden shout made me jump a mile. Braced as I was, I nearly wet myself.

'I told you. Stop. I'll open the pods.'

The Boss's voice cracked like a whip. 'As you were, Farrell.'

'No,' he said, hoarsely. 'You don't lose her like you lost Annie. I'll open the pods for you. Just don't shoot her.'

Relief and shame in equal proportions. 'Don't do it, Chief. I ...'

Someone pushed me face down into the ground. 'Shut up.'

I twisted my head and spat sand, desperate to see what was going on. Someone seized me by the scruff of the neck and pulled me back onto my knees so I had an excellent view of what happened next.

Chief Farrell and Ronan crossed the gritty sand towards the pods.

The Boss called, 'Farrell, you will not do this. Stand down.' His voice dripped with contempt. And a little desperation.

My chest felt tight and I struggled to breathe. This could not be happening. He couldn't be doing this. Of all people, he could not be doing this. Did he seriously think we'd be allowed to go free? He was handing them our only advantage. He'd come back from the future to prevent this very thing from happening. Why was he doing this? I knew the answer to that and felt ashamed. Because of me he would kill us all. Because of me ...

I bunched my muscles, ready to jump. Jump and die. Because if I was dead then he wouldn't have to open the door...

And a voice on the wind that wasn't there breathed, 'Wait.'

Who said that? I looked wildly around and that confusion caused me to miss my opportunity. Farrell had reached TB2. He stood off to one side. Ronan and his henchmen stepped back and fanned out. Much bloody good it did them.

Farrell said clearly, 'Door.'

The ramp came down.

A huge, boiling red-golden rose of flame bloomed in their faces.

Professor Rapson and Doctor Dowson stood in the entrance. The Professor held the industrial vacuum cleaner we'd brought to clean sand out of the pods. Bright flame spurted from one end as he played it right and left. Behind him, Dr Dowson pumped furiously on some kind of homemade stirrup pump attached to what looked like a milk churn. How had they managed to knock this together? They were covered in soot and such hair as they possessed between them stood on end. The Professor was yelling, 'God for Harry, England, and St George!'

Ronan hurled himself to the ground. The two men with him, not so quick, were engulfed in flames and dropped to the ground, screaming.

We had the element of surprise.

The Boss shouted, 'St Mary's – get down!' and we threw ourselves face down. A huge tongue of flame boiled over our heads. Ronan's men fired wildly, torn between either shooting us or being incinerated on the spot. Guthrie hacked the legs from under one of them and grappled for his gun. Others were doing the same. The Boss, unable to get up on his own, laid about him with his stick and caught one across his knees. He went down with a cry of pain and I threw myself on top of him and tried to wrest his weapon away.

Fresh gunfire sounded nearby and I could hear Guthrie yelling for Dieter.

Ronan's man tore free from my grasp and dashed across the sand with Murdoch and me after him. Everyone frantically scrambled for weapons.

A rattle of machine gun fire echoed and clattered off the canyon walls. I couldn't tell from which direction it originated. Murdoch pushed me ahead of him. It saved my life and lost him his. We both fell to the ground. I was underneath, his body covering mine from incoming fire. I twisted my head to look. From the knees down both his legs were shattered. I could see white bone fragments amongst the pulp. I felt sick. His face was inches from mine. He knew. I looked into his eyes. He shook violently, teeth clenched against the pain. Faintly, I heard him through the noise of battle.

'Max …'

I said urgently, 'Dave …'

I wanted to tell him to hold on, that I'd get him out of this, that he'd be OK, but there was no time. I saw the exact moment the light left his eyes and he died and a small part of me went with him.

I wriggled out from beneath him and ran for cover.

Behind me, Professor Rapson and Dr Dowson had left the pod and were still wielding their homemade flame-thrower, playing bursts of fire at everything they perceived as the enemy. God knows how they were still alive. The Doctor was shrieking, 'Awake! Awake! Hereward the Wake!'

And then, the shit, quite literally, hit the fan. Or the flamethrower.

The Professor had acquired a considerable amount of mixed dung. Not knowing how much he'd need, he had gone for quantity. Obviously, they'd located it as far away as possible from the pods, at the north end of the canyon. But not nearly far enough. It was steaming when he'd obtained it. It had festered in the sun for a few days. It had got hotter. And more active. We had methane. And now we had a flamethrower. It was inevitable. St Mary's could explode a sack of soggy tissues.

A long way away, I heard Guthrie shout, 'Look out, Professor.'

I threw myself to the hot sand, assumed the traditional foetal position, and tried to make myself as small as possible.

An endless second passed. A huge inhalation sucked the air from my lungs. Everything went black, and then red, then a crack, then a roar, then more heat and I flew through the air. I hit the ground hard and half a mountain fell on me.

Once, when I was a kid, I was playing on a see-saw and the kid on the other end got off while I was still in the air. I can still remember the shock as I hit the ground. The impact knocked all the air out of my lungs and I lay on the ground, desperate to breathe and knowing that the next breath would be agony. This

305

was exactly the same, but scaled up.

I left it as long as I could, but eventually you have to breathe in, so I did. And again. And again. Red hot barbed wire tightened inside my chest.

I could see, but my eyes stung badly. I tried blinking to bring up some tears, but my eyelids felt like sandpaper. Not that there was much to see. Dark clouds of heavy dust hung around. A lot of other people were on the ground as well.

I turned my head very gingerly. I lay on and under a pile of rubble. My left arm was gone. I couldn't see it anywhere. I was pleased at the lack of pain. My right arm I could see and it was still attached, as were my legs, although nothing seemed to be working properly. I felt my eyes close …

Something grabbed my ankle. The shock jerked me awake and that set the pain off. Every single inch of me hurt. Even my missing left arm. The grip on my ankle was released and something grabbed my leg instead.

Lifting my head again, I could see a dusty figure dragging itself across the rubble and using handfuls of me to pull itself forward. I wished it would stop. I was in enough pain without this as well. An arm reached up and grabbed at my tee. As it did so, it lifted its head and I knew I was in serious trouble.

Izzie Barclay.

I didn't waste time thinking about how she got there. The main issue seemed to be what she was going to do now she was here. As if she read my mind, she scrabbled one handed and came up with a rock.

She looked bad. Her nose was a funny shape and she bled from deep gashes on her head and arms. Blood ran into her eyes and every now and then, she shook her head to clear them. Despite this she never took her eyes off me and her intentions were very, very clear. I'd never seen such blind, vicious hatred. I wasn't going to get out of this.

She said something. I saw her lips move.

I said, 'I can't hear you,' and watched her look puzzled. She was deaf too.

She raised her arm and brought the rock down. At the last moment I turned my head and she missed. It wasn't a powerful blow – she was all over the place, but sooner or later, she wouldn't miss and she would beat my face to a pulp. Her lips were moving continually. I guessed she was telling me how much she'd always hated me. She pulled herself up until she sat astride my chest and held her rock with both hands above her head. This really wasn't the way I wanted to die.

And, as it turned out, it wasn't.

I became aware of a cooling breeze drying the sweat on my face. I sighed in relief. I was dead.

Mrs Partridge sat on a rock and regarded me impassively. Her dark hair was bound up in loose ringlets secured by a silver clasp. She wore an exquisitely draped robe. Her feet were bare. She held a scroll.

I said, 'I'm dead, aren't I?' Which is not a phrase you get to use that often.

She shook her head.

All right, maybe hallucinating, then.

I tried to lift my head, but nothing was moving. Everything had stopped. I felt no pain. The ringing in my ears translated into a small musical noise, as if someone was running a finger around a wine glass.

Suddenly, I knew. It was all there. I knew exactly who Mrs Partridge was. I couldn't believe it had taken me this long. The blow to my head must have shaken things into place. Not Cleo – Kleio! She was Kleio. Kleio, the Muse of History. Who was always around at vital moments? Who prevented me asking Barclay to join us at Rushford? Leon Farrell would certainly not have come to my room if she had been there. Who advised a change of scenery? Who kept telling me to do my laundry so I could discover the fir cone? Who guarded my Trojan Horse and kept it safe until exactly the right moment? Who tried to keep

307

the Boss out of harm's way? And now I had an idea who Sibyl De Winter was as well. No wonder she had laughed at King Dave Superbus. I was lucky she hadn't boxed my ears.

'*You* told me to wait. It was you.'

She nodded.

'You saved my life.'

She nodded again.

'Why?' She hadn't saved Jamie, or Markham, or Murdoch. Why me?

She didn't answer me.

'Why are you at St Mary's?'

A faint voice whispered down the centuries.

'History is important. Far more important than most people believe. And it is under attack. Something is happening.'

Well, I knew that. It was happening now. Most of St Mary's finest were either shot or buried under a mountain of burning manure.

The familiar expression of exasperation crossed her face. She was referring to something else.

'What is happening?'

'It is under the fourth step.'

'What is?'

'The anomaly.'

'What anomaly?'

But she was gone and I was back.

The sun came up over the mountains, bright and eager. A brilliant shaft of light caught Barclay squarely in the face, causing her to screw up her eyes.

I made a huge effort to dislodge her, but to no avail. I really couldn't move at all. And then, out of my view, something went 'thunk'. Her eyes slid upwards and she fell forwards across my face. I fought to breathe.

I thought I heard Mrs Partridge say, 'I never liked you, Isabella.'

She'd never liked me either, and now it seemed she'd killed two birds with one stone. Literally.

I twisted my head to try to get free. I could hear Helen's report now. Despite extensive burns, blast damage, crush injuries, head trauma, shock and loss of limb(s), Miss Maxwell managed to die of suffocation.

Someone heaved Barclay away. I sucked in a huge breath and squinted up at Ronan. One side of his face was burned and so was his hair. He should have kept his helmet on. And still the frightening lack of expression, even though he must have been in agony.

He said simply, 'You,' and levelled his blaster at me. I was staring at the afterlife again.

Another rattle of gunfire and I heard someone call his name. His blaster was still whining; not charged up yet. I heard another shout. More urgent this time. He looked over his shoulder and then back at me. People were staggering to their feet. Shouts rang out. He could wait those extra seconds for the charge to build and risk capture or he could do the sensible thing. He did the sensible thing. He turned and ran. I said faintly, 'No,' and tried to roll over and grab his ankle. I missed.

Our camp was a ruin. The pods were intact, but burning debris and people lay everywhere. All the awnings were down, shredded, and burned.

Thus it was that for the first time, I saw TB2 without its canvas coverings. Some joker had stencilled 'THUNDERBIRD TWO' across the side, in yellow paint. I stared at it, feeling my blood congeal. Suddenly, I was back in the Cretaceous, running for my life and seeing a twisted sheet of metal with the letters RD T written across it.

And then I knew what Chief Farrell and Dieter had been doing in Hawking for three days. I knew why they wouldn't – couldn't – let anyone in and I knew that scene between Farrell and the Boss had all been a put-up job. But what a risk. What a huge, crazy, unbelievable risk. When I thought about what could have gone wrong …

I opened my mouth, but someone clamped a hot, rough hand across it and said, 'Quiet.'

I struggled as much as I could, which was not very much at all and Farrell said again, 'Shut up. Don't say a word. Keep still.'

I watched Ronan take three men into TB2. The rest had dispersed back to their own pods. The ramp went up. For long seconds nothing happened. I felt the familiar hot air rush and TB2 disappeared. They'd got away.

Slowly, he let me go and helped me to my feet. I took a deep breath and prepared to murder him on the spot.

He said to me, 'Are you hurt, Max?'

I said, tightly, 'You bastard.' And then all the mountains blurred and I fell forwards into darkness.

Eighteen

Twenty-four hours later, I lay in the blessed cool of Number Six, along with all the other walking wounded. They'd found my arm. It was between my shoulder and my wrist, exactly where it should have been. I'd been lying on it. I felt a bit silly.

Jamie, Murdoch, and Markham had made their final journey back to St Mary's. The Boss accompanied them. The rest of us were having our bits and pieces patched up and being re-hydrated. I leaned my head back against the wall and tried to make sense of it all.

They'd gone off with TB2. Eventually, they'd take it to the Cretaceous period. We'd turn up, fire the EMP, thereby initiating a countdown to the explosion that would destroy TB2 and take a large number of Ronan's people with it. Maybe even Ronan himself. We knew we'd be all right, because it had already happened to us. Our past. Their future.

And Barclay. Was she dead? She'd been slugged by a vengeful goddess, but with my luck …

And bloody Leon Farrell. Who'd built a bomb and not told me. And I was speaking as his mission controller now. He would have allowed us to live and work in a bloody great bomb. It's all very well to say it was harmless until triggered, but anything could happen to disrupt the power then the whole bloody lot would have gone up.

No, it wouldn't. We already knew – it exploded back in the Cretaceous. We'd been perfectly safe. And he'd done his best to prevent Ronan slaughtering the unit wholesale, without completely giving the game away. He must have been beside himself expecting me to do something stupid. Which I nearly had. And whose fault was that? I was back to being pissed because he hadn't told me.

And what about Mrs Partridge who had stopped me from doing that stupid something? Was she indeed the Muse of History? The daughter of Zeus who sat quietly at St Mary's, manipulating people and events? Did she work for St Mary's? Or did St Mary's work for her?

I opened my eyes to see someone put a chair for the Boss. He was back. Although he still looked desperately tired, he looked a million times better than the last time I'd seen him.

'Miss Maxwell, how are you?'

'I'm fine, sir. Another hour and another bottle of glucose drink and I'll be back out there. Doctor Dowson tells me they'd already unloaded the pots and the Professor says he can still make pitch, although apparently, we all now have to make – personal contributions.'

He seemed amused by that. 'I have some good news for you. When I last saw Mr Markham, he was attempting, somewhat groggily, to persuade Nurse Hunter to engage in a game of cards, the purpose of which, I understand, is to cause the loser to divest herself, or himself, of course, of various articles of clothing. He seemed very determined. I should not be at all surprised if he is successful in his endeavours.'

That news did me far more good than anything the medical team was doling out.

'He's alive?'

'Very much so. His reputation for indestructibility is untarnished.'

I leaned back and closed my eyes, feeling the treacherous prick of tears.

He smiled. 'You're about to have another visitor. Be gentle with him.'

And he left.

'Don't you come near me you devious, double-dealing, underhand, rat-bastard. I'm going to gut you with a rusty breadknife and then stake your honey-covered arse over an anthill in the noonday sun.'

'You're very grumpy today. And after I picked you up out of the sand and brought you into this nice cool pod. How ungrateful are you?'

'I've been shot at, blown up, covered in shit, brained with a rock, and lied to. You're lucky I'm only grumpy.'

'I haven't lied to you. Did you ever say to me, "Have you rigged TB2 to explode?" No, you did not. And as for the rest, you're bullet-free and everyone was blown up, not just you, so stop making such a fuss. And I don't know what you did to Izzie Barclay but she was in a much worse condition than you when she left, so why are you complaining?'

He was calm and soothing and had a reasonable explanation for everything. No woman should have to put up with that.

'Well, answer me this. How did she get free in the first place?'

'I let her go.'

I took a deep breath.

He took a step backwards.

People were edging out of the pod.

'Hold on. Before you go up like the Professor's manure heap, I had to let her go.'

I would have raised an incredulous eyebrow, but my face hurt too much. I had to content myself with sipping my drink in a disbelieving manner.

'There's someone else out there. Someone recruited Sussman and put that money in his account. Someone got Barclay into St Mary's. Someone's providing a safe haven for Ronan to operate from. We – I – thought that if I let Barclay go then she might lead us to him. Or her. Or them.'

'Really,' I said with awful sarcasm, because I'd come to exactly the same conclusion and without unleashing Barclay upon the world. 'And how did that work out for you?'

'Well, obviously it could have gone better. We didn't quite

get the information we needed.'

'You mean she gave you the slip, somehow managed to meet up with Ronan and this mysterious X and you still don't know who or how. And now they've escaped with TB2. And a good part of our equipment. And the pods they came in on. In fact, this could be a new St Mary's definition of the words "total fuck-up". And don't tell me that he's probably plastered all over the Cretaceous by now because I don't want to bloody hear it.'

'You're feeling a bit under the weather,' he said soothingly. 'I know it's natural for historians, but try not to dwell so much on the past. This operation's going to be a huge success. We'll be heroes when we get back and Edward's already scheduling new assignments, so really, you've got a lot to be positive about.'

I remained unimpressed.

'I'll admit to a nasty moment when our two lovable scamps and their home-made flamethrower nearly saved the day, though. Who ever thought we'd live to be grateful for methane?'

The pod was empty by now. An amazing number of sick people had picked up their beds and walked. People obviously preferred the blazing sunshine to the blazing row I was trying to have – and failing.

He moved in for the kill. 'You know I love you, don't you?'

'I know nothing of the sort. You just hurled me across the car and went at it like a crack-crazed rhino.'

He smirked. 'I did, didn't I?'

I sighed in frustration.

He took my battered hand and kissed it. 'I have to go. When this is done – when we're all finished here, I'd like to take you away for a few days. What do you think?'

'Not more camping?'

'Well, this time I was thinking there would be soft beds – big, soft beds and good food and plenty of alcohol. And decent

314

plumbing, of course. Will you come?'

Many, many times, was probably the correct answer to that, but I pretended to consider.

'Somewhere cool.'

'Well, you won't be getting out of bed, far less going outside, so it's not really that important, but yes, somewhere cool if that's what you'd like. Now, are you going to lie there all day?'

After all that, packing the scrolls into pots was comparatively easy. Just hard, hot, back-breaking toil.

We worked inside as much as we could, sorting the scrolls under Dr Dowson's guidance. It was a slow business, mainly because Peterson and I kept unrolling them to look at the contents. I found some kind of a bestiary with some pretty good drawings of lions and crocodiles and a beautifully rendered drawing of some technical device which meant nothing to me but Professor Rapson nearly swooned over, prophesying a world-wide sensation when that was discovered.

We laboured over the hot pitch in the hot sun, but the worst bit came when we lugged the pots up into the rocks and then carefully lowered them down into the cave. We broke a few in the process, but nothing serious. We were in no rush and there was no point in everyone dropping from heat exhaustion. This had to be done exactly right. People had given their lives for this. Imagine if Thirsk and Egyptian archaeologists broke through and only found a load of dust and shattered pottery simply because we'd cut corners.

They lowered the last pot down to me. I stacked it with care, making sure it lay wedged safely amongst the others, straightened up slowly, and thought about the price we had paid for this. Was it worth it? I had been prepared to sacrifice myself to save the pods. Dave Murdoch and Jamie Cameron had actually made that sacrifice. I gave the pots a small nod of acknowledgement and thanks.

And then it was done.

All we could do now was keep our fingers crossed that no one stumbled across them in the meantime. Or the cave didn't collapse. Or flood. Or that the scrolls themselves would stand the test of time …

It took a week to do the FOD plod. We did it once and then I made them do it again. We had to use metal detectors. I got quite paranoid about shell casings, shrapnel – everything. Archaeologists would be all over this site like a rash. The last thing they needed to find was two-thousand-year-old bullets.

All that remained now was for the cache to be discovered. Safe and intact.

The Chief laid in our final co-ordinates. We were returning to St Mary's some six months after we left and nearly three months after Thirsk's expedition set out.

We all went back together. It had been a team effort. We went back as a team. I paused in the doorway to Number One and looked around one last time. We were probably the most exciting thing that had ever happened here. Well, give it a couple of thousand years … I stepped back into the pod, Peterson closed the door and the world went white.

It was announced on the day we returned. The Boss had promised us a surprise when we got back and he delivered big time. He had the big screen on in the Hall. Thirsk had done us proud. World-wide headlines announced their breakthrough into the cave and the discovery of the treasures we had so carefully buried there nearly two thousand years ago. Or last week, depending how you looked at it.

We filed out of the pods; burned, baked, barbed-wire hair and with sand in all our nooks and crannies. The whole building was decked out with medieval banners, strobing lights, flags of all nations, tinsel, paper chains, Chinese lanterns, reindeer with flashing noses, glitter balls, bunting, and very loud music. It was just like us – noisy and gloriously tasteless.

We watched TV all day as the news reverberated around the world. No one was quite sure what they'd found yet, but everyone knew it was going to be big. Just for once, we knocked the Space Programme off the top news spot.

The Chancellor had rung the Boss personally with news of the discovery.

'What did she say?' I asked him.

'No idea,' he said, sipping his champagne. 'She was incoherent. For all I know she was reading me her shopping list.'

We drank. We ate. We drank some more. We sang. We danced. We did the Time Warp – many times. We may have drunk a little more.

Leon and I moved carefully away from the buffet with an armful of good things to eat and searched for a quiet spot in which to eat them and talk. What we did find were Markham and Hunter apparently playing cards in one of the old lecture rooms off the Hall.

She was more than fully clothed. Apart from a large wound dressing, he appeared to be stark naked.

Leon stepped back. 'I'll never eat another chipolata again.'

He greeted us with his usual sunny smile. I kept my eyes firmly on his face.

Hunter grinned. 'He wanted to play cards. We're playing cards.'

Leon put down his plate and picked up the deck. 'These cards are marked.'

'Of course they are,' said Hunter. 'I marked them myself.'

Markham smirked.

'Go away,' said Hunter. So we did.

We sat in the Hall and watched the Security and Technical Sections challenge each other to the traditional tray race down the stairs. As usual, both teams came to grief halfway down, tumbling gracelessly to land in the Hall with a huge crash which

317

made the building tremble. We were lucky nothing was dislodged. Not like the time … not like the time …

I looked up to see Mrs Partridge looking at me from across the room with her '*Finally!*' expression. At her side, Mrs De Winter smiled slightly. I thought I heard a small musical noise, which, given the racket around me was just impossible.

… Not like the time Dieter and I had bounced Number Eight and we'd dislodged one of those decorative pineapple things from above the front door and it had cracked … it had cracked one of the steps outside.

Exactly which step outside?

I stepped over groaning bodies. They'd be OK. The internal application of even more alcohol would soon have them back on their feet again – albeit very briefly.

I weaved my very unsteady way around similarly unsteady groups of people; past Doctor Dowson and the Professor who were amiably discussing whether it was actually possible to die of a surfeit of lampreys and how to set about it, slipped through the front doors and stood for a moment, enjoying the cool evening air. This last assignment had certainly taught me the value of cool. I would never again moan about being cold.

The fourth step was cracked. Web-like fractures radiated outwards from the small, round impact crater at the centre. The Boss had followed me out.

'Ah,' he said, looking down at the damage. 'Yet another result of your unscheduled visit to the Cretaceous.'

I waited to hear how much would be docked from my pay but he seemed in a fairly amiable mood.

I prodded with my foot and a bit of stone came away. I stared hard at it. He watched me in some amusement.

'We should get this fixed,' I said, eventually. 'Hazardous work environment.'

There was a loud bang from inside the building, the sound of breaking crockery and some ironic cheers.

'Yes, indeed,' he said. 'We wouldn't want that, would we?

However, you're right; it should be fixed. Now we have a moment to draw breath, I'll inform SPOHB.'

The Society for the Protection of Historical Buildings was the official body whose task it was to oversee repairs and maintenance to our beloved but battered listed building. We had them on speed-dial. They had us on their black list.

There was another loud bang from inside.

He offered me his arm. 'There's nothing to concern yourself with at the moment, Miss Maxwell. Shall we re-join the party?'

The fire alarms went off.

'Good heavens,' he said. 'At long last. This will make Leon a happy man.'

Actually, there was a much easier way to make Leon a happy man and only slightly less noisy, but probably best not to mention that.

Peterson rushed past. 'Come on, Max! Swans in the library!'

'What? How?'

'Who cares?' Good point.

In the distance, I could hear shouting. And screaming. Familiar sounds. St Mary's thundered past on their way to make a crisis considerably worse.

It was nice to be home.

Epilogue

Three weeks later, we were finished. All our reports were written and filed away and our sunburn fading. We'd had the service for Murdoch and Jamie Cameron. Their names were on the Boards. The worldwide furore continued, but we played no part in that. Thirsk got the glory – we got the cheque, so the Boss was happy. He gave us three whole days off.

On one of the last golden days of autumn we sprawled on the South Lawn under the shade of the cedar tree. One or two people had dropped an optimistic fishing line into the lake and then apparently fallen into a coma. A couple of people were reading, someone strummed a guitar, and a couple of not very serious card games were going on. The entire Technical Section seemed incapable of adding up to twenty-one. Or even fifteen.

'Thick as two short Plancks,' muttered Kal.

I sat next to Leon, enjoying the unaccustomed holiday. Occasionally, his fingers brushed mine.

The peace was shattered as three men, headed by The Man from SPOHB (to whom we had been requested to be polite), trundled around the corner with a wheelbarrow filled with the tools of their trade and started laying into the fourth step outside the front door. St Mary's sat up, the better to enjoy watching someone else do the work for a change.

I was watching Mrs Partridge and she was watching the Boss. The Boss was watching the workers and someone who knew him quite well might have caught a faint trace of anxiety.

A shout from the workmen dragged my attention away. They seemed to be bending over something. The Man from SPOHB took a few steps towards us, shouted something incomprehensible, and waved his arms.

'Occy, I think you're up,' murmured the Boss and Dr Dowson set off across the grass at a hobbling trot, followed by Professor Rapson who didn't want to miss anything.

They all bent over the hole again and then, very slowly and carefully, something was removed and placed reverentially on a wide plank. They disappeared inside the building.

'Goodness me,' said the Boss. 'Do you think they can have found something?'

His entire unit turned to look at him in deep suspicion.

He smirked. He actually smirked. 'Isn't this exciting?'

I found my voice. 'Do you know what they have found, sir?'

'Well, if asked to speculate, which I have been, thank you very much, Miss Maxwell, I would say they may have uncovered a small box, carefully waterproofed and buried under our fourth step some five hundred years ago. Or last February. Ah, here it comes.'

Obviously pre-arranged, two trolleys with champagne and glasses were wheeled across the lawn towards us.

'Gentlemen, if you could do the honours, please.'

Heads swivelled back to Dr Bairstow again.

'May we ask you to speculate again as to the contents of the carefully waterproofed box, sir?' asked Peterson.

'Of course you may, Mr Peterson. I would say – this is only speculation, you understand – but if pressed, I would say it's possible the box might contain a number of documents that, on examination, may prove to be a play and a collection of sonnets.'

I nearly dropped my glass.

Peterson did drop his.

'Sonnets?' he said.

'A play?' I said.

The Boss sipped his champagne and said nothing.

I made an effort to pin him down. 'Sir, are we – are we talking – Shakespeare? Another collection of sonnets? A lost play? Not Cardenio?'

322

'No, this is the last play he ever wrote. He wanted to make sure the main protagonists were dead, obviously. He was reluctant, but for certain promises and a big bag of gold, he allowed himself to be persuaded.'

'But what's the play?' said Kal. 'What's it about?'

'The Scottish Queen. Parts I and II.'

His entire unit regarded him with shock and awe.

Mrs Partridge finally looked at me. I felt a faint stir of disquiet. The anomaly ...

Professor Rapson galloped back across the grass. Long years of practice had given him a useful turn of speed.

'Edward,' he gasped, throwing himself into a seat. 'We have a problem.'

'Don't tell me we've lost it already?'

'Worse,' he said, downing someone's champagne. 'It's a fake.'

'No, it's not. I buried it here myself, five hundred years ago. It's quite genuine and will easily pass the most rigorous of examinations.'

'No, you don't understand. They executed the wrong queen.'

'How do you know that?'

'I may have skimmed through it ...'

'Why?'

'I wanted to know how it ends,' he said, defensively.

'Andrew, my dear friend, we're historians. No one knows how it ends better than us.'

'Actually, Edward, no. Part I ends with the execution at Fotheringhay.'

'Yes, we know.'

'No, no. You don't understand. They killed the wrong queen. It was Elizabeth. They executed the Queen of England. Mary Stuart survived and went on to unite the two kingdoms.'

'Impossible! I stood over him while he wrote every word. I had to. If I took my eye off the bugger even for a second, he was off to the nearest alehouse. You know what writers are like.'

'Did you actually read it?'

'There was no time. I alternately threatened and bribed until it was completed. I grabbed everything, jumped to St Mary's, buried it all under the fourth step, and then got the hell out of there. I certainly didn't proof read the thing.'

'Do you think he did it as a joke?'

'The man had no discernible sense of humour. Have you never read his comic dialogues? We need to get that manuscript back before anyone sees it. We can't afford even the slightest hint of impropriety.'

'Oh,' said the Professor. 'That's not a problem. 'It's here,' and he pulled the priceless document from under his jacket, wrapped in a Tesco carrier bag. The Boss closed his eyes briefly.

'Well done, Andrew. Where are the sonnets?'

'Occy has them in his safe.'

'Well, for God's sake, hang on to them; they clearly reveal the identity of his Dark Lady. And where is the gentleman from SPOHB?'

'Lying down.'

The Boss frowned. 'I gave explicit instructions – there was to be no violence.'

'No, no, he was overcome.'

'With emotion?'

'Nearly right.'

Wisely, he let it go. 'Well,' he said. 'There's nothing we can do about it at the moment. We'll just have to add it to our list of things to think about when we get back to work on Monday.'

Around me, St Mary's glowed gently in the late afternoon sunshine. Mellow and golden. The gold was picked up and repeated with variations in the autumn foliage. Apart from us, everything seemed serene and quiet. Peaceful, even. But for how long?

324

A cool wind stirred the leaves. The sun dropped down behind the hills and long, purple shadows reached out towards us.

I sipped a little more champagne but the bubbles had gone. It was going flat. I looked up to see the Boss watching me, closely. I leaned nearer and said softly, 'It's not over, sir, is it?'

'For the time being, Miss Maxwell, yes. But no, I'm sorry, it's not over.

Not so much the end – more a kind of pause ...

Jodi Taylor